THE HUNDREDTH MAN

THE
HUNDREDTH MAN
JACK KERLEY

HarperCollins*Publishers*

HarperCollins*Publishers*
77–85 Fulham Palace Road, London W6 8JB

www.harpercollins.co.uk/crime

First published in Great Britain by
HarperCollins*Publishers* 2004

1

First published in the USA by
Dutton 2004

A catalogue record for this book
is available from the British Library

ISBN 0 00 718058 6

Set in Minion and Eurostile by
Palimpsest Book Production Limited, Polmont, Stirlingshire

Printed in Great Britain by
Clays Limited, St Ives plc

To my parents,
Jack and Betty Kerley

ACKNOWLEDGMENTS

"Why don't you get your butt out of advertising and write that novel?"

The preceding quote, voiced by my wife Elaine after I'd had a hell-in-a-handcart week in copywriting, ultimately led to this book. Gentler assistance was provided by my children, Amanda and John, who endured manuscript pages spread throughout the house, rants about missing pens, and my commandeering the computer whenever an errant thought arrived.

The Fiction Critique Group of the Cincinnati Writers Project helped me understand what worked, what didn't, and how to turn the latter into the former. Special gracias to Katey Brichto, who set aside her own work to read and improve mine.

Thanks also to Julia Wisdom, my editor at HarperCollins, for her solid input, and to Richard Green, for his powerful cover design.

The folks at the Aaron M. Priest Literary Agency were – and continue to be – amazing: Joy Ritchey (since departed), who started my manuscript on its journey, the buoyant and indefatigable Lucy Childs, the foreign rights magician Lisa Erbach Vance, and the impresario himself, Aaron Priest. A first-time author never had a surer set of guides.

AUTHOR'S NOTE

I exercised broad license in bending settings, geography, and various institutions and law-enforcement agencies to the will and whims of the story. Everything should be regarded as fictitious save for the natural beauty of Mobile and its environs. Any similarities between characters in this work and real persons, living or elsewise, is purely coincidental.

PROLOGUE

Seconds before one of the most long-awaited events of Alexander Caulfield's adult life, an event he'd spent years planning and pursuing, an event marking his ascension into professionalism, a decent salary, and the respect of his peers, his left eye started winking like a gigolo in a third-rate Italian film.

tic

Caulfield cursed beneath his breath. A physician, he recognized a manifestation of *transient hemifacial spasms:* eye tics or flutters in response to events sparking anxiety or posing a threat.

1

tic

Anxiety was *ludicrous,* he lectured himself, squeezing the offending eye shut; he'd performed or assisted with hundreds of autopsies during his internship. The only difference was this was his first professional autopsy. She was sitting twenty feet away.

Caulfield slowly opened his eye . . .

tic

He angled a glance at Dr. Clair Peltier. She was opening a letter in the autopsy suite's utility office, apparently absorbed in correspondence. Caulfield felt blindsided, unprepared, fumble fingered: Today had been scheduled for procedural reviews and meeting new colleagues at the Mobile office of the Alabama Forensics Bureau.

Then she'd casually suggested he take her place during a procedure.

tic

Caulfield refocused the ceiling-mounted surgical lamp over the body of the middle-aged white male on the table. Water rinsed beneath the corpse, sounding like a small brook playing over metal. He glanced at Dr. Peltier again: still studying her mail. He mopped his sweating brow, adjusted his mask for the third time, and studied the body. Would his incision be perfectly midline? Would it be straight? Smooth? Would it meet *her* standards?

He drank in a deep breath, told his hands, *Now*. The blue-white belly opened like a curtain between pubis and sternum. Clean and straight, a textbook opening.

Caulfield slipped another glance at Dr. Peltier. She was watching him.

tic

Dr. Peltier smiled and returned to her correspondence. Caulfield pushed his fear to a far corner of his mind and focused on inspecting and weighing organs. He spoke his findings aloud, the tape recorder capturing them for later transcription to print.

"On gross examination the myocardial tissue appears normal in size and wall thickness. Areas of myocardium in the left ventricle are suggestive of past myocardial infarction. . . ."

The familiar sights and words steered Caulfield onto a trusted path; he didn't notice when the spasms melted away.

". . . liver mottled, early indication of cirrhosis . . . kidneys unremarkable . . ."

The man had been found sprawled in his front yard after a 911 call. The EMTs followed aggressive resuscitation procedures for a heart attack, but the man entered University Hospital as a DOA. Caulfield's initial findings supported a massive cardiac event, though the nondamaged tissue appeared healthy and free of epicarditis or atherosclerosis. Caulfield moved lower in the cavity.

"An obstruction is noted in the descending colon. . . ."

Caulfield pinched the lump in the bowel. Hard and regular in shape, a man-made object. It wasn't uncommon, emergency-room physicians were forever sending patients to the ER to extract vibrators, candles, vegetables, and suchnot; people were inventive in their quest for erotic sensation.

"Using a number-ten blade, a ten-centimeter vertical incision was made through the anterior wall of the descending colon. . . ."

Caulfield retracted the bowel to reveal the source of the obstruction.

"An object can be visualized, silver and cylindrical, resembling a section of flashlight casing. . . ."

Wet metal gleamed through the slit in the intestine, black fabric wrapping one end. No, not fabric, friction tape. Caulfield's finger tentatively tapped the casing. Something about the object glimmered with threat, an intruder in the house.

tic

He heard Dr. Peltier's chair push back and high heels start toward him. She'd been listening. His fingers slid into the passageway and grasped the object. He tugged gently. It slipped easily through the slit, then resisted. Caulfield tightened his fingers around the object and pulled harder.

tic

Simultaneous: white flash, black *thud*. Caulfield's head whiplashed and the floor slammed his back. Red mist and smoke painted the air. A woman's scream spun through the roaring in his ears. Someone above him waved a blunt stick, a club.

No, not a club . . .

The light flickered twice and failed.

When the autopsy was transcribed to printed form, transcriptionist Marie Manolo was uncertain whether to include Dr. Caulfield's final six words. Trained by Dr. Peltier to be clinically detached and thorough, Marie closed her eyes, took a deep breath, and continued typing:

My fingers. Where are my fingers?

CHAPTER 1

"A guy's walking his dog late one night. . . ."

I watched Harry Nautilus lean against the autopsy table and tell the World's Greatest Joke to a dozen listeners holding napkin-wrapped cups and plastic wineglasses. Most were bureaucrats from the city of Mobile and Mobile County. Two were lawyers; prosecution side, of course. Harry and I were the only cops. There were dignitaries around, mostly in the reception area where the main morgue rededication events were scheduled. The ribbon cutting had been an hour back, gold ribbon, not black, as several wags had suggested.

"What kind of dog?" Arthur Peterson asked. Peterson was a deputy prosecutor and his question sounded like an objection.

"A mutt," Harry grunted, narrowing an eye at the interruption. "A guy is walking his mutt named Fido down the street when he spots a man on his hands and knees under a streetlight."

Harry took a sip of beer, licked foam from his bulldozer-blade mustache, and set his cup on the table about where a head would be.

"The dog walker asks the man if he's lost something. Man says, 'Yeah, my contact lens popped out.' So the dog walker ties Fido to a phone pole and gets down on his hands and knees to help. They search up and down, back and forth, beneath that light. Fifteen minutes later the dog walker says, 'Buddy, I can't find it anywhere. Are you sure it popped out here?' The man says, 'No, I lost it over in the park.' 'The park?' the dog walker yells. 'Then why the hell are we looking in the street?'"

Harry gave it a two-beat build.

"The man points to the streetlamp and says, 'The light's better here.'"

Harry laughed, a musical warble at odds with a black man built like an industrial boiler. His audience tittered politely. An attractive redhead in a navy pantsuit frowned and said, "I don't get it. Why's that the world's greatest joke?"

"It has mythical content," Harry replied, the right half of his mustache twitching with interest, the left drooping in disdain. "Given the choice of groping after something in the dark, or hoping to find it easily in the light, people pick the light ninety-nine times out of a hundred."

Peterson lofted a prosecutorial eyebrow. "So who's the hundredth guy, the one always groping in the dark?"

Harry grinned and pointed my way.

"Him," he said.

I shook my head, showed Harry my back, and walked to the reception area. It was loud and crowded, local VIPs churning like a bucketful of mice as they scrambled for position beside an Even More Important Person or in front of a news camera. Guests huddled three deep around the buffet table. I watched a heavy woman in evening wear slip two sandwiches into her purse before puzzling over meat-balls in gravy. A dozen feet away a florid county commissioner babbled proudly for a news crew.

"*. . . like to welcome y'all to the dedication of the new faculties . . . one of the uniqueist in the nation . . . proud to have voted the fundage . . . the tragedy of Dr. Caulfield should remind us to be ever viligent. . . ."*

I saw Willet Lindy across the hall and plunged into the roiling bodies, excusing and pardoning my way his direction. A reporter from Channel 14 stared, then blocked my path.

"I know you, don't I?" she said, tapping a scarlet talon against pursed lips. "Weren't you part of, like, a big story a few months back, don't tell me. . . ."

I spun and ducked and left her puzzling over my fifteen minutes of fame. Willet Lindy stood against the wall, sipping a soft drink. I pulled myself from the current and joined him.

"It's Wal-Mart three days before Christmas, Will," I said,

loosening my tie and wincing at something dark dribbled on my shirt; following the same cosmic dictum that buttered bread always falls sticky side down, the stain was impossible to hide with my sport jacket. Lindy grinned and scooted sideways to give me a piece of wall for leaning. He was four years past my age of twenty-nine, but his gnomish face and receding hairline made him look a decade older. Lindy managed the nonmedical functions of the facility, such as maintenance and purchasing. I'd known him a year or so, starting when my detective status made me privy to the secrets of the morgue.

"Nice renovation of the place," I said. "Looks brand-new." Lindy was a shorter guy, five seven or eight, and I had to speak down half a foot. Not hard, I was told I stooped naturally, a large puppet on slackened strings.

Lindy nodded. "Cosmetic changes aside, we replaced much of the equipment. Plus we have things we didn't have before"—he pointed to a flyspeck dot in a ceiling tile— "security cameras. Miniaturized. If something like the Caulfield incident happens again, the bomb squad can inspect the scene from a distance."

Caulfield was the first-timer pathologist whose hand had been mutilated by a bomb meant to kill a man already dead; a horrifying event, unsolved after six months. "Not a lot of cops here, Will," I said to change the subject.

Lindy raised a dissenting eyebrow. "The chief and deputy chiefs, a captain or two."

I meant *cops*, but didn't have the time, or maybe the

words, to explain the difference. As if cued, Captain Terrence Squill walked by, saw me, backed up. Squill and I had barely exchanged syllables in the past; he was so far up the ladder I squinted to see the bottoms of his shoes.

"Ryder, is it? What the hell are you doing here?" His eyes noted the blot on my shirt and his nose wrinkled. The director of Investigative Services was a compact and dapper man whose precise features and liquid, feminine eyes recalled a fortyish Orrin Hatch. The knot of his tie was so tight and symmetrical it seemed carved from marble. I knew nothing of gray suits but suspected I was looking at one fitted by a tailor.

"I got an invitation, thought I'd come and represent the department, sir."

He leaned closer and lowered his voice. "This is not an affair for junior personnel. Did you con some City Hall bimbo into slipping your name on the list? Or did you sneak in the back door?"

I was amazed at how much anger was in his eyes while his mouth remained smiling. Anyone out of earshot would figure we were talking football or fishing. "I never sneak," I said. "Like I told you, I got an—"

Lindy spoke up. "Excuse me, Captain?"

"What is it, Mr. Lindy?"

"Detective Ryder was invited by Dr. Peltier. She also invited his partner, Detective Nautilus."

Squill pursed his lips as if preparing to speak or spit, shook his head, and disappeared into the crowd. I shrugged off the incident, said I wanted to thank Dr. Peltier for the invite, and dove back into the crowd.

Clair stood at the door of her office, speaking with Alabama's attorney general and his satellites. A simple black dress set off her skin, velvet over china, and I enjoyed watching her dominate her audience. A striking forty-four-year-old woman with cropped anthracite hair and ice-blue eyes, Dr. Clair Peltier, director of the Mobile office of the Alabama Forensics Bureau, needs only spear and helmet to claim center stage in a Wagner opera. The effect is enhanced by about fifteen extra pounds, which she wears in her thighs and shoulders. When the AG and his retinue paraded away, I stepped up. With high heels she was almost tall enough for her eyes to level into mine.

"Will Lindy says you're the reason I'm here," I said, raising my cup toward those amazing eyes. "Thanks."

"No thanks are necessary, Ryder. The guest list was top-heavy with police brass. The media being here, I figured it appropriate to have some detectives in attendance. I chose you and Detective Nautilus because you might be recognizable from the Adrian case."

Carson Ryder and Harry Nautilus, token detectives, so much for the A-list. I doubted we'd still be recognizable; as demonstrated by the reporter, the media's present-tense mentality had filed the year-old case somewhere between the Norman Conquest and the Industrial Revolution. I started to thank Doc P again anyway, but an upwardly mobilized junior prosecutor shouldered me aside and presented his giggly fiancée to "one of the top female medical examiners in the nation."

I smiled as I walked away. "*Top* female *medical examiners. . . .*" Clair was gonna eat that little bastard's soul the next time they worked together.

A heavy black hand squeezed my shoulder. Harry.

"Working the crowd, amigo?" I asked.

He winked. "A bash like this, Cars, all the politicos and wannabes getting half blammed, you can't beat it for getting milk."

Milk was Harry's term for inside information concerning the department or its influences. Though not a political type himself, he loved departmental gossip and always had the skinny, more milk than a herd of Guernseys. He leaned whisper close. "Rumor has it Chief Hyrum is rolling and strolling next spring, summer at latest."

"He's taking dancing lessons?" Harry's rhyming affliction alternately amused or irritated me. Today was irritation.

"Early retirement, Cars. Two years early."

I'd been a street cop for three years, a detective for one. Though I knew of the thicket of departmental politics, I was indifferent. Harry'd spent fifteen years studying them on a molecular level. I requested a translation. He paused, divining.

"Gonna be power plays, Carson. Upstaging, backstabbing, and downright lying. People that do nothing but push paper are gonna make like they're the hottest shit since the devil's stables."

"How much of that manure is gonna land on our heads?" I asked.

Harry scowled at his empty glass and pushed toward the bar, the multitude parting like water for a black Moses in pink slacks and purple shirt. "Don't fret it and sweat it, bro," he said over his shoulder. "We're too far down the ladder to get caught in the shitstorm."

My glass of iced tea was mostly cubes and I strained it through my fingers and swiped ice chips over my sweating face and the back of my neck. The effect was delicious in the night's heat; a cold startle of wet ice and the astringent draw of tannin. I sighed at the joy of small pleasures and leaned back in my deck chair. A gibbous moon swept above, hazy and haloed, the air glutted with wet. Hours gone from the morgue rededication ceremony, bare feet propped on the railing, I watched the golden plume of an oil rig burning off gas three miles across the Gulf. Fire from the dark water seemed as exotic as a parrot in a scrub-pine woodlands.

I live on Dauphin Island, thirty miles south of Mobile, several of them water. By Island standards my place is blushingly modest, a two-bedroom cottage perched on pilings over beachfront sand, but any realtor would list it for four hundred grand. When my mother died three years back she left me enough to swing the deal. It was a time in my life when I needed a safe retreat, and where better than a box in the air above an island?

The phone rang. I reflexively patted where pockets would

be if I'd been wearing clothes, then plucked the phone from the table. It was Harry.

"We're wanted at a murder scene. Could be Piss-it's coming-out party."

"You're two months late for April Fool's, Harry. What's really happening?"

"Our inaugural ball, partner. There's a body downtown looking for a head."

Harry and I were homicide detectives in Mobile's first district, partners, our job security assured by the mindless violence of any city where the poor are abundant and tightly compressed. That shaped our world unless, according to the recently revised procedures manual, a murder displayed *"overt evidence of psychopathological or sociopathological tendencies."* Then, regardless of jurisdiction, the Psychopathological and Sociopathological Investigative Team was activated. The entire PSIT, departmentally referred to as Piss-it, of course, was Harry and me and a specialist or two we could enlist as needed. Though the unit was basically a public-relations scheme—and had never been activated—there were those in the department not happy with it.

Like me, right about now.

"Get there as fast as you can," Harry said, reading me the address. "I'll meet you out front. Use siren, flashers. Gun it and run it, don't diddle around."

"You don't want me to pick up a quart of milk and a loaf of bread?"

The phone clicked dead.

I jumped into jeans and pulled on a semiclean dress shirt, yanking a cream linen jacket from the rack to cover the shoulder rig. I stumbled down the steps, climbed into the unmarked Taurus under the house, and blew away in a spray of sand and crushed shells. The flasher and siren stayed off until I'd crossed the inky stretch of water to the mainland, where I cranked up the light show, turned on the screamer, and laid the pedal flat.

The body was in a small park on the near-southwest side of Mobile, five acres of oak and pecan trees surrounded by a turn-of-the-century neighborhood moving from decline to gentrification. Three flashing cruisers fronted the park, plus a tech services van. Two unmarkeds flanked a shiny black SUV I took as Squill's. The ubiquitous news van had its uplink antenna raised. Harry was forty feet ahead and walking toward the park entrance. I pulled to the curb and stepped out into an ambush, a sudden burst of camera light in my eyes.

"I remember you now," came a vaguely familiar voice from behind the glare. "You're Carson Ryder. You had something to do with the Joel Adrian case, right?"

I blinked and saw the woman reporter from the morgue rededication. She was in full TV-journalist bloom, lacquered hair, scarlet talons gripping a microphone like a condor holds a rabbit. Her other hand grabbed my bicep. She lifted the mike to her lips and stared at the camera.

"This is Sondra Farrel of Action Fourteen News. I'm

outside of Bowderie Park, where a headless body has been discovered. With me is Detective Carson Ryder of the—"

I scowled at the camera and unleashed a string of swear words in three real languages and one invented on the spot. There's nothing reporters hate worse than a sound bite that bites back. The reporter shoved my arm away. "Shit," she said to the cameraman. "Cut."

I caught up with Harry at the entrance to the park, guarded by a young patrolman. He gave me a look.

"You're Carson Ryder, aren't you?"

I looked down and mumbled something that could have gone either way. As we passed by, the patrolman pointed at his uniform and asked Harry, "How do I get out of this as fast as Ryder did?"

"Be damned good or damned crazy," Harry called over his shoulder.

"Which one's Ryder?" the young cop asked. "Good or crazy?"

"Damned if he ain't a little of both," Harry yelled. Then to me, "Hurry."

CHAPTER 2

The scene techs brought portable lights with enough wattage to guide in a 757, all focused at a twenty-by-twenty area spiked with head-high bushes. Trees surrounded us and blotted most of the stars. Dog shit lurked beneath every step. Two dozen feet away a sinuous concrete path bisected the park. A growing audience pressed against the fence where the park met the street, including an old woman twisting a handkerchief, a young couple holding hands, and a half-dozen sweat-soaked runners dancing foot to foot.

Two criminalists worked inside the taped-off area, one kneeling over the victim, the other picking at the base of a tree. Harry trotted toward the onlookers to check for witnesses. I stopped at the yellow tape and studied the scene from a dozen feet away. The body lay supine in the grass as if napping, legs slightly apart, arms at its sides. It seemed surreal in the uncompromising light, the colors too bright and edges too sharp, a man incompletely scissored from another world and pasted to this one. The clothing was spring-night casual: beltless jeans, brown deck shoes without socks, white tee with an Old Navy logo. The shirt was drawn up to the nipples, the jeans unzipped.

Bending over the body was the senior criminalist on the scene, Wayne Hembree. Black, thirty-five, thin as poor-folk's broth, Hembree had a moon face and a sides-and-back fringing of hair. He sat back on his heels and shrugged kinks from his shoulders. His forehead sparkled with sweat.

"Okay walking here, Bree?" I called, gesturing a line between my shoes and the body. I didn't want to stick my feet into something important. Dog shit either. Hembree nodded, and I slipped under the tape.

An old street cop who'd seen everything this side of down-town hell once told me, "Find a head without a body, Ryder, and it's weird, but there's something whole about it. Find a body without a head and it's creepy and sad at the same time—just so alone, y'know?" When I looked down on that body, I understood. In four years with the MPD I've seen shot bodies, stabbed bodies, drowned bodies, bodies mangled from car crashes, a body with a pile of intestines squirted beside it, but never one without a head. The old cop nailed it: that body was as alone as the first day of creation. I shivered and hoped no one saw.

"Killed here?" I asked Hembree.

He shrugged. "Don't know. I can tell you he was decapitated where he's laying. ME folks thinking two or three hours back. Puts time of death between eight and ten."

"Who called it in?"

"Kids, teenagers. Came back here to make out and—"

Footsteps behind me; Captain Squill and his hulking, omnipresent shadow, Sergeant Earl Burlew. Burlew was chewing paper as usual. He kept a page of the *Mobile Register* in his pocket and fed torn pieces between his doll-sized lips. I always wanted to ask was there a difference between sections, Sports tasting gamier than Editorials, maybe. Or did they all taste like chicken? Then I'd look into Burlew's tiny, oyster-colored eyes and think maybe I'd ask some other time.

Burlew said, "Look who's here, Captain: Folgers instant detective. Just add headlines and stir." He swiped his hand down his sweating face. Burlew's centered features were too small for his head, and for a moment he disappeared beneath his own palm.

"Fag revenge killing," Squill said, glancing at the body. "Love to hack, don't they? Good place to do it, park's copacetic after dark. It's a yuppie-puppie neighborhood; Councilwoman Philips lives two blocks down; street gets overpatrolled to keep her in happy world. . . ."

I'd heard Squill had a speech mode for every crowd. With uniformed cops a dozen feet away he was spewing cop-movie jargon. Disheartening, I thought, a seventeen-year police administrator acting like a cop instead of just being one.

". . . killer thumps the vic's melon or pops a cap. The perp pulls his blade and scores a head." Squill pointed to the bushes around us. "Unsub dropped him here so the body'd stay out of sight."

I fought the compulsion to roll my eyes. *Unsub* was short for "unknown subject" and the FBI types used it a lot. *Unsub* was fedjarg.

"Killed and beheaded here?" I asked.

"Something wrong with your ears, Ryder?" Squill said.

Though the body lay partly beneath a bush decorated with small white blossoms, it was free of petals. Just outside the scene tape was a stand of the same bushes; I walked over and fell into them.

"What the hell's he doing?" Squill snapped.

I stood and studied the drifting of petals down the front of my shirt. Hembree looked between me and the body.

"If the vic fell through the bushes he'd have petals on him, but they're"—he studied the corpse and the ground—"they're around the body but not on it. The perp brushed aside the branches, so nothing fell on the corpse. Like maybe our friend here was pulled into the bushes."

I looked deeper into the vegetation. "Or out of them."

Squill said, "Delusional. Why pull the body out of deeper cover?"

Hembree's chunky assistant produced a flashlight and bellied beneath the bushes. "Lemme see what's back there."

Squill glared at me. "The unsub lured the vic here and dropped him where the body stayed hidden in the bushes,

Ryder. If it wasn't for a couple horny teens, it would've stayed hid until the stink started."

"I'm not sure it's hidden," I said, cupping my hands around my eyes to blot the scene lights and looking through oak limbs and Spanish moss at a bright streetlamp fifteen yards distant. I crouched beside the body and saw the streetlamp boxed between branches.

"Can we cut the lights?" I asked.

Squill slapped his head theatrically. "No, Ryder. We got work to do and can't do it with white canes and leader dogs." He looked at the uniforms for his laugh track but they were staring at the streetlamp.

Hembree said, "Lights turn back on, y'know."

Squill had no control over the techs and hated it. He turned and whispered something to Burlew. I was sure Squill's mouth shaped the word *nigger*.

Hembree yelled to an assistant in the forensics van. "Tell the EMTs and cruisers to douse their lights. Then kill these."

The lights from the vehicles disappeared, leaving only the portable lamps. When they went black it took our eyes several seconds to adjust. I saw what I'd expected: The streetlamp sent a thin band of light through the branches and between two large bushes, a spotlight on the body.

"It's not hidden," Hembree said, checking angles. "Anyone coming around the bend in the path looks right at it. Hard to miss with the white shirt."

"Speculative bullshit," Squill said.

22

The tech squirming through the bushes yelled, "Got fresh blood back here, bring me a kit and a camera."

"Dropped in the dark, dragged into light," Hembree said, winking at me. The uniforms nodded their approval. When the scene lights snapped back on, Squill and Burlew were gone.

I did an end-zone shuffle, spiked an invisible ball, and waggled my hand at Harry for a high five. He jammed his mitts in his pockets, growled, "Follow me," and stalked away.

Harry Nautilus and I had met in the Alabama state pen five years before; visitors, not inmates. I'd driven from Tuscaloosa to interview several prisoners as part of my master's in psychology. Harry'd come from Mobile to pump info from an inmate whose jugular had, unfortunately, been slashed a couple hours earlier; Harry was having a rotten day. He passed me in a tight hall and we bumped elbows, spilling his coffee. He studied my clothing—denim intensive, red-framed mirror shades, faded ballcap over self-inflicted haircut—and asked a guard who let the big, dumb hillbilly out of his cell. I'd come from two hours with a boasting pederast and transferred my sublimated aggressions to Harry's nose. The laughing guards broke it up as he was choking me out.

Afterward, we both felt shoe-staring ridiculous. Mumbled apologies turned to explanations of why we'd both been at the prison that day, and what had conspired to give us the temperament of dyspeptic pit bulls. Stupidity gave way to laughter, and we ended the day drinking in the bar in Harry's motel. After a few belts Harry launched into cop stories, amusing and intriguing me. I countered with tales from recent interviews with the South's preeminent psychopaths and sociopaths.

Harry dismissed my interviews with a wave of his hand. "Behind every one of those pieces of busted machinery is a megalomaniac that loves to talk. Reporters, shrinks, college boys like you—the craze-o's tell them anything they want to hear. It's a game."

"You know the Albert Mirell case, Detective?" I asked, referring to the psychopathic pedophile I'd spent an ugly two hours with.

"His last vic was in Mobile, college boy, remember? If you talked to Mirell, all you got was smirks and bullshit. Right?"

I lowered my voice and told Harry what Mirell had revealed to me as spit gleamed over his teeth and his hands squirmed beneath the table. Harry bent forward until our foreheads almost touched. "There's maybe ten folks in the world know that stuff," he whispered. "What the hell's going on here?"

"Guess I put Mirell in a mind to talk," I said, pretending that's all there was.

Harry studied my face a long time.

"Let's keep in touch," he said.

This was when my mother was alive and I was an impoverished student at the University of Alabama. Still, every couple of weeks I'd drive to Mobile or Harry'd make the run to Tuscaloosa. We'd grab a bucket of chicken and talk about his crumbling marriage or my fading interest in studenthood after six years and four majors. We kicked around aspects of cases bothering him, or discussed my wilder interview sessions. Sometimes we sat quietly and listened to blues or jazz and that was fine too. This went on for three or so months. One night Harry noted my usual at-home meals consisted of beans and rice, and going for a beer meant digging under couch cushions for change.

"Teaching assistant's not a high-pay industry?" he asked.

"It's basically a no-pay industry," I corrected. "But what it lacks in compensation it makes up for in scarcity of job possibilities."

"Maybe one day you'll be a famous shrink, Carson Freud, driving around in a big old Benz."

"Likeliest thing I'll be driving is pipe on an oil rig," I said. "Why?"

"I think you'd make a good cop," Harry said.

Ten minutes after we left the park, I followed Harry to a back booth in Cake's Lounge, a dark bottom-dwellers' saloon wedged between factories and warehouses near the bay. Several ragged loners drank at the bar, a few clustered in booths. Two unsteady men played pool.

"Why here, why not Flanagan's?" I asked, wrinkling my nose. Cake's smelled like the air hadn't been changed in a decade; Flanagan's served cheap drinks and decent gumbo and pulled a lot of cops.

"Squill might have been there, and Squill's what we're gonna talk about. That was a dumbass hot-dog trick with the flowers and lights. Why did you want to outshine him in front of everybody?"

"I wasn't outshining, Harry, I was detecting. We had a guy with no head and Squill spewing anything that came into his. What was I supposed to do?"

"Maybe you could have canned the drama and suggested things to Squill, made him think it was his idea. Didn't I hear you used to study psychology?"

"Beaming thoughts into Squill's head would be para-psychology, Harry, one of the few things I never majored in."

Harry narrowed an eye. "Squill's a political shark, Carson. Piss him off and there'll be nothing left of you but a red stain in the water."

I posed a question that had been on my mind for most of a year now. "How does a pus-weasel like Squill make chief of Investigative Services, anyway?"

I can tell I'm being obtuse when Harry puts his face in his hands. "Carson, you're precious is what you are, my apolitical tribesman. You truly have no idea, do you?"

"Infirmative action?"

"You, Carson. You put Captain Terrence Squill where he is today."

Harry stood and gathered bottles from the table. "I'll grab a couple more brews and give you a little history lesson, bro. You're looking like you could use one."

CHAPTER 3

Harry started his lecture halfway back from the bar, two bottles clinking in his hand. "For years Squill was a paper-pushing lieutenant in Crimes Against Property, a drone with one talent: public relations. Spoke at schools, neighborhood meetings, shopping center openings, church socials. . . ." Harry put the beers on the table and sat down. "He polished his act until he became the department's default media rep. For most people that's a no-win situation. . . ."

I nodded. "It upstages the superiors, which tends to piss them off." In college I'd seen tenure-track careers shot down by academic jealousy.

"Not Squill. The bastard knew exactly when to punt to higher-ups. Even better, when the department had a fuckup and the brass wanted to hide, Squill made himself the center of attention, drew the fire."

I said, "Squill? Jumping into bullets?"

"The media loved him, knowing he'd always deliver contrite, pissed off, colorful—whatever was selling that day. 'MPD captain says wrongful arrest concerns the department, news at eleven'. . . . 'High-ranking officer slams ACLU critics as "misguided crybabies," story on page four,' et cetera and et cetera."

Harry plucked a book of matches from the ashtray and fiddled with it. "Then Joel Adrian went on his spree. Tessa Ramirez. Jimmy Narley. After the Porters' deaths the case blew up. But the investigation went nowhere. You can't imagine how bad it was—"

"Who discovered Tessa, Harry? Who stood in a rat-filled sewer and looked down on her body?"

He shook his head. "I didn't mean it like that, bro. I'm talking politics here. Calls for resignations. People cussing the chief out in the produce section of Winn-Dixie. The media ground us like sausage. Everyone was pointing the blame finger at everyone else and suddenly this crazy uniformed cop shows up—Kid Carson."

"I had a couple ideas. You ran interference."

"They pissed on our heads for it," Harry said. "Until there was nothing left to try."

The peckerwoods at the pool table began a beery argument on spotting the cue ball. We both looked that way for a couple of seconds.

"I got lucky, Harry. Nothing but that."

He narrowed an eye. "Luck can be knowing where to look, right?"

It caught me off guard. "What are you saying?"

"Like it's more than just picking a card; it's knowing who's dealing."

"No. Maybe there's, I guess, an intuition, I don't . . ."

Harry stared at me curiously for a moment, then waved my garble away. "After you came up with that off-the-damn-wall theory and nailed the case, it was a political scramble, everybody trying to turn patrolman Ryder's Lone Ranger roundup into a personal win. And who was best set for it?"

"Squill?"

Harry tugged a match from its rank and studied it. "He'd kept the media pipeline full during the ordeal, and afterward he started sluicing in his own refined oil. Ever think how fast you faded from the hero light?"

I thought back. For two days I was the man who stopped the mad Adrian. By day three it was the department's triumph and I was a factotum. By day five I was a misspelled name nine inches into a ten-inch story. Harry said, "Squill's Law: Kiss up, shit down. He pushed you off the horse so the brass could ride it, one of them being him. He rode it all the way to chief of Investigative Services."

I shrugged. "So I got jerked around a little. When the smoke cleared, I was a detective. No complaints here."

The argument at the pool table picked up steam. One

man positioned the ball and the other slapped it away. Harry rolled his eyes at the scruffy duo and lit the match just to watch it burn. Matchlight turned his face to gold.

"You got a detective shield. But Squill grabbed what he'd been after for years, a seat at the big table. It was you that put him there, Cars."

I frowned. "I don't see the big deal."

"You don't see the big picture. Squill likes to think of himself as a self-made man. But when he sees you"—Harry tickled the air in a falling motion—"down crash them cards."

"He can just ignore me."

"He does. For a year you've been nothing but a name on the roster. And PSIT's been nothing but words on paper. But if PSIT gets activated . . ."

I thought it down the line: Activating PSIT put Harry and me on center stage. We'd be the ones coordinating the efforts, signing the reports, meeting with the brass.

"There I am, up front again, in his face."

Harry flicked the dying match into the ashtray. "Yeah. Only, think of it as in his sights."

The pool-table argument turned loud. One man emphasized his point by bouncing a cue stick off the other's ear. The struck man dropped, cupping his ear and moaning. The bartender looked at the pair, then at Harry. "You're a cop. Ain'tcha gonna do something about that?"

Harry put his big fist to his forehead, opening and closing it repeatedly.

"What the hell's that?" the bartender asked.

"My off-duty light."

We stood and headed toward our separate cars in the sticky night.

"Thanks for the history lesson, Professor Nautilus," I said.

"Read it and heed it, showboat," Harry replied.

I drove to Dauphin Island slowly, windows down, letting the night smells of marsh and salt water wash my thoughts like a cleansing tide, but the headless man kept bobbing to the surface. Once home, I lit some candles, sat cross-legged on my couch, and did the deep-breathing exercises recommended by Akini Tabreese, good friend and martial artist. Akini does a lot of deep breathing before busting hay-bale-sized ice blocks with his forehead. Me, I'd do a little deep breathing and pick up a sledgehammer.

Walk the scene. . . . I instructed my oxygenating thoughts. *See the park.*

I breathed away my anger at Squill and Burlew and visualized what the killer saw as he met the victim, perhaps on the path. The streetlight so near, they slip back into the bushes; here Squill seemed correct, sex the lure, if not the motivator. The victim dies, gunshot maybe, or a hard blow. If the head is crucial to the killer's delusion, it should have been removed deep in the shadows, the blade sliding quickly through its task. But, inexplicably, the killer pulls the body into the ribbon of streetlight, petals streaming in their wake. He kneels, performs his grotesque surgery, and disappears.

My mind played and repeated this scene until the phone rang at 2:45. I figured it was Harry. He'd be considering the scene as well, in a lit room with his stereo playing "thought jazz," Thelonious Monk perhaps, the solos where he breaks through the membrane and flies alone in the raw wind of music.

Instead of Harry I heard a trembling old woman. "Hello? Hello? Who's there? Is anyone on the line?" Then, as if years were dropped from the voice, I heard the voice of a woman in her thirties, my mother's voice.

"Carson? It's me, Mommy. Are you hungry? Can I fix you some lunch, son? A nice Velveeta sandwich? Some cookies? Or how about A BIG BOWL OF FUCKING SPIT?"

No, I thought, *this can't be happening. It's a nightmare, wake up.*

"CARSON!" The voice shrieked, no longer female. "Talk to me, brother. I need to feel some of that OLD FAMILY WARMTH!"

I closed my eyes and slumped against the wall. How could he call out? It wasn't allowed.

The caller banged the phone on something hard and shouted. "Is this a BAD TIME, brother? Do you have a WOMAN with you? Is she HOT? I hear when they get hot, juice POURS out of them. Hi, fellas, I'd like you to meet my date, the Johnstown Flood. WEAR BOOTS WHEN YOU FUCK HER!"

"Jeremy," I whispered, more to myself than the caller.

"There once was a girl from NANTUCKET, you wore boots each time that you'd FUCK IT . . ."

"Jeremy, dammit . . ."

"But the men in the town, one by one were each drowned, in the poison that poured out by BUCKETS!" He switched back to my mother's voice, solicitous. "It's all right, Carson, Mommy's here. You haven't finished your spit. Is it cold? Can I warm it back up for you?" He made a hawking sound.

"Jeremy, will you please stop—"

In the background I heard a door opening, followed by scuffling and a man cursing. My caller screamed, "NO! GO AWAY. It's a PERSONAL CALL! I'm talking to MY PAST!"

A loud crack turned to skittering, as if the phone had been dropped and kicked across the floor. Other voices joined in with grunts, cursing, sounds of struggle. I stood in my cool room and listened breathlessly as sweat poured from beneath my arms.

His words became distant and I pictured men in white dragging him across the floor: "THE MURDER, CARSON! Tell me about it. There must be more than a MISSING HEAD, there's always more. Did he take THEIR DICKS? Is he JAMMING SAUSAGES UP THEIR BUTTS UNTIL THEY SHOOT OUT THE NECK HOLE? Call me! You NEEEEEED ME AGAIN. . . ."

More sounds of scuffling. Then nothing.

Channel 14's affiliate in Montgomery must have picked up the beheading-in-the-park story, run it on the late news.

33

Television was one of the few luxuries Jeremy was allowed, and he would have studied the story with a scholar's focus. I blew out the candles and lay on the couch with my face in a pillow. Sleep, when it finally arrived, was paper thin and shot through with rats and the smell of burning silk.

My alarm fired just past daybreak. I stumbled numbly into the Gulf and swam straight into the waves for a half mile, then turned and dragged myself back. I followed with a four-mile beach run that left me sweat soaked and cramp calved. After a grudging, almost angry, session with the weights, I began to see events with a clearer eye, and wrote off Jeremy's call as an aberration; frighteningly resourceful, he'd somehow managed to get hold of a phone.

But hadn't I listened as it was taken from him? It wouldn't happen a second time; the episode was over.

I showered and ate a breakfast of cheese grits with andouille. My mood began to lift and I headed to work. Harry flipped a coin, and tails bought me autopsy duty. I had time before the cut, and headed to the criminalists' offices, a science lab grafted to a computer store. Two white-jacketed technicians studied a toilet float as if it were the Grail. Another tapped a pencil against a Mason jar full of squirming bugs. Hembree sat beside a microscope drinking coffee.

"We got a print hit on the headless man," he said, picking up a sheet of paper.

I made a drum-roll sound with my tongue. "And the winner is?"

Hembree mimicked a cymbal crash. "One Jerrold Elton Nelson, aka L'il Jerry, aka Jerry Elton, aka Nelson Gerald aka Elton Jelson."

"A big list of aliases."

"A pissant list of priors," he said, reading from the page. "Twenty-two years old. Eyes and hair are blue and brown wherever they are. Petty city and county raps for shoplifting, male prostitution, possession of stolen goods, possession of a couple joints. In March a woman charged him with borrowing eleven grand and not paying it back, charges later dropped."

"Hooker and a gigolo con artist? Guess his door swang both ways." I said, turning away. Though the autopsy was an hour off, I planned to head to the ME's office.

"I almost forgot," Hembree said as I was halfway out the door. "That bit last night with the petals and the streetlight was inspired, Carson, pure Sherlock. Squill's got his head so far up his ass, he spies on his teeth from his throat. I loved how you pointed that out to him."

The morgue's front desk was empty and my footsteps in the hall caused Will Lindy to come to the door of his office. The new facility had been open officially only a few days, but Lindy looked dug in, forms stacked on his desk, manuals alphabetized across shelves, calendars and schedules on his wall.

"Morning, Detective Ryder."

"Howdy, Will. I'm here for the post on Nelson. Clair around?"

I was maybe the only person in the universe who called Dr. Peltier by her first name; I'd used it since our introduction and she hadn't torched me yet. She countered by using only my last name, addressing everyone else by first name or title. Lindy looked at his watch. "She's due at nine, which means—"

I glanced at my timepiece, 8:58. "She'll be here in one minute."

We heard a burst of masculine laughter from down the hall and saw a pair of funeral-home staffers retrieving a body for burial. They rolled a covered body toward the back dock like kids playing with a supermarket buggy, weaving the clattering gurney from side to side. Lindy was down the hall like a shot.

"Hey, fellas," he said. "What you do at the parlor is your business. Around here we show respect."

The funeral home guys froze, reddened. They mumbled apologies and continued on their way, slow and silent.

"Good going, Will," I said when he returned.

Lindy gave a half smile; funny how half a smile indicates sadness. "Poor guy's on his last ride, Detective Ryder. There's no need to treat it like a game."

I admired Will Lindy for his stand; too many homicide cops and morgue workers forget the bodies passing by were once the exact center of the universe, to themselves anyway. No one knows why we were chosen to be here, or if we had much hand in the choices we made during our presence. In any event, for the arrivals at the morgue, this level of the journey was over. Bad people, good ones, the indifferent—they'd all crossed to the final mystery and left behind a soft, soon-gone husk, not always to be mourned, but at least respected.

Lindy and I turned to an insistent rapping: Doc Peltier high-heeling toward us. I detected she'd been to breakfast with her husband, Zane, since he was walking beside her and working his teeth with a toothpick. Zane's fifty-nine, but looks younger, with cool gray eyes in a chiseled face, a nose ridge like the spine of a slender book, and a mahogany tan independent of seasons. He wore a charcoal three-piece cut to hide a touch of paunch and walked fast to keep up with his wife.

"A little early, aren't we, Ryder?" she said as I jumped into her slipstream. Her perfume suggested champagne made from roses.

"I'd like to take a look at the body before the post."

I always tried to do this when the bodies weren't badly decomposed, feeling it provided a stronger link with the victims. After the post, the invasion, the deceased seemed different, as if they'd shifted from our world to the ante-room of the next.

Clair rolled her eyes. "I don't have time to indulge you today." She wasn't big on my linkage concept.

"Please, Clair. A minute?"

Clair sighed. We stopped at the door of the autopsy suite. She remembered her manners. "Have you met my husband, Zane?"

"Art museum, months ago," I said, offering my hand. "Detective Carson Ryder."

Zane Peltier had one of those handshakes that stop short of locking thumb to thumb; he shook my knuckles. "Of course I remember," his mouth said as his eyes denied it. "Great seeing you again, Detective."

Clair opened the door. Her husband said, "I'll wait out here, dear."

"They won't bite, you know, Zane."

He smiled but didn't approach the door. I understood his hesitancy—I believe people sense death as precisely as cattle sense lightning forming, an atavistic warning system that'll be with us until we evolve to creatures of pure reason, slim chance.

Clair and I stepped into the suite. "Make it fast, Ryder," she said. "I've got a busy day and don't need distractions."

"Yes, Your Majesty," I replied, drawing a withering glare but no comment. She slid the body from its refrigerated confines, drew the sheet away.

I studied the odd tableau for several seconds. Without the head I took no sense of being, just of loss. All I noted was the victim's physical dimensions, wide of shoulder, narrow of hip, well muscled. Death removes some of the tone and definition, but it was obviously a body the owner had put time and effort into.

Clair watched me with disapproval, then let her eyes wander the body with professional appraisal. She started to draw the sheet back into place, but paused.

"What the hell?" she said, leaning over the pubic region. "What's that?"

"A penis?"

"No, dammit. Above the pubic hair. Make yourself useful, Ryder, get me some gloves."

I ran to yank a wad of latex surgical gloves from a box beside an autopsy table. Clair snapped them on and pressed aside the matted hair.

"It's writing," she mumbled. "So small I can barely read it. 'Warped a whore,'" she said, squinting at words I couldn't see. "'Warped a whore. Whores Warped. A full quart of warped whores. Rats back. Rats back. Rats back. Rats. Rats. Rats. Back. Back. Back.'"

Clair leaned back and I bobbed forward. There, in precise lavender writing, were two horizontal lines of words, just as Clair had read them.

Without turning from the body she called, "Dr. Davanelle, come here."

I looked to the small utility office in the corner where a petite and pale woman studied a file, so mouse quiet I hadn't noticed her. She had dark shoulder-length hair and owlish glasses. Her name was Evie or something, a fairly recent hire, and I hadn't worked any cases she'd handled. She hurried over. I smiled and nodded and she ignored me.

Clair tapped the victim's pubic bone. "Since you were kind enough to show up at work today, Doctor—it being a Monday and all—I wanted to point out the writing here on the pubis. Call Chambliss and get him over here with the microphotography gear and have him shoot the inscription. And check the body for any other writing. Got it?"

"I would have done that in any case, Doct—"

"What are you waiting for? We're not voting on it; go."

Evie or something retreated to the utility office to summon the photographer. The intercom crackled and I heard the voice of receptionist Vera Braden, the Deep South dipped in honey and fried up with a side of grits.

"Dr. Pel-tee-a? Bill Ah-nett from the eff-bee-aye on line fo-wer. Says he got the 'nalysis on yoah tissue samples from las' week."

"I'll take it in my office," Clair announced to the air and clicked out the side door to her office. I took the opportunity to jump into the rest room a few paces away. I returned a minute later to find Zane Peltier had wandered into the suite. He stood white faced beside the body. His knees looked one shiver shy of buckling and he kept whispering, *Jesus.*

"Take it easy there, Mr. Peltier," I said, moving to his side and putting a steadying hand against his back. "Take a deep breath."

"Who *is* that?" he rasped. "Jesus."

"A man named Jerrold Nelson."

"Jesus."

"Breathe," I repeated. He breathed.

"I came to see what was taking Clair so long and, Jesus— where's the head?"

"We don't know that yet."

"Who would do such a thing to another person?" He

sucked down a couple more fast breaths and his color started returning.

"I'm—I'm all right now, Detective. Never seen a body without . . ." He managed a quivering smile. "I wish I'd stayed outside."

Zane deep-breathed his way to Clair's office, looking closer to his true age. In cattier circles it's mewed that the nuptials of Zane Peltier to the former Clair Swanscott was less marriage than merger, him bringing name and wealth, her weighing in with brains and ambition. Zane's money was rooted in antebellum Mobile, one of those snowball fortunes that gathered as it rolled. He inherited several enterprises, was on the boards of several others, but labored about fifteen hours a week, I'd heard. Probably very efficient hours.

Clair stuck her head in the front door of the suite. I saw Zane behind her. He looked ready to leave. Clair cocked an eye toward the utility office.

"I have a disinterment in Bayou La Batre, then lunch with Bill Arnett. I'll be back by three forty-five." Clair turned my way. "This is the way it operates, Ryder. Everyone doing their jobs, working on schedule. Showing up on time."

Not a word of it meant for me.

The door squeezed shut. Clair was off on schedule and Zane, one suspects, was off for a stiff belt. Which left just me and Evie or something—boy and girl alone together in a way-house for the dead. I ambled toward her while detecting on the way: no wedding band. She was filling in lines on a pile of forms.

"I'm Carson Ryder, Homicide," I said to the crown of her head. "I don't believe we've been formally introduced."

She made a few pen scratches before looking up.

"Ava Davanelle." She didn't offer her hand but mine was unavoidable. Her handshake was cool, compulsory, and quickly retrieved.

"You're new here, Dr. Davanelle?"

"If six months seems new to you." She looked back to her writing.

"Seems like you're on the wrong side of Doc Peltier today. You come in late? I was two minutes late for a meeting with her once, and she just about—"

"Ever see a doctor about that nose problem?"

"Nose problem?"

"The way it pokes into other people's business."

I watched her fingertips shake slightly as she wrote; the room was cold.

"I apologize," I said. "I've worked with Clair, uh, Dr. Peltier, for a year now and always feel like I'm on her wrong side. Like maybe she doesn't have a right side. But if she didn't have a right side, how could she have a right hand? And if she didn't have a right hand, how could . . ." I heard myself babbling inanely but couldn't stop, my version of small talk.

Dr. Davanelle gathered her papers and stood.

"Nice to have met you, Detective Carson, but I—"

"Ryder. It's Carson Ryder."

"—have much to do today. Good-bye."

I followed her across the room until she turned like I was a smelly dog sniffing at her legs.

"Something else I can do for you, Detective Carson?"

"Ryder. Carson Ryder. I'm here to observe the post on the Nelson body, Dr. Davanelle."

"Why don't you have a seat in the lobby," she said, punching the word *lobby*. "Someone will let you know when we're ready."

CHAPTER 4

" . . . rats . . . rats . . . rats."

Dr. Davanelle's gloved hands pressed aside the victim's pubic hair as she leaned over the body and finished a slow and precisely enunciated reading of the inscription. "The ink is light lavender and difficult to decipher from a distance. Preliminary findings suggest a writing instrument with a very fine stylus. Slight penetration into the epidermis can be observed. Microphotos are in the case file. . . ."

Summoned from exile after a half-hour wait, I'd found Dr. Davanelle and the ancient diener, Walter Huddleston, positioning the body. A tall, broad-shouldered black man with the strength of a much younger man, Huddleston had eyes like red torches and never smiled. I pictured Halloween's children trooping to his house, the door creaking open to Huddleston's scarlet glare, the kids sprinting away in a melee of screams and flying candy.

Dr. Davanelle finished the visual inventory. There was no other writing, only a tattoo on the scapula, an Oriental dragon. She pulled her cloth mask tightly into place, picked up the scalpel, and the procedure progressed—the Y cut, the revelation of the dark machinery. I was impressed by her economy of motion, gloved hands moving with such floating, independent grace as to suggest each had its own homunculus in the rafters. Clair and the other staff paths, Stanley Hoellker and Marv Rubin, seemed heavy handed in comparison, brusque and mechanical. I watched for a half hour, entranced, a word I never thought I'd connect to an autopsy.

"You've got great hands," I said. "Ever think of playing shortstop?"

She lifted the heart to the scale, dropped it in. "Surely you know the procedure is being taped, Detective," she said. "I'd appreciate your remaining quiet."

"Sorry," I said.

Dr. Davanelle continued down the cavity for another fifteen minutes. She removed and weighed the first kidney, then proceeded to the second. It squirted from her hand and fell toward the floor. Without seeming to look, she caught the tumbling organ in her other hand.

"There you go," I said, forgetting myself. "Shortstop all the way."

45

Her green eyes blazed from above her mask. I shrugged and said, "Forgive me. Just making conversation."

She flicked her head toward the door. "The hall's over there, the way you came in. If you go outside you can make all the conversation you want. One more outburst and that's where you're going."

My cheeks felt hot, like I'd been slapped in the face. I nodded and went silent, though speaking at an autopsy wasn't a capital offense. There was generally a touch of banter, the transcriptionist recognizing it as such and excising it from the record, no big deal.

She continued the procedure, giving the play-by-play into the air, recorded—as she noted—for later transcription. Being a detective, I studied her as she worked and discovered some interesting anomalies: I'd first thought her petite, but realized it was how she held herself that made her seem diminutive. I also found it odd she didn't include her title when we made introductions. Most MDs waved their titles like flaming swords, and wouldn't leave a note for the meter reader without a *Dr.* or *MD* pasted to their name. She was dour, abrupt, and projected the femininity of a hammer—yet her motions verged on symphonic, her skills beyond what I'd have expected of someone with just six months in the game.

A few minutes later there was a break in the action while she went to fetch an instrument. When she returned, I said, "I meant no offense by comparing you to a shortstop. I was trying to relate my enjoyment at your skill. Your hands move like water."

She stared at me like I'd urinated on her Reeboks.

"Didn't I request that you not talk? Not ten minutes ago?"

I took a deep breath, released it. "I've never been at a postmortem where a gag rule applied, Doctor."

She tossed the instrument to the table, spun to face me.

"Here's how it works: I handle the procedure, you handle the observation. It can be done quietly. If you have intelligent questions regarding the autopsy—and some people actually do—ask your question and the answer will be provided. If that's too difficult for you to understand, I can have it typed up and delivered to your superior."

I'm slow to irritate but sometimes make exceptions.

"Look, Doctor, just because you got shit on this morning doesn't mean you have to shovel it down the the line."

Her eyes lit like green fire and she yanked the cloth mask from her mouth. Her skin was ashen and sweat beaded on her forehead.

"I'm not going to take this," she said. "Who do I call to have you replaced?"

I started to respond, thought better of it. I threw my hands up in surrender, made a lip-zip motion, and stepped back to give her room. Plenty of room.

For the next couple of hours I was the Sphinx. I asked three questions, all framed in bland technical lingo. She answered in the same manner, robotic. The autopsy revealed the severing of the head was precise, accomplished with a thin, razor-sharp blade, and probably unhurried. Save for the tattoo and minuscule, cryptic writing, the body was unmarked.

The dark stain of the gravity-settled blood, livor mortis, indicated the victim had remained supine after death. Nothing else, at least not yet.

The procedure finished, she snapped off her gloves, dropped them in the biohazard container beside the table, and started to walk away. Without turning she said, "I'll have an outline of the major points typed up. It'll take two hours. You'll find it at the front desk."

"Doctor," I called to her retreating back. She stopped, turned, glared. I wondered if I'd broken some rule about speaking after the recorder was turned off.

"Yes, Detective Carson?"

"It's Ry—never mind. Listen, Doctor, we got off on the wrong foot and I think it was my fault. I'm a cretin with small talk and make up for it by jabbering inanely. Can we maybe start over?"

When she didn't answer, I said, "It's past lunch. I know a great po'boy joint down by Bienville Square. My treat."

I smiled brightly and jiggered my eyebrows.

She walked away as if I were a coat of paint on the wall. The door of the utility office slammed behind her. I called Harry to see what was up. He said interviewing white trash. When he asked what I was doing, I said not selling a lot of po'boys, be there in a few.

The most distracting aspect of speaking to Jerrold Nelson's aunt, Billie Messer, was her constant brushing of insects from her face when none were there. I first suspected a neurosis, but realized it was her conditioned response to living in a house trailer with rusted-out screens and a busted AC. The fortyish Messer was Nelson's only surviving relative, and Harry'd spent the morning tracking her to a trailer court overrun by weeds and feral cats.

Billie Messer had been an exotic dancer in her younger days, but exotic drooped into pendulous and she now mixed the drinks she'd once hustled. Dressed for work, Ms. Messer wore scuffed black spike heels, a miniskirt noire, and a frilly black bra straining with effort. Frizzed red hair framed outsized features I suspected looked either equine or enticing, depending upon time of night and substances abused. Harry and I leaned against a sun-hot rust-bucket car in her front yard while Billie Messer sucked cigarettes, waved off invisible bugs, and Cliff's-noted her nephew's life in a strangely seductive voice, like a hillbilly Tina Turner.

"Poor ol' Jerry weren't good for but one thing, and that happens in bed. He was damn good looking. Smart, too, more in the clever way than book kind. Always made out like he was smack on the edge of being some famous model. Might a happened 'cept he was so lazy. He made his way on his looks, though, shacking up with men or women. Didn't matter which, long's they gave him money. I asked once, said, 'Jerrold, how's come you do it with boys and girls both?' Know what he said? Said it all felt the same, so what did it matter? I said what you mean, all feels the same? He said, like nothing, that's how it feels, Aunt Billie—don't feel up, don't feel down, just feels like nothing. You know what else he said?"

"What, Miss Messer?" Harry asked, truly curious.

"He thought it was funny folks thought he was so good at doing it, you know, 'cause he could go on at it for so long. He said when you don't feel nothing, there's nothing to make you stop. I asked wasn't there anything made him, you know, jump over the hill? He said he had to bear down hard on thinking about flying. Then he'd do it, he'd have his—you know." Bessie Messer frowned, shook her shock of frizzed hair sadly, and swatted an unseen insect. "Ain't that the damndest thing?"

We headed across town to interview Terri Losidor, the woman who'd filed charges against Nelson. Harry drove, I reclined in the rear talking to the back of his head. Some people claim their best thoughts arrive in the shower or astride the can; for me it was the backseat of a car. When I was a child and the bad things started at my house, I'd tiptoe into the night and hide in the rear of our sedan, spending the night in wispy sleep before returning to bed at dawn. To this day I took comfort lying in the backseat, hands behind my head, watching the buildings and treetops flash by. My backseat meditations didn't bother Harry, he enjoyed driving, though he was a terrifying practitioner of it.

"You've seen maybe twenty times more jealousy-slash-revenge killings than me, Harry. How many have been as neat?"

"Doesn't mean anything. They're all different."

"Come on, Harry. How many have been so damned immaculate?"

Harry grunted; he liked to drive in silence, I liked to think aloud. He grudgingly elevated his right hand, thumb and index finger forming a zero.

"Slicing and dicing, Carson. Fifty stab wounds. Eighty. Or more hammering than John Henry. I saw a shooting where the shooter emptied a clip, reloaded, and start shooting again."

"Right. The anger floods out. This one was neater than a show home."

"The *body* was neat, Cars. What's the head doing now? My guess is target practice. Or taking a good hammering."

A semitractor rig pulled beside us at a light. The driver glanced down from his high perch, startled at seeing a guy in a sport jacket and tie reclining across the backseat of a Taurus. I winked and he turned away. I said, "The head taking the punishment . . . the face symbolizing the whole. It works, I guess. Where we at?"

"Airport Road by University. So how come you don't sound convinced?"

"If that's what the killer wanted, the head, why not break for the end zone soon as it was in his hands? Do a victory mambo. Spike it, whatever. Just like you were thinking. But he hung around and wrote on the body. I'm guessing that's why he pulled it into the light."

Harry said, "Maybe the writing got him juiced. He had to write."

"If he's got the head to hammer his statement into, why make a speech on the body?"

"Good point. Doing a Farley, maybe?"

Farley Traynor was a bitterly angry accountant who cut words into victims he'd never known, telling them how much he hated what they'd done to him. In a curious bit of deranged perception, Traynor figured since the dead were in their bodies looking out, he'd write backward so they could read it easier.

"Just doesn't click if the head's where he thinks the personality resides. Did you just hit a pedestrian?"

"Traffic barrel. Maybe it's a note to us, cops. Whores and rats? Not everybody loves us like we do."

I couldn't buy in yet. "But the tiny writing wouldn't be around long, or at least not visible. Not in this heat. I bet even slight decomposition would obscure it. And if the words are important, scream them: black marker, big letters."

"You're overanalyzing, Cars. I hate to agree with Squill, but I think it's revenge."

"Revenge is anger. If the killer was angry, he or she's got anger as tidy as doilies."

I was balancing my thoughts between fastidious anger and my unimpressive debut with Dr. Davanelle when the car turned hard and bumped upward, pulling into a drive. Harry said, "We're here, bro. Not what I expected either."

CHAPTER 5

Terri Losidor's apartment complex boasted several Beamers beneath the carports, plus other young-executive-type wheels. The grounds were dappled with crepe myrtles, palmettos, azaleas, here and there a tall loblolly pine. A pool featured several tanned and lounging bodies. Not a child in sight.

"Trailer park to yupster singlesville," Harry said. "Darwin at work."

Terri opened her door without chain intervention or asking for ID, either trusting us or expecting us. She had a broad plain face and green, darting eyes. Moderately over-weight, she carried it well and moved lithely, gesturing us to sit on a plump orange couch as she lit a cigarette and sat across from us. She remote-muted one of what Harry calls "chromosomal defect shows," Springer or whatnot. Despite her calm exterior I detected a nervous undercurrent, not unexpected when cops come a-calling. Her apartment was clean, with inexpensive but matched furniture, and beneath the cigarette smoke smelled of lemon air freshener and a recent shower. There was a cat-box somewhere.

She said, "This is about Jerrold, isn't it?"

Harry nodded and Terri Losidor picked up a throw pillow and clutched it to her breast. Harry started with easy questions to let her get used to answering. She was thirty-three and worked as an accountant at a local trucking firm. She'd lived at Bayou Verde Apartments for three years. Children weren't allowed but pets were cool. They used too much chlorine in the pool. This all came out in a nasal twang I knew the drivers made fun of.

Harry shifted to Nelson. While he slow-walked her through memories, I sat quietly and used a year's worth of detective experience to identify cat hairs on the couch. Long and white.

"How well did you know Mr. Nelson?" Harry said. "I'm talking about his past, his friends, his family, his hobbies, and so forth."

"Those things weren't important to Jerrold and me, Detective Nautilus. It was just us and the things we'd do. I didn't need to know anything else."

"Didn't need to know or Jerrold didn't tell you?" Harry loosened his tie, spun a crick from his neck, relaxed. He

54

works in reverse of many cops by leaning forward to toss mushballs and lying back to throw heat and curves.

Losidor looked away. "I asked a couple of times. He said they weren't things he liked to talk about; it was painful."

"So if you didn't know his friends you probably didn't know any enemies."

"Jerrold didn't have enemies. He was so—so friendly. Always laughing and telling jokes." A sad smile. "One of my friends told me, she said, 'Terri, that Jerrold makes my mouth hurt with all his smiling.' No one could be angry at Jerrold, Detective Nautilus."

Harry locked his fingers behind his head and reclined further. "In May you were angry enough to threaten him with jail. Something about eleven thousand dollars moving from your pocket to his."

Losidor closed her eyes, sighed, opened them again. "See, he told me he had a one-time chance to get in on a business—it would take just fourteen thousand dollars to make at least seventy in a year. All I had was eleven but Jerry said it would still work."

"What sort of business?"

There was a clang from the back of the apartment, like something falling on the floor. Terri jumped.

Harry sat up, wary. "Are we alone here?"

"Oh, yes. Just us," Losidor said, reaching for a cigarette. "That's Mr. Puff, my kitty. He's clumsy, always knocking things off the sills and shelves. Crazy cat."

Harry and I listened for a moment. Nothing. Harry settled back into the couch.

"What sort of business did Jerrold say your money was going for?"

"Something to do with computers and how they're hooked together. He explained one office might have one kind of computer and another office had another and the computers couldn't understand each other. He had a friend who'd invented a better way to make them talk. It made sense, since at my office the computers are always messing up like that."

"You ever get to meet his friend? Or hear his name?"

"I just trusted Jerry, you know."

Harry spent one year with Bunco, and this was a familiar conversation. "Once you gave him the money Jerrold stopped coming by as much, didn't he?"

"I don't know—he got busy with things. . . ." Her eyes dropped to the carpet. "Yes."

"Then the business went sour."

Terri sighed. "He said some other company came out with the same thing first. Intel. I asked the guy who fixes the computers at our office about it. He'd never heard about Intel having anything like that; it wasn't what they did. That's when I filed." Terri sniffled and plucked a pink wad of tissue from her pocket to dab her eyes.

"But a week later you dropped the charges."

"He finally told me the truth," Terri said, sniffling.

"Which was?"

"He used it to buy a share of some cocaine being flown into the county—it's like a stock deal. You buy shares. Jerry didn't tell me because he knew I'd never approve. He stopped seeing me because he was ashamed."

"A . . . stock deal?"

"You remember that little plane that crashed up by Saraland? That was the plane—all the cocaine burned up and we lost our money."

I recalled the incident; a Mercedes dealer in a Cessna 180 miscalculated his fuel by about a half gallon and dropped into the trees. There was nothing about drugs to it. Either Nelson was a world-class liar or Losidor was born for plucking. Or both.

Unless, of course, Terri was spinning us a story.

"One more thing, Miss Losidor," Harry said. "How did you and Mr. Nelson meet?"

She paused for a moment. "At the Game Club, by the airport."

The Game Club is a singles bar with a fox-hunting motif: bugles and English saddles on the wall, servers in livery and gravy-bowl hats. I'd awakened to a couple of unsettling mornings that began in the Game Club, but that was months ago, before I'd matured.

Harry noted her hesitation. "Are you sure?"

"I always forget the name of the place."

"Who initiated the contact?"

"Do what?"

"Who hit on who first?"

57

"I was sitting with a couple of friends. Jerry was standing at the bar. I kinda glanced over at him and he winked, y'know."

Harry finished his questions, and we stood to leave. She followed us to the door. "We were real close before the money thing," she said, dabbing a tear with a tissue. "We were in love. Je-Jerrold said I made him feel like he'd never felt before."

Desultory images floated behind my eyes; Nelson atop Terri Losidor, grinding away like he's milling wheat, she thinking she's inspired her lover to dizzying feats of virility. Nelson is simply bored with everything but the chance of money. He pumps himself weary, then, dreaming of flying, empties joylessly, falling asleep on a sweat-damp mattress beginning to smell.

We were turning around in the far end of the lot when Harry slammed on the brakes.

"Looky there, Carson," he said, pointing to a cat scratching at Terri Losidor's front door, a fluffy white longhair with a pink collar. The door opened a crack and the cat flipped its tail and scooted inside.

I looked at Harry. "Mr. Puff, I presume."

"Wonder who was that clumsy-ass cat jumping on her sill?" he said.

Harry dropped me off at the station. We'd meet later at Flanagan's for some chow and a brainstorm session. He was going to gather copies of interviews in connection with the case, and I headed to the morgue to see if the prelim was ready.

The report sat at the front desk, a few pages detailing basic and unofficial findings. I didn't expect any revelations at this point. Since I was already here, I figured to brighten Clair's day by interrupting it. I also wondered if the chronically morose Dr. Davanelle had tattled, maybe telling Clair I'd spent my observation time nattering like an auctioneer and singing ribald sea chanties. Even Clair Peltier, the sultaness of strict, allowed a little light conversation during an autopsy.

I walked the wide hall to Clair's office. The door was slightly ajar and I heard her talking. I thought I'd stick my head in and say hi, but my hand froze on the knob when I heard the tone in her voice.

"This is *ridiculous*, absolutely unacceptable," she said, her words sharp as thorns, acid dripped into syllables. "I can't even read your writing on these reports. They look like they were scribbled by a chimpanzee."

I heard a low response, hushed, apologetic.

Clair said, "No! I don't want to hear it. I don't care how little time you had to get them out. I did three posts a day in my first position and still managed to make my paper-work legible."

Another muffled response.

"Sorry doesn't cut it. This work is simply unacceptable. I need to see some goddamn improvement."

I've never enjoyed hearing someone getting tongue-lashed;

it dredges up too many childhood memories. I felt as stricken as if the words were for me. Clair's voice continued as I backed slowly from the door.

"Then there's the matter of sick days. How many are you planning on taking this year? Six? Eight? Two dozen? It's inconsiderate at best. When you're not here—or when you're late, more often than not, it seems—it throws my scheduling on its ass. No, I don't want to hear lame excuses, I just want you to . . ."

I heard the sound of dismissal in Clair's voice. Footsteps approached the door from within. I tiptoed a dozen feet down the hall. The only refuge was Willet Lindy's office; his lights were off and I figured he was gone for the day. He often arrived before six a.m., left by three. I leapt into the office.

Lindy had a wide window to the hall, the blinds three-quarters open. I flattened against the wall and heard the footsteps approach. I watched Ava Davanelle stop in front of the window and push tears from her eyes with trembling fingers. Her face was gray. She squeezed her hands into white-knuckle fists and held them beside her temples. Her body began to shake as if her soul were being shredded by white-hot pincers. I watched, transfixed by the depth of her agony. She shook until a ragged sob wrenched from her throat and she grabbed her stomach and ran to the ladies' room.

The door slammed like a shotgun blast.

Ava Davanelle's misery left me breathless. I stared into the empty hall for a dozen heartbeats, as if anguish had been painted across the air, and I could not believe the intensity of its coloration. I crept breathless from my hidey-hole, escaping toward the front entrance, and passed Clair's half-open door.

"Ryder? Is that you?" she called. I turned around, affected nonchalance, and stuck my head through her door as I'd done a dozen times in the past.

She said, "What are you doing here?" No venom in her voice, it was her usual no-nonsense tone. I smiled awkwardly and held up the report.

She nodded. "The prelim. I forgot. It's been one of those days." Clair paused, thought. "Was this your first procedure with Dr. Davanelle?"

I nodded. "My maiden voyage."

She slipped on her lanyarded reading glasses and peered into a file on her desk, frowning at some errant tidbit of information. "Davanelle's good," Clair said, nodding to herself. "Got a couple areas that need improvement. But she knows her stuff, a keeper. Have a good day, Ryder. Stay out of trouble."

CHAPTER 6

Three stacks of photographs rested on his green Formica table-top: one large, one modest, one small. The only other items on the table were chrome shears and a magnifying glass. The air was hot and windless but he didn't feel it. Nor did he hear the roar of trucks a quarter mile distant on I–10, or the whine of jets approaching or departing Mobile's airport. He was working with the pictures and they demanded relentless attention.

They would change the universe.

The largest stack, pushed to the table's farthest edge, were the Culls, upside down so he didn't have to look at them. Emaciated twigs or fat as hogs, matted with hair, or puckered with scars. The Culls were disgusting liars and he always washed his hands after touching their pictures.

Why had they applied for the position? Couldn't the Culls read? His instructions, sixty-seven words drafted over three weeks, had been exceptionally precise.

Centering the table was a smaller stack of photos, the Potentials. Chests broad and pink. Hillocks of bicep, globes of shoulder. Stomachs flat as skimboards. But all had minor flaws: a strident navel, or puckered nipples. One had distractingly large hands. The Potentials were second-stringers on the sideline benches, there if needed, but hopefully kept from the field.

He swiped his hands on his khakis to blot sweat and reached for the closest stack of photos. There were five in all: the Absolutes, the chosen ones. From the seventy-seven photos he'd received, five had survived the most intense scrutiny. He arrayed the Absolutes before him like supplicants and studied them from chin to kneecaps.

Until the sound started up in his head.

Not again, please not again. . . .

He sat back and pushed his palms against his ears. She'd started singing in the next room. He knew she wasn't physically there, but the woman sang across time and between dimensions if she wanted. He hummed loudly to blunt her song, but it made her sing louder. The only way to stop her singing was push his pants past his knees and do that thing, his buttocks squeaking against the cupped plastic chair until *down there* made nasty business across the underside of the table and the floor.

It took two minutes to make her shut up. He refastened his pants in blessed silence, then spent five minutes at the sink attending to his hands: hot water, soap up to the elbows, scrub with the brush, rinse, repeat. Dry his hands with a fresh towel, toss it in the hamper.

He returned to the table and picked up a photo from the Absolutes. The pictured man stood grinning and naked against a cream-colored wall, hips cocked forward, the male-fruit displayed shamelessly for the camera. The man had a smile like actors grow, white as snow and lacking only a glint of light flashing from an incisor. He'd flashed the bright smile in the park when they met.

The man at the table picked up the scissors. Carefully aligning blades and photo, he snipped, and the head tumbled to the floor. He retrieved the scrap, tore it into dime-sized pieces, and brushed it from his hands into the toilet. The last piece sucked down the whirlpool was the white smile.

The man cocked his head and listened for her song, but she seemed to be resting. Gathering strength, probably; time was growing short. He'd been exceptionally careful, but she surely sensed he was closing in. He returned to the table, picked up the magnifying glass, and studied the men in the remaining photos—knee to chin, chin to knee—over and over, until he knew his choice was right.

* * *

"Quart of whores," Harry said, "Rats back Rats back Rats back Rats back Rats Rats Rats Rats." He scribbled aimlessly on his pad, then tore off the top sheet, crumpled it, and flicked it to the growing pile of paper balls in the center of the round table. The tables in Flanagan's were too small for brainstorming, I thought. The lights too low. The noise level too high. The floor too wooden. Everything irritated me when the thoughts wouldn't come.

"Eight rats," I said, exasperated. "Four with backs."

Harry doodled on his fresh page. "Ate rats? A-T-E?"

I thought about it. Shrugged. Nothing clicked.

"*Rats* anagrams to 'star,'" Harry continued, drawing stars. "Eight stars, four stars times two, four-star restaurant, four-star meal, twice as good?"

I dry-washed my face. "Who in the hell warped the whores?"

The third round arrived. Eloise Simpkins picked up the dead soldiers, glanced at my pad, winced. I'd sketched a large rat.

"Yuck," she said, wrinkling her nose, ratlike.

I craned my neck, stretching. Medium crowd at Flanagan's, twenty-five or so, about half cops. Most were at the bar or tables near it. Harry and I'd sat up front where we could pull the curtain and look outside for inspiration. I opened the curtain. Rain in such solid vertical lines it could have been falling up. Four lanes of canal with a street beneath it, an occasional car splashing by. Across the way a chiropractor's office, pawn shop, and boarded-up dollar store. A styrofoam fast-food carton rafted down the gutter. I closed the curtain.

"Zodiac," Harry said. "Eight stars. Isn't there a constellation or something—"

"The Pleiedes," I said. "Seven stars, seven sisters."

"Why couldn't they have been the eight rats?" Harry produced another ball of paper and rolled it to the center. I saw gator boots moving to the table and looked up to see Bill Cantwell, a ranking detective in second district. Cantwell was a lanky forty-fiveish former Texan who expressed his birthright through stovepipe jeans, ornate shirts, and tipped-forward Stetsons. Cantwell noticed my rat sketch, made a frame with his fingers, and pretended to study Harry. "That's good, Carson," he deadpanned. "A touch more mustache and you'd have him dead-on."

"Another Steinberg," Harry moaned.

"Seinfeld," I corrected. Harry had one TV, a ten-inch black and white. He was a music man.

"I hear y'all might be handling this Nelson thing under Piss-it rules," Cantwell said, propping a silver-pointed boot on a chair beside Harry. "Tell me again what Piss-it stands for, Harry. I ain't looking through that damn manual, thing weighs ten pounds."

"Psychopathological and Sociopathological Investigative Team, Bill," Harry said. "Piss-it's a lot easier to remember."

Tomorrow Harry and I were meeting second district's homicide dicks about canvassing Nelson's neighborhood and checking the haunts he favored. They were, in fact, already doing it, since the killing had occurred in their territory. But under PSIT procedures information had to be routed past Harry and me, since we were the sole members of the team.

Cantwell nodded slowly. "I guess it makes sense Piss-it handles things. The case's got crazy writ all over it, a chopped-off head and writing by the peter. They'll be some grumbling from the guys, it'll mean extra paperwork. But we'll be fine with it, even if Squill ain't."

"What you mean, Bill?" Harry said. "Squill ain't?"

"He was in this afternoon making noises, y'know. Like we didn't have to be real cooperative if we didn't want." Cantwell scratched at an incisor and flicked something unwanted to the floor. "I got the notion ol' Captain Squill ain't real fond of Piss-it."

Harry raised an eyebrow.

"Don't worry, Harry; we'll be going by Piss-it procedures. We're in till we hear otherwise."

Cantwell rapped the table with his knuckles and drifted back to his group. I looked at Harry. "Why is Squill sticking his finger in our eyes?"

Harry shrugged. "It's Squill. We have eyes and he has fingers."

When there was more crumpled paper than room to work, we called it a night, heading outside as Burlew was coming in, his gray raincoat a sodden tent. Harry was already on the street and Burlew and I passed in the narrow vestibule between outside and inside doors. I nodded and gave him room, but he took a sidestep stumble and shouldered me into the wall. I turned to see if he was drunk, but he'd already passed into Flanagan's, chewing his wad of paper, a tight smile at the edges of his doll-baby mouth.

The next morning we were summoned to Squill's office. He was on the phone and ignored us. We sat in hard chairs before his uncluttered desk and studied his ego wall. If any political or law-enforcement celebrity had passed within three states, Squill'd been there with hand out and teeth shining. After five minutes of listening and grunting, Squill hung up his phone and spun his chair to look out the window, his back to our faces.

"Tell me about the Nelson case," he commanded the sky.

"Indeterminate," I said. "Yesterday we talked with his aunt, Billie Messer—"

"I'm talking to the ranking detective, Ryder. In this office you wait your turn."

I felt my face flush with anger and my fists ball involuntarily. Squill said, "I'll try again. What's happening on the Nelson case?"

Harry looked at me, rolled his eyes, and addressed the back of Squill's head.

"We talked with his aunt, Billie Messer, plus some other folks. They confirm the lowlife lifestyle indicated on Nelson's rap sheet. He used people. We interviewed a former girl-friend, the one who filed the charges. She's a confused woman who still has tender feelings for Nelson, but basically said the same. Today we're meeting with the D-Two homicide dicks to set up a mechanism to review the—"

Squill spun to face us. "No," he said, "you're not."

Harry said, "Pardon me, Captain?"

"You're not doing anything. I've spoken with the chief and he agrees this isn't a psycho case. It stinks of fag revenge killing. We're dumping the file back to Second District. Your involvement in the Nelson case is officially over."

I braced my hands on my knees and leaned forward. "What if it's not vengeance, but the start of a killing spree?"

"I'm not talking to listen to myself. Dismissed."

"It doesn't fit a vengeance pattern. Here's what I'm—"

"Did you hear me?"

"Let me finish, Captain. We don't yet have enough information to decide whether or not this is—"

Squill spun back to the window. He said, "Get him out of here, Nautilus, I've got work to do."

I was shaking my head before we hit the hall. "That didn't make sense. Why pull us before we've done an overview? We don't have the info to decide either way if this is PSIT status. What's buzzing in his shorts?"

Harry said, "I got some fresh milk this morning."

"Spill it."

"Remember the rumor Chief Hyrum is retiring next year?"

"Thumping and bumping, you said."

Harry sighed. "I'd never have said that, it doesn't fit. I said rolling and strolling. Only it's not next summer, it's this September."

I said, "Two months away. The hatchet jobs have to be done in double time?"

Harry nodded. "Pop an umbrella; the blood's gonna fly."

"That doesn't concern us, remember? You told me that."

"The only constant is change, bro, you told me that. There's two deputy chiefs tussling for the job of Big Chief: Belvidere and Plackett. Squill's hitched his wagon to Plackett's star, been buttering his biscuits for years. If the commission recommends Plackett for chief, guess who he'll slip in as a deputy chief?"

My stomach churned. "Squill?"

Harry slapped my back. "Now you're seeing the big picture, Carson. Like Squill, Plackett's more politico than cop. Guy couldn't find his ass with a mirror and tongs, but he knows how to work the newsies; Squill gave him pointers about sound bites, eye contact, spinning a story. On the other hand, Belvidere's a cop. Knows his shit, but has a personality like instant potatoes. A lot of little things add up in the police commission's selection process, but remember who floated the idea of the PSIT. . . ."

"Belvidere," I said. "Plackett opposed it."

"Probably at Squill's advice," Harry said. "Push it."

"If we do good, it makes Belvidere look good, which steals thunder from Plackett, which works to Squill's disfavor?"

"Hocused and pocused," Harry said. "Now try and focus."

I rolled my eyes. "C'mon, Harry, try it in English."

"Look hard. Take it one more step."

I focused. "In the best of all possible worlds to Squill, the entire concept of PSIT would be floating facedown in the Mobile River?"

We passed Linette Bowling, Squill's charmless, donkey-faced administrative assistant. Harry snatched a fistful of droopy flowers from a vase on her desk and handed them to me.

"You're beautiful when you finally get the picture, Carson."

"Nautilus, you asshole," Linette brayed from behind us, "gimme back my fuckin' flowers."

CHAPTER 7

It was eighty-eight degrees at 11:00 P.M. A wet haze smoth-
ered the stars and gauzed the moon. Two days had passed
since Nelson's murder, and the team Squill had assigned to
the case hadn't made any progress. I stood at water's edge
and cast the spinning rig, retrieved the lure slowly, cast
again. I usually fish with a fly rod and know what I'm fishing
for: specs, reds, pompano, Spanish mac. But now and then
I use a spinning rig to dredge the night waters. Sometimes
my line ties me to a shark. Or a big ray. Familiar species.
But on rare occasions I've reeled in bizarre life-forms not
mentioned in my books on Gulf fishing. I never know what
trick of tide or current directs them to my line, but there
they are, wriggling species from unknown depths, daring

my touch. It's strange, but without them I doubt I'd enjoy fishing as much.

It's the soothing aspect of angling that often compels me to fish when troubled, and I had been upset since hearing Clair's buzzsawing of Dr. Davanelle. I hadn't meant to over-hear, nor spy on Dr. Davanelle's private horror, but it was acid-etched in my mind.

Of Dr. Davanelle's choice for the pathologist position, I knew only the edges of the story: she was the second choice for the job, hired only after the horror of Dr. Caulfield's injury. It took a tragedy for her to gain the position in Mobile, her first professional assignment. As Harry had reminded me during our session at Cake's bar, I, too, had stumbled into my position through the misfortunes of others. I knew such a thing could feel like a form of dishonesty. It didn't help that Dr. Davanelle worked with Clair—brilliant, renowned, sought at forensics symposia worldwide—a total perfectionist who demanded nothing less than the best from every staff member, every second.

I reeled in my line and set the rod in the spike. I sat in the sand with my arms wrapping my knees and stared across the rippling plain of water, liquid obsidian burnished by moonlight. After several minutes of reflection I scrabbled through the cooler bag where I'd tossed my cell phone at the last minute. Phone on ice; Freud would have enjoyed that.

Information provided Ava Davanelle's number and I dialed. Her recorded voice was as cold as the device in my hand. She provided her number, referred to the beep, and was gone. I heard the tone, listened to the emptiness, clicked the call dead. Only then did it hit me—had she answered the phone, what would I have said?

"Hello, Dr. Davanelle, it's Detective Ryder. I'm sorry for being a pain in the ass at the Nelson autopsy, I didn't mean to add to your problems. What problems? I was, uh, skulking in Willet Lindy's office yesterday when you came down the hall and watched as you . . ."

I sighed and unzipped the cooler bag, preparing to refrost the phone, when it started chirping.

It was Harry. "Got a call from the ME's man on the scene," he said. "We got us another headless horseman at Eight thirty-seven Caleria. Saddle up and ride, Ichabod. I'll meet you in Sleepy Hollow."

The scene was a large Italianate-style home near the southern outskirts of downtown, a neighborhood of stately historic homes intermingled with apartments. Insects burred from the hovering pines and wide-spread oaks. Several patrol cars fronted the scene, as did the crime-scene van and an ambulance. A news van did a U and pulled to the curb. Neighbors with somber faces milled on the sidewalk. Traffic thickened, drivers drawn like moths to the flashing lights and activity. A patrolman in the street waved his arms and bawled, "Move on, folks, move on." I saw Harry and pulled up on the curb behind him.

"Weasels 'R' Us around?" I asked.

Harry shook his head. "Squill's been at his brother's condo in Pensacola. On his way."

Pensacola was at least ninety minutes away. Given time elapsed, we had maybe a half hour without him.

"Let's hit it while we can, bro," I said. We walked onto a large front porch. Leaning against a white column was Detective Sergeant Warren Blasingame from District Three, who—since we were in D-3—had initial jurisdiction. Blasingame was sucking a cigarette and staring at the treetops.

"What's happening inside, Warren?" Harry asked.

Blasingame drew a finger across his Adam's apple. "That's all I know."

"You haven't been inside?"

"Just ME folk, scene techs, and Hargreaves. She took the call," Blasingame drawled, spitting onto the lawn. "My guys ain't supposed to go in till Squill gets here. Neither are you, probably, no matter what Piss-it rules say about you being in charge."

"Didn't hear nothing about that," Harry said as our footsteps thumped across the porch.

Words scripted around a logo on the door: Deschamps Design Services. A small sign below the doorbell advised, PLEASE RING TO ENTER. A decal on the glass said PROTECTED BY JENKINS SECURITY SYSTEMS. While the place wasn't the Bastille, neither was it open-door policy. Directly inside was a small pastel-hued reception area that screamed Designer at Work: Chagall-hued abstracts spotlit by track lighting; a puffy blue-leather couch; a frame-and-fabric chair more like a kite than a sitting device. One wall held framed awards for best this and that in design. The place had a subtle astringent smell, like disinfectant, or strong cleanser.

"Could chill beer in here," Harry said, cinching his tie. We walked a short hall. I heard a muffled sob from a room to the left and gently opened the door. A slender woman sat at a small conference table with patrol officer Sally Hargreaves. Sal had been first on the scene. She was talking softly with her hand over the woman's wrist. Sal saw me and came to the door.

"Cheryl Knotts, victim's fiancée," she whispered. "Flight attendant out for three days. She got here fifty minutes ago to find one Peter Edgar Deschamps dead in his studio."

"Impression?" I asked, knowing Sal's got the magic.

"She had nothing to do with it, I'd bet the farm on that. She's devastated."

By magic I mean Sal has that rare sense letting her read people fast and dead on. All cops grow the ability to detect bullshit better than your average citizen, but some are prodigies, polygraphic Mozarts. On Sal's take alone I pretty much X'd out the fiancée as a suspect.

"Get her to answer some questions in a few?" I asked.

Sally nodded, touched my arm. "Walk light if you can."

Sally's got a hint of wet in her eyes; the magic has its price. I kissed her lightly on the forehead. "Did I tell you I dreamed about you last week?" I said. "I was a nurse and you were a Viking. . . ."

76

Sal smiled for the first time and pushed me down the hall. "Go take care of Harry before he does something weird," she said.

The victim was on his back next to a drawing board. Beside the board was a desk with a Mac, and a monitor with a screen larger than the one on my TV. The man's garb was white-collar casual: blue Oxford-cloth shirt, pressed khakis, webbed belt, brown loafers. The deceased was solidly built—not a hardcore gym rat with ham biceps and steroid-worm veins, but a guy with a hard and regular regimen. His shirt was unbuttoned and the slacks unzipped, the pants bunched low around his buttocks. Outside of the scarlet collar there was no sign of blood or other violence on his clothing. Hembree'd caught the case.

"What's the word, Bree?" I asked.

"Looks like you and Harry are going to pull some overtime."

"Cause of death?"

"Just like Nelson. Can't find anything on the body. But a head wound. . . ."

"Could be floating past the Dixey Bar lighthouse about now."

Hembree nodded. "If the perp's using a gun, I'd bet a twenty-two. Most of the time the slug goes into the skull and ricochets around inside like a Ping-Pong ball. No exit wound, no splatter. Just brain pudding."

I thought about what the mind might make of a pellet bouncing within its confines like a metal wasp. Could a brain comprehend its own destruction? Hear itself scream?

"What about the blood when the head comes off?" I asked, rubbing my hands together, suddenly cold.

"Heart's stopped, blood's not moving. Less exsanguination than you'd think. Was me I'd slide a towel under the neck to sop blood, then remove the head. Wrap the head in the towel, drop it into a bowling-ball bag, and wave good-bye."

"Just don't get the bags mixed up on league night. Any writing?"

"Been waiting for you to ask."

Hembree slid the deceased's briefs past his pubic hair. The same minuscule writing, but in two lines. The top one said, *Warped a quart of whores. Quart of whores. Whores warped. Quart of whores. Warped whores. Quart of whores. Warped whores.* This was followed by *Rats Rats Rats Ho Ho Ho Ho Rats Rats Rats Rats Ho Ho Ho Ho Ho Ho Ho*

An icy finger tickled the base of my neck.

"The whores angle again," Hembree said. "You guys went that road?"

I nodded. We'd contacted vice and homicide departments across the Gulf Coast, expanding to national crime-stat sources. No unsolved killings in our area, at least not within our parameters. Whatever this was, we had an exclusive.

Hembree pointed to the second line. "*Ho* as 'whore'?"

"Or *ho* like in laughing at us, Bree."

Hembree closed his eyes. "Oh, man, anything but that."

Taunts from psychopathically disordered killers were a

chilling sign. The killers felt certain they could get away with anything. Some did, especially if they had iron-hard self-control, like the control to precisely sever a head and write in tiny, perfectly defined letters. Such people could live anywhere, be anything: janitor, schoolteacher, bank president.

Hembree said the ME's tech had approximated TOD at two or so hours before, give or take. Harry said, "I'll go look around the rest of the place. See if you can get anything from the woman. Girlfriend?"

"Fiancée," I corrected. "Sally thinks she's clean."

"Good enough for me," Harry said, familiar with the magic. He buttoned his jacket. "Damn, it's colder'n a tomb in here."

I returned to the room with the fiancée, not looking forward to what I might become to her. In a grocery store I once unknowingly stood in line behind a woman I'd interviewed about her daughter's violent death. When our eyes connected she turned white, made kitten-mew sounds, and ran out the door, her groceries still riding the belt. Now, entering the worst moment in this woman's life, I prayed her mind blanked me out after tonight, and when nightmares screamed open her eyes, it wasn't my face printed on the ceiling.

"Excuse me, Ms. Knotts, I'm Detective Carson Ryder, and I'd like to speak to you for a few minutes if I may."

She took a deep breath and nodded. "While it's still . . . fresh, I know." I had to strain to hear her.

"Peter didn't tell you about any kind of meeting today? Anyone he was going to be talking to?"

"No. But he's wearing meeting clothes, long pants, dress shirt. He'd work in cutoffs and a T-shirt, unless . . . someone must have scheduled at the last minute."

I heard voices and footsteps at the front door. Sally closed the door for privacy.

"Did clients come here often?"

"No. He goes to them. Peter's big on service."

"Walk-ins?"

"Sometimes people'd see the sign and ask if he did business cards and stuff like that."

"If he was going to meet someone and wrote it down, where would he keep the information?"

She closed her eyes. "I gave him a PDA last Christmas. It's probably in the front desk. Top drawer."

Sal slipped away, returning a minute later with a device hardly larger than a credit card. She'd put on latex gloves. I joined Sal in the hall. She tapped the keypad and studied the display a long moment before turning it to me.

Today's date. Under that was entered: *8:00 PM mtg.w/Mr. Cutter.*

"Well, isn't that just bold as hell," Sally said.

I stepped out to tell Harry about Mr. Cutter and ran into a straight-arm block with a wall of meat behind it. "Whoa, there, Ryder," Burlew said. "Where you going, sport?" His breath smelled like manure and onions; maybe he should have chewed Listerine ads.

80

"I have to talk to Harry."

"Phone him, hot dog. From outside."

I yelled. "Harry, you back there?"

He pointed to the front. "Door's the other way, bucko."

"Where's the captain, Burlew?"

"Sergeant Burlew to you. Now haul ass before it gets hauled."

Squill stuck his face through the doorway of Deschamps's studio a dozen feet down the hall. It was like the world had shifted on its axis and everyone got thrown into different positions. "I've got the scene now, Ryder," he said. "Go take statements from the neighbors."

"Where's Harry, Captain? It's important."

"Didn't you get enough air at birth, Ryder?" Squill said. "I gave you a direct order. Get outside and start interviewing."

I'd read the revised manual about a hundred times, mostly in drop-jaw disbelief at the autonomy supposedly granted the PSIT. In cases judged to be under the unit's purview, Harry and I were to be the ones coordinating the efforts.

"Excuse me, Captain," I said, "but this scene, combined with the Nelson murder, displays evidence of a disordered mind, pyschopathologically or sociopathologically, that means—"

Squill jabbed a manicured digit toward the door. "Door," he elucidated.

"Dammit, sir, hear me out. The evidence indicates—"

"Swearing at a superior officer? That's it. I'm done talking, Detective."

81

"Then how about listening, Captain? We have two men beheaded, and we have—"

"You, Officer," Squill barked to a young patrolman by the back door. "Yes, you. Wake up. Get over here and escort Mr. Ryder from the house, now."

"—clear evidence of a disordered mind. . . ."

Burlew's hand tightened around my bicep like a vise and I yanked it free. "Off me, Burl. Shouldn't you be washing the captain's socks or something?"

Burlew wheeled to me and spat a gray plug of newsprint on the floor. "Anytime," he dared, a foul-breathed Gibraltar with clenched fists, cannonball biceps bulging beneath his jacket. "Got the balls to try it?"

I shifted my balance low in my hips and felt the buzz of energy just below my navel. I could smell heat coming off Burlew. His penny-sized eyes blazed with anger, but behind it I sensed fear.

"Sergeant," Squill commanded. "Get over here. We have work to do." Squill gave Burlew a come-hither twitch.

I spoke low. "Captain needs a foot rub, Burl. Best get on it."

Burlew tried to set me on fire with his glare, then tongued his lips and turned toward the studio, a heavy shoulder nudging me as he passed. "Your time's coming, asshole," he whispered.

The uniform was at my side. "I'm sorry, Detective Ryder," he said, "but could you please step outside, sir? Please."

Shaking with anger, I went to the porch and heard Harry's whistle. He walked up from the shadows beside the house.

"Welcome to the B team, Carson. We B out here while Squill's in there. He showed up while you were with the fiancée and it was like the Marines landing."

"Explain this to me, Harry. Am I missing something?"

Harry pointed to a big command SUV pulling onto the front lawn, engine revving needlessly, tires breaking traction and spitting grass. *Look at me,* the machine seemed to say as it lurched to a stop. The passenger door opened. After a five-second pause to let camera lights frame the scene, Deputy Chief Plackett emerged as if born of the dark vehicle. He straightened his tie, showed the newsies his palm, and no-commented his way to the house. Bile roiled in my stomach—I got the message: Squill and Plackett were doing the brass-hat dance, Squill performing for Plackett, Plackett for the cameras and public. While inside the house a dead and mutilated human body functioned as a prop in an act of ego theater.

"Excuse me, Detective Ryder?"

I turned to the uniform Squill had walk me from the house, a young blond guy looking like he'd skipped directly from the Cub Scouts to the MPD.

"I'm sorry about the action in there, sir. The captain ordered me and I—"

"Did what you had to do. Relax."

"It's bullshit if you ask me, Detective. It seems if anyone should be in there, it should be you. This crazy stuff . . . wasn't it you solved that Adrian case by yourself? I mean, didn't you?"

His words were innocent, but they wrapped dread around

me. From the corner of my eye I saw Harry's head angle my way, watching my response.

"Not really," I told the patrol officer, trying to talk through the sand in my throat. "I just got lucky that other time. And I had a lot of help."

"Carson, you NEEEEED ME AGAIN. . . ."

I didn't tell him where the help had come from. Or how just thinking of going back for more made my knees weak and my spine cold. I looked at Harry. He was studying the sky like it was a movie screen.

I drove home with the windows down, the AC blasting, and a knot in my gut the windstorm in the car couldn't blow away. Created in the wake of the Adrian killings, the PSIT was the rarest of all public-relations contrivances: one that—accidentally or not—served a purpose. But, like so many blue-ribbon-panel creations over the years, the PSIT seemed destined for an unmourned death. Quietly excised from existence in the next iteration of the procedures manual, its transitory purpose would be served, its vaporous delusions no longer required. Until the next Joel Adrian. Or maybe whatever the hell was out there now.

When I arrived home, drained and angry, the light on my phone signaled a message. I pressed the Play button.

"Hello, Carson? Are you there? It's Vangie Prowse. Pick up, please. I want to talk to you about Jeremy. We have some things to discuss. Carson?"

The message beeped to an end. I pressed Erase and fell into bed.

CHAPTER 8

"Is Piss-it coordinating this case or not," I asked Lieutenant Tom Mason when he arrived at 7:30 the next morning. "We've got two headless corpses. Are we waiting for the killer's shrink to call and say, 'Yes, Cutter's wacko, yours truly, Dr. Igor Hassenpfeffer'?"

I sat heavily on my desk, upending a mug of pencils.

"Hassenpfeffer? Is that a real name?" Tom asked, bending to retrieve pencils from the floor. Tom's head of the Crimes Against Persons unit and our main line of defense against the brass. He's a rail-thin fifty, has a face like a suicidal bloodhound, and is utterly without guile. I'd been stewing about last night's confrontation when Tom walked up. Harry, just in and peeling off his chartreuse suit coat, was right behind.

"Listen to this," I said, lifting the revised procedures manual from my desk and declaiming the PSIT section with the zeal of a jailhouse lawyer.

Tom nodded. "Read that this morning myself."

"Is it pud-pulling, or is it for real?"

Harry sat down with a cup of coffee and gave me his indulgent look. Tom said, "Harry, you remember that rotten ol' scow our river-patrol boys used to have? That itty-bitty boat?" It took Tom most of a minute to say the sentence. He'd come up on a watermelon farm near the Mississippi border, in the deep-back country, where folks talked about as fast as melons grew; if Tom talked any slower he'd talk backward.

Harry nodded. "The leaky tub with the iffy bilge pump."

Tom put his foot on a chair and crossed his arms over his knee. "Carson, back around '99 we got us a brand-new boat donated by Mabry's Marine. Twenty-four foot. Hundred-fifty-horse motor. Stable as a granite Cadillac. Even had life jackets."

I sat tight and waited it out. Tom couldn't bless-you a sneeze in under five minutes.

"Comes the day to dedicate that boat, Carson, y'know, christen it. A big ol' to-do. Told the politicos, called the newsies. Except nobody's told the chaplain. The band played, the politicians yapped. The people stood and stared. But no christening."

My attention started to drift. Harry nudged my arm, pointed at Tom, *Listen up.*

"The very next night some dope-boater comes hauling weed through the fog and slams a log north of the causeway. Rain. Heavy chop. Waterspouts in the bay. But we still had to fish bales from the water before the tide sucked them away. You know which one of them boats the boys took out?"

Harry poked me and said, "They took the old boat because the new one hadn't been blessed, Carson. They weren't going to trust their asses to it without the blessing of a higher power. The PSIT's real, but it's basically brand-new. No one wants to trust it until it's been blessed."

"And when do we know if we're receiving this anointment?" I asked.

"Should be pretty quick," Tom said, tapping the crystal of his watch. "The chief's called a meeting in twenty minutes."

Three words came to mind when I thought of Chief Hyrum: *chain of command.* If the chief was beside me while I choked on a gumball, he'd walk to his office and call a deputy chief of support services. The DCSS would inform the major in charge of the Criminal Investigations Section, who would alert the captain of the Investigative Services Division. The captain would inform the lieutenant in charge of the Crimes Against Persons Unit, and the lieutenant would send a sergeant from Homicide to Heimlich my corpse.

Structure was his insulation from reality. Or, to be kinder, from decision making. He'd been thrust into the position three years ago when the then-chief suffered a heart attack and retired. Hyrum made several well-intentioned missteps in restructuring the department and most resulted in negative publicity and general internal bellyaching. Made wary by the experience, the chief now preached straight from the book and leaned toward the familiar passages. He approached recent experiments—the PSIT, for example—like a blind man nearing the sound of unfamiliar machinery.

We got to the conference room a few minutes early. I drank a cup of coffee by the urn, then filled another and sat as the others filed in. It was an improbable assemblage of rankings, starting at the pinnacle with Chief Hyrum. Below him was Deputy Chief Belvidere, and because Belvidere attended, so did DC Plackett. On the next stratum was Blasingame from District Three, Cantwell from Two, and Tom Mason. Then, dicks from the districts where the murders had occurred: Rose Blankenship from Two and Sammy Walters from Three.

The chief and Squill entered, nodding and gesturing in conversation as Squill patted the chief's shoulder. Chief Hyrum was fifty-three, maybe six feet tall, and gave the impression of solidity, though a few pounds of belly drifted over the belt line. The room fell quiet as he sat and looked out over the expectant faces.

He held on mine.

"I understand you were involved in some miscommunication last night, Detective Ryder. Would you care to explain your side of the story? Now's your chance."

I felt my stomach fall and churn. "Explain what, sir?"

Squill cleared his throat. "Chief, sometimes mistakes are made and apologies are necessary."

Hyrum said, "I can accept that, Captain."

Every face turned my way. I felt like the lead in a play that closed before I'd read the script. It seemed Squill had gotten to the chief before the meeting and poor-mouthed me over last night's incident. I was obviously required to apologize to him.

"What's happening here?" I asked.

Hyrum said, "I say let bygones be bygones, Detective. It's best to forget mistakes and—"

I smacked the table with my palm. Coffee splashed from cups to the table. Grumbles.

"No, dammit. I demand to hear what you've been told about last night."

Beside me Harry moaned so softly only I could hear him. Chief Hyrum gave me a three-count glare as he sopped spilled coffee with his napkin. "Captain Squill said you and Detective Nautilus were doing an excellent job of processing the scene under PSIT directives when the captain mistakenly established command under standard procedures, resulting in some confusion."

Harry moaned again. Hyrum continued. "Captain Squill also told me—"

"That I deeply regret any mistakes," Squill interjected in a mortician-smooth voice. "I assure all in this room and especially Detective Ryder that I've since read the procedures. Twice. No, three times."

A sprinkling of laughter at Squill's self-deprecation. He was doing *mea culpa* and I was doing *me an asshole*. I'd expected him to lie about last night and he'd trumped me by telling the truth.

"Can we move on, Detective Ryder?" Hyrum asked, a baleful eye glaring my way.

I nodded. Please. Quickly. I shot a glance at Squill; he was stroking his chin and smiling out the window. The chief focused on Harry. "You've been at both scenes, Detective Nautilus. What's your opinion?"

"I've been more involved with interviewing bystanders, Chief, so I'll punt to Detective Ryder."

It was Harry's way of lifting me back in the saddle. Suitably chastened and without a single drop of coffee spilled, I ticked off a list of facts.

"Cold blooded," Rose Blankenship said when I'd finished. "Any take on the messages?"

I followed with a quick review of where Harry and I had been: anagrams, astrological symbols, mythical symbols, basic letter codes, nothing feeling right except the notion that the killer felt secure and in control of the situation.

"Why don't you piece together the events leading to the murder as you see them, Detective Ryder," the chief said.

I nodded and started my timeline, trying to sound as professional and assured as a network news anchor. "The perpetrator arrived for an eight p.m. meeting arranged, I'm sure, by phone. He overpowered Mr. Deschamps and killed him. The mechanism of killing can't yet be determined.

Using an extremely sharp implement, he beheaded Mr. Deschamps—a process Forensics informs me could take less than a minute. Before the decapitation the perpetrator spent ten or so minutes writing on the body, using—"

Squill interrupted. "Ten minutes? You're sure?" He liked to keep speakers off balance with scattershot questions. Unless, of course, the speaker ranked above Squill, who then hung rapt and mute on every word.

I kept the irritation from my voice. "I figure it was somewhere in that range, Captain."

"How did you arrive at that number? Forensics?"

"Not exactly, Captain. It's sort of an independent experiment, a way to—"

Squill nodded triumphantly, as if he'd caught me in a baldfaced lie. I heard another low moan from Harry's direction. "Detective Ryder, I know we're blue-skying here, but we assign times to actions only after a qualified judgment from Forensics."

"I think it's qualified, sir," I said. "Empirically at least." I hadn't had time to run it by Harry, he'd been at court.

Chief Hyrum frowned. "What are you talking about, Detective Ryder?"

"Like I said, a kind of experiment, sir."

"Explain, please."

I stood and dropped my pants.

Harry sounded like he was having an attack of appendicitis.

CHAPTER 9

Mr. Cutter sat in his car in the morgue lot and waited for her. He hadn't thought of himself as Mr. Cutter originally, but after using the name with Deschamps, he'd come to enjoy it, like a good joke. Deschamps had certainly seemed attached to it, saying *Mr. Cutter* this and *Mr. Cutter* that, but everything about Deschamps had been likable; he was so eager to please. He'd even fallen supine; Mr. Cutter did not have to wrestle him over so the blood would pool in his back and not discolor the important parts.

They'd built a firm relationship from that first phone call: "Mr. Deschamps, I'm Alec Cutter, and I'd like to discuss the creation of a logo and other corporate identity materials for my new company. I'm hoping you might work up both some typographic solutions and perhaps some graphic treatments. . . ."

Mr. Cutter chuckled at the memory—it had taken fifteen minutes in the library with an advertising primer to glean enough jargon to avoid suspicion.

"Don't worry, Mr. Cutter, I've had plenty of experience with logos and corporate ID. I'll show you some samples when you arrive. You said eight? I look forward to it."

Mr. Cutter knew his man would be alone. After Deschamps became one of the Absolutes several months back, Mr. Cutter dedicated over a hundred hours to the artist's schedule and habits. His female always left Monday and returned late on Thursday. Though Mr. Cutter worked a day job, his schedule was flexible, allowing him to devote the necessary hours to stalking his quarry.

Nothing in the universe was more important.

Mr. Cutter arrived at the house at 7:50 P.M. and Deschamps suggested meeting in the studio. He turned his broad back and led the way, showing a strong roll of shoulder and shapely cut of bicep beneath the short-sleeve dress shirt. Perfect. And untainted, as Mr. Cutter already knew. Deschamps wasn't the type for scarifying trends like tattoos and piercings; he was picture perfect from neck to knees.

He'd even sent Mr. Cutter the picture to prove it.

Mr. Cutter conducted his true business, then cleaned the studio like a maid possessed. Removing every mote of evidence wasn't overly difficult with knowledge and planning. Time wasn't an issue—Deschamps's woman never arrived before 22:00 on Thursday. He didn't want her late, but delays—sometimes long ones—were inevitable in her line of work, and Mr. Cutter dropped the thermostat to its lowest point.

Nelson had been even easier than the artist. Mr. Cutter instantly recognized a man driven by greed. The phone call had been almost delicious.

"You don't know me, Mr. Nelson, but we have a friend in common."

"Tony? Rance? Bobby?"

"Now, now, you know not all of your friends want to be, how shall I say, friends in the morning. Just night friends. Nameless night friends. Generous nameless night friends."

Laughter from Nelson. He loved little games, you could tell.

"I'd enjoy just meeting you, Mr. Nelson, somewhere quiet, out of the way. . . . I'm a man of simple tastes and ample wallet. . . . There's a little park not far from me. . . ."

It had worked so wonderfully. Nelson, too, was perfect from chin to knee, just like his photographs had predicted.

A pickup truck pulled into the morgue lot. Mr. Cutter bent low and reached to the glovebox as if looking for something, face averted. When the truck passed by, he sat up and returned to his reflections.

Two of his projects had gone well, one had gone to hell.

It was his first attempt. Horrible. He'd been deceived by a man-child and should have beaten the bastard's face into paste right there in the farm-field dark with the music and watermelons. After seeing the disgusting thing the little scummer had scrawled on his chest, Mr. Cutter head-bashed the bastard with a rock, then slipped away unnoticed, leaving the drugged-up fools to their glowing necklaces, water bottles, and filthy clutchings.

Thirty-seven and a half hours of research and planning turned into vapor. Fortunately, Nelson had sent his particulars a week later. He'd been so easy it almost made up for the time spent on . . . what was the little bastard's name? Farrier?

Mr. Cutter glanced at his watch. Almost noon, almost time for her to step out for lunch, clockwork. He pulled the visor down and leaned back. Thinking of her, his heart began racing in his chest, pumping a delicious mix of fear and joy to every cell in his body. He needed to see her walk outside into the hard sunlight. It scrinched up her face in that crazed bitch-anger, one of her moods set to crash over her like a glass wave, hot shards slashing everywhere.

The first time he'd seen her, since she'd come back, she was outside. Outside walking inside. Angry; not sun anger but her wild hidden fury, bitch-hot fury full of lies and promises.

He'd seen it even through her pathetic lying disguise; a kiss is just a sheath over the biting.

He recognized her as Mama.

And knew the universe had granted him a second chance.

"I used what's called a Rapidograph technical pen," I said, pointing to my thigh, my pants around my ankles, "and

95

wrote the words found on Deschamps. The lab's micro-photographs indicate the writing was done stroke by stroke to keep the ink from pooling due to skin porosity. I tried three times and the fastest inscription took over ten minutes."

"I barely see the writing," Deputy Chief Belvidere said from across the table, squinting. "Almost like he didn't want it seen." Chief Hyrum seemed uncomfortable around burgundy briefs. "Very, um, thorough, Detective Ryder," he said. "I think that's all we need."

I retrieved my pants and sat down.

Squill said, "I congratulate Detective Ryder for his independent research and hope he checks it against that of our experts. That's the beauty of the combining PSIT with proven investigative technique: the theoretical and the practical can mix and merge; when fanciful flights are tempered by reality, they can sometimes be instructive."

Fanciful flights tempered by reality. Zing.

Hyrum *ahem*ed uncertainly and addressed the room at large. "We formed the PSIT to respond to the growing numbers of, well, freakish crimes. Detectives Nautilus and Ryder proved themselves in the Adrian case. That's why Detective Ryder was promoted from the uniformed division, and why he and Detective Nautilus received extra training. Though this is the trial run of the PSIT, they deserve a modicum of latitude in investigating these murders."

"Yes," Harry whispered. I held my breath. Were we about to be blessed?

"I agree completely," Squill said. "Both of the affected

neighborhoods have citizens who are frightened. And vocal. Both are near downtown. We can't have people afraid of those neighborhoods, not with the mayor's urban revitalization plan under way."

Hyrum listened intently, his head bobbing to the cadences of politics. Politics had structure.

Squill continued. "Which is why I welcome the PSIT's involvement. By combining in task-force mode we'll maximize our resources to the fullest."

Out of nowhere the words, "task force." I knew *task force* in departmental lexicon defined a rigid vertical structure perhaps overarching the procedural revisions of the PSIT. Everyone's eyes moved to Hyrum; investigational structure was his call. He reached for a legal pad. After a few halting marks he displayed the results: a single baseball-sized circle at the top of the page. He tapped its center with his pen.

"Here's how I want it organized: Detectives Nautilus and Ryder will lead field investigation of the cases, all information channeled their direction. . . ."

I glanced at Harry. He raised an eyebrow. Hyrum continued tapping the page, thinking, structuring.

"Detectives Ryder and Nautilus will work with the"—he put the pad on the table and drew another circle directly below the first one. He held the pad up and tapped the second circle—"district detectives assigned to the case. Information freely shared, copies of the murder books to everyone involved. . . ."

We were top circle! Underneath us was the investigative

team we'd assemble. I was thinking Larry Twilling from Four, Ben Dupree from Two, maybe finesse Sally Hargreaves on board.

"We're blessed," I whispered to Harry.

Hyrum started drawing again, a final circle at the bottom of the page to indicate Command's position as recipient of data, hands off, but kept in the loop, of course. He worked slowly, making it compass perfect, the end seamlessly joining the beginning.

"Now," Hyrum said, nodding at his sheet, "by assigning this case task force designation, I'm putting—"

Hyrum flipped the pad upside down and tapped what was now the top circle.

"—Captain Squill in overall command of the force and its configuration, plus continuing to act as liaison to myself and the deputy chiefs. He'll also handle media inquiries, demonstrating the task force's, uh. . . ."

Squill pretended to write in his own pad. "Preplanned proactive structure, Chief. I'm working up the deployment plan now."

Hyrum finished the meeting by scribbling arcs between circles, intending to convey cooperation and flow of information. It didn't matter, everyone had carefully noted our true position as butt-bottom on the snowman.

"Good luck gentlemen," Hyrum said. "And keep me posted on results."

Tom shot me a sad smile, knowing Harry and I'd just been backed into the blades. Harry deflated with a growl.

Chief Hyrum looked quizzically at Harry. "What's that, Detective Nautilus? Did I hear you groan?"

"Sorry, Chief," Harry said, kneading his thigh. "Cramp in my leg."

CHAPTER 10

After the meeting Harry went to check some financials on the victims. We hardly spoke; we'd been blindsided and there was not a damn thing to do about it. Having been present at Nelson's autopsy, I was the de facto body man, and headed to the morgue for Deschamp's procedure. I knew Dr. Davanelle was to be the prosector; I'd spoken to Vera Braden about the time of the procedure and offhandedly asked who was scheduled.

I planned to ask Ava Davanelle out. I wasn't sure why. And had no idea how to do it.

Will Lindy was at the front door as I arrived, diddling with the lock, a screwdriver in his mouth, tiny parts scattered across the floor. I was always impressed by anyone with mechanical prowess; I relied on duct tape or super glue. If either failed, I was up the creek.

"Can't you hire people to do that, Will? A locksmith?"

"Urn er bubdit?" he replied. "Pap chat."

"Come again?"

He took the screwdriver from his mouth. "On our budget? Fat chance. If I save a hundred bucks here, I'll put it toward something we actually need."

"I thought you guys got wheelbarrows full of bucks when the place was redone. Put in the new gear, furniture, security cameras, and whatnot."

"Government dollars," he said, smiling. "Spend 'em or lose 'em."

I went inside, waved to Vera, and ambled back to the autopsy suite. Be humble, be charming, be professional, I told myself. And be them all while keeping your mouth shut.

The procedure was under way as I entered, Ava Davanelle bent low over Deschamps's groin, speaking the inscription into the air for the recording system. She knew one of the things I needed to see and nodded at a table against the wall.

I found a stack of photos taken by Chambliss, his usual excellent work. The words above Deschamps's pubic hair were displayed beside a ruler, block lettering between three and four millimeters tall, lavender, precise. I waved the photos at Dr. Davanelle.

"Thanks," I said, smiling her direction. "Good seeing you again, Doctor. How's it going with—"

I caught me before she could. I winced, mouthed, *Sorry*, and turned back to the photos, shuffling them through my palms. There was a variety, from shots of the full inscription down to individual letters. I couldn't fathom why anyone making a statement would choose such a hard-to-read color and write in microtype, but it would be as logical as subtraction to the mind behind these crimes.

I sat and studied the photographs until seeing them with closed eyes. Now and then I'd shift my attention to Dr. Davanelle. Her voice was monotonic, her eyes focused on her tasks. She was gowned in blue from crown to knees. I tried to discern the shape of her calves within her beige slacks, and concluded they were slender but not skinny.

The task took three hours. It would soon determine Peter Deschamps had been murdered by some form of head trauma, the head removed by a blade similar to that used to behead Jerrold Nelson, if not the identical one. I walked over as Ava Davanelle stripped off her mask and head cover. I popped the question before she could escape.

"Would you care to do something this evening, Dr. Davanelle? Something quiet and simple? Get a bite to eat, take in a—"

The door opened and Walter Huddleston appeared. He launched a pair of scarlet flares my way, then ignored me completely. In less than a minute Deschamps was carted and rolling away. I returned my attention to Ava Davanelle, now shutting off the table's irrigation system. Without the gentle trickling of water through pipes and across the metal table, the room was blank with silence.

"I was about to ask if . . ."

My words trailed off when I realized she was staring at me. Not the glare I'd come to know, but something more akin to a gentle perplexity.

She said, "You phoned my house the other night, didn't you, Detective?"

My heart seized up. Busted.

"I, ah . . ."

"This is a technical age. Even answering machines can have Caller ID. May I ask what you wanted at eleven thirty-seven in the evening?"

I boiled my intentions down to essentials. "I wanted to apologize for the other day. I spoke out of turn. You're the prosector, you call the shots. And my remark about you shoveling down was rude and uncalled for."

She pursed her lips and raised a slender eyebrow. It made her look almost pretty.

"It took you two days to come to that conclusion?"

I shook my head. "No. It took me a half-hour to come to the conclusion and two days to find the courage to call."

Was that a hint of a smile? The footprint of a hint? I wasn't being hand-on-Bible honest, but wasn't about to mention overhearing the scene in Clair's office; it swerved a little too close to eavesdropping.

I said, "My offer stands, Doctor. Would you care to have dinner? Nothing fancy, I'm thinking quiet and simple. We could grab a sandwich and watch the sun drop into the water."

She said, ". . . No."

But she said it a beat past a hard-and-fast no, the no of dead ends, slammed doors, and fallen bridges. I knew this no. It was the no people used when asked, *You sure you don't want more gravy on those taters?* It was a yes in disguise. Or maybe a maybe.

I said, "Please. It means a lot to me."

Her mouth started to say no again. The next no would have had time to set, and be irrevocable. I held up my palms to cut her off. "Just think about it," I said. "I'll drop by later this afternoon."

This time I was the one who spun and retreated.

The man at the end of the bar sobbed into his hands and no one paid the slightest attention. A mirrored ball in the ceiling threw spinning diamonds of cut light over men slow-dancing to a torchy Bette Midler ballad. Though it wasn't quite five, the dark bar was filling with the Friday crowd, adding to the others who'd skulked here since the door opened. A fat man with cow eyes gave me a once-over and licked his lips. I sent him a wink and a glimpse of shoulder holster. He disappeared like smoke in a hurricane.

Squill's "deployment plan" meant putting Harry and me on the shoe-leather trail, aiming us at gay bars around town. Harry'd taken his own list and gone a-hunting.

Though the bars had been checked once, we were retracing with Deschamps's photo.

Canvassing bars is easy on TV, where one bartender works around the clock and knows every client down to shoe size. In reality even a modest bar might have a half-dozen regular barkeeps, plus part-timers on call. Even if you sat all the employees in one room and showed them the photos, it'd still be a crapshoot. My dictum for the experience in six words: memories are faulty and people lie.

The bartender was a guy with cartoonishly huge muscles and a penchant for black leather: cap, vest, belt, chaps. His sideburns looked like black leather pasted in front of his ears. He wasn't a tall guy, five ten or so, but nail a chrome grille to his chest and he'd have been a Kenworth. His skin looked oiled under the black vest, the better to define the pecs, I guessed. I flashed the shield and set the photos on the bar.

"Seen either of these gentlemen?" I asked the Steroid King.

"No," he said.

"You didn't look at the pictures."

"True." He pumped his fists to make the muscles in his forearms jump; they looked like steaks wrestling beneath his skin. He gave me bunker-slit eyes and said, "Good-bye."

I pointed to a corner booth where several men vamped and giggled. "Look over there, Meat. I'll bet each one's carrying something. Smoke, Ecstasy, acid . . . I'll walk over and check them out. They'll mask fear with belligerence. I'll become frightened for my safety and call for backup. Cops will rush in, the place will clear out. What will that do to your tips?"

The steaks went wild. "You think you're a tough guy?"

I sighed. "Worse. I am a busy guy."

Meat stared at me, pursed his lips, then shrugged and put his elbows on the bar. He studied the photos.

"Oh," he said, and—inappropriate to his image—tsk-tsked.

"What?"

He pushed Deschamps's picture aside and tapped a sausage finger on Nelson's face. "This one. He's been around. And I mean that both ways."

"Enlighten me, Buddha."

"A charmer, knows how to talk and act above his station. He'll come in occasionally, pick off some old queen who'll keep him for a while."

"Know anyone who'd like to see him boxed and shipped?"

It took a second to sink in. "He's dead?"

I nodded. The barkeep flipped the photo back. "Sad. I remember him as kind of goofy; a dreamer. He never really hurt anyone, maybe broke a few old men's hearts." He paused, thinking. "He was in here a couple-three weeks back. I remember because he usually drank well booze, but he'd switched to top shelf. Buying rounds instead of hustling them. Said he found himself a bottomless honey jar and life was going to get sweet." The bartender shook his head, grunted a laugh. "Like I've never heard that one before."

"You didn't believe him?"

The barkeep was still laughing when I walked out the door.

After two hours of dark bars, worn-out faces, and cigarette smoke as thick as jam, I was ready for a final run at the elusive Dr. Davanelle. She sat in her small office working up the preliminary report. Her face seemed washed of color. I wanted to say something charming, pithy, and witty. Instead, I stood in the doorway and settled on the truth.

"Look, Dr. Davanelle, I can be a wiseass at times. If I've said things to offend you or make you think I'm a jerk, I apologize. When I asked you if you wanted to do something quiet and simple tonight, I meant only that. My intentions are so honorable I might have an ascension at any moment. That said, it's Friday night. Before I ascend would you like to grab a sandwich and watch the sun go down?"

Her head was shaking no before I finished the sentence. But this time her eyes weren't looking at me like cold pork gravy with a hair in it.

"I've got to finish the preliminary report on Deschamps, then drive over to Gulf Shores. My stereo receiver's being repaired. If I don't pick it up tonight, I won't get to it for a week."

"Need company? I know the area," I said, instant tour guide to Greater Mobile.

"The store provided me with clear directions, but thank you."

Mobile Bay encompasses four hundred square miles, a vast, shallow pan of water extending approximately thirty miles from its wide Gulfside mouth to the Mobile and Tensaw rivers that feed freshwater into the northern delta. The city of Mobile is on the northwest side of the Bay, in Mobile County, appropriately enough. Baldwin County is on the eastern shore of the Bay, and has no signature city. Tourists might disagree, tending to think in terms of two motel- and condo-laden beach locales, Gulf Shores and Orange Beach.

Though Baldwin County has rural areas of charm and beauty, it's not only temporary home to tourists, but permanent home to former Mobilians looking for the "country life." Driving to Gulf Shores on one of the major thoroughfares is an exemplar of what inrushing money can do, especially teamed up with bulldozers—development after development, billboard following billboard. Strip centers. Big-box stores. Fast food and service stations. I was once traveling through the city of Daphne when I heard an excitement-voiced tourist call back to the Winnebago: "Get in here and take a peek, Marge, southern BPs are just like the ones we have in Dayton!"

I was seized by inspiration: suggesting Ava return to Mobile via the ferry between Fort Morgan on the tip of the eastern Bay, and Dauphin Island on the western side. I ran to my car, returned with a map, and traced the route with a highlighter. The ferry cost a few bucks and wasn't much of a time saver, I explained, but the view beat the hell out of the alternative.

She glanced at the map. "Uhm-hum," she said, furrowing her brow.

"It's a date," I said. "I live on Dauphin Island. Stop by on your way home and I'll show you my collection of sand."

"Date? I don't think I—"

"I didn't mean date like in *date*, Doctor. I'd just like to get your input on the autopsy. Bring a copy of the prelim by. Ten minutes. Max. You'll be home before dark."

"Home while it's light?"

What did it matter—was she a vampire? I crossed my heart. "I promise."

"Give me your phone number," she said. "I'll call while I'm in Gulf Shores. If I'm able to stop by, that is."

It was a dodge worthy of a Gypsy with legal training. Requesting my number implied intent, thus mollifying me, but she left her escape hatch wide open, not having to phone at all. Still, I penned my number to the map, which she stuck in her purse without a glance. Leaving, I turned to wave and saw her walking away like she'd slipped into another dimension.

CHAPTER 11

A week after moving into my house I was seized by a fit of domesticity and bought a vacuum cleaner. Or, judging by the looks of things when I'd unboxed it earlier this evening, several vacuum cleaners: tubes, brushes, cords, bags, and all manner of vaguely obscene, mouthlike devices. Finally assembling a working instrument, I'd given everything a good suctioning. I squeaked gray film from my windows with rubbing alcohol. The toilet bowl received magic blue dust that fizzed and bubbled. Stacks of clothes were tucked into drawers. After an hour the place dazzled, in a relative sense.

By 7:30 I was sitting on the deck contemplating the slender odds that Dr. Davanelle might appear. The sun slid through its last degrees of arc. A squall to the east pushed toward Pensacola, but the remaining sky was warm blue. The phone rang and I popped up like anxious toast. *Be Ava*, I wished, reaching for the phone.

"Carson? This is Vangie Prowse."

My heart dropped to my knees. "Hello, Dr. Prowse. What a surprise. I haven't seen you in—"

"Jeremy called you a few night's ago, or early morning, rather?"

Her voice always split the difference between question and statement, a good voice for a psychiatrist.

I said, "I didn't know he was allowed to call out."

"He isn't. He slipped a cell phone from an attendant's pocket. I left a message for you the other night, to call me? I wanted to apologize for the lapse."

My mind-photos of Dr. Evangeline Prowse, taken a year ago, gave her brown eyes as penetrating as those of a snow owl, fortune-teller eyes. In her mid-sixties, she had more pepper than salt in her hair, the salt more silver than gray. Her loose-jointed knees and elbows conferred the gait of a retired marathoner. She would be calling from her office, high ceiling, shelves dense with books, an intricate carpet from some country where rugs have meaning.

I said, "He was manic, spinning. Is he any better?"

"Overall? We try to keep him stable, Carson. Never think he'll be better, not in the usual sense." She paused. "He wants to talk to you."

"You mean now? I have a friend due any minute, Dr. Prowse."

111

"It's Vangie, Carson. You mentioned you'd stay in contact? I'd hoped to hear from you more often."

"I'll call back. Now's just not a good time."

"Jeremy wanted me to say it's been a long time since you two connected? He also says he thinks you both have current events to discuss."

"I'm very busy right now, Vangie. Seriously."

Her voice dropped away. Never try to match silences with a shrink, they'll wear you down every time. I finally said, "I have a few minutes."

"Thank you, Carson. If he can't speak to you he'll start obsessing, and that creates problems. I'll have him brought to a room with a phone? Hang on."

She put me on hold. Three minutes passed. Five.

The line clicked open. I said, "Jeremy? Is that you?"

"Jeremy is that you?"

Like an echo my voice returned to me; he was a brilliant mimic of men or women, a mynah. Then his true voice, midrange, musical, a wet finger making a wineglass sing, one octave lower.

"Yes, it's me, Carson. How nice of you to remember someone with whom you once shared a womb. A few years apart, but shared nonetheless. Cold in there, wasn't it?"

"How've you been?" The words sounded ridiculous as I spoke them.

Jeremy cupped his hand over the phone as if talking to someone in another room. "He asks how I've been." A

112

different voice called back, but still his. "Tell him the cookies were delicious."

He took his hand from the phone. "The cookies were delicious, Carson. But I can't quite get it clear in my head, brother—did you send them on the first or third year I was here?"

"I've never sent cookies, Jeremy."

"No cookies?" pouted a little-girl's voice. "Don't you wuv me?"

"I'm busy here, Jeremy. Can I call you back tomorrow?"

"NO! YOU CAN NOT CAN NOT CAN NOT! Holding this fear-crusted, sweat-dripping phone is the first freedom I've had in A YEAR! Speaking of that, we have to talk. How does one get ahead in the world, Carson?"

I sighed. "I don't know, Jeremy. How?"

"A knife is always helpful." He laughed. "Get it? A knife's helpful to get . . . a . . . HEAD! It zeems to me like you haff a leetle problem in Moe-byle, Carson. A free spirit. Need some help? If one is traveling to Iceland, one should take along someone who speaks ice, *n'est-ce pas?*"

"Jeremy, I don't think—"

"Our first dead lad was—or perhaps still is, depending on various philosophies—one Jerrold Elton Nelson, age twenty-two, beheaded in Bowderie Park, sharp instrument, body dressed in et cetera, et cetera . . . the *Mobile Register* offered such a sterile recitation. COLORLESS! Then yesterday I find another poor boy's gone to bed without his head. A French name—Duchamp? I hope he didn't lose his beret as well. It

113

was on the news for all of ten seconds. Are they your cases?"

"I can't discuss—"

He banged the phone on a hard surface. "HELLO? HELLO? This is your REALITY CHECK service." He put a hand over his mouth and made hissing radio-interference noises, abruptly stopping.

"There, Mr. Ryder, your lines are CLEAR. How about your conscience? You can't discuss, can't discuss? . . . dear sir, did we not spend hours and hours *hotly* discussing a previous incident? Does the name JOEL ADRIAN come to mind, dear sir, esteemed sir? Was I not of some simple, humble help to you in that instance, good sir, dear sir, most honored sir? DID I NOT SOLVE THE BLOODY FUCKING CASE FOR YOU, CARSON?"

I listened to my heart. What seemed like a thousand beats later, I said, "Yes."

"We're going to have so much fun on this one. I can hardly wait. I'm thinking of having a decorator in, redo the place, get it all nice and cozy for your arrival."

"Jeremy, I'm not—"

"You can bring all the photos and files and we'll pore over them like happy old ladies looking at scrapbooks of friends who've passed away."

"I'm not planning on—"

"DON'T INTERRUPT, CARSON, I'M WORKING A TOUGH ROOM HERE. . . . You'll have to call Dr. Prowse, Prowsie, Prussy, Pussy, and let that dried-up old pussy know you'll soon come a-calling."

"I won't be up, Jeremy," I said. "Not for a while."

"Oh, yes, you will," he stage-whispered. "You've got a boy down there on the old reverse diet, one I know so well."

"You're talking past me, Jeremy."

"Reverse diet? It's real simple, Carson. The more you eat, the hungrier you get. See you soon, brother."

He hung up. I looked out the deck door. The day, bright and beaconing minutes ago, seemed overwhelming, the sunlight a too-loud voice, raucous and grating. I walked window to window, shutting the blinds.

"We're going to have so much fun on this one. . . ."

I cranked up the AC just to hear it spill into the quiet. Boxing myself in again. Retreating into my Mesmer box. Jeremy's phone call hung in my head like wet smoke.

". . . come up and visit . . ."

I started the horrible tumble back in time, walking down the dark hall, six years old . . . my mother at the sewing machine . . .

I was pulled from my dark time travel by the sound of tires on sand and shells. I looked out the window. A white Camry pulled across the drive to the twin parking spots beneath my stilt-standing home. The car stopped. The door opened and closed.

Ava Davanelle.

"Hello? Detective Ryder?" she called out from below, feet kicking through crushed shells. "Hello?"

I ran to open the shades in the kitchen, pulled the curtains open to the deck. *Yes!* I ran to the bathroom for gargling and spitting as tentative footsteps began the wooden ascent to the small porch on the land side of my house. *Yes!* One last swipe of rag across the counter as I moved toward the door, past the mirror, seeing me—square grinning face brown from the sun, shadow of beard that never disappears, khaki shorted, aloha shirted, pulling off the faded Orvis cap to slap sprigs of untamable black hair.

Feet on the porch planks, outline through the curtains on the door. I turned from the mirror, smiling. Frightened?

Knocking on the door.

A woman I barely know swam fifteen years into the past, grabbed my collar, and pulled me back to *thankyouthankyou* now.

"Hello? Anyone home?"

I opened the door to find a smile as wide and bright as a mid-summer sunrise. I gestured Ava inside, sniffing in her wake a whisper of perfume and mint. Her motions were music, her hair shone. A blue, short-sleeved shirt tucked into a white skirt touching modestly at her knees. She walked on the long and shapely legs of a figure skater. There was bounce in her steps, the air wanting to carry her. Was that a hint of shyness in her eyes?

I was breathless at the transformation: Was this the dour-faced woman in the floppy lab coat?

Ava nodded at my interior decor of posters and driftwood and shells and walked to the doors opening to the deck. The Gulf was slate blue with waves burnished amber by the low western sun. A dark tanker dotted the horizon.

"What a view. This place is yours? How do you ever affor—" She caught herself and turned, touching pink lacquerless fingertips to her lips. "Whoops," she said. "That's not polite."

"An inheritance. Don't worry, everyone asks that question, if not always out loud. Can I fix you a drink and if so, what's your preference?"

"I'll just go with a vodka and tonic. Light, please. I'm not much of a drinker."

"Twenty watts, coming up. Get your stereo repaired?"

She waved her hands above her head and shuffled in a circle, an impersonation of local cable-access preacher Beulah Chilers. "I have mew-sic again and heard its glow-ree and I have been sank-tea-fide by it, pra-a-a-a-ise Jay-sus!"

I nearly dropped to my knees and hallelujahed. Was this the same gray-humored woman who minced bodies for a living?

"Damn, it's colder'n a morgue in here," Ava said, and with great difficulty I avoided noting her nipples thought so too. We took our drinks to the deck. Ava seemed to have brought a breeze and for the first time in a week the air didn't feel like hot syrup.

"So you boated over," I said as we angled chairs toward one another and tapped glasses in a toast to the boundless spirit of Friday nights everywhere.

"Getting to Gulf Shores was a nightmare. But returning

across the bay made up for it. Someone told me we passed over the site where the guy said, 'Damn the torpedoes, full speed ahead.'"

I nodded. "Admiral Farragut during Battle of Mobile Bay, August fifth, 1864, the curtain coming down on the War Between the States."

Our eyes held one another's longer than usual for a one-line history lesson and startled us into looking away. Ava jumped up and wobbled slightly. "Sea legs from the ferry," she said, walking to the railing and looking out over the Gulf. A sailboat ran east with the wind toward the mouth of the bay. The wind nestled Ava's clothes against her slender body and I knew Reubens was wrong and subtle curves curved best. Ice chimed against her lips as she sipped.

For a half hour or so, we conversed like friends too long apart. The weather. The dearth of Indian restaurants. Mobile's once-famed Azalea Trail. The serene and stately glory of Bellingrath Gardens. I told her how Mobile had danced to its own version of Mardi Gras years before New Orleans put its shoes on.

I discovered Ava Davanelle was thirty years old with an orthopedic-surgeon father and a mother who taught French. She'd grown up in Fort Wayne, Indiana. Reading her father's copy of *Gray's Anatomy* when she was thirteen inspired her career. She'd lived in Mobile for six months, and today was the first time she'd been on the beach. I discovered she understood quiet, and our silences were comfortable and contemplative.

Then, over a period of fifteen minutes, her silences became forced, almost troubled. Her eyes wavered from mine and their incandescence waned. Ava sat forward and rubbed her forehead. "Doggone," she said, "I brought you the copy of the preliminary report. It's in my car. I'll be right back."

"I don't need it now. I'll wait for finals."

"After I've brought them here by land and sea? You're getting them." Her smile was strained, like trying to smile while lifting weights.

"Just summarize. Similarities and differences in twenty-five words or less."

She rubbed her forehead. "I was struck by how similar the bodies were, like twin brothers, except, had they been brothers, Deschamps worked out two hours for every one of Nelson's: more pronounced musculature, primarily in the upper body."

"Great," I said. "All I needed."

She stood. "I'll get the report."

"I'll come with you," I offered. "Show you the exotic sights under my house. You'll love my kayak."

She handed me her glass. "Fix me another, please. Light. I'll be right back."

Shapes of the past: Ben "The Bear" Ashley, my first partner, finding reasons to get me out of the car. "Gimme a pack of gum, Carson," "Run in and grab me some smokes, bud." Bear sent me inside fast-food joints for the food instead of using the drive-through. I also recalled Bear's low moods before he'd command some odd errand. Until learning the truth I thought it a rookie initiation or show of pecking order.

After mixing two more drinks I returned to the porch and waited, a weight pressing my heart. Ava stepped outside with a manila folder. A new scent of mint suffused the air. She rolled her head as if loosening her neck. Two minutes later she was laughing like a tickled bell.

The indications were there, but I needed to know for sure. I smacked my forehead. "Damn," I said. "I've got to take out the trash. If I forget I'll find ants everywhere in the a.m."

"Ants! Of coursh," Ava slurred. "Pesky things."

I grabbed a half bag of trash from the container and wrapped it for show, heading downstairs. She'd locked her car and I got the slim-jim from mine, a two-foot strip of thin steel slipped between door and window to pop the lock. Ava's door opened in seconds. The glovebox had the usual automotive records, plus several packs of gum, breath mints, and other scented candies. I patted beneath the passenger seat. Nothing. My hand crawled beneath the driver's seat and found a long brown bag that sloshed as I retrieved it. Inside was a liter of bottom-rung vodka, a third empty. A sales receipt fell out. Beneath the imprint of the package store was the name and price of the vodka, plus date and time of the purchase.

7:01 P.M. Tonight.

Jesus. Ava had sucked down eight or so ounces of liquor before she'd arrived. No wonder she'd looked incandescent at the door; she was lit up with first-flush alco-energy, blazing. But it's a fire ravenous for fuel and her feather-weight drinks lacked the voltage, so she'd hustled to her car for an eighty-four-proof jump-start.

Bear was an alky who pulled chugs from a bottle under the seat when I picked up smokes and burgers. Ten months with him taught me if Ava could drink that much and still present a sober facade, she'd had practice handling it. She was experienced enough that leaving the report in the car let her socially birdie-sip her drink, having an excuse to head to the well if the itch started. Alcoholics are master planners at sneaking drinks.

The slurring had started. With a fresh surge of ethanol in her system she'd start showing its effects, but perhaps be too affected to realize it. Letting her drive back to Mobile was unthinkable. I felt like an amateur juggler handed two lit blowtorches and a Roman candle: how to proceed without getting burned?

"How's your trash prollem?" Ava said loudly as I stepped back outside. Her glass was fuller than when I'd left, and I realized she'd slipped inside and poured one. It didn't seem the best way to begin a relationship, she sneaking my booze while I broke into her car.

I said, "It's solved. No ants in my pants tonight."

"What about your pantch?" Her esses had moved from slippery to slushy.

"Nothing. Just a comment on entomology."

"Etta-molgy? Where words come from, right?"

She squinted slightly, a reaction to blurring vision. After

several seconds spent studying her watch Ava jumped up as if bee stung.

"Pas' my bedtime. Gotta run." She started to walk but wavered. "Whoopsie," she said, covering. "Leg fell asleep." She bent and pretended to massage sparkles away.

"And a very nice leg at that," I said.

She grinned crookedly. "Thanks. Got another'n just like it over here."

She wobbled again. If she got in her car I'd have to call the Dauphin Island cops and have her stopped. I couldn't sober her up quickly, but I could push her the other direction.

"Just one more small one?" I suggested. "A light light for the road?"

"Nope. All done." But her eyes weighed the notion and her feet weren't moving.

"Please, just one more with me," I said. "Sit, darling."

"Darling?" she echoed as I went to the kitchen. A minute later I handed her three shots of vodka with tonic to take it to the rim. I'd added a hefty squeeze of lime, hoping its citrus bite masked the potency. Ava was past sipping for show and drained a third of the glass in a single swig. She cocked her head my way and her eyes took a two-count to focus.

"Carshon, did you call me darling before?"

"Yes, I did, Ava."

"Why?" she said, turning the word into two syllables.

"It seemed appropriate."

Ava rose with a waver and walked toward me. She leaned

my way and I thought her equilibrium was failing until her lips found mine. She tasted like lime perfume and her lips were cold. But her tongue was warm and we held tight as her hands stroked my back and kneaded my buttocks. Between the lime and vodka I smelled the heat of her need. We half walked, half staggered to the dimly lit bedroom. I sat her on the bed and she nibbled between my neck and ear. Despite the circumstances I heard the amoral beast of my body howling.

"Wait here, darling," I said. "I want to take a quick shower. But first let me get your drink."

"Oh, God, pleash hurry," she said, and I wondered if she was referring to the shower or the booze. I brought her another thermo-nuclear blast of vodka.

I sat on the toilet seat and ran a cold shower for several minutes before climbing in myself. Fifteen minutes later she was sprawled and snoring. When I tugged the cover up to her neck, my knuckles touched the warmth of her lips, and I let them rest there. I had so far seen two Ava Davanelles, the first a joyless, brooding ghost, alert to slights and quick to anger, the second a sun-bright dazzle of the delicious, all smile and wit and sweet, laid-back laughter. Were both no more than fables from a bottle? If so, where between the extremes resided the true Ava Davanelle?

Was it the woman I saw in the hall outside Willet Lindy's office, her fists knotted tight and her face a white horror of conflict and struggle?

I should have felt anger and betrayal, not by the woman

whose breath warmed my hand, but by myself. My self-serving need to understand and battle discord had drawn me to a place where I lacked knowledge or solution. I could not understand the situation, but since it had crossed into my life, I could not in good conscience turn and retreat.

Or could I? None of this was of my making.

I oversaw Ava's sleep for twenty minutes, then went to the deck and watched the stars assemble until their noise overwhelmed me and I went to bed.

CHAPTER 12

I once found Bear on his knees in front of the toilet, hand jammed in his mouth and tickling the back of his throat to jump-start the retching that pushed the binge-toxins from his stomach. At 6:30 I awoke to the same sounds behind my bathroom door.

I knocked tentatively. "Ava? Are you all right?"

"Give me a few minutes," she said. "I'm—I'm ill." A muffled moan. More gagging. I put bread in the toaster in case she needed something in her stomach. Five minutes passed before the door opened, last night's ethanol glow replaced by the starchy pallor I'd seen at the morgue. Her eyes were wet and red. Beads of sweat covered her forehead. I'd opened the windows and the sound of the Gulf poured in.

"I, um, I'm so embarrassed," she said. "I must have the flu or something. I guess the drinks must have gone to my head." She pushed strands of hair behind her ears with shaking fingers.

"You were pretty gone."

"Flu," she said. "It's been going around at work."

"Sure."

"Uh, did we—that is . . ."

"We were the epitome of propriety. You got tired, I steered you to the bedroom. I took the couch." I hoped my collar hid the bite marks she'd sucked into my neck as I'd wrangled her to the bed.

Relief dropped her shoulders a full inch. "I'm sorry to put you out, I—I don't remember much. Didn't I just have two drinks?"

Groping through the blackout.

"Maybe three," I said. "Are you sure it's the flu?"

"I—what do you mean?"

"I got the impression that you had a few pops before you arrived."

"What?" A show of surprise. *Moi?*

I shrugged my shoulders "An impression."

"Are you saying I showed up drunk?" An edge to the question. I noticed her color was returning.

"I'm saying you got pretty blitzed for a couple light-light drinks, Ava."

"Maybe they weren't as light as I asked for."

Nobody does defensive better than a guilty alky. Her voice

was getting stronger and her shakes were gone. "I thought it was the flu," I said.

She'd stopped sweating. Her eyes were clearing. They flared at me. "Maybe that's just part of it. Maybe you got me plastered. Maybe you—"

"Maybe I'm the one who planted that stash of vodka in your car."

Her eyes went saucer-wide. "You looked in my . . ." Guilt and anger fought in her face and anger won. "I think you're a *bastard*," she hissed, grabbing her purse from the table. She blew by me and I saw wobble in the legs, smelled sweat and vomit and an astringent tang in her wake. The door slammed shut and seconds later came a grinding of sand as she fishtailed away.

I pretty much knew what I'd find before I went to the cabinet. I shook the vodka bottle and watched it bubble abnormally and heard a hiss as I unscrewed the cap. Watered. I checked the bathroom wastebasket and found a crumpled Dixie cup hidden at the bottom. It smelled as expected, making her morning passage easy to map: she awakened with the craving, pulled a cup from the bathroom dispenser, and tiptoed to the liquor cabinet to fill it. She replaced the removed vodka with water and returned to the bathroom to alternately drink and vomit until she absorbed enough alcohol to start the buzz. When the door opened she was already getting straight, if that's what you'd call it—shakes leaving, eyes clearing, mind defogging. Right now she was working on the vodka under her car seat. Hair of the dog that bit you, it was humorously called. But I knew this dog. It didn't bite; it ate you whole, and there wasn't a damn thing funny about it. I gave Ava twenty-five minutes and phoned her home. No answer. I gave it another heart-pounding five before redialing.

"Hello?" she chirped a little too loudly, but pleasant and controlled. Juiced again, but at least she was home. I gave silent thanks to whoever pulls the levers and gently hung up.

Harry and I headed toward downtown to interview a woman who'd known Deschamps both personally and profession-ally. I was in a funk and lying in the backseat with my arms tight over my chest, a doleful mummy.

Harry shook his head with regret. "That pretty little doc, a drunk. Sad."

Like me Harry didn't use the word *drunk* as a pejorative; we both knew too many recovering alcoholics—AA folks, mainly—who easily referred to their drinking selves as drunks, alkys, boozehounds, or whatnot. I figured it for a badge of courage, the guts to look in the mirror and tell the truth. Then get healed if you stayed honest with your reflection.

"When she gets found out it'll be her job," he said. "And she'll get found out."

Harry was right; when Ava's alcohol abuse was discov-ered she'd be sent to a rehab program and reassigned to a lesser position, like filing. Another pathologist would be hired. Ava'd eventually get eased out the door like a bulldozer eases aside a sapling. It'd be a fast track to the street—Clair wasn't long on sympathy.

Harry spoke over his shoulder. "What you figuring on doing about it, Cars?"

"Why would I be doing something about it?"

"You got a feeling for the girl, don't you?"

"I barely know her, Harry."

He swung the car down a side street and jammed on the brakes. I felt the front tire bang the curb, roll up over it, fall back down. Harry parking.

"Come and sit up front, bro."

I got out and switched seats. We were in an old neighborhood and the street was bordered by spreading oaks and tall pines thick with cones. I figured some of the trees predated the War Between the States. The antebellum houses sat distant from the pavement behind azaleas, magnolia, redtips, and myrtle, as if hiding in the past and eavesdropping on the present.

Harry said, "We got a full plate, what with the murders, Squill hijacking the PSIT. It could turn into a king-hell political mess, eat us alive. If that little lady's got the alcohol sickness, and you got a feeling for her, you can get ate up from that side too."

"You telling me leave it alone?"

He smiled with a touch of sadness and shook his head. "You're gonna do what you're gonna do. I know it, you know it, and all the angels above know it. I'm just saying to watch out for yourself."

I stared out the window. Down the street a frail and elderly woman watered her flower garden. She looked like an ornament, she was so still.

Harry said, "You keep pretty tight inside yourself, Cars. Nothing wrong with it. But you find those old wires tightening around you, don't go nowhere but to me, right?"

His phrasing struck a disconcerting note in my head. "What old wires? What are you talking about?"

He looked away, put the car in gear.

"Don't get yourself tore up, that's all I'm saying."

Harry drove the final few blocks to the next address on our shoe-leather list. We got out in front of Les Idées, an art gallery on Mobile's near-south side, a slender yellow New Orleans—style two-story with scrollwork iron on the balconies and plum-colored shutters. There were flower boxes. A cobblestone walk. A small trickling fountain. The place was *precious*. Harry eyed the coffee shop across the street; the coffee smell was thick in the air.

"Go grab a cup, bro," I said. "I think I can handle the interview."

Harry crossed the street, looking relieved.

Though Deschamps was primarily a commercial artist, he relaxed by painting watercolors, mainly seascapes. Françoise Abbot was the proprietor of Les Idées. She'd exhibited Deschamps's works for several years and occasionally socialized with him in a group situation, before and during his engagement.

Abbot was a slender fiftyish woman dressed in a red velvet wrap just west of where caftan meets kimono. A smoker, she affected an ebony cigarette holder, a device I'd considered passé to the point of antique. Her black hair had one of those abbreviated anticuts that sent shaggy sprigs flailing in all directions. She led me to several Deschamps watercolors, workmanlike, but lacking the insight to spark illustration into art. I thought they'd have made decent covers for blank-page New Age journals with titles like *My Daily Reflections* or *Notes From a Life*.

Madame Abbot's low voice matched her conspiratorial demeanor and she punctuated phrases with an elastic assortment of facial displays. I suspected someone once told her she looked cute when wrinkling her nose and she'd decided to diversify. Customers were absent and we sat at a small ornate table in a back corner. I said, "Everyone I've spoken with considered Mr. Deschamps next in line for beatification, lacking only in that he was Baptist. Is that your impression, Ms. Abbot?"

"*De mortuis nil nisi bonum,*" she stage-whispered with a flaring of nostrils that segued into a squint. "Surely you know what that means." She gave me three quick expressions that bet I didn't.

"Of the dead speak nothing but good," I replied. "That's inexact but sufficient."

She dropped her jaw and wiggled it, followed by a wink and a thumbs-up. She pointed the suck end of her cigarette holder at me. "That's excellent, Detective Ryder."

I said, "It's a phrase often connoting ill that might be revealed, but is left unspoken."

Abbot winked and wrinkled her nose. "Really?"

"Perhaps Mr. Deschamps didn't quite lead the straight-arrow life I'm being led to believe."

She shot her brows and pursed her lips. "For the most part I think he did."

"What about for the least part?"

Abbot went through another series of facial contortions meant to convey, if I'd had to guess, some form of consternation. She said, "Two months ago a friend of mine double-dated with a friend of hers over in Orange Beach. A friend of my friend's, that is. Her friend. And guess who my friend's friend brought along as her date?"

While I unlinked the chain of friends, Abbot produced a facial display of such distracting variety I had to turn away to think.

"Was it Peter Deschamps?"

Abbot looked side to side as if crossing a busy street and leaned toward me. "This was two months after he'd proposed to Cheryl."

"Friends out for an innocent night together."

"It's possible." She winked three times and smiled.

"You believe it was more than that?"

"My friend's friend is, how shall I put this, an energetic woman, *physically* energetic." Abbot batted her eyelashes. "Does that say it?"

"Someone who . . . celebrates her libido?"

Abbot winked, nodded, pursed her lips, grinned, grimaced, and frowned.

I took it as a yes.

"We heading over to see this 'friend's friend'?" Harry asked.

"Stop at the morgue first?"

Harry didn't say a word. He U'd the car to a cacophony of horn blowing while I shut my eyes and gripped the door handle. He pulled up to the morgue a few minutes later.

"I won't be long," I said, closing the door and walking away.

"Carson?"

I turned. Harry had his thumb in the air. "Good luck," he said.

Ava was at her desk doing paperwork. I stepped into her office and shut the door.

"Get out," she snapped. Her eyes were bagged and bloodshot.

"I'd like to take you to lunch or to supper. If you're busy today, how about tomorrow?"

She scribbled on a form, pushed it across her desk, grabbed another.

"No way in hell."

I moved forward to the edge of her desk. "We should talk about Friday evening."

She started to initial a form but the pen tore the paper. She threw the pen into the wastebasket and glared at me.

"There's absolutely nothing to say."

I said, "I'm scared."

"You're *what*?"

"Maybe worried's a better word. Listen, Ava, I consider you a friend—"

"And I consider you a snoop and a meddler. I suppose you've already told half the town."

"I've told no one. It's not their business." I didn't mention Harry; telling him was like writing her secret on a slip of weighted paper and dropping it into the Marianas Trench.

"Oh, I'll bet. I'll just bet."

"Listen, Ava, I know some people who've had experience in things like this. Good people. Maybe you could use a little assistance with—"

She stood with such force it rocketed her chair backward to the wall. "I don't know what the hell you're talking about with this 'assistance' business, Detective Ryder. Maybe I had too much to drink the other night. It was a mistake and it'll never happen again. I didn't like your insinuations then and I like them less now. We have to work together professionally, I can deal with that. But I want nothing from you on a personal level and that means conversations, insinuations, prevarications, advice, or lunch. If you really want to be helpful you can close the door from the outside. If you can't figure out how it's done, I'll call security and they'll be glad to help you."

"How'd it go?" Harry asked when I dropped into the passenger seat.

"What's that big-ass river in Egypt?" I asked, shutting my eyes against a too-bright sun.

"De Nile," he said, not missing a beat.

Abbot's friend's friend was named Monica Talmadge. She was in her mid-thirties and lived in an expensive brick home in West Mobile with a perfectly manicured lawn and a canary-yellow Beamer in the drive. Monica was not happy to see us.

"I've never heard of Peter Deschamps. You've got to believe that."

She wore open-toed high heels, lavender jeans, and more makeup than midafternoon generally required. Her bra made the most of small breasts, the tight, scoop-neck pink shirt not hurting either. Auburn waves of hair hung halfway to the outswooping of her derriere, as round and succinct as an orange.

"Look, guys, officers, whatever, my husband's going to be here any minute."

Harry looked at his watch. "Maybe he can help us with the Deschamps question."

"No! I mean, he doesn't know anything."

"Doesn't know anything or doesn't suspect anything, Mrs. Talmadge?" Harry asked softly.

Monica looked down like memorizing her toes for a test. I could have given her the answers: perfectly tanned, pedicured, and pinkly lacquered. I knew she was debating whether or not to tell the truth. When she looked up her face held harder eyes and harsher shadows.

"Peter and I went out a few times, a friendly kind of thing."

Harry said, "Discreetly friendly?"

There was a long silence and her eyes narrowed.

"Look, my husband's what they call a man's man. That means when he ain't in fucking Montana or Canada with a bunch of other men hunting for mooses or beavers or whatever, he's out fishing the blue water for days at a time. When he's not being the American Sportsman, he's halfway across the world selling generators. I grew up in a single-wide in Robertsdale and I like all this a lot"—she gestured around her, meaning the car, the house, the neighborhood— "but there are a few other things I like too. I'm just trying to keep a little balance in my life, y'know? So when Peter answered my ad—"

I said, "Your ad?"

"I put an ad in that ratty paper, *NewsBeat*? Personals. Semi-attached woman looking for a semi-attached man. Someone for intelligent, adult fun, no strings and no tales."

A vehicle approached and Monica froze. When she saw it wasn't her husband she released her breath. Harry said, "What happened after the ad ran?"

"I got a bunch of responses. More than I ever thought I'd get. Peter enclosed a photo, and he looked and sounded nice. It fit perfect he was engaged and had to be careful too. We had a few dates, nothing serious, just good fun, you know?"

"Did you get the impression this, uh, dating was something he'd done before?"

"No. I think he wanted a final fling before getting married. He as much as said so. Made sense to me."

"Did you get any sense Mr. Deschamps might have orientation other than heterosexual?

"God, no," she said. "He was very masculine. You're not telling me he—"

"No. But in any murder we have to ask all sorts of questions."

"I cried when I heard about it. Such a good guy. Great body. I feel so sorry for his girlfriend."

"Why'd you break the relationship off?"

"We both sorta did. I think we just ran out of things to say."

I heard the roar of a big diesel engine. Her eyes looked past us to the street. "Oh, my God, it's Larry. Please don't say anything about this, please, please, please."

I saw a black truck gearing down for the driveway, eyes glaring through the windshield.

"Smile and shake your head, Mrs. Talmadge," I said.

"What?"

"Smile real wide but shake your head no."

She caught on and did it, adding a little tinkle of laughter lost in the shuddering engine sound at our backs. I winked at Harry and we waved farewell to Mrs. Talmadge. We turned to see her husband leap from a dual-tracked 3500 Dodge Ram diesel with a tailpipe like a howitzer muzzle. What wasn't painted was chromed. Lettering on the door proclaimed, ATLAS INDUSTRIAL GENERATOR SALES, YOUR INDEPENDENT

POWER COMPANY. Larry left the door open and the engine running. He went an easy six three, two fifty, with a neck to match Harry's. Clouds of graying hair puffed from the collar of his Polo shirt. His face was red, his chest expanded in full turf-protection mode; we were probably walking places he'd pissed.

"Hey," he bellowed, "what the hell you guys doing?"

"Thanks again, Mrs. Talmadge," I called over my shoulder. "Sorry to bother you."

"I asked what you're doing here?" Larry growled.

I smiled, *Nice doggy.* "You must be the mister," I said politely, flipping open my badge wallet. "We had a bad hit-and-run in the Bankhead Tunnel yesterday. A witness got a partial tag number and said it was a yellow sports car—" I talked loud enough for Monica to hear me.

"You wouldn't believe how many yellow vehicles have similar numbers," Harry said, sounding exasperated. The Harry and Carson show.

My turn. "We're going to all possibles looking for damage to the right front fender. Obviously"—I looked at the Beamer—"it wasn't your wife's vehicle."

"Well . . . damn right," Larry huffed.

We drove away as Larry pulled suitcases from the monster truck. Monica and I shared a glance. She mouthed, "Thank you," then turned a warm and welcoming face to man's-man Larry, home from the hills and home from the sea.

CHAPTER 13

Save for me, the Church Street Cemetery was deserted. Behind Mobile's main library on Government Street, the small cemetery was a place to walk slow beneath ancient trees, ponder headstones, and count the passing of years. Harry'd needed to drop a couple books at the library, and I'd been drawn to the cemetery's hushed commitment to the past.

When the Adrian case was an explosion of sirens in my head, rats and fires and the burned-out cinders of a young girl's eyes, I often came to sit beneath the trees and listen to the quiet. The death of Tessa Ramirez had been unspeakably violent, yet the graves here seemed so peaceful, as if Death paused in its journey between whatever worlds it traverses to let the chosen cast off the memories of dying, gathering themselves in cool shade and simple surroundings. Though Tessa had been buried in Texas, I felt one graveyard was all graveyards, conjoined beneath—or beyond—the ground. I'd hoped the Church Street dead called the petite dark-haired girl to their midst; perhaps this was where they mentored her, gave her understanding.

There must be understanding, I thought; why else for the universe to utter us into existence than to allow our individual voyages of discovery—detection, if you will—with the threads of all passages finally woven into the Ultimate Understanding, a great cosmic cooing of "Yes. Why didn't I figure it out? How elegant. How simple."

Or maybe it's all random. Our most brilliant lies are those we reserve for ourselves.

"Invisible lines everywhere," Harry said, jolting me from a reverie about reverie. He was back from the library and bending to study a grave laid thirty years into the nineteenth century. *Invisible lines* was Harry's term for lines connecting seemingly unrelated events in homicide cases. Invisible at the onset, they gradually revealed themselves until we saw we'd been tripping over them all the time.

"It's in the words on the bodies," I said. "They're messages with meaning and purpose."

The messages had been withheld from the media and public to weed out those who exorcised God knows what past horrors by confessing to every bizarre killing. No one admitted killing street-corner dope boys, but let a woman be found steeped in savagery and the wild-eyed confessors lined the block.

"Meaning and purpose if you're balls-to-the-wall nuts," Harry said. I sat on an elevated grave and Harry sat beside me. He sighed and looked up and studied the clouds or the treetops. When he turned back to me his eyes held a sadness and concern I hadn't seen in a long time.

"I've been worrying about you, bro."

I stiffened. "You mean the thing with Ava? I'm concerned about her, sure, but it's not—"

"Not that. You're not doing anything on your own, are you? On the headless cases?"

I jumped up. "What the hell would I do on my own, Harry?"

His eyes searched my face. "Like independent research. I know you get wild hairs sometimes."

"Do you think I'd hold something back, Harry, is that it?" My voice came out clenched. I heard guilt beneath the anger.

His voice was calm, reasoning. "I didn't say that, I was just wondering if you were doing any blue-sky. During the Adrian days it was like you were calling some psychic hotline, y'know. The shrinks and profile types saying the fire over the victim's eyes was a form of hiding, that Adrian knew the vics. Then suddenly—like out of air—you get the idea it was a bonding mechanism."

"It was a chance idea that panned out, nothing but serendip—"

Harry cut me off with a lifted finger. "Next, you decide all the victims were chosen by proximity to another fire in their recent pasts. It turns out true. You suggest shadowing the fire department, checking scenes of potential arson, trying to find a guy scoping out his next vic. We do and—bingo!—you see that guy with the hair-pulling deal, what was that called?"

I looked away, hating how the Adrian case and its flotsam kept floating into today, bumping my ass.

"Carson, what was that hair stuff? Yanking it out?"

"Trichollomania, dammit."

"Yeah. You saw that guy at the fire pulling out his hair like he's shredding a rotten sweater. And there he is, Joel Adrian."

I fought the compulsion to walk away. "I was there, Harry. I remember it."

"Maybe there's other stuff you don't remember. Or don't want to."

My attempt at laughter broke before leaving my lips. It came out as a croak. "You think I'm getting senile? That it?"

"What I remember most is after the case. You laying in the hospital with that breakdown and—"

I rushed toward him, hands jabbing the time-out signal. "Hold it, whoa . . . stop. No it wasn't, dammit."

Harry looked up with innocent puzzlement. "Wasn't what?"

"A breakdown, dammit. It was stress and lack of sleep. Nothing else, nothing mental."

"Did I say mental breakdown? I don't think I did. I meant physical breakdown, exhaustion. Like you said, stress, hurrying and worrying, lack of winks. I do recall the word *depression*."

"Lack of sleep combined with stress can mimic chronic depression."

"All I know is you could barely walk or talk for about a month."

I stood and looked at my watch without noting the time. "Maybe we can make something out of this day. Do some work." My voice came out angrier than I'd expected.

Harry put his hands on his knees and pushed slowly erect, like hoisting a bag of concrete on his shoulders. "All I'm saying, Cars, is you did a helluva job on the Adrian case, but it did a helluva job on you too. Just keep me in your loop, let me know what you're thinking. It's always good to bounce stuff off your partner, right?" He pointed to his head. "Gets lonely in here sometimes, Cars. People make fast decisions, don't let anyone in on them."

"Whatever you want, Harry." I said it over my shoulder, a dozen feet gone and moving away, wondering what in hell that had been all about.

A 3:00 A.M. shooting at a notorious after-hours hangout left two dead and five injured. While the shooting wasn't in itself notable, the twenty-year-old daughter of an activist minister was one of the injured, preliminary findings revealing she may have received her thigh wound in practice of the world's oldest profession. The media was in full-court press, the detectives' room chaos, cops running in and out, people yelling, phones ringing as snitches peddled useless lies and the media tried the back doors.

We retreated to a closet-sized meeting room and spread files and photos across the tiny table. Neither of us visited Nelson's apartment or had a decent chance to study the inventory of his personal belongings, so we buried ourselves in the notes of the assigned detectives. The inventory wasn't large, but we sifted sand for the nuggets linking Nelson and personals ads, since they'd connected Deschamps to Talmadge.

"Here's something," Harry said, jabbing his page. "Page three, item twenty-seven: 'One silver metal (aluminum?) file box in closet. Personal papers. Insurance forms. Check stubs and financial records. Correspondence. Newspaper clippings.' Newspaper clippings? I wonder what paper? Be interesting if it was the *NewsBeat*."

"I'll get the car," I said.

Nelson had lived in an apartment complex not far from Brookley Airport. The long common hall smelled of grease-cooked food. The rug had patches of mildew, or maybe mange. Someone at the far end of the hall had "Whip It" on the stereo. Harry and I followed the manager, Briscoe Shelton, to a brown door with the number 8-B scribed on it with Magic Marker. Shelton was a skinny, rusted-out redneck in his mid-fifties who smelled of cigarettes and WD-40.

He wore stained painter's pants and a sleeveless T-shirt that had once been white. A heavy chain jangled from his belt to his back pocket. When he flipped the chain a rattling clot of keys popped from his pants and landed in his hand. You could tell he'd spent hours practicing the move. Harry verified the scene tape was intact, then sliced through with a penknife.

"I never liked the little sonofabitch, y'know," Shelton testified as he poked at the lock with key after key. "Never paid his rent on time, but always managed to get it in just before I could legally evict the smartass."

"Did he have any regular guests, Mr. Shelton?" I asked.

"He had a damn parade through here. Men, women, boys, girls, and some whatchamacallits I couldn't say what they were, y'know?"

"Anyone stand out?"

"There was the chunky girl with the vanilla-pudding face and Minnie Mouse voice. Spent a lot of time here a couple months back. Real lovey dovey at first, then later a lot of yelling and shit."

Given the time frame and the description, I figured that was Terri Losidor. Shelton held the clot of keys in front of his face and squinted at it, separating a key from the rest. "And there was one guy I remember cuz he was so different from the riffraff and perverts. Older guy, compared to the rest of the circus. Always came at night. He'd pull up at the far end of the building and hustle in like he had fire in his britches. After a while they'd come out and take off and sometimes I wouldn't see smartass for a few days, y'know."

"When was this?" I asked.

A key fit and the door swung open. Hot, stale air poured out like trapped memories. Harry's run to the AC probably made the folks downstairs think the roof was caving in.

"Maybe two months back. Sniffed around regular for a month or so, then I didn't see him no more. Didn't mean he weren't here, just means I didn't see him. I don't spy on my people. Even perverts."

Shelton stayed by the door as Harry and I scoped the place out. "You get done be sure and pull the door. How long's it gonna be 'fore I can rent the fucking place?"

"I don't know, Mr. Shelton. Perhaps a week until we release it," I said.

Shelton screwed up his pasty face. "That means a month 'fore I can rent, y'know."

"Why's that, sir?" Harry asked.

Shelton showed us yellow teeth. "Cuz it's gonna take least three weeks to air the stink of faggot outta here."

"Fun guy," Harry said, as Shelton's bootsteps disappeared down the hall. "Wonder does he do parties?"

While Harry checked for the file box, I promenaded through Jerrold Elton Nelson's life. If I'd been handed a dictionary and allowed one word for the surroundings, I'd have circled *meagre*, choosing the Brit spelling to add a Dickensian twist to the sparseness. The furniture looked like rental-company repos: just enough use left to make it salable.

The TV was a nineteen-inch make I'd never heard of. The flatware pocketed from cheap restaurants. The bed a king-size box spring and mattress on the floor. A squat chest was beside the bed and in it I found a twenty, two tens, and a fistful of coins, mostly pennies. A weight bench centered the living room, weights, barbells, and dumb-bells scattered around it. When closed the mirrored closet doors reflected the bed.

The only place abundance ruled was the bathroom. Nelson had more primping supplies than a poodle parlor: shampoos, conditioners, rinses, holding sprays. There were mouthwashes, skin washes, hand washes, creams, lotions, jellies. I counted seven hair brushes and three blow dryers. He owned four different kinds of tweezers. What and where did he tweeze?

While I counted colognes—I was at eleven—Harry came in with the aluminum box and held it up for my inspection. Larger than a lunch box, smaller than a briefcase. Handled. A hinged opening at the top.

I said, "And?"

Harry flipped the box upside down and the top dropped open. Nothing fell out.

"Empty but for echoes. No forms, bank statements, or newspaper clippings."

"They've got to be there," I said. "They're on the list."

Harry tossed the box on the bed. "Yeah, that's what I used to say at Christmas, Cars. Somebody got here before us and whatever's in that box is as gone as my high round ass."

I stood in the middle of the shabby apartment and stroked my chin exactly the way perplexed detectives do on TV.

"My, my, what do you make of that?" I puzzled.

Squill had instituted daily 4:30 P.M. meetings since our get-together with the brass. It was him, Burlew, Lieutenant Guidry of the Crimes Against Persons Unit, Tom Mason, and any other precinct detective who felt they could make a contribution. Today, this was Jim Archibold and Perk Delkus from D-2. Usually this meeting was to report leads from snitches on the street, which, like most snitch-generated leads, were constructed from hope and horseshit. Hundreds of man-hours went into chasing snitch-generated phantoms. Squill reported our meetings to the brass, giving him a stranglehold over information. I'd seen the chief exactly once since our ecumenical assembly, on television, where he was calm and reassuring and used Squill's vocabulary.

Squill entered and assumed head position at the table, the omnipresent Burlew beside him, chomping his pulp.

"Let's make it quick, folks, got a crisis brewing with Reverend Dayton's five-bucks-fucky-sucky daughter. Anything new on the Nelson-Deschamps cases?" Squill's eyes glittered and I figured it was because the preachers'-kid incident had him working the media, his only true talent.

The meeting commenced with other teams speaking first and often redundantly. We'd already shared info this morning without a big table, without Squill as a moderator, and without a combined ten man-hours lost. Tobias and

Archer had discovered Deschamps was involved in a civil suit, trying to recover money owed for a design job. Nelson had been arrested for soliciting in Pensacola two years back. The incidents needed pro forma checking, but neither seemed to have a bearing on the cases. Squill would nonetheless tell the media two promising new leads were being investigated.

When the others finished, I added our info.

"We've got an odd incident, Captain. When Nelson's apartment was tossed, the report mentioned a box containing bank statements, correspondence, newspaper clippings, and the like. Harry and I checked the box—its contents were gone."

Squill waved an imperious hand and revisited an apologia designed for budget-request meetings. "A mistaken entry in the catalog," he dismissed. "Happens all the time, much as we'd like to believe the contrary. Too many cases, too few personnel, tired eyes doing the cataloging. . . ."

"Bill Harold and Jamal Taylor did the cataloging. Taylor definitely recalls going through the box and itemizing."

"It was a thief, then, Ryder. We can't put a twenty-four-hour guard on everything."

"The tape was intact. Plus this thief ignored a TV and about fifty bucks in order to steal a handful of paper."

Squill shook his head as if amused. "Are you going somewhere with this?"

"It's in the report. Deschamps and Talmadge met through the personals in the *NewsBeat*. I wanted to see if any of the newspaper clippings mentioned were from the *NewsBeat*, or the personals section of the *Register*. Maybe Nelson was contacted the same way. It's a long shot, but I want to rule out personals ads as the victim-selection process."

Burlew emitted some form of noise, a burp or a grunt. Squill looked at him before aiming his eyes back at me. "It's not your goddamned job, Ryder. You and Nautilus are supposed to be the Psychopathological Crime team. If I remember from the forming of this cobbled-together unit, that's the angle you're supposed to be working. The psychological aspect? Like what does the writing on the bodies mean?"

"I have no idea."

"No idea? Great. How about, do you know if the writing's important?"

"To the killer, yes. But it may be so intensely personal that—"

Squill smirked. "You think it's important. But here you are chasing your tail about some supposed newspaper scraps."

"It's all we have."

Squill shook his head. "Damn right it is. For all your squatting and grunting you're producing nothing. Nada. Zip. Who is this guy? What's he think like? What do the words on the bodies mean?"

"You don't just rub your hands over the words and they come to you."

His smirk turned to shark teeth. "Don't you smart-mouth me, mister."

"I was explaining why papers removed from the home of a dead man might have significance."

Squill sat back, suddenly disinterested, and made his pronouncement. "Let the district detectives handle the day-to-day work, Ryder. If Piss-it does nothing but walk the tracks of the other teams"—he flung his hands up—"what the hell good is it?"

Harry said, "It was walking the tracks of the other teams that gave us the missing papers in the first place."

Squill ignored Harry and stood. "Anyone have anything else to say?" His tone said he wouldn't be happy if they did.

"Dismissed," he said. "Next time let's try for some hard leads."

As he strode out the door he spat the words *Piss-it* just loud enough for everyone to hear.

Harry and I sat at the table and studied our hands as everyone filed out. Tom thumped us each on the shoulder as he passed. "Y'all really eating the shit sandwich on this one, guys," he said, dolefully. "I'll be damn glad to get you back."

"And we'll be damn glad to get there," Harry growled.

We returned to the office and I flung my notes on my desk. "Squill calls us in, he waves us off. He wants us on the street, he wants us off the street. He's got no idea what the hell he's doing."

Harry sat heavily in his chair. "It's Squill, Cars. He knows exactly what he's doing. Trouble is, we don't."

I tumbled thoughts over in my head. "Harry, if the PSIT

turns up leads, but someone else pursues them to a bust, does the unit get any credit?"

Harry's sad eyes provided the answer. We'd been ripsawing the cases night and day and in return had just been informed we were incompetent screw-ups, an opinion now churning up the pipe to the brass. But if we did uncover something, Squill could subvert it by claiming the leads had arisen within the normal parameters of the investigation and had had nothing to do with the PSIT. I began to hear the clocking ticking on the unit. Or the first faint notes of a death knell.

The offices of the *Mobile NewsBeat* were in a strip center on the south side of town, tucked between an alley and defunct hobby shop. A hand-lettered sign was taped inside a front window ghosted with the lettering of the previous occupant, AAA-Printing. Darkness hung behind the window and a magnetic sign inside the glass door informed me I was a half hour late. Hands cupped against the glass, I peered inside at cheap plastic furniture in a waiting area. A long counter separated the front from the rear work area, and a sign taped to one end of the counter said, ADVERTISING—DISPLAY AND PERSONALS. There was a sense of bare-bones, ramshackle enterprise, and I surmised the optimum employee would be a reporter who could run a printing press while selling advertising space. Opening time noted, I picked up the latest copy from a rack by the door and headed home. I was rolling south on I-10 when the car suddenly veered off an exit and turned north, as if responding to a distress call from another world.

Ava lived in a compact white Creole near the end of a cul-de-sac. I drove by slowly, staying low, wearing shades, my cap pulled down. Flowers and a sextet of crepe myrtles bordered her drive and several flower boxes sat on the porch. A Japanese magnolia stood in a circle of pine straw. Everything wanted water, including the yellowing lawn. The morning paper nudged the front door. Her Camry was in the drive. I phoned the morgue and Vera Braden answered. I Yankee-voiced her, talking fast, pushing flat sounds through my nose.

"I need to talk to Dr. Davanelle and right now."

"Ah'm sorry, she's not in the o-fice today," came Vera's creamy drawl. "May Ah take a message, sir?"

"Is this her day off? This is Sanderson. I'm the sales representative from Wankwell Testing. Dammit, I thought she'd told me her day off was tomorrow. Listen, I've got some new products I want to show your people—"

Vera spiked her southern cream with venom. "She was s'posed to be in today, Mr. Sanders, but I do believe she called herself in ill. How 'bout I have her phone you up when she feels perky enough to trouble with it."

Click.

My next call was to Ava. I left nothing at the beep, and drove away.

I made it two blocks before returning to park behind her

car. There was a hose falling from the side of the house and I gave everything a good soaking, almost hearing the dry lawn drink its way back to green. I found it oxymoronic that the word *dry* described sober but *lush* meant drunk, when few things parch body and mind more than addiction to alcohol. I stayed fifteen minutes and didn't knock at the door. If she was awake she knew of my presence, and the choice of coming out was hers to make.

CHAPTER 14

Morning took me straight to the *NewsBeat*'s offices, hoping for information to set my day's structure. Harry had a meeting at the DA's office on a previous case, and would spend most of the day either there or in the courtroom. I smelled wet ashes before turning onto the *NewsBeat*'s block. Where yesterday stood an alternative newspaper, today squatted a fire-gutted building. The interior was a sodden pile of wreckage with the blackened carcass of an offset press and scorched file cabinets. A tall, stovepipe-lanky woman in a black shirt, jeans, and work gloves kicked disconsolately through ashes at the rear of the building.

A siren whooped as a cruiser slipped beside me, Officer Bobby Neeland's thick wrist over the wheel. Neeland was a square-built thirtyish peckerwood who never smiled when he could smirk or laughed when he could sneer. Even the most desperate cop groupies at Flanagan's avoided Neeland and gigglingly referred to him as Baby-Dick behind his back. His excessive-force complaints needed a separate folder, but since there were never witnesses beyond the aggrieved, he dodged them all. Neeland slowly lowered his window and peered over dark shades.

"Why you here, Ryder? No one died." The blackheads clogging his nose looked like pencil leads.

"I'm following up on something, Bobby. What the hell happened?"

Neeland slipped off his glasses and stuck a sidepiece in his mouth, sucking noisily as he talked. "Somebody busted the window and tossed a can of gas inside." He sneered. "Bye-bye hippie paper."

"Any idea who did it?"

"Check the alley side, Ryder. It's autographed."

I walked to the side of the building. Spray-scrawled against the discolored brick was WHITE POWER in letters two feet high. Actually, it said, WHITE PO . . . , the last three letters a horizontal swipe toward the back alley.

When I returned, Neeland was gnawing his glasses with tiny sharp teeth. The clicking made me queasy.

"Whoever did it was more interested in running away than making a statement, Bobby."

"Huh? What say?"

"Forget it. Not important."

He stuck his spit-wet frames on and stared through black ovals. "Heard the paper'd been writing about the white power folks lately. Guess them boys got a little pissed. Shit, Ryder, you're a college boy, you tell me, hows come the ni—blacks can have all their shit like the NCPA, but white people want to stand up for their own and it's a big deal? I mean, where the fuck's the justice in that?"

Inside the front of my skull a hornet started buzzing. I said, "Know who the woman in the building is?"

"Owns the paper. No, *owned* it. She ain't s'posed to be in there on order of the fire marshal. I kicked her skinny ass out an hour ago and I'm about to do it again. Stay and watch, Ryder. It'll be fun, she's a real cop-hating cunt."

"Keep your pimply ass on the seat, Neeland. Drive away."

"Hell, you say."

"Go tickle your baby dick."

"You can't talk to me like that, you fuck."

I stuck my face in front of his, provocation for the terminally insecure. "I'm believing I just did, Bobby."

Neeland's knuckles were white on the wheel. I felt his hatred through the sunglasses; must not have been polarized. His voice shook with anger. "Get outta my face, cocksucker, or we're gonna have trouble."

I snatched his glasses from his face and tossed them over my shoulder, stepping back as I pulled his door open. Without the glasses his eyes stopped glaring and started blinking. He jutted his fat jaw and screamed at me from inside the cruiser. "I know what you're doing, you crazy bastard! I beat your ass and who goes up on charges? Me. *You* ain't getting *me* busted down, Ryder. I know your shit."

I gave Neeland his redemptive moment of grabbing the door and slamming it shut. He screeched away howling curses. His sunglasses lay on the pavement glistening with saliva. Not wanting rabies, I let them lie. Then, not wanting anyone else afflicted, I stepped on them.

An aluminum awning hung off the building. I enjoyed its shade until the fortysomething woman trudged from the wreckage. She seemed overpoweringly familiar until I realized she looked like Abraham Lincoln. First, it was the eyes, deep set under cragged brow, as dark and honest as coal. Her cheekbones were high and prominent and her chin was firm and square. Black hair rose like a wave before being pulled back and secured behind her neck by a blue bandanna. Though her motions were reserved, her feet lifted high and coltish when she stepped, gangly frame following the large boots like it was surprised where it was going. She sat on the step to the parking lot and pulled off her gloves to reveal lovely hands. She leaned back on her elbows and closed her eyes.

"Salvage anything?" I asked.

She looked up, squinting against sunlight. "What do you care?" She'd seen me with Neeland, knew I was Cop.

"Just do, I guess."

"We've published enough negative stories about your people that I doubt it."

I sat down beside her. The smell of smoke was thick on her clothes. "My people? On my daddy's side or my mama's?"

The nuggets of coal inspected me. I said, "I read the article on the white power movement last night."

"And?"

"It made me angry at people whose hatred of others is based on something as transparent as skin color or personal beliefs. Then I realized most of those folks have been stewed in those prejudices since they slid into the world."

"Don't apologize for them. They can change."

"Many do. The ones that don't spend ugly lives wallowing through inner poisons and never seem to be happy or grow into anything remotely worthwhile. Their hate-diluted lives seem ample punishment for the venom they squirt into the world. Still, it's a damn shame on all sides."

She thought for a moment, and pointed an elegant finger at a storefront bakery down the street. "Grab a cup of coffee?"

We made introductions on the walk to the bakery. I learned Christell Olivet-Toliver was the editor and publisher of the *NewsBeat*. I gave her my impressions without giving away too many of my facts.

"Let me get this straight," she said, stirring sugar into steaming coffee. "You're not totally convinced it was the white-power types last night?"

"I'm just saying immediately I start poking into the *NewsBeat*'s personal ads you get burnt down. Coincidence fascinates me."

She cocked an eyebrow. "Is it the headless murders that you're investigating?"

"Without going into details, yes."

"What do you need from me?"

"Basically, how the personals work."

She cradled a ceramic mug in her violinist hands. "Let's say you want to run an ad. All you do is write your ad, and e-mail it to the *NewsBeat*. We assign your ad a code number and run it. If someone, let's say Muffy Duffy, wants to respond—"

"I could never hit it off with someone named Muffy."

She flipped a stir stick at me. "*Hortense* goes to the personals section of our Web site and e-mails a response. Our computer system directs it to your assigned number."

"How does one pay?"

"Our personals are like a club, there's a small fee both ways. Pay online, or mail a check or money order to our office."

"Doesn't sound secure, especially using check or plastic."

"There's no way the public can know who's placing an ad or responding. People trust us, and we don't violate that trust."

I wagged a skeptical finger. "But computers will be computers; I'll bet somewhere in its innards is a record of the electronic addresses of the respondents. I imagine a tech type could dig them out."

"Maybe. With a court order"—she jabbed a long thumb at the charred building—"and the computer."

"Everything's gone?"

She smiled sadly. "Ashes to ashes and all that."

So much for the personals. I switched gears. "Anyone strange hanging around lately?"

"White-power types? Skinheads? Tattooed bubba boys. Like that? The other cops already asked me. I see weird characters all the time."

"Anyone set off alarms?"

She tented her hands and her fingertips tapped together like butterfly wings drying in the sun. "Just one little thing. Two days ago I saw a car parked across the street from the office. I had taken the trash out about a half hour earlier and I saw the same car going down the alley as well."

"What kind of car?"

"A Jaguar. XJ series. With the three-seventy horsepower Super V-eight and the long wheelbase."

I gave her a look.

"Hey, even us tree-hugging, ball-busting, feminazi communist anarchists can dream."

"Your titles on the paper's masthead?"

She sighed. "From my mail."

"How much did you see of the driver?"

"I only saw it side-on and it had the deep window tinting. Nothing."

"Plates?"

"I looked at it for a half second and thought about it for two. Then something else grabbed my thoughts and . . ." Her hands made flyaway motions.

"You recalled the car because it's your dream machine?"

"Partly. But there's nothing across the street from us but a second-hand clothing shop and a busted-down Laundromat. The car didn't belong. It was just a tiny wrong note."

Wrong note, wrong note . . . Ms. Olivet-Toliver's words echoed in my head all the rest of the day and on the way home. They pursued me through the stand-up fueling from a bowl of cold red beans and rice, and out to the deck, where I propped my feet on the rail. The sun was fading and several beachcombers sifted the surf with their little white nets. Watching them sift, I slowly realized Abraham Lincoln's message: This case was discordant.

Discordant. The wrong notes, maybe. Or the right notes played incorrectly, something awry in timing or interpretation. I've always been attuned to discord, sensitized, perhaps, so that even slight akilters can be measured.

Something about this case had been out of true from the first moment I laid eyes upon the topless corpse of Jerrold Nelson. It was not so much the incongruity of the body lacking a head that tilted my psychic equilibrium, but rather the lack of expression in the crime or the scene. If the motive was, as Squill sold and resold at every opportunity, vengeance killing, where was the vengeance, the anger? Not in the textbook-precise removal of the head, nor the time-consuming inscriptions on the flesh. Both seemed more the work of a ghoulish accountant than a hate-charged spree killer or ritual-driven murderer. And if so, where was the sense of spree, of abandonment to savage and wanton destruction?

The more I thought, the stronger my sense of dischord grew.

I grew up attuned to discord, my child's antennae sifting the air for the subtle vibrations that presaged violent change, much as seismologists use lasers and mirrors to measure hair's-breadth motion between mountains. We all want warning before the earthquake strikes.

I learned to want it more than most.

Truth be told, my first memory is of a kind of earthquake. I had no warning and no one outside of our house felt it. Though it was twenty-fours years ago, I remember the event with a clarity unmarred by time, perhaps even sharpened by its passage.

It's night. I rise from bed and walk in dreamlike detachment through a narrow gray corridor that seems to span miles. Ahead is a black square set into the wall that reaches to the sky. It is the hall of our house outside of Birmingham, and it is gray with moonlight through glass and the dark square is the doorway to my brother Jeremy's room. Screaming pours from the dark square.

I am six and my brother Jeremy is twelve.

I stand at the threshold and listen quietly, knowing somehow I must not enter. I need to visit the bathroom and, continuing down the hall, pass my mother's room. She is a seamstress specializing in wedding dresses. My mother sits at her sewing machine as white fabric flows through it like liquid. Her hands are motionless above the cloth and her eyes are focused on sewing. The high whine of the sewing machine mutes the grunts and shrieks from down the hall. A floorboard creaks beneath me and she turns. Her eyes are wide and wet and she speaks, not knowing that I will remember her words, keep them forever.

"I know it's wrong," she hisses through clenched teeth. "But he works so hard. He's a professional man, an engineer. Who would think that someone like me could marry an—" A scream slices down the hall like a scythe. My mother's brow furrows and for a moment her hands fly out of control like startled sparrows.

"And what could I ever do anyway?"

Mother contains her hands and turns back to her sewing but becomes still and her head droops. White fabric covers her lap like a deflated ghost. She whispers, *Go back to bed, it will be quiet soon . . .*

At an age when most children are learning to handle a bicycle, I became a student of the transformations that preceded these events, every two or so months at first, then with accelerating frequency. It seemed I could feel the air in the house charge with negative particles that gathered in force and intensity until discharging in a night of black lightning. I learned to take shelter at the first hint of the gathering storm, to hide in my treehouse in the woods, or in the backseat of the car at night. After the storm's passage

I would seep back inside, antennae quivering for vibrations of the next explosion, ready to run.

And then, in the lazy span of a summer's afternoon, it was over.

. . . the woods behind our house are thick with slash pines and loblollies, the ground covered with a soft mattress of brown needles studded with fallen cones, and I spend my days sheltered by the soft-spoken trees. I built a tree-fort in an ancient live oak and though the fort is a rickety jumble of chipboard and two-by-fours and other rescues from construction site burn piles, the heavy branches of the oak hold it securely. I feel safest in the woods, in my tight and shadowed fortress a dozen feet above the ground. Lately my father has been making me more scared than ever. He is starting to see me and he's never done that before.

His eyes are so angry. He says I'm stupid.

I am nine.

Once from behind the boards I saw my brother . . .

Jeremy is fifteen.

Once, from behind the boards of my fort I saw my brother come running into the woods with a squealing shoat under his arm, a baby pig from the Henderson's farm down the road.

I laid flat on my belly and watched my brother wire the pig to a tree and do loud things to it with a big knife. I was sure he looked up and saw my eyes between the broken wood and leaves. But he must have been looking at something else and started up with the pig again. It took a long time, and then he buried the red things deep in the pine-needled ground. He wiped the knife on leaves and stuck it in his pocket . . .

Then, one day not long after, I saw flashing lights at our house. I was alone in my tree fort and ran to find the county police right in front of our house.

Up close the flashing lights hurt my eyes and I looked instead at the policeman's hands. The knuckles were like rocks and he held his hat over his privates. His eyes were hidden under mirrors. Jeremy watched from the porch glider, one foot on the floor, softly swinging the glider to and fro.

"We don't know how it . . ."

"Close down the county roads until we find . . ."

"Coroner there now, he's . . ."

"You don't want to go there . . . your husband . . . it's not a fitting sight for . . ."

"We'll find this madman, ma'am. I'm so sorry for your . . ."

After a while, the policemen pulled away. I lifted my eyes from the ground and saw only dust above the road. Mother was a gray statue in the front yard. I saw how she must have been talking to Jesus, her words were so quiet.

And I saw Jeremy wink at me and make the sound *oink*.

CHAPTER 15

There's a short story by Sartre called "La Chambre," and in it a man named Pierre is tormented by malevolent statues that buzz around his head, driving him deeper into insanity. His sole control over them comes through his *zuithre*, strips of cardboard glued together in a spider shape. On one strip is the word *Black*, the words *Power Over Ambush* on another, a third holds a drawing of Voltaire. I was sitting in the dark with the heads of Jeremy and my parents buzzing around me like shadowy statues, wishing I had a *zuithre*, when a car crunched into my drive. I heard a long bleat of horn and saw a taxi in my driveway, the white dust of crushed shells drifting past its headlamps. It bleated again and I yanked open the door thinking, *God grant me a* zuithre *for the idiot taxi drivers of the world as well.*

"I didn't call for a cab," I yelled. "You got the wrong damned address."

A heavyset guy with a black pompadour leaned from the driver's window. My security light was in his eyes and he porched his hand above his brow like a salute.

"You owe me sixty-three bucks," he called up. "Fare from Mobile."

"Listen, buddy, I don't owe you—"

The back passenger-side door opened and Ava stumbled out. She took two halting steps toward the house before her knees crumpled and she dropped to the ground.

"Carson, help me, please," she cried as she tried to push from the sand, her voice a slur of tears and alcohol.

The driver and I wrangled her up the steps and onto the couch. I peeled four twenties into his palm and he looked happy to escape. Ava tried to push herself up, brushing sand from her face and mumbling semicoherently. "I got drunk, Carshon, I fuck tup and got drunk and I wasn't goin' to again but I got drunk and—"

"Shhhh. You don't need to explain."

"I need *assistance.*"

She stunk of booze and sweat and fear. I stripped her to her underwear and guided her to the floor of the shower and adjusted a spray of tepid water. Her head was on her knees and she shivered and sobbed while I sponged water over her.

Several minutes later I helped her to stand, covering her with a robe as she fumbled from bra and panties. She was more coherent and her words made halting and desultory pictures of her last few hours. She worked Saturday, with Sunday and yesterday off. She'd gotten drunk Saturday night after work and couldn't stop drinking. This morning she'd arisen sick and ashamed. She'd called in ill and gotten Clair, who'd tongue-whipped Ava for her absence, an increasingly common event.

Ava looked at me through eyes more red than white. "I thought I'd sober up today an' go in tomorrow and get through it somehow and I'd stop this . . . ugliness. Yesterday would be the last." She hugged herself and shivered.

"But as soon as you hung up you started drinking."

Her hands made the hard gripping motion I'd overseen from Will Lindy's office. "I can't *stop*. What's wrong with me what's wrong with me what's . . ."

"You have to go to a detox center, get the poison out of you."

She grabbed my sleeve with the iron fingers of someone at the edge of hysteria. "No! I can't. People'd find out. I can't *do* that. No. NO!"

"All right, it's fine, calm down. We can do it here."

"You didn't tell anyone about Friday night. . . . I kep' waiting for people to look at me, to know. You said you didn't and you didn't. . . ."

"Of course not. It wasn't anyone's business."

She wiped tears from her eyes with the back of her hand.

"I don't know anyone else here . . . I feel so *alone*. Then I saw you at my house, I saw you . . . You didn't tell anyone and then you came over and watered. I wanted to, I couldn't go out, I couldn't let the neighbors see—"

"Sleep time," I said, taking her hand and leading her toward the bedroom. "We'll talk tomorrow, get you well."

"She hates me," Ava blurted. "She just hates me. I don't blame her, I fuck up so much, ever since I got there—"

"Who hates you?"

"Dr. Peltier. Even when I'm at my best she hates me, I—I—"

I grabbed a wastebasket and Ava got sick. I waited it out and guided her to the bed.

"All I ever wanted to do was my work and I'd study more at night and review and try to learn more and more and the more she'd hate me the more I drank and some days I JUST WANT TO DIE. I JUST WANT TO DIE I JUST WANT . . ."

I got her calmed and covered and put a wastebasket beside the bed. She stared at the ceiling and squeezed an invisible ball in her fists. Tears poured silently down her cheeks. I closed the door and tiptoed away.

Ava tossed and moaned most of the night, her rhythms ripped apart by three days of drinking. At daybreak she found deeper escape and her face looked at peace when I inched open the door. I hoped she'd pull some strength from the peace before waking to the hard choices in her path.

* * *

Mr. Cutter sat motionless in a steel folding chair in the dark of his closet. The rise and fall of his chest was his sole motion. He hadn't been tempted to cheat just because no one was looking. Inside him everything pumped and squirted and oozed. You couldn't help that.

He'd sat in the chair for hours, spine erect, knees together, hands atop his thighs. He'd been a good boy.

Until an hour ago. He'd been unable to hold his water and though he'd fought it—no quiver of hand, not a single bounce of leg—he'd had to let go. Just a few drops at first, but instead of giving relief, it only heightened the agony and he'd finally relaxed his insides and let the liquid flow out.

Once there would have been hell to pay, he'd thought, the release spreading hot and acrid down his legs, pooling in the cupped seat. But not anymore. Everything was changing. His pictures were coming true: he was making them come true.

He thought about going to the secret room where he kept his dream and worked on it. But today was a business day and he had outside work to do and the outside face to wear.

After several minutes Mr. Cutter stood haltingly and kneaded his frozen thighs and cramped buttocks. He walked stiffly to the bathroom to shower. On his way he selected his tie for the day. Socks. Shoes. He inspected his pants, picking at lint, being a good boy, tidy. He almost passed through the kitchen without stopping—today was a busy day, had to crank it in gear—but his favorite drawer called to him. Everyone had a secret helper. He removed a long knife, a bread knife—Mama's bread knife. She made good bread but he'd have to behave to get it. Since he'd peed himself he wouldn't have been allowed any bread. *Bitch!* A sharpening steel came out next, and Mr. Cutter whisked the blade over the steel. The sound was music. He'd once been to an ice hockey game and his heart screamed its joy at hearing skates make the same sound cutting over ice, in their wake the flakes of perfect cold, whisk whisk whisk.

Pulling into the morgue lot caused the bottles to rattle in my trunk. Every bit of liquor in my house was back there. I'd even pitched in the Listerine; to a sick drunk alcohol is alcohol.

Ava had reached the threshold of Truth: admitting the problem existed. It was my job to pick up a squirming, biting Truth in both arms, dump it squat in the middle of Clair's lap, and hope Ava still had a job afterward. I pulled into a protected hearse bay by the side entrance. It was early and the door was locked. I hit the buzzer. Willet Lindy, carrying a toolbox, let me in.

"Don't tell me you do the plumbing, too, Will."

He rattled the box. "If it's busted, I fix it, if it's needed, I requisition it, if it's impossible, I lie about it."

"I need to see Clair. She in?"

Lindy winced. "Yes. But it's annual budget time and we're one prosector short today. Keep your distance so you don't lose an arm."

Walking the hall to her office I kept pasting a bright smile on my face and it kept slipping off like a Halloween mustache.

"Morning, Clair," I said, eyeballing through her half-closed door. She wore a dark jacket and simple white blouse. Beneath the desk she'd have on a skirt and heels. Clair's lanyard-strung reading glasses perched on her nose as a fountain pen hovered above an official-looking form.

"I'm busy, Ryder. No time for chit-chat."

"It's important, Clair."

She reluctantly gestured me inside. "Mind if I close the door?" I asked.

Clair narrowed a puzzled eye and nodded. I sat in a worn leather wingback chair opposite her ancient oaken desk. As a high-ranking public employee, ME, Clair could have demanded the full decorator treatment including thousands of public dollars' worth of furniture, drapes, shelves. Instead, her only concessions to office were the removal of the over-head fluorescents in favor of warmer light from floor and desk lamps, and an ergonomic chair that probably cost ten bucks more than the ones supporting the chunky gals at the license bureau.

In my line of work reading upside down is helpful. I saw the header on the official-looking form beneath Clair's pen: REPRIMAND.

I pointed to the form. "Is the reprimand to Dr. Davanelle?"

"I don't think that's any of your . . ." Clair paused and wearily closed her eyes. "Why do I think a bad morning is about to get worse?"

"She's at my place," I said. "She couldn't work today and yesterday because she was drunk. She's been drunk since Saturday. She's a mess, Clair."

She tossed the pen on the desk and rubbed her eyes. "That explains a lot. In the past six months she's called in sick seven times. Four of her sick days were Mondays. 'Lost weekends,' probably."

"Probably," I admitted.

"You know how I run this place, Ryder. I have three paths to handle the bulk of the medical procedures. I handle as much as I can, but mainly I'm up to my ass in administration. I need people who show up on schedule and work."

"She'll get treatment. It's a disease, Clair."

She picked up the pen and poised it over the reprimand. "I can't have an alcoholic here, Ryder, even one in treatment. The position demands attention to detail. And in the end, no matter how capable or well meaning she is, it's not her ass on the line, it's mine. My department, my reputation. She's out of here."

The penpoint pressed at the paper. I caught the word *capable* in Clair's description and threw a desperate rope to it. "Dr. Davanelle is good at her job, capable, as you say?"

"Allowing for age and experience, she's the best I've ever seen. When I was interviewing for the position only one person came close, Dr. Caulfield."

Caulfield was a fresh-from-school pathologist hired six or seven months back. He was performing an autopsy on a low-life S & M practitioner named Ernst Meuller when a bomb in Meuller's lower bowel detonated. It was speculated Meuller had crossed someone inventive with explosives. Dark-humored cops dubbed the perp the "Bottom Bomber," and figured he'd gotten Meuller pass-out drunk, inserted the device, and left Meuller to awaken, attempt to remove the device, and die horribly. The hard-living Meuller foiled his nemesis by succumbing to a heart attack in his drunken sleep. The only casualty was Alexander Caulfield, who lost three fingers and a career. The case remained unsolved, an enigma.

I said, "If Ava was so good, why'd you hire Dr. Caulfield?"

Clair took a deep breath. She set the pen aside, stood, and walked to the window. "I don't expect you'd understand, Ryder."

"I've amazed others. Try me."

There was a long pause as she stared into the clouds.

"I'm inflexible and unyielding," she said as if reciting from a sheet of paper. "I demand excellence from my staff every minute they're here, and have no desire to involve myself with their lives when they're not. This is a hard job anywhere in the country, especially for a woman." She reached out and put her hand against the window as if confirming its existence. "Don't take that as whimpering, Ryder; the hardships are ingrained in the system and will be for years to come. I have to be tough to make it work." She turned from the window. "But I wasn't sure I could be completely unyielding with a woman pathologist.

I'd remember the struggles I'd encountered, make allowances, maybe even . . ." Clair grasped at the air if if trying to pluck the perfect words from it.

"Become empathetic?"

"Whatever. The whole dynamic and personality of the office might change."

"With a man you could maintain distance."

"Only after Dr. Caulfield's . . . incident did I question why I'd hired him, what my motives had been."

"And you hired Dr. Davanelle."

She sat behind her desk again, the reprimand beneath her fingertips. "It was always her or Caulfield. They were on a different level than other applicants."

"But you managed to avoid empathy, though, didn't you, Clair? You pushed hard."

Her voice tightened, defensive. "She was new and new people make mistakes, Ryder."

My gut tightened. "I'll bet you were right on her about her mistakes, right?"

"When she screwed up I let her know. She had to *know*."

My hand slapped the desk and I spoke through clenched teeth. "Damn right, let her know. Put her through what you went through! No sympathy, no empathy, no quarter. Whip the little bitch. Show her how bad Clair Peltier had it. Shovel it into her face."

The words scalded my tongue; I didn't know where they came from. Clair jumped to her feet. "You've got no goddamn right to talk to me like—"

"She thinks you hate her, you've always hated her and wish she'd never come here."

"Don't you dare think you can . . ." My words registered and confusion clouded the fire in Clair's eyes. "What? Say that again, Ryder."

"Ava thinks you hate her and want her gone. Is it true?"

"Hate her?" Clair looked unsteady, as if the floor had softened beneath her. She lowered herself, reaching for the arms of the chair with unsure fingers. "My God, no, I—I think she's exceptional, I think . . ."

"You don't dislike her?"

"My God, no. I never meant for her to think . . ." She turned her head away and blinked several times. "Maybe I—"

"It's time for some empathy now, Clair. Maybe even overdue."

Clair closed her eyes and took a deep breath. When she opened them she reached for the pen and tapped it on the reprimand. Fourteen times. She slipped the pen in her pocket.

"She gets this week and the weekend, Ryder. I'll put her down for emergency family leave. Next Monday I want her back here clean and sober. One transgression, no matter how minor, and she'll be gone while her footprints are still warm on the floor."

I was halfway to the door and letting my breath out when Clair spoke.

"Ryder?"

"Yes?"

"Why did she come to you? Are you two romantically involved?"

"No. I guess she's a friend."

I was closing the door when she spoke again.

"Carson?"

I leaned my head in. "Yes, Clair?"

"I know you're carrying double baskets of shit with the headless cases, but give her all the help you can spare. Please."

I nodded and closed the door. I'd never heard Clair say please, and I'd never seen her look so beautiful.

CHAPTER 16

"I'm making a few changes in the assignments," Squill said, dealing papers around the table like cards. I slapped down the one that flew at me. "Don't read ahead, Ryder," Squill said. "I'll walk you through it."

Today's meeting held the usual crowd. Plus Blasingame had brought one of his sergeants, Wally Daller. Burlew was doing pushoffs from the wall and further straining the seams of his rumpled brown suit jacket. I smelled a gray sweat coming from him, like opening an old gym locker. He waited until his master passed out all the papers before sitting.

Squill said, "One of the reasons this case is going nowhere is diffusion. No focus, and poor communication."

"Excuse me, Captain," I said, "but we have meetings every morning."

Squill threw his sheaf of papers down. "Another reason it's in the crapper is I can't get two words out without you contradicting me, Ryder."

"I'm not contradicting, I'm enlightening."

"I've had all the smart-mouth I can take."

Harry nudged me with his leg. "We're listening, Captain," he said.

Squill waited until the silence in the room turned uncomfortable before continuing. "Everyone's running the same ground. We need to become specialists. Each team has to take a portion of the puzzle and dissect it."

I started to speak, but Harry's knee smacked me quiet. Squill flicked his sheet with a shiny tailored nail. "I've made new assignments. I want Nautilus and Ryder to concentrate solely on Deschamps. I want to know everyone he talked to in the last six months, every meal he ate, who he fucked in his wet dreams."

My hands squeezed the table's edge. *Stay down. Breathe.*

Squill continued. "As for Nelson, I want his investigation to continue in the same fashion, but with Sergeant Daller at lead."

Wally Daller?

"Take it easy, Cars," Harry whispered.

I liked Wally. Everybody liked Wally. He was our comedian, more off-color stories than a Shriners convention. But he had analytical tunnel vision; ask him to investigate a road and he'd give you the total number of white stripes down its middle. I figured Nelson was an intersection of invisible lines: the first chosen, the missing papers, a lifestyle more likely to touch aberrant psychologies. Wally didn't know dysfunctional psyches, he knew, *"There's a priest, a rabbi, and a hooker in a pork dress . . ."*

"Begging the captain's pardon," I said, "but Harry and I've established relationships with people close to Nelson. We're unraveling threads that might—"

"You've gotten too near these people. We need fresh eyes and new threads."

"Fresh eyes? You mean start from the begi—"

"You're running in circles, it's not working," Squill snapped.

"In the Adrian case I moved between the victims to establish—"

"Get the hell out of this room, Ryder."

"You said running in circles? What's that mean?"

"Now. Go outside, Ryder. You're done here."

"There are dead people. I'm not done." I felt hot sand rising in my throat, my voice rasping.

"Git," Harry whispered.

Squill said, "Every time I try to speak you're in my mouth telling me what I'm doing wrong. Insubordination is a big deal in my department, mister. Get the hell out of here while you're still a detective."

"Insubordination? If you think—"

"*Git*, dammit," Harry hissed.

The assignment sheet crumpled in my fist like foil as I

closed the door behind me. I went back to my desk and waited. Harry reappeared ten minutes later. I was up before he got halfway across the floor.

"Wally! He put Wally Daller in charge of investigating Nelson, Harry. He wants us off Nelson. Why?"

Harry sat heavily and pressed his knuckles to his temples.

"Come on, Harry, give. We can't let—"

"Shut up, Carson. For once. Please just give my aching ears a rest."

"There's a guy out there chopping off heads, Harry."

He banged his desk with his fist. Everything on the desk jumped an inch. "You think I don't know that? You think I don't care? What? You think you're the only person in the whole department, Carson-fucking-Ryder, give me a high five, Harry, we whipped their asses, Harry?"

I jabbed my finger toward the meeting room. "You didn't say jackshit in there."

Harry's jaw twitched. "Don't you tell me when to move my lips."

"Why didn't you back me up?"

"Same reason I don't bet on three-legged horses."

"I was trying to keep our hands in Nelson's case. That's where the break'll come from."

Harry flung his hand up, thumb and index finger touching. "You came about a shit-hair's distance from getting us kicked off everything, that's what you did."

"Squill wouldn't do that."

"He's doing it right now, you're just too dumb to see it.

182

He pokes, you squeal, he runs and tells Hyrum you're an insubordinate pain in the ass who got lucky once but who's now upsetting the applecart. Hyrum nods and says, 'Do what you have to do, Terrence.'"

"We can nail this if he'll give us room to move."

Harry rolled his eyes. I said, "What? Squill doesn't want it solved?"

"On his terms and putting the glory on him alone. Here's surprising news, Cars, you're not the only detective in the department."

"It's a Piss-it case, Harry. It's ours."

"Did those pretty birdies come with your crib? The ones spinning above your head? Grow up, Carson, what's ours is what Squill tells us is ours."

"The manual says—"

"If the manual said it was going to rain pussy at noon, you'd be out there with a net, wouldn't you?"

I opened my drawer just so I could slam it shut. Harry had his phone on speaker and the desk clerk announced a call. "Says his name is Jersey, Harry. Said you wanted him put through."

Harry clicked off the speaker and turned away with his hand cupping the phone. I figured Harry was talking to old Poke Trenary, a janitor at City Hall. Several times while in that citadel of mirrors I'd seen Harry glide the slow-mopping Poke to a quiet corner for a fast milking. Harry put down the phone and whispered, "Damn."

"Damn what? Yankees? The torpedoes?"

"I was thinking because Hyrum retires in September the chief decision would be in September. I forgot about get-ready time. The commissioners decide early, then work on transition crap. The decision'll be made at the next executive session, when they get to close the door. They won't vote or anything, but they'll weigh the input, and make the decision, and it'll hold until the official announcement in a few weeks."

"And this unofficial coronation will be when?"

"Eight days from now."

"Eight da—No wonder we keep getting cut off at the knees."

"You got it. Squill's gonna keep us bottled and throttled until then. After that it doesn't make a bit of difference. He'll either be a deputy chief or not."

I asked, "How's Poke putting the odds?"

Anyone with a jones for political intrigue suffers a touch of paranoia. Harry glanced around the room to make sure no microphones were aimed our way. "No one hears about this," he whispered.

I slapped my forehead. "Shit. Dan Rather's offering fifty grand to hear what Poke gets from scruffing through trash bags at City Hall."

Harry sighed. "Tell Danny-boy odds are running about five to three in favor of Plackett . . . and that Squill guy hanging off his tit."

"For nine days we're gonna be shoved away from Nelson? Just so we don't get lucky and break the case, maybe making the chief decision an even race at best?"

"Squill's set to make a two-level jump, Cars. He doesn't want even money."

"Tell that to the next guy looking Mr. Cutter in the knife."

Harry went to fetch a coffee. I watched him walk slowly through the maze of desks, giving himself time to think. He returned three minutes later, hard resolution in his eyes.

"It's looking more and more like we're gonna have to nigger this case, brother. Do most of the work for none of the credit. You cool with that idea?"

"It's what we're doing now," I said, standing and rolling up my sleeves. "Let's surf 'em and turf 'em."

Harry shook his head sadly.

"That don't mean a damn thing, Cars. They got to mean something."

Apartment manager Briscoe Shelton wasn't thrilled about being pulled from his TV viewing, a fuck opera by the sounds through his door, bass-heavy synthetic music and moan-inflected ululations. I'd returned, unsatisfied after yesterday's toss of the place got chopped short by Squill's meeting. Harry was pounding pavement, revisiting Deschamps's contacts. He did what we were supposed to do, I did what we hoped would work, making one final run before Wally hippoed through. If Squill found out, I'd be humping an oil rig, handing Harry tools.

"How's about you folks git through looking at this place so's I can rent it," Shelton whined after the key-flip bit again.

"How's about you get your sorry ass back in your office

and continue your jack-off session?" I replied. Screw public relations, sometimes it's just not worth it.

It was a steam room inside. I hit the misnamed High button on the wheezing window AC and looked for fresh ground to plow. The contents of the aluminum box hadn't magically returned, so I turned to Nelson's junk drawer, where all the orphan crap goes to die. For Nelson it was matchbooks, broken combs and brushes, bent tweezers, a couple of screwdrivers, pliers, cracked candles, matchbooks, a half roll of duct tape, and a stack of menus.

I crouched in the tepid wind of the AC and flipped through the menus. Pizza. Sandwich shops. Gumbo joints. Rib shacks. More pizza. Lots of delivery menus. Made sense; judging by the paucity of gear in the kitchen, Nelson hadn't apprenticed at Spago. I was set to move on when I noticed a room-service menu from the Oaks Hotel in Biloxi, part of the sprawling High Point gambling complex.

A woman friend and I had stayed at the Oaks a few months before, though we'd started at the Day's Inn. After an afternoon of cheddar on Triscuits and experiments in fluid dynamics, we'd sashayed to High Point's casino to try the blackjack tables. A well-timed jack had left me staring at over a thousand dollars. We'd shifted our experiments to the Oaks and left the cheese and crackers for some lucky housekeeper.

Two nights at the Oaks turned my windfall to vapor. Or, more romantically, to memories. I remember a bed large enough to confound a surveyor, a spa with gold-plated fixtures, and an honest-to-gosh bidet, which continues to perplex me. Though the experience was a kick, I was relieved when we left, like I'd reached some sort of limit.

So the question was, what was a sidewalk-level hustler with a small wallet and big dreams doing at the Oaks, if he indeed really had been there? I flicked the menu with my thumbnail and remembered back to the casino, how the one-eyed jack winked when I lifted the edge of the card.

Maybe it was time for a little more luck.

"I'm busy here, bubba," the flat voice growled over the phone. "You get one minute."

Ted Friedman was assistant director of security at the Oaks Hotel, an unhappy guy with a flat midwestern accent, Detroit maybe, or the hard side of Chicago. He spoke around a cigar. I laid out a sketch of what I hoped for and heard keystrokes in the background.

"If your boy was a hotel guest in the past year I can tell you. Lessee . . . Nalen, Naughton, Navis, Naylor . . ."

While Friedman talked I pictured a scowling, boiler-chested guy in a fog of stogie smoke, scrolling through a screen of guest names, the walls of his surrounding room filled with security monitors peeking down hallways and into elevators.

". . . Nebner, Neddles, Neeland, Neeler, Neffington, Nekler, Nelson. Three Nelsons in the past year. Linda Nelson from Opeleika, Russell and Patricia Nelson from Green Bay, and John and Barbara Nelson from Texarkana. That's it, bubba. Any help?"

"Not what I wanted."

"Nice talking to you, bye."

I recalled Nelson's affinity for aliases. "Wait a minute, Mr. Friedman, my man's got a thing for reshaping his name."

"Time's up."

"Two minutes, Mr. Friedman. Five at the max."

"Hanging up now, bubba. I just went on break." I heard the phone leave his ear.

"You ever a cop, lardass?" I yelled.

I swear I heard Friedman's phone rise back up; his air must have been scratchy with cigar smoke. "BATF. Twenty years with *real* law enforcement."

"Always hated working with the locals?" I asked.

A satisfied snort. "Especially bubba locals."

"I'd never have guessed. Fun to dish it out?"

I heard his smile through the wires. "Turnabout's fair play," he crooned around the stogie. "Ain't too bad."

"What'd I do to you?" I asked.

"The runaround. The tickets. The general small-town-cop horseshit."

I said, "I guess I don't remember you."

"Musta been one of your brothers."

"Why don't you slap that boulder off your shoulder, Friedman?"

"Why don't you ride the bone, bubba. I gave you what you asked for."

"That Nelson I'm interested in? He's on the cold coast over here. No head. Got another just like him one drawer over. I'm expecting triplets any day. When it gets out some fatass at the Oaks could have made a difference, it'll hit the papers big time. Especially when it turns out he's an ex-fed. You might want to consult your PR director on this. Thanks for the help, Friedman."

There was a five-beat pause before Friedman spoke. "You bought yourself two more minutes, bubba," he said thickly; I wondered if he'd bitten off the ass end of the cigar. "What the hell is it you want?"

I heard Hembree's voice in my head: *"Jerrold Elton Nelson, aka L'il Jerry, aka Jerry Elton, aka Nelson Gerald aka Elton Jerson."* I remember this stuff perfectly until a case is closed, then *ka-whosh*, my mind flushes it.

"Try Gerald. Can you do first-and last-name searches?"

Friedman sighed. I heard the cigar snuff out in a metal ashtray, followed by keystrokes. "I've got no last names 'Gerald' but two firsts: Gerald Staunton from Montreal and Gerald Boyette from Memphis."

"Nope."

For five minutes we tried every combination of names I recalled. Then Friedman cleared his throat and spoke up. "You know, I just noticed that the name 'Elton' anagrams into 'Nolte,' like the actor."

"Run with it."

Another series of keystrokes followed by a pause. "Well, well . . . I've got an E. J. Nolte of Mobile."

Nelson's initials and anagrammed middle name. My heart took a five-beat time-out. Friedman said, "He was here for four nights in May." He gave me the dates.

"How'd he pay, cash or card?"

"Cash upon checkout."

"That unusual?" I knew what Friedman would say.

"Huh-uhn. Yokel comes in, hits, decides to stay here instead of the Piddle Inn. We take a credit card imprint. If the bill's paid in cash the imprint's torn up. We won't have an imprint anymore, just the basic sign-in. Got a space for home address and company name on the form. Elton lists Bayside Consulting, Three twenty-one Water Street, Mobile. That's all."

I wrote them down. "Anything else, Mr. Friedman?"

"Judging by the charges, Nelson had a fine time. Heavy room service, looks like every meal. A lot of bar tabs, also in-room. They racked up over three grand in four days."

"They?"

"First night I got a single entrée and salad going to the room; next three nights we're eating for two. Unless your boy's got a split personality down to his appetite. . . ."

"Gotcha."

"Anyway, looks like we got two folks ordering from room five nineteen—suite, by the way, four seventy a night."

"Your professional take on the situation, then, is . . ."

"To me, Detective Bubba, this looks like two people taking a room, hanging out the DO NOT DISTURB sign, and having a rock 'n' rolling good time without coming up for air."

* * *

A check of the phone directory showed no listing for Bayside Consulting. The operator came up empty too. The address was a dummy. I drew blanks with the Chamber of Commerce and Better Business Bureau. If the company was incorporated there'd be records somewhere. I didn't expect to find anything.

Chances were Nelson's trip to Biloxi had zero ties to the murders. The switch-hitting hustler probably had boy-toy usage at hotels and motels across the region. But right before his death he'd bragged about finding the mother lode, a sugar daddy or mama who might spend a few grand on a long weekend's private partying.

I called my house, no answer. It was after 8:00 P.M. I'd gotten Ava at 6:30, worn voice straight from sleep, said I'd soon be home. She went back to sleep, I told myself; didn't hear the phone, or felt too rotten to talk. I left Harry a note detailing my day, and headed for Dauphin Island. My next chore was telling Ava I'd ratted her out to her boss.

"*I trust you. . . .*"

Where the hell was that *zuithre?*

CHAPTER 17

I entered just after eight with my hands full of groceries to feed my starving shelves, plus sports drink to help flush Ava's system and keep her hydrated. I'd also bought thiamine and other vitamins. The drink and vites were on the recommendation of my former partner, Bear. I called him on my drive home and asked what to expect from Ava. He predicted a spaghetti western: Good, Bad, and Ugly. Problem was, Bear said, you went through a shitload of the last two before the first one kicked in.

The bedroom door was closed and I pictured Ava sleeping it off. Kitchen cabinets were ajar and I suspected she'd been searching for hooch. I was glad the Listerine was in the trunk. Figuring she'd returned to bed, I tapped at the door and, hearing nothing, entered. Not there. I checked other rooms, closets. She wasn't anywhere in the house. Something else was missing—sixty bucks from my bureau drawer. She'd left a barely legible IOU scrawled on a napkin.

The phone rang. My mind flashed to a scenario of the Dauphin Island cops calling—they'd found Ava wandering the streets and were checking her story. Even if she'd gotten hooted I could likely get her released into my care. I grabbed the phone.

"Carson Ryder."

"Hello, brother. Can you believe those stupid fucking attendants lost another cell phone? I've been hiding this one. They're so small all it takes is some plastic wrap and a little bit of—"

"I'll call you back, Jeremy. I got an emergency here—"

"NO, YOU DO NOT! Every time I call you try to HANG UP ON ME!"

"I'm not kidding, Jeremy. A friend's in trouble."

"Oh?" His voice dropped to a hiss. "Is it a womb-man?"

"What's it matter?"

"She'll keep. They're SURVIVORS, Carson. She'll be here long after the cockroaches have gone belly-up. Just don't ask them for help and you'll be fine."

"I'm hanging up now, Jeremy." I started to put the phone down.

"NELSON AND DESCHAMPS, CARSON!" He shrieked. "WHERE'S THE PASSION, BROTHER?"

I lifted the phone back to my ear.

"Hi, Carson, welcome back. I read the papers. They were covering the headless twins until the preacher's daughter's soap opera took center stage. All I gleaned was the heads had been severed. No mention of gunshots to the body meat, no axes, no thumpity-thump of the ball bat. Was it nice and clean, brother?"

"Dammit, why have you fixated on these cases, Jer—"

"FIXATED, HE SAYS? I'm not FIXATED, brother. I'm not FACT SATED, either, since you won't TELL ME ANYTHING!" He adopted a matter-of-fact tone, a college lecturer. "What happens when you tell me things, dear brother, is that it allows me to travel from my current confines, vicariously, of course, seeing the pathways of the world through your brown eyes. It's nice to be out and about again, just like the old Joel Adrian days. And I thought I might again be helpful with some map reading. Was I not helpful in the past, brother? I'll take your silence as an affirmative." He shifted to the quivering voice of an old woman. "Tell a weary old traveler about the bodies, Carson. Pretty please?"

I took a deep breath and looked at my watch. One minute, that's what I'd give him. I said, "There was no . . . *expression* in the killings. . . ."

"Ah, lad, you're an amazin' fella you are. But it's not expression. It's *passion*. BLOOD! FEAR! SEX! FIRE! There MUST be passion, Carson. Bites. Or cuts. Or leetle-teensy pieces chopped out and taken away to dry. SOUVENIRS! Were words cut into the body? Messages? Was a finger missing? A dick tip? Smoke signals squirting from torn assholes?

WHERE'S THE PASSION, CARSON? Perfect hate or perfect love, perfect anger or perfect joy. Either or both, but NO MIDDLE DISTANCE!"

I watched the second hand arc around again. "We were thinking the express—the passion might have been demonstrated elsewhere. On the heads."

"Ahahaha," Jeremy said. "*Sur la tête*. The ol' cabeza. Take the canvas, leave the easel."

"There were some attempts at communication, seeming nonsequiturs."

"Oh, ho—in dribs and drabs my brother tells his tale. Words?"

In the distance I heard a siren. *Ambulance*. Pictures of Ava drunkenly walking down the middle of the street invaded my mind. "Yes, dammit, words on the body. I have to go, Jeremy."

"Tell me the words, Carson. QUICKLY!"

I recited them and he started laughing. "Sounds to me like our boyo isn't finished with his head-challenged friends. I'll bet he wants more from them, brother. Promise you'll come see me. Promise, promise, promise."

"I promise. Soon."

"We'll discuss the words. Already they're making me tingle. Promise again."

"I *promise*."

"Don't fib to me, Carson. I know phones: the tongue gets in front of the mouthpiece and just lies there."

"I said I'd come see you, Jeremy. I goddamn well meant it!"

"Ahh," he cooed. "A spike of emotion. Yes. I believe I'll see you. Almost on the anniversary of our last little escapade. You'll have to talk to Madamoiselle Prussy. Tell her to reserve you lots and lots of time alone with your brother." He cupped his hand over the phone. "Oh, this is so exciting, Mama, our boy's coming ho—"

I hung up and almost bolted out the door but stopped. First dictate of fishing: Fish where the fish are. Second dictate: If you don't know where the fish are, get a guide.

I called Bear again.

Ava stumbling across Bienville Boulevard, a car full of partying teens racing down the street, distracted . . .

"Yo, Cars, what can I do for you, brother? How's that problem with—"

"She rabbited before I got home, Bear. Probably not long ago. What kind of place would she look for to go drinking? She's whitecollar professional. . . ."

"The first place she finds. She's not looking for conversation among her social equals, Carson, she's looking to stop the pain. She know the neighborhood?"

"No."

Ava taking a drunken walk on the beach, deciding to swim, a rip current sucking her far past the breakers . . .

"Did she pass any bars or package shops on her way in last night?"

"A couple. But she was sozzled."

"Was she conscious? Able to make some conversation?"

"Yes."

"Alkys' eyes pick up drinking holes like owls scope out mice. She'll have crawled to one if she had to. She gets a couple drinks in her she'll relax and maybe look for ambience."

"Thanks, Bear."

"Like I said, I got a chair for your friend over here, Cars. It's in a real safe place."

"Here's hoping, Bear. Later."

I started out the door and remembered her clothes. They were in my dryer. What was she wearing?

Like every nautically themed bar from Boston to Boise, the Wharf Bar & Grille had nets strung from the ceiling, life rings on the walls, and false pilings lashed with sisal. The waitstaff wore pirate hats. Owner and barkeep Solly Vincenza smiled and ambled over.

"I'm looking for a woman, Sol. Brown hair, slender, maybe five seven—"

"Wearing a big-ass T-shirt saying '*Laissez les bons temps rouler*' and probably nothing on under it? And a ball cap says Orvis?"

My shirt. My hat. "That's my girl."

Solly wagged his Etruscan head. "Came in an hour ago, said, 'Double vodka and grapefruit juice.' She grabbed it with both hands, banged it down in about five seconds, and called for another. That's when I saw her eyes, them bad, haunted ones. I said, 'That's the last one, lady, I think you'd be better off at home.' She called me a name or two, tossed some bucks on the bar, and rubber-legged out. Having some problems, Cars?"

"Not a night I'm gonna frame, Sol," I said. "Where'd she go?"

The sad head again. "Last I saw her she was heading down toward the inlet past the marina."

The closest bar to the inlet was a dive frequented by blue-collar locals, service people, charter-boat crewmen, and the like. It reminded me of the beery, atmosphere-deficient places my snitches preferred. Inside it was chilled to the point of condensing breath without freezing out the stench of stale beer and vomit. The barkeep was a heavyset guy with hooded eyes, razor burn, and a blue chain tattooed around his neck. If he'd been a bulldog, I'd have named him Spike. Spike was counting cash into the register and talking to the only patrons, three roofers, judging by the tar on their clothes and shoes.

"I'm looking for a woman—" I called over the jukebox spew of eighties heavy metal, theme music for the lobotomized.

"Ain't we all, sport," Spike interrupted.

I smiled. "She's five seven or so, slender, brown hair, T-shirt . . ."

"Like a vir-gin," one of the roofers sang as his buddies hooted. The place was a regular comedy club.

"It's important," I said. "She might be in trouble."

"If you're her boyfriend, sport, I'd say she is," Spike said.

It takes me a while to catch on, but I do. Since I'd started my day with Clair, I'd dressed up, tie and light suit. I'd sparked a touch of class consciousness with the mokes in the bar. You don't often see it on an island catering to the wealthy, but when it breaks through, it can be ugly. You can fight it or roll with it and I figured rolling was faster. I pulled out my wallet and flipped a fifty on the bar. I put my finger on the bill.

I smiled self-consciously. "Aw, c'mon, guys. This is important. You know how it is, we had a little argument and if you can lead me in the right direction I'll pick up the drinks tonight."

Suddenly, they had a choice: continue the taunts and lose the fifty, or get skunk drunk on found money. Spike eye'd that money hard, since it would all end up in his till.

He said, "She had a few, then took off. Feeling damn feisty too."

"Which way'd she go?"

"Went off with the Gast brothers. They got a boat down on the—"

"I know where it is," I said, heading for the door as the roofers started calling out their drink orders. I heard Spike's happy voice as the door slammed shut. "You don't want to mess with them brothers, sport. They'll rip your face off and shit in it."

For two hundred bucks and up depending on the season, you can get a private or semiprivate fishing charter for a half day. Your money buys a competent captain who knows tides and currents and where the fish are running. Forty to sixty bucks buys you space on a "party boat," standing shoulder to shoulder with a hundred others and crossing lines for four hours. Twenty percent of the customers will be beered up and get violently seasick. They'll be the ones standing next to you.

The Gast brothers ran the *Drunken Sailor*, a slum with scuppers and the ugliest reputation of all the party boats on the island. Tourists didn't know this, so the Gasts scratched a living out of puttering a few miles out and handing customers a fishing rig guaranteed to jam, back-lash, or flat-out disintegrate. If a mark wanted to keep his catch, the Gasts charged a usurious fee to toss a couple of ice cubes over it, and a buck for a plastic bag to put it in. The Coast Guard was always hauling the Gast brothers' boat back to the dock and I figured they planned it that way to save on fuel. No one sailed the *Drunken Sailor* twice.

The Gasts were even dirtier and uglier than their boat, white trash on water, as amoral as sharks. They lived in a cinder-block sweat haven on the mainland and only crossed to Dauphin to run their ratass enterprise.

The *Drunken Sailor* bobbed against pilings. Shoreside was a small picnic area with figures moving in the semidark, lit by a sputtering yellow light on a phone pole. The air was thick with the smell of rotting fish. I cut the headlamps and parked on the crumbled macadam and jogged the hundred feet to the picnic area. Ava was sitting on a picnic table and sucking from a quart of Dark Eyes. My shirt wasn't doing a good job covering her. Johnny Lee Gast, about two hundred twenty pounds of tall white trash, had a grubby paw on Ava's thigh. Earl, a loudmouthed runt, was leaning against her, laughing and sucking a beer so loudly it sounded like he was gargling.

"All right, party's over," I said, coming into the light.

Ava turned to me with a cockeyed grin. "Carshon! Guess what? Jimmy and Lee are gonna take me on a boat ride. C'mon 'long." She waved the bottle like ringing a bell and took a gurgling swallow.

"Come on, Ava, we're heading back," I said easily, knowing it wasn't going to be easy at all. I knew how the Gasts fought. Little Earl was the bait and Johnny Lee the trap. I also knew that Johnny Lee didn't know when to stop hitting, and he'd done three years on a manslaughter conviction to prove it.

"Ah, c'mon, Carshon. Have a li'l drinkie."

"Private party, Ryder," Johnny Lee said.

"Let's go, Ava."

"I said private party, boy," Johnny Lee growled from somewhere around his groin. "Move on."

Earl had a whiney singsong voice straight from the playground. "What you gonna do, Ryder? Maybe you're a dee-tective in Mobile, but here you ain't shit. My brother says git, you better git, bitch."

"You guys be nice," Ava said and followed it with a burp. She giggled. "S'cuze me."

There are important lessons learned as a street cop. One is that street fights have no rules; the trick is to take out the other guy before he can hurt you. If you prefer not shooting anyone, one of the best assets is the nightstick. I'd been taught how to use it, legally and otherwise, by two wood-slamming pros, one being an Okinawa-te expert in the shore patrol, the other my ice-breaking bud, Akini. He'd taken the Koga method of baton usage and added a good deal more kendo. I always kept a short, straight stick in the truck as a fish billy. It was currently jammed down the back of my pants with my shirttail over it.

"Come on Ava," I said, "I'll mix you a drink back at the house."

Her eyes lit up. "Promise?"

"Cross my heart."

Ava wobbled off the tabletop. Earl grabbed her, a hand cupping her breast. She was more concerned with checking the level in the bottle.

"Good-bye, Ryder," Johnny Lee said. "Ain't saying it again."

Ava chirped, "I think I'll go with Carshon. Thanks, guys," She tried to step away from Earl. He grabbed her wrist. "You got shit in your ears? Is that why you ain't listening, Ryder?"

Johnny Lee was slipping almost imperceptibly to my side. Earl pulled Ava to him and cooed at me over her shoulder. "Hey, Ryder, hey, Ryder. Missy here says she's a doctor. You play doctor with her, Ryder? Hey, Ryder, look at me. I asked do you like to play doctor with little missy here? Give her a checkup?"

"Stop spitting in my ear," Ava whined at Earl, trying to push away from him. "An' get your hand off my boob."

"Let her go, Earl," I said, reaching for the stick.

"Fuck you," Earl spat, shoving Ava toward me.

Johnny Lee slammed behind my legs like a wheelbarrow full of bricks. Ava spun away as I hit the ground. My chin smacked my shoulder and blue sparks exploded behind my eyes. Earl scuffed a hard kick off my back as I rolled away. Johnny Lee came at me and I cracked the stick across his shins. He howled and jumped back. The lights of the marina swooped and whirled as I rolled to the edge of the oily water. Somewhere in there I dropped the stick. Johnny Lee thumped a kick off my hip and I heard a yell, mine. I scrabbled in the dark for the stick when Johnny Lee slammed a kick off my bicep. If it had hit my face I'd been finished.

I grunted and rolled and the stick prodded my back as I went over it. I got a finger through the handle loop as Johnny Lee dropped on me and snaked a ham-thick arm around my neck. He pushed my face into the sand. The world started to blur. I tasted blood and heard the sparkling hiss of approaching unconsciousness. I heard Earl laugh, about a hundred miles away. I pushed up on my elbows and got my face slammed right back in the sand. My head whirling toward black. I gripped the stick in both hands and speared it over my shoulder with the last of my breath.

A howl nearly blew out my eardrum and I felt Johnny Lee's arm pull away. I stumbled to my feet, fell, stumbled up again, sucking air, waiting for the world to stop spinning. Johnny Lee was squirming like a cut worm, hands over his eye, screaming he was blind. Figuring he needed something to take his mind off his eye, I bounced the stick off his shins and shoulders, sharing my thoughts about men who preyed on intoxicated women. Earl was a hundred feet gone and gaining speed. When my arm got tired of hammering Johnny Lee, I let him crawl off, leaving a snail trail of stink and body fluids.

Ava was passed out by the picnic table. I eased her over my shoulder and limped to the truck. "Ava, this would be damned funny if it wasn't damned serious," I lectured. She vomited down my back by way of response.

CHAPTER 18

Until I was introduced to Bear's shuddering treks back from a binge, I'd had no idea of the snake-venom toxicity of large amounts of ethanol. At 6:00 A.M. I came in from breakfast on the deck, stacked my dishes in the sink, and heard low moans from Ava's bed. She had spun herself into a tangle of blankets and was shaking uncontrollably, fists knotted beneath her chin. The shaking hit in spasms; attack, relent, attack. Bear described this phase as being eaten by buzzsaws.

I sat by her head and slipped wisps of hair from her eyes. She pulled the covers tighter. Her lips were parchment and I brought her a large glass of apple juice and held her head up to suck at the straw. She fell back, an arm thrown over her forehead.

"What happened last night?" she whispered, hiding under her arm.

"You took a walk. Thankfully, I'd pinned a note to your collar with my address on it."

She saw the scrapes on my face and closed her eyes. "Do you have anything to drink?"

I tapped the cup beside her. "Apple juice. Soda water. Gatorade. Tea. Coffee."

"Something stronger. Just a little bit. I hurt so bad. I really need a drink, Carson. God, I swear I do, just one. It'll help me make it to work."

"You're not going to work."

"I'll lose my job. I've got to get home, clean up, and head in." She pushed herself up on an arm and her eyes floated with vertigo. I pulled the wastebasket over and she emptied her stomach into it. She fell back, eyes red and wet, sweat beading her forehead.

"One drink, that's all. I *need* it. I'll lose my job, Carson."

I closed my eyes and took a deep breath. "You're not expected at work today, Ava. I told Clair about your problem. It's all ri—"

"Oh, Jesus, no . . . you *didn't*. Tell me you didn't."

"If you can stay sober she'll—"

"Why did you do that to me? Oh God, oh fuck, oh God . . ."

I tried to explain but she recoiled at my words and spun deeper into the covers. Time was a failing commodity; Monday was five days away and if Ava didn't get more help than I could give, she'd never make it. I went to the kitchen, called Bear, made plans, and returned to the bedroom. I figured there were two ways I could push her toward a meeting with Bear: Calm and reasonable and reassuring, easily the safest. Or I could go in swinging, using sarcasm, insult, even ridicule. If I'd thought she was weak in spirit, corroded in her underpinnings, it could only be the former. I made my choice as I entered the bedroom. Her red eyes blazed through pain as she wrestled free of the bedclothes. Her hair looked styled by a tornado.

I said, "Come out, come out, wherever you are."

"Screw you. I'm out of here. I'm already out of a job."

I leaned against the wall and crossed my arms. "That's up to you."

"You're the one that told Dr. Peltier about my—"

"I told her the truth. You can't work. You can't even stand up."

"I would have made it through the day, gotten better. But, no, Carson-fucking-Ryder has to tattle to the great Doctor Peltier."

"How tough is it to do a post when you're toasted, Ava?"

"I've never gone to work drunk!" She steeled her jaw and looked away.

"Too proud to go in juiced, is that it? Admirable. Step right up, ladies and gentlemen, and see the pride of the county morgue, Ava Davanelle, hangover queen and martyr extraordinaire. But don't stand too close, not if your shoes are new."

"You're a sick and ugly bastard."

I sat at the foot of the bed. My hand touched her covered leg and she jerked it away. "How far do you have to fall, hangover queen? Don't answer me, just answer it to yourself. How much farther are you going to fall?"

Her eyes said that if she'd had a knife I'd be singing with the castrati. I stood up and hitched my hands in my belt. "Here's the way it's going to work, vodka girl. I've made an appointment for you. Don't give me that look, it's not a hospital or detox unit, it's with a friend named Bear. We'll stop by your place, you can clean up, get fresh clothes."

"Screw your meeting. You've ruined my life. Take me home *now*."

"You're staying here until you promise to meet Bear." I couldn't guarantee she wouldn't back out after giving her word; it was just something I felt.

"No fucking way. I want to call a cab."

I handed her my cell phone. She fumbled at it. "It's not *doing* anything."

"I took the batteries out. I locked the other phone in the closet."

I ducked as the phone zinged over my head and exploded against the wall, plastic and circuitry flying like shrapnel.

"I'm getting the cops, say you're holding me against my will," she wailed.

"Order the meat loaf."

"What?"

"The jail contracts with the Windbreaker Café. The meat loaf is excellent."

"*I'm* calling the cops on *you!*"

I started laughing. "Too many people saw you crawling the bars last night like a drunken hooker, babe, the cops won't listen. Plus I have a cabdriver who'll swear you couldn't pay the fare. I've got bartenders who saw you spending money. Remember stealing sixty bucks from me? Or did that get lost in the blackout too?" I neglected to mention the IOU.

Her mouth opened and closed like a beached fish. "You rotten *bastard.*"

"You have two ways home, Ava. Promise you'll do what I ask, or . . ." I snatched her hand and studied it. "Is your thumb sober enough to hitchhike?"

She jerked it away and woozily struggled to sit upright. "I'll fucking well do it, I will." She tipped over.

I ticked off the situation on three fingers. "Do you want to go home? Then I want you to meet Bear. And I want your promise to meet him."

"I want to go home *now!*"

What she wanted, according to Bear, was for the pain and the guilt to stop, and that meant more alcohol. My act made me feel lower than a stable worker's bootheel, but Bear had told me to stand firm. He also suspected if Ava got drunk again she'd be ruined for working Monday. Her shoulders were hard against the bricks.

"I want out of here, *now!*"

I pointed to the door. "Out is that way, Ava, as you recall from last night. Wait. You don't remember last night, do you? Here's the gist: Our lovely young pathologist went barhopping. She ended up with the Gast brothers, dirty, amoral lowlifes. She wore a T-shirt and a cap and no under-wear. I found her sitting on a picnic table with her legs spread and her tits jiggling. Earl Gast was playing with our lady's boobs but she was too drunk to notice. The three playmates were about to take a nighttime cruise."

I stared into her eyes. "A dozen miles out in the Gulf with the Gast brothers. Guess what the price of that cruise would have been, Ava? Paid over and over and all night long."

She clenched her eyes tight and tears squeezed from them. I heard waves crash and repeat a dozen times before she spoke.

"I promise," she said angrily, though I knew the anger was not at me. "You win."

"It's not a competition," I told her. "We're on the same side."

Ava said she'd need fifteen minutes and went to her bedroom and closed the door. Too late I realized she might have liquor squirreled away in her room. I flung wide the drapes in her living and dining rooms and let the light pour in. Her furniture was eclectic, Shaker to contemporary, and everything fit against everything else. There was art on the walls, well-wrought repros of van Gogh's Arles period, the fields and flowers of France, plus some lilies courtesy of Monet. I noted several small multimedia works by an artist I didn't recognize—glittering concoctions of paint and silk and metal foil, abstract birds frozen in time against her roseate walls.

I opened and closed cabinets in her kitchen until I came across a half gallon of Dark Eyes hundred-proof vodka, one-third full. No mixers or liqueurs. No bottle of port or brandy to celebrate special occasions, just high-speed obliteration for the brain. The booze went down the drain and I put the bottle back in the cabinet.

I was in the living room admiring one of the jewellike paintings when Ava reappeared. Her weary frown said she hadn't kept a stash in bedroom or bathroom. She wore faded jeans and a tee from St. John's Hospital. Her hair was wet from the shower. The strings of one white Reebok slapped the floor as she walked.

We were on the porch when she tapped my arm. "Whoops. Forgot my purse. I'll grab it. Please, Carson, get the AC running in your truck."

Bear told me AA members define insanity as doing the same thing over and over and expecting different results. I got in the truck and waited for Ava to discover her bottle was empty, half expecting she'd simply lock her door until I went away, the easy way out.

She charged out the front door a minute later, slamming it hard enough for me to feel the concussion twenty feet away. She strode to the truck and got in, cold fury on her face.

"Let's get this the hell over with," she said.

*   *   *

Mr. Cutter brought the photos to his office. He had decisions to make and time was growing short. He had three choices left, though only one more was necessary for the project's completion. His eyes scanned them from behind the security of his locked door. The men in the photos were from the same mold: broad shouldered and slender of waist and hips, differing mainly in hair and eye color and degree of musculature.

Something wasn't right.

It had to be exact. This selection was the most important, the final incarnation: Boy, Man, Warrior. Boy and Man had been perfect, but Warrior needed raw fury and unbridled power. And size. Mama could melt steel with a glance and needed a man equivalent to the task. He picked up the photos and studied again. His choice for Warrior seemed to have shrunken in the past few days.

Or maybe he was growing beyond his own dreams.

A new vision of warrior formed in his head and he set the photos on his desk, picture side down. He already knew the man, had seen him, heard him speak. You could tell he was a fighter, an avenger. Was he a fit adversary for Mama? The one to take her, kill her, save her?

Yes. He was a warrior and had the strength.

Mr. Cutter relaxed into his desk chair. The universe had answered again. First Mama, then the boat, now the Warrior. It was beautiful. All he had to do was claim the warrior as his own, *whisk, whisk, whisk.*

Footsteps outside and the voices of his coworkers. The

drones were returning. They'd soon be scratching at his door.
I need, I need . . .

Mr. Cutter gathered the now unnecessary photos and
notes in an edge-aligned stack and pulled an envelope from
his jacket. He carefully placed the photos in the envelope
before folding it over, aligning the blank end with the return-
address end, the one printed *Bayside Consulting.*

"I don't want to be here."

"Nobody does their first time. After you."

I pushed open the side door of a small former church on
the south side of downtown, now a meeting place for
Alcoholics Anonymous. Ava reluctantly entered a spacious
room with tables and chairs, a pool table, an ancient pinball
machine, and two pop machines. A bulletin board advertised meeting times and alcohol-free dances. Beside it was
a rack of literature. Steps near the back led upstairs. There
was a small snack counter. Behind it an older guy with
Einstein hair attended a restaurant-sized coffee urn. Four
guys played cards at a back table. Two women were shooting
pool and trading barbs with the guys at the table. Words
passed between the pool players and card game and they all
started laughing. A man in a business suit sat alone near
the back, sipping tea and reading *The Wall Street Journal.*
He whistled and fiddled with his tie. Ava studied the faces
from the corner of her eye.

"Where are all the . . . people with problems?"

"They've got us surrounded."

"Have they been drinking? They're laughing."

"They're laughing because they haven't been drinking."

Ava started shaking and sprinted to the rest room with her hand over her mouth. The guy behind the window smiled. "New," he said.

"First-timer," I affirmed.

"She's in the right place. You in the fellowship?"

"No. But a believer, nonetheless."

He gave me a thumbs-up and returned to his coffee ministrations. Ava returned two minutes later, face red and eyes wet. She still shook, withdrawal jitters kicked in by fear of this place, at first telling her only what she was instead of what she could become.

"I can't take this, let's get out of here, Carson. Let's come back tomorrow."

Footsteps thundered down the stairs beside us, big feet with a Bear above them, a bear in jeans and a blue sweat-shirt, a cap from Bass Pro Shops covering an ursine shock of brown hair. A two-hundred-eighty-pound embrace lifted me from the floor like a sack of feathers. Bear's delight was electric, transferable; jumper cables for my attitude.

He said, "Damn, just look at you: lean and mean and that same stupid-ass grin."

"It's not the same stupid-ass grin, Bear, it's an upgrade."

Bear yelled to the coffee guy. "Hey, Johnny, this is my old partner, Carson."

Einstein shuffled back to the counter. "You're the one stole the wheelbarrow and rolled him in here?"

Bear turned to Ava. Her hand disappeared in his massive paw. "Hello, Ava. Carson's told me all about you."

Ava turned to me as if I'd betrayed her again. Bear laid his arm lightly around her shoulders. "A bit rocky?" he asked, turning her toward the steps. "You should have seen my first day—Carson dumping me on the floor like a load of bricks, me howling mad, shaking like a dog shitting peach pits. . . ."

Bear turned to me and winked. Then he guided Ava upstairs, one step at a time. She stayed for an hour and then I took her home. We'd both fulfilled our parts of the bargain.

"You'll be all right?" I asked.

She looked toward her house and back at me. "Listen, Carson. I want to say—"

I shushed her with a finger over her lips. "Just stay safe."

We had an awkward moment—nodding and mumbling until she turned away. When her door shut I heard a high whine in my head as I tried to remember how to drive, what lever performed what function. My hands lost the notion of grasp and I forgot what I was doing and where I was going. After a deep breath I finally coordinated the machinery and began pulling away into air as coarse as burlap.

"Carson, wait!"

I jammed on the brakes, turned, and saw Ava running stiffly toward me.

"I'm afraid of what could happen. Could I—would it be too much to ask . . ."

Her hand clutched tight to my arm. She looked ragged; spun and wrung and flung a hundred directions. But I saw something else too: a sense of resolve, loose but gathering, like pieces long apart but finally, with the seamless and inexorable pull of gravity, coming together, needing to be whole.

"Let's go pack your bags," I said.

Just like that the air turned to velvet.

CHAPTER 19

"From this Friedman you figure Nelson was humping and pumping in Biloxi," Harry said, pulling off his lime-green tie and jamming it in the side pocket of his jacket. The tip hung out, looking like the head of a flattened frog.

"All expenses paid, from the sound of it."

A group of day-shift patrol officers charged into Flanagan's, hooting and hollering, out of uniform, free for another day. Harry and I nodded to familiar faces and turned back to the table. I'd settled Ava at my place and returned to meet Harry for brainstorming and a bowl of gumbo.

Harry was in a contrarian mood from a day filled with too many walks down dead-end streets. He pitched his spoon into his empty bowl. "Probably has nothing to do with anything."

"There's the shadow man Shelton saw with Nelson. The one that wasn't like the others. Plus Nelson's blabbing about having found his bottomless honey jar, easy street."

"So? Messer said that was his theme song, always on the edge of a major score."

"Nelson was the first. Someone's grabbed stuff from his apartment. There's got to be lines right to Nelson."

Harry flicked an invisible string in the air like plucking a harp. Silence.

"Yeah, I know," I said, slumping in the booth.

"What's eating you most about this thing?" Harry asked. I watched across the barroom as a patrolman demonstrated how a DUI bust had failed the walk-the-line test. The cop held his arms out like stepping onto a tightrope, teetering, putting one toe inches in front of the other. The onlookers howled and clapped.

"It all comes back to the lack of passion," I said, quoting my brother, again running on his ideas, hating it because it was my only choice. "It's not vengeance killing or serial killing. It's something different. There's no sense of finality. He wants more from them than their deaths."

Harry shot me dubious. "Like zombies, you're saying? The living dead."

"The working dead. They have a job to do. I just don't know what the hell it is."

Across the room the patrolman finished his act by pirouetting into a stumble and falling facedown on the floor. The crowd went wild. Harry glanced over, frowned, looked back at me. "I don't know, Cars. My head's jammed up enough just trying to lay scenes and vics over one another and come up with places they match."

"Bodies are similar," I said, tapping my swizzle stick against my cocktail glass like ringing a bell, *bing*. "Ages are close" *Bing*.

"That's about it," Harry said. "Even the venues don't have many matching points."

I tolled the venue information. "One outside, one inside." *Bing*

I tolled the time of day. "One daylight, one night." *Bing*

I tolled coloring. "One guy rather fair, the other dark." *Bing*

I tolled status. "One white-collar guy, one bottom feeder." *Bing*

Harry grabbed the swizzle stick, snapped it in half, and handed it back. "Even the damn temperature was day and night. I cooked at the park and froze at Deschamps's."

I thought about it a moment. "It was cold there, wasn't it; not just me."

"I put on my jacket. It was an icebox."

The plucking of a distant string, soft, but distinct. I said, "Even with the door opened and closed, people coming and going. Maybe the killer bottomed out the AC to keep the body fresh as long as possible."

"I got an uncle could live naked in a meat locker, you can see your breath in his house. Maybe Deschamps was the same way."

"His fiancée step-hopped from the West Coast on Thursdays. Miss a step and she's hours late. What if the killer knew it?"

"What about Nelson's body—what preserved it? Sprawled in the park on a hot night? If it wasn't for a couple horny kids, Nelson would have cooked for hours."

While Harry wrinkled his nose at the thought, my mind focused on Bowderie Park. The body in the light. The deserted park. The fright in the faces of the onlookers. The sweat-soaked runners at the periphery, legs pumping as they watched from the street, staying loose.

Runners.

The winding path that ran the length of the park.

I almost ran to the phone booth for the directory. "Philips, Philips, Philips," I said, my finger dropping down the listings.

Harry frowned. "The councilwoman?"

"She lives in the Bowderie Park neighborhood."

I called councilwoman Norma Philips and explained myself. She was concerned and polite and excused herself to check her neighborhood's phone list. She said the person I wanted to speak to was Carter Sellers, adding to call back if there was anything else she could help with. I made a mental note to vote for her.

"Sellers residence," the voice on the phone said. I heard a TV low in the background.

I identified myself, then jumped into it. "I understand, Mr. Sellers, you're one of a neighborhood group who run on a regular basis."

He chuckled. "The Night Rangers, we call ourselves. Nobody has time during the day, so we get together a couple times a week and knock out some Ks in the neighborhood."

"Regular route?"

"We measured out a five-kilometer route, or close."

"Does it take you through Bowderie Park?"

"Be a shame to set up a route and not go through the park. Sure."

"Would you have run through it Thursday night if the murder hadn't occurred?"

"At ten forty-five p.m., or damn close."

"Pretty precise, Mr. Sellers."

"An old guy who sits on his porch calls us Mussolini's train; we always run on time."

"Every Thursday?"

"Tuesdays, Thursdays, and Sundays, rain or shine."

I made one more call to a person I did not enjoy disturbing, then turned to Harry. "Cheryl Knotts, Deschamps's fiancée, says the thermostat had been dropped to fifty degrees. She couldn't explain it, said the temp was the one thing she and Peter used to argue about: she liked cool, he was warmer blooded."

Harry nodded, started feeling it. "The killer couldn't control the temperature at the park, but his surveillance told him that the Night Rangers would chug through at ten forty-five."

"On the dot," I said. "He spotlighted his merchandise not just to show off . . ."

"But to get it to the cooler as quick as possible. Didn't want the meat to spoil."

"Who watches after a body's found?" I needed to hear it said.

Harry ticked the participants off on his fingers. "Cops show up. The ME's office shows up. Criminalists show up. Fingerprints. Techs. Detectives. Ambulance drivers. Passersby."

"Take it to the morgue."

"Attendants. Pathologists. Doc P. More forensics types, maybe. Cops. Then the afterward folks; funeral homes."

"Maybe the killer's sending messages to someone in the chain, Harry. I think we can write off passersby and the shifting cast of fire department and ambulance personnel. They're transients. Ditto the afterward folk."

"Leaves morgue and criminalist folk. And us."

I cupped my hand behind my ear. "Do you hear it, Harry?"

He flicked a nail against his glass.

Bing.

CHAPTER 20

"I started drinking when my brother died. Two years ago. Heavily, that is. I'd always liked it, from the first time I had a beer when I was sixteen. It made me feel, I don't know, smart. I got the grades and did all the right things, but always felt dumb. Like I was faking it."

Ava and I walked slowly along the beach. It was midnight deserted, just us and the waves and the slightest thread of breeze. Our footsteps crunched in the dry sand. I said, "Your brother, you mentioned him once. Lonnie?"

"Lane. He was four years older than me. I called him Smoke. It was my pet name for him because he moved so softly and quietly. I'd be sitting on the porch reading and he'd drift up and point at a cloud and begin describing the shapes in it. . . ."

She'd started talking when I walked through the door, a flood of disparate thoughts connected only in that she wanted them out. I also felt she wanted to talk about her drinking, to pick it apart and study it. She wanted to under- tand how to ground herself when shadow lightning hissed and sizzled in her head, how to channel the current harm- lessly into the earth.

"We could spend an entire afternoon studying the clouds. Or I'd watch him draw. . . ."

We started toward my house, crossing the roll of the small dunes.

"As early as I can remember he was an artist; not a kid who did art. He'd amaze people with his insights and skill. I have six of his paintings at home."

I recalled the brilliantly crafted abstracts on her walls, controlled explosions of color, joyous. "I saw them. No, that's wrong: I was pulled into them."

"The one by the couch? Red and gold and green? It's called *Crows*. Most people see dirty black birds, Lane saw beyond, into their beauty. That's how I felt when he was with me, he saw places where I was beautiful that were hidden to me. He used to call me or even come visit when I was in school. He kept me going, focused. I felt so alive when he was here."

"How did he die?"

She stopped. Behind her, far down the strand, I saw whirling stars. Kids out burning sparklers, the Fourth wasn't too far away.

"He committed suicide," she said. "It turned out he had been seeing a psychiatrist for years. Depression. It tore our family to pieces."

I watched the sparkling stars, said nothing.

"I thought back through all the times he'd seemed so happy, so alive. But he had this—this mental cancer in him, a thing with tentacles that kept growing until it tore him away from me, from our family, from everything.

"That was when I first fell apart. My anger turned to drinking and I took leave from school and stayed drunk for a semester. Sick, rotten drunk. The school knew about Smoke, about Lane. They thought I was just taking time off to deal with it."

I wrapped her shoulders with my arm. "You were, Ava. Just not correctly."

"When I started working here . . . there was no Smoke to call at night, no one to tell me I'd be fine. I'd have a bad day with Dr. Peltier and I'd go home and have a drink and suddenly it was morning and I was on the couch with an empty bottle in the kitchen. I'd fight it until the weekend and fall apart again. Then I'd be so ashamed I'd—"

She hung her head. "Damn, Carson, I have an MD and I can't even begin to explain alcohol addiction. For an alcoholic to drink is a supremely irrational act. And yet, as scientifically and logically trained as I am, I drink. It's insane."

We stood quietly and watched the sparklers etch silver against the dark until they shrank into black. We headed back to the house. I heard music, Louis Armstrong blowing

"Stars Fell on Alabama" through the sea oats. Harry was in my drive, sitting in his old red Volvo wagon and sipping from a bottle of beer. He heard us crunching through the sand and turned off the music.

"Sorry if I'm interrupting, Cars, but I wanted to run a couple things by you."

I did the perfunctories as we climbed the steps. "Harry, Ava Davanelle, Ava, Harry Nautilus."

"We met at a couple of posts," Harry said to Ava.

"I probably wasn't the best of company. I apologize."

"I didn't notice, Doctor; I tend to keep my distance when the chitlins are showing."

We went inside. Ava picked up her AA book and said she was going to read. Harry sat on the couch and leaned forward, clasping his hands on a bouncing knee. "She doing any better, Cars?" he asked when the door closed behind Ava.

"Worn and shaky, but talking it out some tonight. Bear said that's a good sign. What brings you to the water's edge, bro?"

Harry scowled at the iced tea I'd set in front of him. "You got anything stronger, Cars?"

"In my trunk."

"Sure could use a tot of scotch."

I went to my car under the house and fetched the Glenlivet. Holding the gurgling bottle made me recall scrabbling through Ava's car and finding the vodka. I stood below the bedroom and heard Ava's footsteps creaking across the floor above.

My box in the air above an island.

The tide was receding, the waves a gentle hiss a hundred yards distant. I listened to Ava padding across the wood and hoped my small retreat might be where she found comfort. That it might do for her what it had done for me.

While in my first year of college, tired of the questions— "Are you any relation to . . ."—and the lies I answered with, I'd changed my name from Ridgecliff to Ryder. I took the name from Albert Pinkham Ryder, the nineteenth-century painter whose most enduring works are of men in small boats on dark and boiling seas. Changing my name was one of many changes back then, all designed to destroy the undestroyable fact that I was the son of a fiercely sadistic man and the brother of one who had murdered five women.

I'd quit college, joined the navy, returned to college, changing majors like changing shoes, finally planting deepest in psychology. Girlfriends came and went like meals. I changed hair, vehicles, speech patterns, magazine subscriptions. I once had five addresses in a year, not counting my car. I changed my name.

But every morning I still woke up me.

My mother died. I intended to use the inheritance money to buy a single-wide trailer and let the rest spin a tight but viable existence. When you sleep upward of a dozen hours a day, basic existence is not a hard nut to make. One day, fishing the surf, I saw this place. It stood in the air, but its underpinnings were sturdy. The windows were wide. The deck overlooked boundless water. It had a For Sale sign.

I couldn't push the place from my mind and even dreamed

of it, sometimes as a house, sometimes as a helmet with visor. I bought it two weeks later, knowing I'd have to work to keep it. Spurred by Harry's remark about me making a good cop, I joined the police force and found the work honorable and necessary. It also let me see clearly, for the first time, what had been in front of me for years.

In the first few months on the street I learned vast helpings of the misery I encountered came from the participants' inability to tear free of their pasts. Old slights simmered into grudges, grudges into gun-shots. Crackheads shambled inexorably from last bust to next vial. I watched hookers link and relink with the pimps who would eventually kill them, directly or indirectly. *Don't do it*, I'd plead into faces confused by paths they felt driven to walk. *Stop. Think. It doesn't have to be like this. The past is nothing but a series of recollections; it doesn't own you. Change before it's too late.*

Talking to myself.

One aspect of a tectonic shift in self-awareness—a revelation if you will—is it is ineffable, beyond description. So I can only say that on a normal afternoon one thousand and fifty-two days ago, I went to a locked footlocker in the farthest reaches of my closet and withdrew a black-handled knife I'd seen plunged into a squealing, desperate shoat. A knife Jeremy had hidden in the basement of our home. I tucked the knife beneath my shirt and took the ferry across the wide mouth of Mobile Bay. Midpoint in the journey, without ceremony or even a second glance, I sent the knife to join the broken craft of older wars.

The ferry brought me home, which is here, not there, now, not then. I figure if we are prisoners of the past, we are jailer as well.

I turned to go back upstairs and again heard Ava's footsteps creak across the floor. She stopped directly above and for a moment we aligned from sand to stars. A need arose in my fingertips which I resisted as a quaint and silly notion, yet reached to touch the joists above my head. They're wood, rough hewn and salt crusted, but to my fingers they seemed a kind of holy relic, one mingling human frailty with ceaseless faith . . . the bones of light, perhaps.

I heard the door open and Harry called my name into the night, wondering where I was.

CHAPTER 21

I poured Harry a scotch and soda and we sat in the living room.

Harry rolled his glass between his hands and said, "After you took off tonight I hung around at Flanagan's. Guess who comes in? Rhea Plaitt."

"From legal."

"Witchy woman, sexy and hexy. We get to talking. Bayside comes up and she says, no problem, the state's got a database of incorporations. Suddenly Rhea's got a teensy computer wired into the wall and her lovely fingers are tapping away. Bingo, Rhea's reading about a company called Bayside Consulting. Incorporated a couple years back. A sole-proprietorship, something with evaluation of medical equipment. Vague."

I felt an electric prickle run up my spine, leaned forward. "One owner. Usually a smaller business. And?"

Harry looked at his size-fourteen black loafers and shook his head.

"What? Come on, give." I said.

"I think the lines are getting confused."

"Harry? What are you—"

He looked at me and said, "Bayside Consulting is owned by Clair Peltier."

My breath stopped. I closed my eyes and heard the low burr of the refrigerator, a drip of water from the shower head in the bathroom, Harry's breathing. I heard Ava turn a page in the book she was reading two dozen feet away behind a door.

"There's a simple explanation," I said.

"Doesn't the doc spend a lot of time out of town?"

"She's a consultant, Harry. She consults out of town. It's in the job description. She also goes to seminars, symposia."

"I'd be interested if she was symposiating when Nelson was in Biloxi."

After Harry left I tried relaxing on the deck, but it was a windless night and the mosquitoes were a crawling blanket. When I retreated to bed my head showed unwanted movies: Nelson, Clair; penumbras of distant worlds converging in muddy shadow. I heard the bedsprings bouncing beneath Ava; Bear said she'd have a tough time sleeping; alcohol impairs the body clock and sends dense, creepy dreams. After slipping into a T-shirt and shorts, I knocked on her door and said I couldn't sleep, either, maybe it would help if we both didn't sleep together. She was beneath a quilt and patted beside her. I lay down and we both yielded to a welcome, temporary darkness.

Dawn was at the curtains when my vagabond dreams evaporated. My eyes focused on Ava, turned toward me with her head snuggled into the pillow and slender hands tucked to her chin. I moved slowly getting off the bed, keeping her safely in sleep.

I awoke fully in the surf, the waves chilled by an offshore current, saline taste in my mouth and salt sting in my eyes. The sun was hazed, the air already curdling with heat. I sluiced off the salt in the cold-water shower beneath my house and went inside to the scent of coffee. I dressed and came out to find Ava at the kitchen table reading the newspaper. A glass of orange juice and plate with toast crumbs sat by her elbow.

"I was watching you swim," she said. "Why so far out? Why not back and forth along the beach?"

"I swim straight out until I'm breathless and can't go another stroke, then turn around."

She gave me a raised eyebrow.

"I hate exercising," I explained. "I either keep swimming or drown. It's good incentive."

She shook her head. "I actually understand that."

I studied her. "You look better."

She gestured at her garb: pink ribbed tank top, white

jeans, hair held back with a golden scrunchy. "DKAA. Casual wear for the recovering alky."

"I meant you," I said. "You're getting color. Your—"

"—hands aren't shaking as much," she said, holding her OJ semi-steady in front of her. She took a sip and set it down. "I slept good," she continued. "Other . . . bad times, I—no, dammit, on other *drunks* I always sleep rotten after quitting. But when I woke up, I heard you breathing and I thought, *I'm safe*, and went back to sleep."

I walked behind her and my fingers found her shoulders, lightly kneading. She spun a kink from her neck, let her cheek rest against my hand. The sun crested the roofline of the house to my east and the kitchen slowly brightened through my curtains. Dust motes glittered in the sunlit air like pinpoint flares. I watched them burn and felt strangely at peace.

Ava said, "I've been thinking about what we talked about the first night. It's a little fuzzy, but I remember discussing the physical similarities between Deschamps and Nelson; how they were basically the same, just that Deschamps had a more pronounced musculature."

I sat beside her. "Twins, or brothers, you said, one worked out more than the other."

"Something else popped into my head." Ava sipped juice and probed her memory. "We had a head trauma victim the second day the new facility opened. A nineteen-year-old boy from a party in the north end of the county. The county police brought the body in and I did the post."

I remembered the incident, but it was out of our jurisdiction and I hadn't paid much attention to it.

"He had the same basic body type, tall and long-limbed, plus his skin was smooth and unblemished, nonhirsute as well."

"Musculature?"

"Very similar to Nelson. Probably high-rep lifting of lighter weights resulting in more definition and less bulk, especially in the arms and shoulder."

"Cause of death?"

"He was struck in the head with a round, blunt object. A softball-sized stone, judging by the wounds. Or something similar."

My connection to Sergeant Clint Tate of the Mobile County Police was a patch-through and the signal struggled to reach his cruiser in Citronelle.

"There'd been a rave, buncha kids in a watermelon field," Tate said, a constant crackle beneath his words like someone crumpling a pretzel bag. "Never seem to find out about raves till they're done, couldn't do a helluva lot if we did. They pay some farmer a couple hundred bucks to rent a few acres, haul in a generator for lights and music, and it's a party. The vic you're talking about's a kid named Jimmy Farrier, a student at University of South Alabama. No brushes with the law, nothing. A decent kid that heard about a party and thought he'd give it a try. We're still digging but we're spread kinda thin."

"How'd it happen?"

"Nearest we can come up with is he must have pissed someone off. Blunt-force head trauma in a dry creekbed in the woods, about three hundred feet from the rave proper. He took a while to die."

"Who found the body?"

"Anonymous call about two a.m. Fake voice. Kid voice, girl. Scared. Probably off in the woods stoned and fell over him."

"Anything unusual about the body? Maybe marks on the neck where someone tried cutting?"

"All I recollect is that the clothes were"—there were a few loud pops and Tate sounded like he was drowning in flames—". . . bit . . . zipped . . . neck."

"I missed that, Sergeant. Repeat please."

"I said, his clothes had been pulled around a bit. Pants unzipped. Shirt yanked up to the neck."

"Any leads?" I said, yelling over the electronic warfare. For a moment the signal cleared enough for me to hear Sergeant Tate sigh.

"Got about two hundred half-naked dope-addled kids dancing in a little circle of light with nothing beyond but woods. A killer's dream party, Detective."

"When you get done, Carson, just drop 'em off to my desk."

Vera Braden left me and the three files in one of the morgue's small meeting rooms. Neither Clair nor Will Lindy were in this morning, something to do with a budget meeting. Vera didn't know when they'd be back.

I pulled a facial shot of Farrier from the shots taken when he entered the morgue. A square and beardless baby face with eruptions of acne. Prominent ears and shave-sides haircut. There was dirt on his lips and teeth from the field where he'd fallen. I traded the facial for a full-length photo and held a similar shot of Jerrold Nelson beside Farrier.

I saw the bodies of twin brothers. Size, muscles, definition, skin tone, all similar. Even navels and nipples seemed interchangeable. There was a quarter-sized tattoo of a leaping swordfish above Farrier's left nipple. Nelson had also been tattooed, the oriental dragon above his right shoulder blade.

I pulled a photo of Deschamps from its file and held it beside the others. It was like a third brother entered the room, older perhaps, stronger, with bulk added to the arms, shoulders and thighs. I pushed Deschamps's photo aside and concentrated on my twins.

Why behead Nelson and not Farrier?

I studied Nelson's frontals. Like Deschamps, he'd been supine, facing upward. The discoloring livor mortis was confined to his back. I noticed Farrier had two darker stains in the livor mortis and shuffled through his file. In the close-ups they looked like bruises.

Footsteps by the door. I resisted the urge to hide the photos. The door opened with Walter Huddleston, the diener, behind it. His eyes pierced me like scarlet lasers, then traveled to the photos. He grunted and pulled the door shut, heading back to his coffin, maybe.

I read Farrier's autopsy report, hearing Ava's voice declaim it into the air for transcription. *"Contusions over the rib cage indicative of sharp blows delivered before death, and consistent with semi-rounded shoe, athletic style or similar—conjecture: two hard kicks as body lay on ground. . . ."*

I gathered the materials and took them to Vera at her desk. I snapped my fingers as I was turning to leave. "Just remembered, Veer—I'm putting together a timeline and need to see the May post schedule."

She looked over her reading glasses. "All that monthly stuff gets put in a file and goes direct to Dr. Peltier. They're locked in the credenza in her office."

I shrugged. "No big thing, I'll check 'em next time through."

I passed Clair's office on my way out. The door was open and I looked inside, not looking for anything more than a sense of a woman I admired and thought I knew.

CHAPTER 22

"I didn't go to the rave," Dale McFetters said, stroking an emaciated mustache. "Working that night. Pizza Junction." McFetters had a shaved head, a recent defoliation judging by the way he kept reaching to twist invisible locks. He paced the living room, working his absent hair and tugging a silver ear loop. His jeans appeared to be entering a second decade without laundering. He was shirtless and skinny, ribs countable to anyone so inclined. A blue tattoo resembling barbed wire circled one broomstick bicep. "It could have been me, y'know. I'd have gone if I hadn't had to work."

McFetters and Jimmy Farrier shared a shotgun duplex near the university. Furnished with twenty bucks and a blue-light special on yellow paint, the place was like walking through the interior of a lemon.

"It wasn't you," I said, leaning against a bright wall. "It was Jimmy. I need to know why."

McFetters threw his hands up in the air. They were grubby hands and I hoped he'd never made a pizza I'd eaten. "I told all this to the state police," he protested.

"Now you get to tell me. Merry Christmas."

He flopped into a battered recliner, probably rescued from a Dumpster. "I don't know nothing else." A computer-science major.

I crossed the room to a corkboard beside the phone, carry-out menus thumbtacked to it. There were some photos. One showed Farrier and McFetters sunning in a lawn chair in the small front yard of the duplex. I leaned close and studied it. The boys were shirtless, squinting from the bright sunlight. Jimmy looked bemused while McFetters affected a "white-boy-as-gangsta-rapper" pose. McFetters's body was pasty and anorexic, Jimmy Farrier's tan and toned. His face looked soft, closer to child than adult—beardless, a vulnerability in the eyes, acne on his cheeks and forehead. It was obvious he worked out. His biceps and triceps were firm and expanded, his shoulders thick, his pecs blocking out. Washboard lats above his denim cutoffs. A small bright swordfish leapt above his nipple. The dated photo was almost a year old.

I turned back to McFetters. "Was Jimmy going to the rave to meet someone, Dale?"

He shrugged. "Never said. Maybe."

"No regular girlfriend, female acquaintance?"

McFetters studied the citrine ceiling and stroked his lip-cirrus. "Chicks? He had, like, a lot more hope than luck."

"Not a pick-up artist."

His laugh resembled a seal's *arwk*. If he'd slapped his hands together I'd have tossed him a fish. I said, "He ever try and meet girls through the personal ads?"

McFetters gave me an odd look, then slid out of the chair and went to Farrier's bedroom. He returned with an old copy of the *NewsBeat* bent open to the personals ads.

"By his bed," McFetters said. "He was always scoping 'em out. Sending letters, but—" McFetters twitched his bony shoulders.

I said, "You don't know about responses?"

"Huh-uh."

I said, "His stuff still in his room?"

"His mom said they was gonna come over and get it, but they haven't."

I stood. "Mind if I take a look?"

He waved toward Jimmy's door. "Knock yourself out."

A typical student's room. Posters for some band I'd never heard of, skinny androgynes wearing black clothes and mascara-enhanced sulks, nihilism with a beer sponsor. The bed was made. A desk in the corner had a computer atop it. A shelf held textbooks, papers jammed between pages. Free weights sprawled around a lifting bench. The standard clothes in the closet, plus a skimboard and some snorkeling gear, decent stuff.

I opened the top desk drawer. Pencils and pens and paper-clips, Post-its. Class schedule. A small framed photograph of Farrier with Mom and Dad and Little Sister. Mountains in the background, everyone smiling, arms clasping one another's shoulders. There was genuine warmth in the faces, a close-ness. Beneath that was a loose photo—Farrier and his mother on high school graduation day, the kid in his black gown, mama beside him with her head on his shoulder. Proud smiles. They looked comfortable together, happy. I noted the photo-graphs weren't atop the desk where his roommate or visitors might see them, but not upside-down in the bottom of the closet, either. I tried the side drawers. The top one held note-books from various classes, the bottom a six-pack of Coors Light and a twelve-pack of Ramses condoms, unopened.

Party on, Jimmy, wherever you are.

I fired up the computer and did a name search of files: Personals, ads, NewsBeat . . . nothing. I shifted to a file-by-file scan and under *Misc.* and discovered a sub-file, *PerLets.* It turned out to be short for Personal Letters and held responses to ads in the *NewsBeat,* seven in the eight months since the *NewsBeat*'s redux.

Jimmy's response to each was a variation on a basic theme:

Dear (ad number)
I saw your ad in the NewsBeat and would love to meet you. My name is JIMMY and I'm a student at USA

studying Computer Science. I LOVE the beach and would be there every day if I wasn't in school or studying. I'm kind of quiet but I can also be wild if I'm with the right person. I have dark brown hair and blue-green eyes and like to work out with weights. I'd LOVE to meet you and maybe we could meet soon. There's a place near USA called THE CUPPA where they have coffee and live music on Wednesday, Friday and Saturday. Maybe we could get together there or anywhere else you want. I hope to hear from you.

Jimmy

I printed the letters and Jimmy's list of response dates, and left Dale McFetters sitting in his lemon world.

"Cutter *advertised* for them, Carson?"

I crossed my arms behind my back and studied the car's gray ceiling. There was a footprint beside the dome light. It seemed my size. A horn behind us honked and Harry accelerated.

"It's a thought. Deschamps met Talmadge through the personals in the *NewsBeat*. Now Farrier turns out to have used them."

I handed one of Farrier's letters over the seat to Harry. He studied it while driving, which always made me nervous. He flipped the letter back a minute later.

"OK, Cars—say the killer selected Farrier from this. Then why'd he reject him?"

"I don't know. Something about Farrier wasn't right."

I stared at the treetops passing by. Something was bothering me, some discord, but it was at the edge of my consciousness, indistinct. My mind kept returning to a picture of the tattoo on Farrier's chest: crisp and prominent, bright as a Sunday newspaper cartoon. I saw the smiling faces from the photos in Jimmy Farrier's desk. Heard his mother's worried voice . . .

"Jimmy, a tattoo? You didn't. It's not you."

"It's all right, Mom," Jimmy replies, smiling. *"It's a . . ."*

I slapped at my pockets for my notebook, opened it to a number just added, dialed.

"Huh?" the voice answered.

"Dale, it's Detective Ryder. I was just there."

"Uh-huh. I remember."

"Tell me about Jimmy's tattoo, Dale; was the swordfish real?"

Confusion. "The fish? It was, like, a drawing."

"I know, Jimmy. But it wasn't a real in-the-skin tattoo, was it?"

The seal *awrk* again. "Nah, man, not Jimmy. It was a temp-tat, like a decal. You put it on with water, rub it off with alcohol. You can tell they're fake usually, the color's so, like, intense."

"Did Jimmy wear them much?"

A long pause. "Um, like, just when we'd hit a party. We'd get back and he'd wipe it off, worried his dad or mom'd drop in without calling—they did that sometimes—and he was afraid they'd flip out thinking he'd turned, like, biker or something."

"Just a couple more questions, Dale. Jimmy probably sent out photographs of himself with some of his personals letters, right?"

Again the long pause as gears engaged. "Pictures. Yeah. I even took some at the beach last spring."

"Was his shirt off?"

"He was just in swim trunks."

"Think hard, Dale. Was he wearing a tat in the photo? He liked the swordfish. Was he wearing it?"

We drove three blocks. I said, "Dale, are you there?"

"I'm like, thinking."

I apologized for disturbing him. Three more blocks passed. "I remembered now, man," McFetters blurted. "He told me some chicks dug tats and some didn't. He didn't want to turn any of them off with the picture, y'know?"

No tattoo.

Not in the photos sent to *NewsBeat*. Jimmy Farrier's belly was as unmarked as a baby's. But he'd pasted a temp-tat on for the rave, probably figuring it'd be cool there. I turned the phone off, dropped it in my pocket. Harry's eyes studied me in the rear-view; he had questions, but knew I was working on the answers. I settled back down in the seat, closed my eyes.

Walk the scene, I told my mind. *See the rave . . .*

I stood in a watermelon field and watched the dancers, sweating appariations with glowing necklaces and water bottles in their hands. In the distance I saw a baby-faced kid bobbing his head to the music and sucking at a beer, self-conscious, not one with the crowd. Waiting for someone; at least that what he hopes. From the black pool of the woods a shadow glides to him. Something's whispered or maybe shown: a beer, a blunt, a tab.

"Come on, brother, lighten up, it's a party, be cool . . ."

Be cool, the piper's incandescent call to the young. The pair stumble through the vines, step over a copulating couple, skirt a man whispering to a melon about God. In the whirling, grinding, music-blind mass, the pair are invisible. Then the trees brush their faces and the rave becomes a bonfire in the distance. A tap on Farrier's shoulder and he turns into an explosion of pain and a dark, seeping taste far above his tongue. He's on the ground in a tight copse at the edge of the field, on his side in a dry gully. The shadow has a flashlight, a pen, and somewhere a long sharp blade. Farrier's pants are unzipped, prepared for the writing. His shirt is pulled up . . .

Tattoo.

Out of nowhere; unexpected. Blue and red and green against the pink-brown flesh. It's all wrong, all the work, all the stalking, all the chances. All desperately wrong. Enraged, the killer kicks Farrier twice and leaves him to die, head on, his damaged brain spilling memories until there's nothing left but primal impulse; Farrier dies with his mouth in the dirt, trying to nurse.

Suddenly I was bolt upright, slapping Harry's shoulder.

"The Farrier the killer wanted wasn't the Farrier he got," I said. "Pull over."

He yanked the wheel and we skidded into a car wash lot. A half dozen black guys were toweling off a white Mercedes. Curious faces watched me exit the backseat to sit up front. They looked at Harry, saw the cop eyes, and turned back to serious towel action.

"Cutter selected Farrier from a photo the kid sent with his letter," I said, closing the door. "Farrier wasn't tattooed in the picture; he used fake tats, like decals. But he only wore them occasionally, like at the rave. Cutter culled Farrier out and killed him, but when he lifted the shirt to write . . ."

Harry nodded. "Surprise. It appears the boy's got ink."

"For some reason the tattoo kept him from decapitating Farrier."

Harry held up his hand to slow me down, did devil's advocate. "Maybe Cutter just got interrupted."

"According to Sergeant Tate, Cutter could have done anything he wanted."

Harry thought a moment. "Jerry-boy had a tattoo, Carson, the dragon; he still lost his head. How you explain that?"

My spine started tingling with the feeling of another sense coming on. It happens when I think there's an invisible line nearby, and we have to walk blindly with our hands out until we touch it. I saw the morgue photos in my mind and rifled though them. Posterior stains on Deschamps and Nelson, two backs dark as bruises. But the anterior bodies were lighter, almost natural, free of settled blood.

"Livor mortis," I whispered. "Deschamps and Nelson were on their backs, Harry. The blood wouldn't pool on their anterior bodies, discolor them. He doesn't just want them on their back so he can write on them—the appearance of the front of the bodies is crucial."

Harry's thumbs drummed the steering wheel. "Farrier was on his side because it didn't matter?"

"Exactly. Once Cutter saw the tattoo, figured it was real, Farrier became useless."

"Appearance," Harry mused. "Body art, the body as art. Could that be his thing? His treasure? Something as simple as a photo of the perfect body? The perfect corpse to deliver his perfect message to whoever?"

"The perfect messenger. Damn, Harry, what if he's sending avatars?"

"Copies of himself?" Harry asked.

"More like stand-ins," I said.

"Where do we go from here, Carson? Your call."

I felt something glide over my palm, a strand of web. I closed my hand but it was gone. I told Harry about the scheduling records at the morgue and that I'd finesse them from Will Lindy. We turned our attention to Farrier and his connection to the *NewsBeat*. I looked at my copy of Farrier's responses.

"I have dates Farrier responded to ads, but no ads to cross-check against."

Harry frowned. "Just the ads, that's all you need? The ones in the paper itself?"

"The records are smoke, but we'd know which ads Farrier responded to by the numbers; each ad has a code number. It's straws in the wind, but . . ."

Harry thought for a moment. He said, "Remember that guy up by Flomaton? Lived in a house full of every kind of map he could get his hands on? It was in the newspaper last year."

I remembered; too strange to forget. I'd snipped the article and filed it in my *Weird World* folder. "Maps from everywhere that would send him one. Tokyo. Murmansk. Ulan Bator. Satellite maps, topo maps, maps of geologic faults, population density, dogs per square acre."

"Collecting maps. What's your take on that?"

I searched my jargon file. "Obsessive-compulsive behavior. Maybe even delusional depending on what purpose he ascribed to the maps."

Harry jammed the car into drive and we squealed from the lot just ahead of a pack of vehicles released from a red light. Irritated horn blasts followed us down the street.

"Talk about purpose," Harry said, oblivious to the cacophony. "I want you to see a place and tell me if it really exists."

CHAPTER 23

The two-story clapboard house sat on a deep lot overrun by kudzu, the broad leaves shrouding trees, utility poles, most of the back and side yards. We parked on the crumbling macadam street and walked past two battered bicycles leaned against a pecan tree, a Radio Flyer wagon clothes-roped behind one. An old Checker sedan sat in the gravel drive, its paint so faded it seemed to have evaporated. A car buff once told me whenever Yellow Cab's Checkers reached five hundred thousand miles they were sold to the Mexican Army to be fitted with ordnance and used as tanks. I never knew when he was kidding.

We heard cranes from a nearby scrap-metal yard dropping metal into boxcars. The air smelled of rust and salt water. A full minute after Harry knocked I heard dead bolts snap free. The door opened to a wizened and bald black man wearing a faded blue jumpsuit over a frayed white shirt and black bow tie. He might have been sixty years old, he might have been three hundred. Bowing at the waist, he said, "The Nautilus has surfaced." He repeated it three times, an incantation.

We entered a large paint-peeling foyer. There was a desk and an ironing board in a room to the right. Several newspapers were stacked on the board and a vintage iron drizzled steam toward the high ceiling. I looked into three adjoining rooms. Newspapers to the ceiling. The old man studied me warily, as if I might represent a biting species.

"Have you brought uncertainty?" he asked softly. "Challenges from the State?"

I searched my memory for a quote from a long-ago poli-sci class and replied, "'Given the choice between a government without newspapers and newspapers without a government, I would not hesitate a moment to support the latter.'"

The old man studied my face as if memorizing it. He reached out and cradled my fingers, then bent at the waist, and touched his forehead to my hand. "I know the same songs as Thomas Jefferson," he whispered.

I could only nod, *Of course.*

Harry explained what we were looking for. The old man led us through a maze of rooms, often sidestepping through particularly narrow passages, noses to yellowing newspapers. He had a curious way of walking, part skating, part jumping rock-to-rock across a stream. We stepped quickly to keep him in sight. The stacks we passed were in perfect alignment, folded papers stacked to alternate thinner edge and thicker fold. Had I a level, I suspect the top paper in any given stack would have centered the bubble.

On the papers I saw names of Alabama papers from cities big and towns small: *Mobile Register, Dothan Bugle, Jackson Daily News, Huntsville Times, Cullman Times.*

"New York Times?" I asked. *"Washington Post?"*

He shook his head. "Not my responsibility."

We sidled up creaking stairs holding step-stacked copies of the *Montgomery Advertiser* dating back years. A brittle and yellow Richard Nixon leered from a front page. Light flicked on in a dark room and the old man led us to a foot-high newspaper stack in a corner.

"Mobile NewsBeat," he recited from a perfectly typed card in his head. "Published weekly on Thursday. First date of publication was May eleventh, 1996. Suspended publication on August seventeenth, 2002, due to financial difficulties. Purchased by a new owner last October and resumed publication."

Harry nodded. "We'd like to borrow the recent ones if possible."

The old man bowed again. "For you, Harry Nautilus, anything."

Harry bent to the papers and the old man whispered to me. "Five years ago I kept my work in Mobile. The city called it a public nuisance and a fire hazard and was going to take it to the dump. Harry Nautilus found this place and helped us move." He snuck a speculative eye at Harry, then whispered, "He can be meaner than the devil, but sometimes he grows wings, this Harry Nautilus."

We retraced our haphazard passage, Harry carrying the short stack of *NewsBeats* flat across two upturned arms like a crown on a velvet pillow. The old man followed, nodding approvingly. We passed a short stack of papers that caught my eye and I picked up the top one. Turning to the man, I displayed the fresh copy of *Le Monde* and gave him a *What's this?* eyebrow.

"A guilty pleasure," he said, smiling like the *Mona Lisa*.

We returned to the office and evicted two pinochle-playing janitors from the small meeting room. I called Christell Olivet-Toliver for the codes on the personals ads. She was delighted when I told her we could lend her copies of *Mobile NewsBeat* going back to November, and didn't question it when I asked if she'd iron them before returning them. I explained Christell's alphanumeric coding to Harry and we began reviewing ads, starting with the most recent of Farrier's responses.

Harry stretched his arms out until the small print focused. "Two inches before I need glasses," he said, and read the ad. "'Need a Friend. SWF, twenty-four, sks friendship first then maybe LTR w attractive fun-loving, honest man twenty-one to twenty-eight. Enjoys walks in park, dancing, snuggling, and I love the beach.' What's LTR?"

"Long-term relationship."

Harry grunted. "I figured it was short for 'litter.' A singles way of saying they want to get married, settle down, and drop some pups."

"Farrier was a beach boy. He was probably responding to the beach reference in the ad."

Harry riffled through another paper, read. "'Soulmate Wanted. Active, Outgoing SWF twenty-seven w/blnde hair and brn eyes sks sweet soulmate for dinner, movies, moonlight hikes on the beach. Should be fit and enjoy working out. Friendship first, then . . . ?'"

"Beach again. Fitness aspect. Nothing stands out."

We went through the next four ads quickly. They were all basic clones of the first two in tone and interests, and I began to feel bricks smacking my forehead again. Harry picked up the last *NewsBeat*. He snapped the paper open and let his finger drift down the page, reading silently. His finger stopped, retraced.

"Sheeeee-it," he whispered, and spun the paper 180 degrees, finger tapping the ad. I read it, and I knew that nightmares, like prayers, could be answered.

New in Town and Looking for Someone Special—*SWF seeks SWM. I have an absolute crazy craving for a man 6'–6'2", 175–185 pounds, 20–30 years old. I love a smooth, clean, almost hairless chest, noticeable biceps, and hard round shoulders. No appendectomies or other scars. I love flat abs. I'm a SWF executive, 5'7", 120 pounds, blond*

hair, long legs, and full breasted with lots of secret and
special needs. If you're in a relationship, I can be very
discreet. If the above description fits you to a T, send
letter, photo (nude or swimsuit please—face doesn't have
to be in photograph if you're shy), and phone please. All
replies answered if received within a week.

"Face doesn't have to be in photograph," Harry said, "—cuz
you ain't gonna be wearing it very long."

"How many responses do you think he got?" I asked,
amazed at the brazen recruitment.

"The only qualification I got is the height," Harry replied,
"but I would have written back all day long."

"Terri's got to be lying," I said. "She met Nelson through
the personals. Cutter did too."

Harry said, "Only two reasons to fib, bro, something to
lose if you don't or gain if you do."

This time Terri was more circumspect about letting us in,
spending several seconds at the peephole before we heard
the chain fall and dead bolt slide.

"GCBC?" Harry whispered, meaning Good Cop-Bad Cop.

"Always nice to revisit the classics. I call BC."

"Yes?" Terri said warily through a half-open door.

"More questions," I said. "Open up."

"Won't take but a couple minutes, Miss Losidor," Harry
offered. "Then we'll be on our way."

She led us to her kitchen. She'd stopped at a supermarket

after work and was stashing groceries. "I told you every-thing the other day," she said, tucking a twelve-pack of diet soda under the counter.

I stood against the sink as Harry passed Terri items from the Winn-Dixie bags on the table. "We took the photos of Jerrold to the Game Club—where you said you met Jerrold?—and no one there remembered him. Could you tell us what your waitress or waiter looked like? We've got questions for them."

Terri stood on her tiptoes to put the peanut butter on a top shelf. "I don't really remember, ah—"

"Miss Losider," I said suddenly, "why didn't you tell us you met Jerrold through the Personals section in the *Mobile NewsBeat?*"

Her head snapped toward us and the p-butter went bouncing across the floor.

"Love those plastic jars," Harry said approvingly.

Terri turned. "I met him at the Game Club. I told you that."

"You met him through the personals. I know it, Detective Nautilus knows it, and now we're just waiting for someone to tell you."

Terri pondered a moment. Her head slumped forward and she rubbed her temples. The motion looked stolen from a high-school play.

"You're right," she said, raising her head, doing pity-me eyes. "I'm sorry."

"You're sorry I'm right?"

"I'm sorry for misleading you, I just . . ."

"Just wanted to go to jail for obstruction of justice."

She studied her folded hands. "My mom always told me personals ads were for, well, people more interested in . . . sex than relationships. I was embarrassed."

"You write this stuff yourself or do you have comedians on staff?" I rolled my eyes and snickered wickedly. Maybe that was in the high school play too.

Harry said, "Be civil, Carson. It's all in the open now."

"I'm getting tired of her filling my ears with shit."

"Hey, watch your language," Terri snarled. "I fuckin' live here."

I said, "Yep. You and Mr. Puff. Remember the last time we were here? Mr. Puff knocked some stuff over in the bedroom?"

He eyes went wary. "He knocked a book off a shelf. Why?"

"This the same Mr. Puff likes to wear his white hair kinda long and full, prefers his collar to be pretty pink?"

"I don't know what this has to do with—"

"The same Mr. Puff we saw come in your door right after we left?"

Terri Losidor's mouth made shapes but not sounds. It took several seconds for them synch up. "You're nosing in my personal life. It's time you left."

I said, "Did you bag Jerrold after the money thing? Or did you keep scr—seeing him?"

She pointed to the door. "I want you both out."

"We're here until I hear the truth," I growled, moving into

Losidor's personal space. Her jutting jaw wanted to stay but her feet moved back.

Harry patted my shoulder. "Carson, chill out and let Ms. Losidor and me talk a bit."

I leaned against the wall and pouted. Harry turned to Losidor. "We're just trying to get our facts straight, ma'am."

Terri repeated her assertions, her routine nailed down to the word. The more time I spent with Terri, the more I saw her as softly innocuous on the outside, hard and driven inside. I wanted to cut to the core, see what lurked there. But we had no leverage: all we held were a couple pebbles with no idea what direction to throw them. I shouldered off the wall and chucked the largest one. "I'll bet she knows what Jerry-boy was doing in Biloxi. And who he was doing it to."

The stone landed heavier than expected—fear flickered in Terri's eyes. She masked it with volume. "What in the *hell*? What are you talking about?"

"Lady, I got three dead bodies and a killer crawling through the personals in the *NewsBeat*. Why didn't you tell us that's where you found Smilin' Jerry, the Love Machine."

She jabbed her finger at me in time with the words. "You . . . are . . . freaking . . . nuts!"

Harry slipped between Terri and me. "Carson, this isn't getting us anywhere. Go somewhere and relax."

Terri whined, Harry coddled, I backed to the counter. There was an ashtray on it, empty save for two lipsticked butts and something resembling an insect chrysalis, gray. I'd seen similar objects in ashtrays at the station. Terri was looking at Harry and I flicked the object with my fingernail.

Amazement.

It felt right. Could it be? I started to pick the thing up, but Terri angled my direction, still holding to her Game Club story.

I thundered across crossed the kitchen and shouldered Harry aside.

"I've had it with you, lady! You lie anymore and you're gonna wake up in the slammer with MORE DYKES AROUND YOU THAN THE FUCKIN' NETHERLANDS!"

She shrieked and bolted for the bathroom. I returned to the counter, pocketed the object, and nodded at a wide-eyed Harry, *Let's haul ass.* Losidor leaned around the door frame, shaking her fist and threatening lawyers if we weren't gone in seconds. Harry showed her his palms as he backed away, pretending to pull me with him. "We're leaving, Miss Losidor. Sorry about the inconvenience. My partner's having a bad day, his ferret died this morning. Thanks for your time. Bye now."

We climbed into the car. "I don't know what you were trying in there," Harry said, "but it was Oscar quality. Miss Terri's working a shuck. I smell it."

"Does it smell like this?" I asked, fishing the object from my pocket.

Harry eyeballed it. "Dirty gum?"

"Chewed newspaper, Harry," I said, bouncing the dried wad in my palm. "Know anyone with that odd habit?"

*   *   *

"You gonna start getting your mail here?" Briscoe Shelton asked. His door was chained and he peered between door and frame. He wore the same T-shirt and painter's pants he'd worn the past two visits. Watching the same porn video as last time, by the sounds of it. The man needed a vacation from his life.

"You mentioned seeing a guy with Nelson, someone hanging around now and then."

A moaning male from inside, *"Oh, bay-bee you make me need to . . ."* Shelton looked down and his neck reddened; capable of embarrassment, a surprise. I'd copied a photo of Burlew from the files and floated it just outside Shelton's pupils.

"This the guy?"

A woman on the tape made a sound like yodeling. Shelton grimaced, talked louder. "Huh-nuh. Head's too fat. He can see outta them slitty little eyes?"

I slipped him the photo. "Study it. Be sure."

"Ain't the one." Shelton pushed it back. "Ugly bastard, ain't he?"

"Big and ugly. But uglier than he is big. And he's damn big."

I put the photo in my pocket. The players on the tape were in contrapuntal harmony now; the male grunting, the female emitting monosyllabic imprecations.

Shelton raised an eyebrow. "Big like a football player? That kind of big?"

"Six three or so, two seventy maybe."

259

"I was chopping hedge over by Building B—Nelson's building—and saw a guy getting into a car. Week back? Wouldn't a thought twice 'cept the guy was a gorilla. Didn't see his face, he was either turned crosswise or back to me."

"You seen this woman?" I held up a publicity photo of Clair. Shelton took a long time studying it.

"Huh-unh, nope. That I'd remember real good."

The female on the video vocalized a gale-force orgasm, the male trumpeting in her wake. Maybe I looked at Shelton with pity; he caught my eyes and glared. I thanked him and he slammed the door in my face. When I was almost outside he opened his door.

"I don't give a fuck what dirty things you think about me, Mr. Bigshot Detective," he yelled down the hall, his voice breaking. "My wife's in the hospital on one of them machines and I ain't gonna cheat on her while she's alive."

It was a long walk to the car.

I drove through the morgue lot. When I didn't see Clair's shiny gold Lexus in its space, I parked and jogged inside. I discovered she'd been called to a scene in Mount Verson, but hadn't planned on being gone long. I saw Will Lindy in his office and and stuck my head through his door, said good morning. Lindy's office was large, furnished with filing and larger cabinets, a long credenza, television monitor, even its own pantry-sized record storage space. He turned from arranging videotapes on a large shelf. "You here to tell me the blamed thing's been found?"

"What's been found?"

"The table?" His eyes scanned my face. "You didn't know? We had a thief last night."

"In here?"

"Outside." Lindy shook his head, amused and bewildered. "Somebody clipped an autopsy table from the loading dock."

"Who the hell'd want an autopsy table?"

He shrugged. "It was in an unmarked box about the size of a refrigerator. Maybe that's what the thieves thought they were getting. Love to see their faces when they open the box . . . if they even know what it is."

I pictured a bunch of crackheads eating at a gleaming table, wondering why it had gutters. "When'd you guys start doing autopsies on the loading dock?"

He chuckled. "We didn't have time to get it installed before the dedication; takes time to assemble and needs a plumber. It was going in this week. Anyway, that's my problem. What can I help you with, Detective?"

"I'd like to see the scheduling sheets from back in May."

He nodded. "Who was in and who was on-call?"

"Those am the ones."

"One of the few files I don't have. They're what we call Prosector Activity Reports; Dr. Peltier keeps them." He fetched a key from his desk and we ambled down the hall. I glanced out the window and didn't see her car in the lot. He said, "You need the reports for a case?"

I sighed, a fellow worker burdened by tail-chase minutia. "Trying to determine a time line. No big deal."

"Good. Because they're not set in stone. More to make sure everything's covered. Dr. Peltier's intense about making sure we're completely staffed, vacations and professional days don't overlap, that kind of thing. She spends a fair amount of time out of the office and wants everyone present and accounted for."

A large vase of fresh-cut flowers sat on Clair's desk and perfumed her office. Lindy pulled the file from a locked cabinet and we crossed the hall to a copier room. Walter Huddleston hovered above the machine, copying various forms. I nodded and he tried to burn me down with his eyes before leaving.

Lindy made my copy, returned the file, and went back to filing tapes. I turned the corner and saw Clair coming through the front door. The ladies' room was behind me and I jumped inside. Five seconds later the door opened. I slipped into a stall and hopped up on the toilet, wondering what I'd say if Clair opened the door.

"If I can cut the entry cleanly I'll nail a nine-eight . . ."

She took the first stall and was in and out in an efficient minute, simultaneously handling nature's call and a call to her landscaper. I slid outside, feeling less ashamed than I should have.

I got in my car, set the schedule on my lap, and ran my finger down the dates.

CHAPTER 24

The back room of Mr. Cutter's house was always safe and quiet, his second-favorite place in the world. The first was the boat, always the boat. Though the boat from his childhood looked different from the boat of today, they were the same. The universe pulled things way from you, spun them in circles, maybe changed their outsides, then set them in your path again.

Like his boat. Like Mama.

He felt like giggling. He rolled the chair forward and pressed controls, saw Mama talking lies to him, heard the slow and precise tone she loved. Then, with a few motions of his hand, he made her eat her words, suck them back into her head. He arranged the words however he wanted.

Mama's head moved toward him. He made it stop, then made it go backward. He would have loved to have spun her head on its lovely, hateful neck.

"Boston," he said. Then again, stretching out the word: "Bosssston." It sounded right. He tried Kokomo, the same way, short, then long. He wrote the words on an index card, ready for use. This was hard work, here in the dark with the pictures. Listening, analyzing. The time spent tracking Boy-Man-Warrior was nothing compared to this.

Light and shadow, words and pictures. Mama and the Bad Girl.

This part of the project, when the Bad Girl was pleading, was the most difficult. He worked in increments—moments, syllables. He was careful not to make the entire picture appear at once, she was too strong. She could rearrange his insides and make him think so different, it was like he disappeared in one place and appeared in another.

Oh, damn. Like she was doing *now*. Singing.

Mr. Cutter closed his eyes and caught his breath. He forced his heart to stop its wild pounding. His hand had been fumbling for his belt but he checked himself.

Control.

Control.

He opened his eyes and his hands repositioned themselves above his work area. He made Mama suck her words back into her head, and like an anthracite sun sinking beneath a snow-white sea, she left Mr. Cutter to work through the night.

*   *   *

"Burlew has to think we're threatening Terri, that she might break loose with whatever she's holding back." I looked around to make sure no one was listening. The detectives' room was quiet, Naylor and Scott at a desk grinding out paperwork, Pendery whispering in his phone, talking to a snitch or one of his interchangeable pneumatic blondes. Everyone else was working the street or working on giving that impression.

Harry did devil's advocate. "What if we're wrong, she's got nothing? Clean?"

"She smells like a kennel, Harry. You've said that a dozen times."

Unless Terri had a friend who sucked wood pulp, Burlew and Losidor were tied together. The lines still disappeared around a blind corner, but ragged ends were showing. It was time to grab the nearest one, yank hard, and listen for what tumbled.

Harry said, "When we admit to working Nelson, Squill's gonna blow a valve. Claim DDO maybe."

Disobedience of a Direct Order meant a month without pay and generally preceded a downtumble in the department. It would spell the end of PSIT.

"I can wear this hat myself, Harry. It was me tossed Nelson's place and called Friedman."

Harry shook his head. "Huh-uh, bro. We are the right brothers, and this plane's a two-seater. Time to put the vise to Burlew. Trouble is, we don't know where the juice's gonna squirt from. He'll pop it and slop it."

"Keep that umbrella handy."

Harry went silent, found my eyes. "You know, don't you, we'll maybe squeeze Doc P as well. You ready for that?"

The morgue schedule had confirmed my worst fears: Clair took four days of vacation in March, three overlapping the days Nelson spent in Biloxi.

I nodded. "I'm ready."

"No, you're not," Harry said. "But you're as close as you're gonna get."

Squill'd shifted our daily meetings to 5:30. The grumblers said he did it to keep us from supper a bit longer. They were probably right. The usual crowd attended, including Burlew. He leaned against a wall, squeezing his hands together, either isometrics or he was congratulating himself. Harry shuffled pages, looked at Squill, and started.

"We're pursuing a line of inquiry related to Nelson. We think this woman, Terri Losidor, knows more than she's saying."

I said, "We want to bring her in for questioning. She's cool in her living room, but let's make her feel like we're crawling down her windpipe."

Burlew stopped his squeezing. Squill half rose from his seat, his face a sudden scarlet. "Nelson? I told you to concentrate on Deschamps. No, I ordered you—"

I said, "The two vics aren't hermetically sealed, Captain. Paths crossed in front of us and we tripped onto Nelson's again."

His voice was clenched, barely audible. "This came from that box crap, didn't it. Lost papers or whatever?"

"No," I said, revising the borders of truth. "This was new information presented in the course of the investigation."

Squill's eyes seared into mine. A vein pulsed blue in his pale forehead. *Here it comes*, I thought. *Tossed off the case . . .*

A chair squeaked like a wounded fiddle and all eyes turned to Wally Daller. He stopped swiveling his chair, laced his fingers behind his head. His rumpled jacket fell open, tie askew across his large belly. "Ah, hell, Captain. What's it matter as long as we're moving ahead. That's the point, ain't it? Solve the goddamn thing?"

Squill started to speak, but nothing came out. There was a long pause and heads started nodding. Grunts of assent. Rose Blankenship jumped in, probably as tired of watching us get beat up as we were of taking the shots. "If you think this Terri's got a lead, I say haul her ass in here."

Blasingame rapped the table with his knuckles. "Hell, yes. I'm sick of bumping my head on the wall."

Hembree from Forensics said, "The scenes have been cleaner'n a nun's whistle. You got somebody to squeeze, I say take the shot."

"I'd love to have a search warrant for her place," I said. Though there was nothing to justify it, I wanted to see Burlew's reaction.

He stood as still as a man carved from stone, not even breathing.

"Can't do that," Tom Mason said. "Unless you got something you're not telling about, Carson."

"Working on it," I said, implying we maybe had more without saying it, since we didn't.

Rose said, "If we bring her in and she squeals for a lawyer, that'll tell us something in itself."

Heads nodded. The dynamic in the room slipped from Squill's grasp and moved toward police work. I could have kissed Wally on his big pink brow. He looked at me and winked.

Wally, you sly dawg . . .

I kept the momentum going. "I don't think she's directly involved, I think it's something peripheral, something to do with Nelson's last days. She's tough in her living room, but"—I gestured widely with my hands, meaning the whole place, sound and smell and flinty-eyed men and women walking around with large guns hanging off them—"we all know what a little ambience can do."

Harry grabbed the reins. "Terri's never had any brush with the law, probably never been in a place like this before. She'll come in tough, be singing two minutes later."

I stole a look at Burlew. His face was impassive. But I saw fear in those tiny eyes, and sweat crescents beneath his arms. Squill looked confused, like he was missing something important and didn't know whether to bull forward or step back.

Sergeant Bertram Funk stuck his head into the room. "This the meeting on the headless murders?"

It gave Squill a chance to be officious. "We're very busy here, Sergeant. What is it?"

Funk handed Squill a message. His lips moved as he read it. He stood. "It seems a severed head was found just off McDuffie Island. It's on its way to the morgue and Dr. Peltier is standing by. This may have a bearing on the case, let's see what the ME has to say. I want the regulars on the case at the morgue in one-half hour."

Terri Losidor fell off the agenda for now. Burlew mumbled about an appointment and was gone before most of us were standing.

It took less than fifteen minutes for Burlew to pound on Terri Losidor's door, run inside, and return moments later with an expandable file folder tucked under his arm. Terri slammed the door behind him. Burlew squirmed into his unmarked, jammed the folder under the seat, and left the blue smoke of burnt rubber in his wake.

"I got the feeling we're about to get this hog pitted," Harry said as we pulled out from behind a Dumpster in Terri's parking lot, giving Burlew a block-long head start. "We're gonna kill it and grill it."

"Snark it and bark it," I said, rising to the challenge. Harry looked at me like I'd come from the john with a saucer-sized wet spot on the front of my pants. "Hopeless," he said, rolling his eyes.

Burlew drove straight to the morgue. He hadn't done anything with the folder; still beneath his seat. Squill showed up a few minutes later and the pair went inside. Burlew walked lightly as he entered the morgue, like a burden was rising from his shoulders.

Harry dropped me out front and I headed through the door. Once inside, I turned and saw him pull beside Burlew's car. Harry slipped out, a slim-jim tucked against his side.

The head on the autopsy table was in sad shape, dark flesh hanging like half-cured rubber cement. Clair gently plucked at it with shiny tools. Squill stood against the wall and held three overlapped masks to his nose. I figured this was the second or third time in his life he'd been in the morgue.

"Where the hell's Nautilus?" Squill said, the masks muffling none of his irritation.

"He stopped in the can, Captain."

Squill looked disgusted, but I couldn't tell if it was from Harry's tardiness or the stench of the putrifying head. Burlew was impassive, his jaws punishing a fresh scrap of paper.

"Definitely Peter Deschamps's head," Clair said, holding up an X-ray sheet. "Dental records clinch it."

"Is there damage to the head, Doctor?" I asked.

She frowned. "It's been here less than an hour, Ryder. I can say I've found a puncture in the parietal lobe, the size of a clean entry of a .22 or .25 bullet. No exit wound unless it exited an ear or nostril, which does happen, but is rare enough I'll bet the slug's inside."

"Does it shake like a maraca?" Harry asked, coming through the door. The smell hit him and he went for his handkerchief. Harry winked at me through watering eyes. He'd copped the folder.

"No, Detective Nautilus, it does not."

I said, "Other damage or abuse? I mean, given the time you've had to inspect it, Doctor Peltier? Signs of a beating, for instance."

"I again stress we're just getting started. But right now it appears the head was simply removed and discarded."

"He won't be happy when he finds the folder gone," I ventured, in the front seat now, too adrenaline-charged to recline.

When nothing monumental had been revealed at the morgue, Squill dismissed the troops. Harry and I resumed our lag-back tracking of Burlew. We hung three quarters of a block back, keeping ample traffic between the vehicles. Harry said, "He'd jammed the stuff way under the seat. He won't grab for it until he gets where he's going. Home, judging by it."

Burlew slowed, turned down the street he lived on. Tidy, midsize two-stories built in the fifties were shadowed by tall, mature trees. The lawns were well watered, verdant. A white-haired woman walked a glossy retriever. It was pretty enough to be a movie set, a Disney street. Until Harry had checked Burlew's address, I figured he lived in some grimy ranch house in a one of those cookie-cutter suburbs installed in the fifties. Or a cave.

Harry K-turned in a drive and we broke off before passing

Burlew's house. I said, "Pull off somewhere and let's see what sort of fish we caught."

We parked behind an elementary school two blocks away. I gloved my hands and dumped out a sheaf of papers and an eight-by-ten envelope. I picked through the papers and found a page torn from the personals section of the *NewsBeat*. I read it aloud.

"Gorgeous Man Wants A Loving Friend—SWM, twenty-two, bi, safe. Blue eyes, dark brown hair, very good looking and masculine, buff build, beautiful smile, can be mild or wild, traditional or experimental, loves to travel and is a great companion. Seeks older man, distinguished and generous. . . ."

"Nelson's ad," Harry said. "Generous? That mean what I think, Cars? Put down some money 'fore you reach for the honey?"

I nodded and kept reading through a few more descriptives and a request for a photo.

Harry said, "Anything else in there, like Cutter's ad? Or something from Losidor?"

I found another ad, very similar to the other, but aimed at women; they were both compelling ads and I figured Nelson, with a little training, could have been an ad copywriter.

But that was all that seemed to pertain to the cases. Nothing else stood out, like they were simply a wad of various forms clipped together for convenient storage. I set the papers aside and opened the eight-by-ten envelope.

"Pictures of Nelson, I'll bet," Harry said. "Smiling for the audience."

A stack of photos and a wallet of negatives shook out of the envelope. I studied a photo. Another. Then riffled through them like playing cards.

"Shit," I said, handing the photos to Harry. He glanced at several, then dropped them back in his lap.

"Bales of it and pails of it," he agreed.

CHAPTER 25

"This is difficult," Zane Peltier said. He sat on a red velvet sofa and stared at the Oriental carpet. Beside him was the folder. The photos were in a file on a crystal table in front of him, upside down. Harry sat on a piano bench, a black Steinway gleaming behind him. I leaned against an ornate high-backed chair, a Louis the something-or-other. I could never keep my Louies straight.

Clair sat in a wing-backed chair to the side of her husband. Zane aimed his wet eyes at her. She looked away.

Their home was on the eastern shore of Mobile Bay, in Daphne, on a high bluff overlooking the bay. The House of Peltier was an amazement of columns, arches, high embellished ceilings. Chandeliers seemed the norm, light from the tall windows sparkling through countless facets of dangled crystal. The furnishings fit the space: grand piano, looming wardrobes, marble-topped buffets of rare and burled woods. Impressionistic paintings stood easeled at eye height. The snow-white carpet flowed so perfectly, it seemed to have been poured rather than laid. Yet, despite the diversity of objects and effects, I noted no cosanguinity of furnishings, no sense of two human beings living here, and only the barest feeling of life at all. The only hint of breath came from battered running shoes beneath a chaise, women's shoes.

It was late afternoon, time for moisture evaporated from the Gulf to be dragged inland and dumped. It's pocket rain, sun splashing the east side of a field while the west side's beaten flat by raindrops the size of marbles. Through the cathedral window I saw dark clouds lined up to the horizon, cumulonimbus hanging like gravid bellies. Tucked between clouds were thin veins of blue sky, invisible until almost directly above. Harry shifted on his piano bench. I cleared my throat and addressed Zane.

"You were in charge of paperwork," I said.

Zane inspected his lustrous black shoes through wet eyes. "I'm the businessman, Clair's the doctor."

"You set everything up."

"She occasionally evaluated equipment for manufacturers. I suggested she turn it into a bona fide business, taxes and all. Bayside Consulting."

I looked at Clair. She was the great stone face and I couldn't imagine what it was hiding. We'd come to speak to Zane, but Clair appeared and snatched the folder away. She studied three photos, more than enough to tell the story, and handed them to her husband without a word.

Ten very long minutes ago.

I said, "Seeing Nelson's body in the morgue shook you so much because you recognized it."

"His hands. His skin. His—" Zane sunk his face in his hands. His fingernails shone like mica. He wore a small gold wedding band and a larger silver pinkie ring. Clair shuddered and looked away.

I said, "When you needed a cover for your trip to Biloxi, you had Bayside pay. Clair never sees the paperwork."

He pinched the bridge of his nose. "She signs a few forms at tax time."

"You met Nelson through the *NewsBeat*."

"I was looking through it one day. I saw an ad. . . ." He looked at Clair. "Just for someone to talk to, just talk."

Clair's hands began to flutter, the motion quickly staunched. Zane continued. "We met and that's when it all started. It was—I don't know. . . ."

"You had nothing to do with his death, did you?" I asked.

His eyes went wide, horrified. "My God, no. Even though—"

"Even though he and Terri Losidor started blackmailing you. You were his big payoff, the one he bragged about."

I figured that when Terri filed charges against Nelson, he offered to share the proceeds from blackmailing Peltier. By this time Terri would have discovered Nelson's greed was stronger than his talent for larceny and she wriggled deep into planning the scam.

"Peltier's wife's going away for a few days? Jerrold, you get him to take you to some fancy-ass place we can hide one of those little cameras. . . ."

Zane said, "He wanted a hundred thousand dollars."

"Probably not all that much to you."

"I knew Jerrold well enough to know he—they, would keep coming back. I confessed my situation to an officer who coordinates security at various events I hold—stock-holders meetings, charity benefits . . . a Sergeant Burlew."

"One of the perks of being Squill's spear carrier," I said to Harry. "You get to cherry-pick the cushy overtime gigs."

Zane said, "I told the sergeant if he found and destroyed the materials in question, I'd pay him twenty thousand dollars."

I saw where this road was headed. "But Burlew turned on you, didn't he?"

"When Jer—Mr. Nelson, was killed, the sergeant said I was now linked to a murdered homosexual with a record of drugs and prostitution, an incredible scandal; I'd be the butt of ridicule."

"Burlew picked up where Nelson left off, started black-mailing you, right?" The lines were no longer invisible; they were a black picket fence in a field of snow. I figured when Terri was working with Nelson, she'd kept the photos. That she'd retained possession meant Burlew and Terri had forged a new partnership. She was proving a very resilient lady.

Zane nodded. "Sergeant Burlew demanded two hundred thousand dollars. And a job in one of my companies."

"Director of security?" I ventured.

Zane looked me straight in the eyes for the first time. "He wanted to be a horticulturalist."

I stared at Zane as if he'd spoken in Swahili.

"Horticulturist? You mean like. . . ."

"Plants, Detective Ryder. Trees. Flowers. I have part owner-ship in a large landscaping-supply business. The sergeant wanted to be a horticulturalist, the position guaranteed until he wished to retire. He was adamant." Zane looked at me and shrugged.

"Did he ever mention Captain Squill?" I was still trying to figure out horticulturalist.

Zane's eyes dropped. "I can't recall."

"What about the fire at the *NewsBeat*?"

"The sergeant was concerned they'd have a record of me responding to Mr. Nelson. Something the investigation might uncover. I have no idea if he set the fire."

"If it went public Burlew's hold turned to vapor," I said. "But you checked the paper out yourself."

"I drove by a couple times, just to look, think."

Driving up I'd seen the back of the Jag in the five-bay garage. Zane started weeping. Clair sat beside him and put her hand on his shoulder. But her eyes remained on the dark clouds out the window.

"Somehow I figured this was where the action was," said a voice from the doorway. Burlew strode into the room. Clair stood angrily. Harry stared from the piano bench. I spun to Burlew, fists clenched.

"Oh, come on, Ryder," Burlew said. "Grow up."

"Sergeant, I want you out of my house this minute," Clair said.

Burlew blinked his infant eyes and turned to Zane. "There's no problem here, Mr. Peltier. None."

Zane said, "No problem? I'm about to become a laughing-stock, and you're about to go to jail."

"I don't remember a thing," Burlew said slowly.

"You were blackmailing me with—"

"I don't remember a thing," Burlew said. "Good words to know, Mr. Peltier."

I saw it coming. Zane's nostrils started twitching as though smelling fresh air from an unexpected source. "What are you talking about, Sergeant?"

"Unless you press charges against . . . whoever, there's no trial. No trial, no negative publicity. No pictures entered into evidence for the world to see." Burlew smiled, a tiny red bow. "You know my favorite? The one I call Duckwalk, where you're—"

"Out of my house, Sergeant," Clair demanded. "This instant."

Harry leaned back and rested his elbows on the instrument's keyboard. A low bass note sounded. Harry smiled softly as he watched Burlew, then turned to me. "I ever tell you about a partner I had once, Cars? Back, oh, a dozen years or so?"

Burlew reddened. "Fuck you, Nautilus."

Harry stared calmly at Burlew. "You'd best giddy-up, Burl," Harry said. "Yee-hah, ride 'em cowboy."

Burlew eyes widened to almost normal size and he turned apple red. He started to say something, but stopped. He spun, reteating on legs as stiff as fence posts. When we heard Burlew's engine fire up, Zane stood and shot his cuffs, consternation creeping over his face.

"Who was that fellow?" he said to no one in particular. "What on earth was he talking about?"

Clair looked at her husband as if she was going to vomit, and strode from the room. Harry tapped my arm and craned his head in a follow-me motion. We walked a dozen feet and stopped, heads together. He said, "So does this have to do with our case what I think it does?"

"Right," I affirmed. "Absolutely nothing. It's a complete sidetrack."

Harry shook his head, cursed Burlew under his breath, and left. I retrieved the photos and quietly slipped to the door. Clair intercepted me in the foyer.

"Whatever's involved in this," she said, "I want it pursued like any normal case."

"There is no case, Clair. It hinged on Zane's testimony against Burlew. There's no other evidence against Burlew except Terri Losidor, and she's riding his bus."

Clair's laugh was humorless, metallic. "Zane won't talk.

He's in there contriving some pathetic story to make me pity him." She gently touched my arm. "Following this led you down the wrong path, didn't it?"

"We were looking for an elusive someone with close ties to Nelson. We thought it might lead us to the killer, not—"

"To my husband."

I shrugged.

She shook her head. "Does it put you back at square one?"

"We're also investigating the idea that the bodies are messengers, avatars. It's what we were looking at when we got . . . sidetracked."

Clair walked outside and I followed. Mobile was eight miles across the Bay. It was raining there, sky and city connected by a curtain of gray. We walked a flagstone path through waves of azaleas and arbors of roses. "Much of this is my fault, Carson," she said, stopping beneath a trellis. "My own damn, ridiculous, stupid fault." The scent of the flowers hung in the air, counterpoint to her bitter-spoken words.

"I can't see that, Clair."

She looked out over the cloud-gray water. "I knew Zane was a weak man before I married him. I even suspected his bisexuality, rumors, though it's probably closer to asexuality. But he was the ne plus ultra of what girls with my upbringing were supposed to treasure and trap, Ryder: he owned wealth, position, influence. . . ."

"Clair, you don't have to—"

Her blue eyes aimed at me, and I fell silent.

"Zane sold himself as a step into that world, the one of inherited ownership and influence, instant history, and I presented myself as a unique material acquisition. You see, Zane, like most others in his world, did nothing for what he has but open his eyes. I struggled years for technical expertise, professional accomplishment. All I lacked was a stage on which to let others see how far I had come."

"You're respected across the country, Clair. Beyond."

She smiled sadly. "Vanity is a cleft that widens as it's filled, Ryder. Professionally, I stood on my own, but I didn't stand apart; I'm one of many talented and regarded people. But not in Zane's world. There, I was an anomaly: a self-made woman in a world of glittering bubbleheads whose accomplishments mirrored Zane's, inherited, purchased, or married into. But how did I get to where I could stand beside them to tower above them?"

Her eyes told me I had to fill in the blank.

"Married Zane Peltier," I said.

She laughed without mirth. "A wicked piper, vanity. I walked down thinking I was stepping up."

Across the Bay the veil of rain over Mobile turned golden on its trailing edge, the sun burning through. Clair pondered it a moment. "My introspection is recent, Ryder, occurring only since you came to me about Dr. Davanelle, Ava. After you left, I realized my first response was not, 'How can I help?' but rather, 'I can't allow a potential blot on my record.' It was despicable thinking; I'm a self-centered fool."

I shook my head. "I think you've set a measure mark two inches above your head so you'll never reach it, Clair. It screws up priorities."

Clair reached to the trellis and cradled a pink rose. "Zane's act of weakness, his submission to Burlew, has sickened me past all tolerance. Not at Zane, at me." She nodded toward the house. "This was never my place, my life, this monstrous overwhelming of *things*. All I've ever truly loved was my work, my ability to—" She paused and clenched her fists until her knuckles turned white.

"Damn. Here I am doing it again, Ryder, the world of *me*. My life. My things. My job." She turned away to dab at her eyes with a wrist. "How's Ava? Is she going to make it? Tell me she's fine, even if she's not."

"Clair, I think she's—"

Clair put her finger to my lips before I could finish. Her perfume spun my head. Or maybe it was the roses.

"Just for today, tell me she's fine. Tell me she's going to make it."

She lifted her finger. I said, "She'll make it, Clair."

Clair smiled brightly, an extraordinary act of will. "Without a doubt. She's young, she's strong. She'll be wonderful. Everything's going to be fine. The world is diamonds and roses, Ryder. No, screw the diamonds, they're just dirt with an attitude. The world is roses."

Her smile broke like white glass and she fell toward me. I held her and she wept softly, more breath than tears. I felt the warmth of her lips brush my cheek. Then she stood back, wiped damp eyes on her sleeve, and pushed me toward my car.

"Things to do, dear," was all she said.

I watched her straighten her back, set her mouth, and stride into that cavernous house. I knew it signaled the trip I'd been avoiding. Our case had just rocketed into a wall and now it was my turn to straighten, set, and stride. Though I'd called the number perhaps six times in my life, I pulled the phone from my pocket and dialed Vangie like the number was branded across my soul.

CHAPTER 26

The night, muted breezes and a pearl-white crescent of moon, would be beautiful if I were anywhere but here. But above these grounds the glowing moon, like the stars, was incongruous. This was a place beyond beauty, a land where even the shadows were shadowed and light was irony. Driving the mile from the road to the gate, my hands gripped the steering wheel so hard they cramped. Shaking them out I remembered I had been here four times and each time I lied and told myself it would be the last.

The gate guard took my name and checked his clipboard against my ID while his flashlight stayed on my face. I wasn't offended; it's the way things are done here, no room for error. I parked in the lot and went to the door, where another guard treated me as if the guard at the perimeter was only a warm-up. I entered amid a burring of locks and clanging of doors.

Though it was late, Vangie was there. She knew my mood and we didn't converse beyond pleasantries. A guard arrived to escort me to Jeremy's room. I told him unless I specifically called for him, he was not to open the door or the slat window. I'd requested the camera monitoring his room be turned off and Vangie had reluctantly agreed. The guard looked at her with skeptical eyes.

"He knows what he's doing," she said.

"He better," the guard replied.

We walked a long white hall with several solid steel doors, slatted, the slats closed. A siren started down the hall, rising in pitch. I thought it a fire alarm until I realized it was a human scream, though I couldn't fathom what hellish vision could inspire such a sound. The scream lingered in the air as if trapped between molecules, then disappeared into another dimension. I saw the guard studying me with a strange, exultant smile and I realized he was energized by working where anguish and horror were the norm. I wanted to punch his grinning mouth, to see his head snap backward as spit and blood trailed a comet pattern down the wall.

It's this place, I told myself. *Stay calm.*

We stopped at a door. "I'll be right outside," the guard said. He slid the slat aside and peered inside before sliding a plastic key into the electronic lock. The door hissed open.

I entered.

If anything, it resembled a dorm room: built-in drawers, an open closet, a long table that served as a desk, chair beneath it, another chair in a corner, and a futon-style bed. The furniture was made of soft plastic. There was a bookcase, full and neat. A sink and toilet and shower stall recessed into a wall. The full-length mirror was Mylar. Its reflections were skewed, like viewing yourself in mercury.

Jeremy sat on the bed with a green book in his hands. Slight and fair, with yellow-blue eyes and cornsilk hair, he lacked my father's powerful build, but had his coloration. Jeremy wore gray sweats and white socks under institutional slippers. He glanced up as if this was our nightly routine. I leaned against the wall with my arms crossed.

He tapped the book. "Ever read Lucretius, Carson?"

"Not since my sophomore year, I'd guess."

"Oh? Which sophomore year? Just kidding. Here's one of my very favorites: 'For as children tremble and fear everything in the blind darkness, so we in the light sometimes fear what is no more to be feared than the things children in the dark hold as terror and imagine will come true.'"

He wrinkled his brow, perplexed. "But my question is, who should fear when the trembling children are correct, Carson?"

I looked at my watch. "I'd like to start back by—"

His voice dropped an octave. "Who should fear, Carson, when the trembling children are correct?"

"It's been a long day, Jeremy."

"WHO SHOULD FEAR, CARSON? IT AIN'T BRAIN SURGERY!"

Though he suckled from emotion, I couldn't keep the anger from my voice. "The parents, Jeremy. How's that? Question and answer. Call and response. Sound and echo. Are you done?"

He canted his head as if hearing faint music in the distance. "Is Mother all right?"

I sighed. Always the game.

"I asked if Mother was all right. She's fine isn't she?"

"She's dead, Jeremy. She's been dead for three years."

He raised a curious eyebrow. "Oh? A pity. Was there much pain?"

"Yes, Jeremy, there was pain."

White pain, black pain. Pain that scorched her small hands into iron knobs and she turned almost transparent before its snow-white fire. She never touched a pill nor, until the end and she could not resist, allowed me to do anything for her. She needed to go through hell just in case there was a heaven.

"Enough pain for three?" he asked. "I'm not including you in this list, of course. You escaped the flames. Oh, maybe you were a bit inconvenienced, a bit neuroticized, but your soul didn't get burned. You were saved from the flames. Did your soul get burned, Carson?"

"You know, Jeremy, we could have handled this by mail: Question. Did your soul get burned? Please circle Yes or No."

"DON'T YOU DARE MOCK ME! YOU NEED ME, I DON'T NEED YOU! I'll try again: Did your soul get burned, Carson?"

I yanked the chair from beneath the table and sat eye-to-eye in front of him. "No, Jeremy, it did not."

"How unusual, given the flames that seemed to be everywhere. Why?"

"You tell me, Jeremy. You seem to have little else to think about."

Jeremy leapt up his bed, screaming and pig-squealing. "BECAUSE I KILLED THE BASTARD, THAT'S WHY! I wired that SQUEAL to the SQUEAL and I SQUEALED until his SQUEAL and his SQUEAL were pouring down his legs like tube worms and black honey. I stuck my face in his dripping SQUEAL while he was alive to watch. That's why your soul didn't turn to ashes, brother. I SAVED YOU!"

Jeremy jumped from the bed and paced the room, once, twice, then crouched before the mirror in a batter's stance. He winked at me through the shifting image of the mylar.

"Maybe all of this could have been avoided if dear daddy had played ball with me instead."

He lowered his voice and affected a perfect imitation of our father's voice. "*Hey, son, what say we go outside and throw the old pill around.*"

"Stop it, Jeremy."

"*No, son, that's not the right way to grip a bat, hold it like this.*"

"Stop it."

"Dammit, boy, I said hold it like this."

"Don't." I stood.

"Hold it, you little fucker!"

I jumped toward him. "Jeremy!"

"I'll show you you little bastard I'll fucking show you I'll show you I'll—"

I grabbed his shirtfront. Jeremy threw back his head and a shriek from a corridor of long ago pierced the heart of today. My mother turns to me and says, *Go to bed it will be quiet soon.*

The door slat snapped open.

"Everything all right?" the guard asked. His eyes scanned the room to find Jeremy smiling calmly, me against the wall soaked in sweat.

I yelled, "Keep that window closed!"

The slat closed slowly and I went to the sink and splashed cold water over my face. Jeremy sat on his bed and smiled. "Now that we have the opening ceremony out of the way, what do you want to talk about, Carson? Let me guess . . . the recent incidents in good ol' Mobile? I knew you'd need a little advice when the answers wouldn't come. Did you bring the photos and files for me to diddle over for a day or two? Oh, and a lighter?"

It was midnight when I crossed to Dauphin Island. A heavy storm approached from the south with low exhalations of thunder, lightning diffused through clouds. I hoped Ava was asleep, that I could drag myself to bed, tumble into the black

I craved. When I turned the corner and saw Harry's Volvo in my drive, I jammed on the brakes and stared at his car. What could he want at this hour? I felt my head listing and eased ahead and parked. It was difficult to walk up the steps, as though the space between them had doubled.

Harry and Ava were as still as marble. Harry was a statue in a chair; Ava a statue on the couch, a cup of tea poised between breasts and lips. Someone tossed hot paraffin over me as I moved through the doorway; the wax slowing my motions as it hardened.

"Why are you here tomorrow?" I asked the Ava statue, hearing the words twist out wrong, trying to remember what I had meant to say. I tried again and got, "I mean there Harry late . . ."

While I waited for my tongue to clear, the floor shivered, as though lightning had struck soundlessly at the foundation. It ignited the pilings because the far end of my house began to founder and sink. *The pilings are failing*, said a calm voice in my head. *But why isn't the furniture sliding down?* I watched in fascination, my house had never done this before.

"Thar she blows," I said.

I heard cold strands of harp music. The statues levitated from their seats and flitted to me like butterflies.

"Hold it just like that. Out a bit more. That's it."

Ava's voice was on dry and failing recording tape, a constant hissing and crackling behind her voice.

"How bad is it?" I heard Harry say, recorded on the same tape.

"Second degree. Looks worse than it is. Infection's the first concern."

Sounds resolved. Another strike of thunder, distant and muffled. The hissing was hard rain on my roof. I opened my eyes, swimming from deep water toward surface sparkles. I tried to sit up but Harry's hand blocked my chest. "Don't move, bro," he said. I felt stinging beneath my bicep. My shirt was off and I lay on the couch. Ava smoothed on a medicated cream that smelled like paint made from spoiled cabbage. Harry held my arm tight as I winced and jerked.

"Where you been tonight, Cars?" he asked.

"Camp meeting," I said, the room creeping into focus. Ava wrapped me lightly in gauze from shoulder to elbow. Harry gently lifted me to sitting position as Ava plumped pillows to brace my arm. She went to the kitchen.

Harry leaned close. "Was Jeremy at that meeting, Carson?"

My breath froze; Harry knew. I closed my eyes. "I talked about him while I was out, didn't I?"

"You didn't say a word."

"Then how—"

"I know about Jeremy, bro. I've known for a year."

My mouth didn't form the question but my eyes did. He said, "I'm a detective, I detect." Ava returned with a glass of scotch in her hand. She knelt beside me and brought it to my lips. "Stuff's bad for you," I mustered.

"Bad for me, good for you. Drink."

The warmth hit my stomach and spread. Lightning flashed outside and the lights flickered momentarily. Thunder echoed. Harry scooted a chair over and sat by my head. The pain beneath my arm started to subside and with it my sense of disconnect.

"You followed me to the hospital last year?" I asked Harry.

"Back then you couldn't see a tail pinned to your forehead; I almost tailgated you to the door. And if that's a hospital, Fort Knox is an ATM."

"You couldn't let it go. Not your style."

Harry said, "Did I do some digging? Hell, yes. I'm still not sure what I found. I know Jeremy Ridgecliff is your brother. Were you going to him for advice about Adrian?"

I couldn't meet his eyes. "I wasn't sure if what I was doing was right, Harry."

Ava said, "Could one of you please tell me what's going on?"

I looked away. Harry scooched his chair to face Ava. "A year ago a patrol officer followed some crackheads into a rat-infested sewer beneath the city. He tripped over a girl from the projects, twelve-year-old Tessa Ramirez. Her eyes, face, were horribly burned. Forensics determined silk had been placed over her eyes and ignited. She was alive when it was lit."

His words sparked unwanted pictures in my head: Tessa Ramirez, sprawled face-up among the rats and broken glass, her eyes dark cinders burning into my soul. *Help me,* she cried, though she'd been dead a week.

Ava said, "My God."

Harry said, "A month later an old wino was found the same way."

"Nothing to go on?"

"Zippo, nada. Then, from nowhere, a street officer tells me the burning silk pads might be a bonding mechanism between killer and victims. This cop also suggests the victims were chosen by a 'bonding fire' before the killings. I thought he was mouth-foaming nuts, but we checked—both vics had been at arson scenes in the previous six month, gawkers. We told the brass. But the department had called in the feebs—FBI—and their profile types were saying the fires were a form of hiding, the bonding-fire idea was lunatic ranting."

"What about the arsons?"

"Coincidence, the brass said. The fires were big—an old apartment building downtown, a ramshackle farm near Saraland. Hundreds of onlookers. The patrolman and I got our asses chewed ragged for interfering."

Ava looked at me. "You were the patrol officer."

I nodded reluctantly and was glad a rolling surge of thunder prohibited speaking. Harry poured another glass of Glenlivet and continued.

"Cynthia Porter and her twenty-year-old daughter were found slain, eyes burned to cinders. Ms. Porter's husband was a well-known auto dealer. He contributed heavily to both political parties. Unlike the previous instances the family was upper-income white. Everything went into uproar mode. The department created a parallel investigation, giving me and Cars a little room to pursue the bonding theory. Not believing it, natch, but wanting to cover all bases for PR reasons."

Ava said, "Had the Porters been . . . selected . . . by a previous fire?"

"Selected? Good word. A month prior they'd been at the scene of a mysterious blaze at a strip center. Out shopping, saw the smoke, stopped to gawk. Carson figured we had to hit fire scenes, especially those that might be arson. He told me there was a good chance the perp used the fire to smoke out his victims, so to speak."

She looked at me. "You were right, weren't you?"

A blast of wind shivered the house and I waited it out before speaking. "There was a major fire in an abandoned warehouse by the state docks. I was following the fire department frequency and got there fast. I scanned the crowd and saw a guy more interested in gawkers than the fire. I snuck behind him and watched him yank out hunks of hair with his fingers, not flinching. It's called trichollomania and a trichollomaniac—"

The MD in Ava jumped in, nodding. "Pulls hair for pleasure and a tension release. I've read about it. Rare in adults, one of the impulse control disorders, like compulsive gambling, explosive anger, kleptomania and. . . ." She paused, raised her eyebrows.

"Right," I said, "pyromania. I watched Joel Adrian pull a notebook from his pocket and walk to a dockworker. Adrian took notes before he booked. The dockworker told me the man was a reporter needing quotes for his story. He also told me the 'reporter' took his name and address for verification."

"What about Adrian?"

The story approached the ending. Harry, sensing my unease, jumped in. I lay back into the pillow, trying to listen to the storm, hearing little but Harry.

"Cars caught up to Adrian and got his tag number. We shadowed him, every hour, every day. Four days later Cars followed him to the home of the dockworker. Adrian conned his way inside, the reporter angle. Carson called in backup and slipped to the window to see the dockworker wired tight and laying on the floor. . . ."

Ava stared at me. I closed my eyes and saw Harry's words become a movie. Adrian soaking a red silk pad with gasoline as the dock-worker struggled in wire bondage. Adrian putting the fuming pad over the worker's terrified eyes, kissing him on the brow. Adrian pulling a lighter from his pocket, one of those pistol-grip tubes he'd fashioned to resemble a magic wand. I dived through the door. Adrian clicking the lighter's trigger, smiling at me like we were about to share a wonderful dinner. . . .

"Carson?" Ava's voice, far away, again under rain.

The explosion of my gun was numbing. I scrabbled behind the couch, heart roaring, not knowing what I'd hit, if Adrian was armed. I heard loud thumping, like someone hammering erratically, and peeked out. Adrian was bucking on the floor, head and heels pounding the wood. He moaned, spasmed, hacked blood from his mouth. I watched it turn from a spray of pink to a torrent of red. He tried to squirm away from death, a broom-wide swash of red following him across the floor. . . .

"Carson? You killed him?" Ava's voice pulled me into Now.

"He did what he had to do," Harry said, looking at me. "Don't start that thinking, Cars."

I shook my head; the moment never resolved. "Maybe I could have distracted him. Waited for the backup. He could have been studied for future—"

Harry stood, jabbed his finger at my face. "I don't want to hear that psychobabble again; you're a cop, not a fucking psych student. Another second and the dock guy's head would have been a ball of flame."

Ava reached out and touched my hand. "You never told Harry about your brother? Where your ideas were coming from?"

I looked at Harry. "He figured it out on his own."

Our strange moment at the Church Street Cemetery soared back to me and I realized Harry had been telling me not to go to Jeremy alone this time, we'd run it down the pike together.

I was ashamed to look at him. "I lied, Harry. I played Jeremy's ideas like my own. Like it was me came up with all those leads to Adrian."

Harry snorted. "Not telling ain't the same as lying,

Carson. If you had to lie to eat you'd weigh a pound and a half."

"I wasn't straight with you."

"You were going to tell me you were getting ideas from a psycho? I had a hard enough time believing when you were selling them as yours."

"You found where the ideas came from. And stayed in."

Harry's pointing finger came out again. "Not at first. I found out who you were visiting. I had no idea you were pumping him for info. I only figured that out when you kept adding pieces to the theory after visits. If you'd started off telling me you got your ideas from a mass murderer, I'd have busted down the door getting away. Don't overestimate the length of my neck, Cars."

Ava sat on the edge of the couch, watching and listening, nervous, something stirring on her tongue. She started to speak, but thunder rolled and she waited. When she spoke her voice was as sad as her eyes.

"You've been burned before. On your other arm. Badly. There's tissue seared away."

Harry froze. Turned to Ava. Back to me. Before I could move he gripped my arm in his hand, looking at the year-old scars.

Whispered, *Jesus.*

"Tell me about the past," Ava said. "Everything."

CHAPTER 27

The heart of the storm covered us. A chair on the deck pitched over in a gust, the rain cutting at a hard angle now. Wind moaned through the joists beneath the floor.

"My father was a civil engineer," I began, "who crossed between sanity and insanity as easily as he could lay a bridge over a shallow gorge. He was a dark force who fed on fear and pain and panic."

Ava said, "Yours."

"Jeremy's. He abused him in ways beyond desperation. My mother's pain was excruciating, but wholly mental."

"He didn't touch you?"

"He hardly saw me. Not until I grew large enough to catch his attention."

Harry said, "How old were you when—"

"I turned ten the day before Jeremy lured my father into the woods and ripped him apart."

A siren in the distance, the fire department racing to a lightning strike.

"My father discovered my brother when Jeremy was ten. Like he'd suddenly materialized. I think ten was an age of significance to my father. Something from his own history."

Harry said, "You think Jeremy killed your father to save you?"

"Himself as well. It was too late, he'd become the past."

"Where was your mother?" Harry asked.

"She was a seamstress. Whenever things slipped into nightmare mode she went to her room and sewed wedding dresses, her speciality, great flowing cocoons of silk and lace. She was a simple woman whose only strength was a transient youthful beauty, and who found herself in a situation she couldn't describe, much less affect."

Harry said, "Jeremy continued killing. Women."

The room stopped spinning; I pushed up on my good arm. "Though he'd exorcised the father demon, he had to keep killing Mother over and over again. For never standing between father and him."

"Why didn't he kill her, Cars? I mean, *her.*"

"The other killings didn't start for five years. Like they were fermenting inside him. And had he killed her I'd have been sent to a foster home or whatever. He didn't want that."

"But why does he burn you? Is it something to do with Adrian, the burning?

"Not directly, but it may have been what gave him the idea. It's how I'm supposed to share the pain with him, the burden. That's how he sees it. In return for his giving me a child-hood."

"It's savage, it's . . . evil."

I fell back into the pillows, laid my forearm over my fore-head. "It's mental illness, Harry, a sickness beyond all control. He's extremely intelligent, seemingly rational at times, but the way he sees the world has no basis in what we call reality."

"How could you let him do it?"

"If I hadn't let Jeremy exact his moment of what he terms equality, Adrian might still be out there."

Ava crossed the room to the deck doors. The rain pelted the glass like hail. She touched the glass, her fingertips lingering over it for a moment, then turned to me. "It's not over, is it?" she whispered. "It's happening again."

"Yeah, it's over," Harry said. "Look at what happened to his arm tonight. He's paid up."

Ava walked over and stood above me. "No. It's not over. He's going to burn you again. Tonight was what? A test? A down payment? Next time he's going to really *burn* you. Just like before."

Wind rattled the house, died away. I said, "I lent him certain materials that might be helpful in solving the beheadings. . . ."

Ava stared at me, waiting.

I looked at the floor. "I'm required to return for them."

She started shaking, then crying soundlessly, the tears flowing down her face. Her chest heaved and bucked and the ragged sobs broke through. She clenched her hands into fists and beat against the air. Harry and I ran to her but she waved us away as though we were a cloud of wasps. As though my house had filled with indescribable pain, Ava opened the deck doors and escaped into the rain. I moved to follow her.

Harry, smarter than me, held me back.

We heard a few long loud moans like she was finding the key, and then Ava grabbed the railing, threw back her head, and started screaming like the world giving birth. Howls, shrieks, growls. She picked up a plastic chair and winged it off the deck, screaming between the bolts, beside them, and above them. She screamed to turn the night and the storm inside out. She grabbed the small table and flung it over the railing. The lightning flashed the world white and black and she screamed like she was going mad. Thunder rattled the foundations of my home and she screamed like she was going sane. She pulled off her left shoe and threw it at the rain. She howled, she moaned, she bellowed. She sounded sad and angry and together and apart and all pounded by rain and electrified by the night. She pulled off her right shoe and threw it at the sky. The storm roared at her and she roared back, charged and defiant. She peeled away her clothes and gave them to the wind.

Harry turned away and began pulling on his raincoat.

I went out to join Ava.

The morning smelled pure enough to drink when we awakened at dawn. The storm slipped north around 3:00 A.M., the only relics of its passing were breeze in the sea grasses and the pockmark stippling of the sand. I opened the window to the sound of waves.

Ava rolled toward me, her eyes calm and steady. "I wasn't thinking of such things last night, but we could have been electrocuted, you know, on the deck."

Her forehead was warm beneath my kiss. "Yes, and wouldn't that have confounded them that found us?"

It had amazed me last night, the possibilities of joy, even in a weakened condition with one working arm. First on the rain-swept deck, the rain only against our skins, far away from where we were, then, later, rocking the bed as the rain softened to a sussurious undercurrent.

The possibilities continued afresh: We spent the opening hours in experimentation with the new. Whether to be shy while naked and dressing (neither of us was stricken with false modesty), whether to touch in passing (yes, lightly), who would instigate another session of lovemaking (a tie). Ava inspected my dressings and applied another round of the salve. Neither of us mentioned the cause of the burns, a tacit agreement allowing refreshment at the small oasis blooming in our lives. It was only mentioned as I left for work.

"When you go again," Ava said, "to see your brother?"

"Yes?"

"I'm coming with you. Don't give me that look. I'm as good as there."

At four Harry made a run to the bank, and I'd started a half-hearted run to Billie Messer's, Nelson's aunt. I was going to reinterview everyone if that's what it took, hoping to shake something, anything, loose. My phone rang, Harry.

"Cars, we've got another one. A beheading. I'm there now." Harry gave me the address. His voice was tight, clipped.

I said, "What's the physical type?"

Harry took a breath. "You know how big Burlew is?"

"The vic's as big as Burlew?"

"Same exact size," Harry said. "It is Burlew."

I'd never seen anything like Burlew's home that wasn't in a hothouse. Orchids flourished everywhere: shelves, low tables, hanging baskets, driftwood fixed to the walls. Some bloomed pink trumpets, others squirted pearlescent bells. There were red cups and blue saucers, yellow lanterns and lavendar chandeliers. A small solarium off the dining room seemed the incubator, cuttings and plantlets getting their legs in small brown pots. The air smelled dense with fecundity, as if you could sprout seeds by letting them drop from your palm.

Burlew's headless body was supine in the kitchen. Squill had been and gone. I figured there were heavy-duty meetings among the brasshat clan. Hembree and his people were finishing up, two techs stowing gear. Harry and I stood in the living room, pressed close by the plants at our backs.

I said, "I been meaning to ask about what you and Burlew were walking around yesterday. Giddy-up?"

Harry studied the peaceful jungle around us. He reached to a shelf and touched a white cascade of tubular blossoms. "Look like candles, don't they?" he mused.

"Burlew and you shared a car?" I asked. "You were partners?"

"Not long after he'd left his training officer. I was twenty-eight, he was twenty-four."

"You and Burlew on the streets together? Strange brew."

"Back then he wasn't the Burlew you knew. You could talk to him. He even looked different, a tall, lanky, wide-shouldered country boy."

A wall-mounted branch beside Harry's head cradled an orchid: a garland of jingle-bell blossoms dangling from a spray of leaves. Harry flicked a blossom and seemed surprised when it didn't ring.

"We got a call to the Tallrico Apartments, that sprawling scruff-hole out northwest. Resident said she'd seen a man with a gun running around. It was maybe two a.m. We rolled up and rolled out, Burlew left, me right. I ended up with some woman babbling about a giggling guy waving a gun and running crazy around the place. I left her and went off to see what Burlew'd come up with, but couldn't find him."

Hembree waved me into the kitchen. I flipped my index finger up, *one minute.*

"I heard a commotion from the left and doubled back that way. Heard sounds from the back of the building, voices. I crept back to the trash bins."

Harry made sure no one else was near and leaned close enough to warm my ear with his breath. "Burlew was stark naked on the ground with this skinny little guy riding him like a horse. The guy had a brain-load of uppers and downers and acid and was zooming with the asteroids. He'd gotten Burlew's gun and was jumping him through the hoops he'd always fantasized about putting cops through. Burlew was crying, crawling in filth, pissing down his thigh, hands and knees ripped up from busted glass. The guy's banging his gun against Burlew's head, yelling giddy-up and whoopy ti-yay. He's got Burlew making horsey sounds, whinnying."

I closed my eyes and saw the pictures. "You dropped the guy."

"The looney's waving the gun like a flyswatter. I waited until he'd swung it off Burlew and I stepped around the corner yelling, 'Police. Freeze.' I had about another half ounce to go on that trigger. The guy smiled like I was his mama bringing him a bowl of warm oatmeal and laid the gun on the ground. He sat next to it and started picking at his face."

The fingerprint guy walked past, bag in hand. Hembree was waving me over like a windmill.

I yelled, "One minute, Bree. Hang on, dammit," and turned back to Harry.

"That night Burlew broke down and told me how he hated being on the streets; how his old man, a cop, made Burlew be a cop, no choice. He had an uncle was a landscaper, gardener; that's what Burlew secretly wanted to be."

"Was that Burlew's last day on the street?"

Harry nodded. "Next morning he applied for an admin position."

"When'd he become the bottomless box of toothaches?"

"He started lifting, power stuff, bulk. The bigger he got the meaner he got."

Harry studied a small bloom in a hanging basket, a chartreuse pennant the size of a dime. "Burlew put on muscles like a costume. Then he had to drag the muscles around with him, too. He got hitched up with Squill's detail a few years back, became his de facto adjutant. I think Squill liked to have a guy Burlew's size with him like a short guy strutting behind a pit bull."

"Burlew ever talk about that night?" I asked.

"He never looked at me again unless it was on his way to look past me."

Harry shook his head and let the pennant drift from his fingertips. "Every year when I was little my aunt used to read *A Christmas Carol* to me. I loved it but it scared me. What got me most wasn't the Ghosts of Christmas, but the picture I'd get in my head of Jacob Marley, this faded old guy bound up in all the chains and moneyboxes of his past. I swear I could hear the clanging and banging as he dragged his shit across eternity."

Harry looked around and I saw his nostrils flare as he breathed in the subtle perfume of the blossoms tinting Burlew's hidden life, his real life. My previous concept of Burlew forbade him a capacity for devotion, but as I studied the books, the misters, scissors, the bags of plant food and moss, my surprise at Burlew's ability to nurture gave way to mourning for the missed and misplaced, and for pasts that, allowed to dry and set, formed the path of our futures.

I said, "He thought you'd told me about that night. It's why he always went out of his way to jump on my feet."

Harry shrugged. He looked through the door at Burlew's body, then turned back to me.

"Think people ever shake off those chains to their pasts, Cars?"

"Never happens, Harry. The trick is to keep adding links so you don't pull it forward with you."

"I'm coming with you tomorrow. You know that."

I put my hand on his shoulder. "Thanks, amigo, but Ava volunteered. She wants to be my *zuithre*."

"What the hell's that?"

"Power over ambush, Harry," I said. "If you hold it just right."

"Come on, Carson," Hembree pleaded. "Check this out so we can get rolling."

I dodged tables and plant stands on my walk to the kitchen, each crowded with blooms and petals and thickets of green. Hembree and his assistant had the body on its side, Hembree pointing at Burlew's back. I knelt and saw a

308

broad expanse of flesh turned crimson and purple by the settling of blood. All across Burlew's back were words. Not the tiny writing, but maybe half- to three-quarter-inch letters, running from the back of his truncated neck to his buttocks, a nonstop scrawl of black ink.

"Looks like our boy's graduated to epistles," Hembree said. "Happy reading."

CHAPTER 28

Like so often happens, the moment that Ava had been dreading—her return to work, seeing Clair—passed by almost without touching. Clair sat behind her desk peering at correspondence over half-glasses. She seemed to barely notice as as Ava and I walked by.

"Good morning, Dr. Davanelle," Clair said. "Good to have you back."

"It's wonderful to be here."

Clair tucked back into her paperwork and that was that. Ava checked her in-basket and correspondence, set a few pieces aside, then dressed for Burlew's postmortem. Ava had been scheduled to handle today's first procedure before I told Clair about the drinking; Clair hadn't changed the roster, even after knowing it would be Ava's first day back.

It was faith rewarded when Ava stepped into her role with the quiet command I'd seen before, the powerful yet economical motions, the sense of respect for the deceased. I studied the photos of Burlew's back as Ava recited them for transcription.

You were with,
weren't you   doesn't she girl
bad things inside of you Mama
We have to make sure She makes how
Time to get the bad things Mama
that girl again out   you lie you
She's to get her out   deep I'm scared makes us pure
What do you know   What did you say
Don't me in you I have pain
No   Don't   Don't me there
Hurdy-gurdy   Namby-pamby   Willy-Nilly   You're
* scaring Roly-poly*
Very scary   Don't scare

At the bottom, across Burlew's coccyx, was written:

Boston and Indianapolis please touching   Will it be
Big Boston or Little Indy?   Kokomo   Booooo Peeeeee
Mama

Squill arrived after schmoozing the media outside, this case now pulling heavy newsglare. Harry and I had laid the tattered history of events before Hyrum, Squill, and the three deputy chiefs. They'd winced and grimaced through the entire presentation. Consensus was reached: Displaying Burlew's untidy closet would only embarrass the department and the Peltiers. Clair was an innocent caught in the taint and Zane was too monied to cross, especially since he'd been guilty of nothing beyond carnality and general stupidity. That left only Terri Losidor, and her indictment would lift the lid from the garbage can.

I suggested Zane demonstrate his kinship with the Fourth Estate by sponsoring the resurrection of an alternative newspaper. He seemed amenable, especially since I was the last person seen with the photographs.

Ava finished the post and went to wash up, leaving just Squill and me in the suite. During the procedure he'd stayed in the farthest corner, studying anything but the autopsy.

"You checked on Peltier?" Squill said, walking up from behind me. "He's clear?"

"Zane couldn't slice bologna without instructions. Besides, he's alibied." At the time of Burlew's death Zane Peltier was with his personal attorney, discussing details of an impending separation.

Squill said, "We're shit-canning Piss-it, Ryder. The task force'll take this over. Burlew fucked up, but that's life."

I expected this. Squill'd gotten smudged by his adjutant's

actions and the only way to get clean was putting his task-force types into full-court press. That meant locking PSIT out. But with the threads of Burlew and Losidor and Zane pulled from the box, Harry and I had a clearer picture of what was left.

Plus tonight I was discussing the case with a pro.

I said, "It isn't going to fall that direction, Captain. Harry and I are in till the end."

"Guess what, junior? It just ended."

I stared into Squill's liquid eyes. "Why were you trying to keep us away from Burlew, Captain?"

"Who's saying that?"

I pulled a folded sheet of paper from my pocket and handed it to him, pertinent sections highlighted in yellow. "Notes from our meeting where Harry and I told you about the missing papers. Anyone reading those notes might be inclined to think you were leery of us coming up with the papers. Especially since we did. Remember, the ones leading to Zane?"

Squill studied me like I was dog leavings on his shoe. "How could I possibly know Peltier was a fag?"

"You didn't. But I think Burlew insinuated he had some kind of chain around Zane's neck. He'd maybe give it a few tugs for you before he left the department. Burlew owed you; guy didn't have to do cop work for years—just ran your rinky-dink errands."

I expected anger, got smug instead. "You're saying I put the brakes on the investigation, Ryder? That what I'm hearing?"

"What's a few more days of maybe keeping a head-chopper on the loose if it ups your chances of becoming a DC?"

He shook his head, a ghost of smile haunting his thin lips. "You think you're something, don't you? I'm going upstairs, Ryder. Better put a bucket on your head when I get there."

"I know you got juice, Cap. Somebody told me Plackett owes you. Seems like you're the one turned him into a media dandy, a first-rate sound-bite slinger. And probably the next chief."

Squill made sure no one had slipped into the room. "Just between you and me, Ryder," he gloated, "I made Plackett. I took a piece of shit-clay and sculpted the new Chief of Police."

"Meanwhile, you kept tossing nails in our road."

He smiled and winked. "It only looks that way to a paranoid like you, Ryder. Go back to your unit and solve some nigger shootings."

"You're a hell of a cop, you know that, Squill? If we'd been able to see things without Burlew's little games, he might not be laying there."

"The breaks. Like in breaking my heart. You're off the case."

"You know Zane Peltier has an in with the Police Commission, don't you?"

He tapped a hand over his heart and feigned surprise. "No way."

"Zane's CEO of Mobile Marine Resources. The president

of the company chairs the commission. You knew it; you know every piece of lint on the scale. Was Burlew going to add a little something to his demands? Get Zane to pull some strings? Just for insurance?"

"Here's a little advice for you, Ryder: don't meddle when adults are playing."

"You're going to win at any cost, aren't you, Captain?"

He laughed and punched my arm on his way out. "You're not a win, Ryder, you're an ant I step on. Don't elevate yourself."

Before preparing for my night's work I called the Indianapolis, Boston, and Kokomo homicide departments and asked if they'd had anything similar to what we sere seeing here. No, the people I talked to said, not even close, good luck. Glad it's yours and not ours.

I passed Ava's office on my way out and hugged her and told her she'd done a great job. A crystal vase of fresh-cut flowers overwhelmed her desk and brightened the air, a gift from Clair. Ava passed me a thick folder with copies of photos and reports from several cases. I put them in my briefcase.

"How about that other little matter?" I asked. "Were you listening?"

"I heard you clear as a bell," she said, handing me a small white envelope. I tucked it in my pocket.

"Tomorrow I'm taking you out to celebrate your return to the world of the living," I told her.

"I'd rather it was tonight," she said.

"Tonight we have places to go, things to do. Are you going to be ready?"

"If being scared is getting ready, I've been set all day."

CHAPTER 29

"What's THAT?"

My face was congenial, introducing two old friends at the market. "Ava Davanelle, meet Jeremy, my brother."

Ava offered her hand. "Hello Jeremy, I'm ple—"

"What is it DOING HERE?" Jeremy jumped from his bed to face me, indicating Ava only with the slightest flicks of his head. "We can't talk with IT in here."

"She'll sit in the corner if you wish. Out of the way."

"I won't talk, I won't. NOT with IT here."

I shrugged.

"You promised me we would TALK and then . . . MY NEED."

"Nothing's changed."

"*SHE'S* here!"

"I invited her. She stays."

He closed his eyes and crossed his arms. "I refuse to say another word."

"Then our deal is—" I waved my hand, *Nothing.*

Jeremy false-charged Ava, snapping his teeth before retreating, a display I'd seen in monkeys establishing dominance and territory. I started toward him, but Ava's eyes told me, *Stay put.* He circled her, lolling his tongue and slurping; he made claws of his hands and raked them toward her, hissing. He growled and shrieked, hawked and spat on the floor beside her; he mimicked masturbation, moaned, and pretended to ejaculate over her.

She yawned.

He turned to me, pleading. "IT CAN'T STAY! PLEASE send it, her, away, Carson. I have my needs, our . . . ritual. We need time together."

I looked at my watch. "Our time has already started."

He crossed his arms and tapped his foot. "You won't hear what I know. I know, Carson. I know who it is."

"You know how to manipulate. It's your only real talent."

He began a child's singsong voice: "I know who it is, and so do you. . . ."

I didn't know if he was lying or his augar-twisted mind had found a connection we'd missed. I was betting he had as much a need for me as I did for him.

I said, "She stays."

Jeremy gritted his teeth, snapped twice at the air, and

retreated to the corner. He pretended to study his nails, glancing at Ava from the corner of his eye.

"So tell me, dear lady," he said, polishing his nails on his shirt, "do you whore much?"

"I whore never," she said cheerfully.

"All women whore. It's in their SOULS! What do you do that makes you think you don't whore?"

"Are you inquiring about my job, Mr. Ridgecliff? I'm an assistant pathologist with the county morgue."

Jeremy pushed from the wall. He began circling Ava. I tensed, moved closer.

"OH, FOR THE UNHOLY LOVE OF GOD!" he screamed, pushing at the sides of his head. "When will all this POLITICALLY CORRECT BULLSHIT CEASE! A tender li'l thing like you wading through dead bodies? Do you pick at them? Touch a pinch of tissue here, a strand of sinew there? Or do you just watch and point as A LOWLY MAN DOES THE WORK? Say, you, sir, could you pluck out that purple thing there? Looks like a greasy tomato? Put it in this pickle jar. It's a Christmas gift for a lover. What DO you do with dead bodies, sweet thang?"

Ava stepped in front of Jeremy and stopped him cold. He slid to one side, she moved in front of him. He sidestepped, she blocked. They looked like Latin dancers. Jeremy froze, nowhere to go. Ava smiled sweetly into his eyes.

"I do a lot of things with dead bodies, Mr. Ridgecliff," she crooned, "but most of all I like to slice open their bellies, climb inside, and paddle them around the room like canoes."

319

Jeremy twitched as if prodded by voltage. His neck clenched and he hissed through his teeth. He retreated to his bed and sat, eyes closed so tightly it seemed he was trying to keep even thoughts from entering. He sat for a full minute before his eyes opened, already staring at Ava. His voice was frost on an ivory window, as cold as the smile creeping over his lips.

"You just bought yourself a seat at the table, girly. Hope you enjoy the view."

He turned from Ava and snapped an open palm toward me. "Did the drugstore process the latest glossies, brother?"

I passed Jeremy the photos of Burlew. I had previously brought everything on the beheadings. He'd this time asked for rundowns on every unsolved murder for the last year. Jeremy set everything beside him on the bed and started by studying the photos of Burlew. A hellish smile lit my brother's face.

Mr. Cutter wiped sweat from his brow, set the level on a shelf with other tools, and gazed proudly over his evening's work. The new autopsy table sat in the center of the room, gleaming beneath a hooded utility light hanging from the cabin's low ceiling. Getting the table was the purest form of providence; the universe intervening again. He'd shunted the drain out through the hull, neatness counting. The nearest paved road was two miles away and there were no power lines, so he'd rigged up an electrical system from banks of car batteries in the bilge. A small Honda generator charged the batteries, but he rarely used the noisy contraption.

He went to the pilot house. The wheel, instrumentation, and most everything else had been stripped out. Years ago some optimist had hauled the boat from the river to its high storage blocks, planning a refit. But it had fallen into decrepitude, waiting for Mr. Cutter to boat by on a scouting run and realize the universe was bringing back the pieces, setting the board for another game.

Mr. Cutter watched the moonlight wash over the field and, two hundred feet to his left, across the short channel of river branching from the main course. He couldn't see the river itself, the view blocked by a thick stand of brush almost encircling the shrimper. He returned to the cabin. Time to put the final images in place. The ones telling Mama the story.

In her own words.

Just in time too; that damned detective was crawling around asking questions, smelling something. No matter. This part of the journey, the only part the detective could affect, would soon be history. Mr. Cutter would remove his mask and makeup and shine as himself.

Jeremy spent a half an hour with the photos, then another hour with written reports. Ava and I sat to the side as Jeremy grunted at the photos, sniffed them, ran his hands across them as if secret messages were imprinted in the colors, then scattered them across the floor like confetti.

"Why didn't you tell me about the pathologist who had his ticklers removed by a bomb? This changes EVERYTHING."

Jeremy held up the investigative report on the Caulfield incident and pretended to study it through a lorgnette. It had been included as a sidebar report on the Mueller killing.

I said, "Caulfield? There was a murder attempt, but it was aimed at Mueller."

"So I read, brother. Someone stuck a bombaroo up Mueller's fundament knowing when he awoke he'd attempt to remove the obstruction and jellify his exhaust system. The man's lifestyle prepared him for such discoveries. Yawn, what is it this time . . . a pumpkin? A cocker spaniel? Who could anticipate the man's heart would explode first and he'd be sent to the morgue."

I said, "The bomb wasn't meant for Caulfield. It was horrible misfortune."

"Put yourself in Caulfield's booties. He's worked years for the moment, he's given a postmortem he's not expected to have, and gets his touchy-feelies turned to paste. Bye-bye, career."

"What do you mean, the post wasn't expected?" I plucked the sheet from Jeremy's hands.

"It's all there. Mueller's postmortem was scheduled for Dr. Peltier. She graciously stepped aside and let Caulfield be head chopper." He raised an eyebrow. "Oh, my, was that Freudian?"

I read the report. At the last moment Clair gave the post to Caulfield. This was all new to me; it hadn't been our case. Jeremy sneered. "Maybe good doctor Caulfield got a little pissed about the substitution."

"How do the words fit in? I can't connect them."

"DON'T START with the WORDS! They don't have to make sense to YOU!"

"I want them to mean something," I said, confounded that the thick scrawl of phrases didn't resolve into order, lacked the fingersnap moment of *That's it!*

"Mean something? MEAN SOMETHING? What do you know of meaning? Did you know what the burning silk pad over the eyes of Adrian's little dolly meant? Your people were saying it was a way of hiding. I told you it was a bond of love. . . . Didn't I tell you Adrian loved his fires far more than any female could ever love any male and didn't I send you away from here looking for arson? The first step in—may I call him Joel? Thank you—Joel's selection process? That Joel would find people at his fires and follow them until LOVE HAD ITS WAY?"

It didn't make sense for Joel Adrian to see fire as a spiritual entity. It didn't make sense for him to believe his set fires tapped his victims for death. I hadn't seen it, but Jeremy had, as well as the fires selecting the next four victims. I couldn't see into the world of Joel Adrian, for which I daily thanked God, but Jeremy could. How could I doubt him?

I nodded. "You were right, Jeremy. I can't argue that."

Ava spoke up. "Your participation saved lives, Mr. Ridgecliff."

Jeremy turned to Ava and his lips curled into a sneer. "You see it as saving lives, witch. I see it as BETRAYING JOEL ADRIAN!"

323

Ava startled and her purse fell, its contents spilling across the floor. The red lighter spun on the white tile.

"Oh, don't get so excited, honey," Jeremy said, smiling at the lighter. "We'll get there."

He stood and began circling again. "Caulfield lost his career on the first day he went to work, Carson. Years of work gone in a"—he smiled—"fingersnap. I think your boyo is a wee bit PO'd at his old boss for slipping his digits in the blender. Think of the bodies as—postcards, that's a nice analogy. Postcards from hell. Miss you, wish you were here. She will be, if our boy has a word in the matter."

Ava said, "Why no heads?"

Jeremy jerked his head to her, veins cording in his neck. "Because SOMETHING has to be MISSING, girly, and missing fingers would point to him. Is that an oxymoron? And consider: Can even the most perfect body function without a head? No. Can even the most perfect pathologist function without a hand?" He said, "Tell me, how were the heads removed?"

I replied, "With near-surgical precision."

Jeremy crossed his arms and tapped an impatient toe. "Is that not a signature for a man dedicated to slicing and dicing?"

Ava frowned and said, "It wasn't surgical precision. There were hesitations, he was off track."

"He's got half a fucking hand, WHORE!"

Suddenly Jeremy was on the floor and my hands were around his neck. He made no attempt to fight. Ava was over me, pulling me away. "Carson. Stop!"

I released my grip. Jeremy looked at Ava, confused. "Thank you, dear," he said, recovering and standing. He glared at me.

Ava said, "If he hates her so much, why doesn't he—"

"Remove her hated head? He's making something, laying a foundation. He's suffered, and he's planning for her to pay back the pain with heavy interest."

Jeremy smiled and took a bow. "Our work here is done, Tonto," he said. He turned to Ava. "Got that lighter, sister?"

CHAPTER 30

"Perhaps my brother explained our little arrangement," Jeremy said, rubbing his hands together as if trying to strike fire from his palms. "My words for his . . . music. At first I thought your presence would hinder our ritual. But you, my dear, have touched the magic pretties, swam amid the stink-flowers that bloom within. You have been up to your delicate little wrists in"—he reached over and stopped just short of touching her fingertips—"the glorious. Maybe you'll even learn something."

He turned to me. "Why don't you slip that shirt off now, brother. I know you're anxious to tell the world about Dr. Stubbyfingers's adventures, and I do have my paycheck coming."

I nodded at Ava. She opened her purse and removed the lighter, a simple red Bic, seventy-five cents' worth of plastic and stamped metal and butane. She held it on her palm and offered it to Jeremy. His hands shook as they reached for the implement, fingers figuring how to pluck it from her palm without contacting flesh.

"Get what you need, Jeremy," Ava said. "But make sure it's a lifetime's worth."

He paused in his reach.

"What do you mean, lifetime?"

Ava's arm slashed the stack of photos from the table. They drifted across the white floor like exotic leaves.

"What are you DOING?"

She said, "Wasn't it fun while it lasted, Jeremy? Having rare blossoms brought to you from the far side of the walls?"

He turned to me. "What is it SAYING?"

Ava held the lighter on her palm like an offering. "Breathe deep, Mr. Ridgecliff. Today's the last day you'll ever smell the magic blooms."

His eyes darted like baitfish beneath an osprey. "What is it SAYING? What does it MEAN?"

I looked away.

"You know, you have lovely hands, Jeremy," Ava continued. "Look at them. So soft, so pink. But think of an old man's hands. White and blue and wrinkled up like claws. Even when you have hands like that, hands of fifty years from now, you'll never again have touched outside this building. Because the only way you can ever touch outside is through

Carson. And if you touch him with fire tonight, I swear, it's over."

She moved the lighter toward Jeremy and he shrank back, looking between my face and the lighter. I said nothing, this was Ava, skating on the far edge of the ice.

"Look at your hands, Jeremy," she said. "The next thing they touch outside of here will be the grave."

He studied the lighter as if divining entrails. His nostrils flared. He slapped her hand and the lighter flew across the room. He sat back and crossed his arms and legs, looking away, affecting disinterest.

"Oh, very well. You win, pathologist. But only because you pulled him off me. Good deeds and all that. My own brother wanting to STRANGLE ME." He smiled, frost over steel, then leaned forward and tapped my hand with a cold finger.

"But just so we understand, Carson, this little, uh, abeyance is only valid for the present purchase. Next time my deal will have all the loopholes negotiated out."

"Thank you," Ava said. Jeremy waved her words away.

He remained seated as Ava and I stood. There was something behind his eyes that frightened me, figures moving through smoke. The conclusion was too fast, too simple. Jeremy should have screamed, ranted, weighed Ava's every word and countered with his own maimed logic. Never before had I left without him screaming imprecations or singing foul songs or asking for a final recitation of our mother's pain. Something false rang loud through my head, the dull throb of a leaden bell, and I was followed through the door by its blunted, thudding toll.

"It's my habit," Clair said the next morning. "I always let a new path think the first day is going to be nothing more than a get-acquainted day, practices and procedures and learning paperwork. If there's an autopsy, I offer it to them. I like to see how they handle the request."

It was 8:00 A.M. We were in Clair's office. I'd picked up a box of pastry on the way in. Everything had shifted to Caulfield. I couldn't resolve the words on Burlew's back—nor the messages on Nelson and Deschamps—all I had was Jeremy's avowal that they were part of Caulfield's internal landscape, and no amount of illumination would render them sensible to a sane mind.

"I was scared to death when you asked me to perform the procedure," Ava said. "And when it was over I felt like I was part of the group, the team."

"It's being asked to cross the deep end on the first day of swimming lessons," Clair nodded. "Poor Dr. Caulfield's eye was twitching." She closed her eyes. "But he never finished."

"No one here talks about him," Ava said. "Like a curse."

"It's stuck in the air," Clair said. "It was the motivation for renovating the facility. The autopsy suite was sprayed with blood and I used the tragedy to press for a complete renewal. It took months, but it got done."

"You have Caulfield's address?" I asked Clair.

She nodded and walked toward her office. "A post office

329

box somewhere in the Talladega Mountains. He receives a monthly check as part of his settlement."

She was back in a minute with a photo of Caulfield taken for his ID card. He looked like a nice guy, pleasant, like you'd buy him a beer just for standing next to you in a bar.

The steep and rutted road in the Talledega Mountains made me glad I'd spent extra for four-wheel drive, the truck like a boat grinding up a churning stream, prow bouncing, slamming down, veering, leaping again, a wake of gray dust streaming from my stern. After fifteen minutes of punishing my truck and my kidneys, I found Caulfield's house where the kind lady at the post office had said it would be: on a gentle slope to my left, the land rising fast and hard behind it. To the right the mountain dropped like a waterfall. Judging by the condition of the road continuing up the mountain, this was about the end of it.

I pulled in beside a dusty blue Cherokee and rubbed eyes tired from five hours of driving. The house was modest but well kept, a fresh coat of white paint over the wood, the front yard clear of the spent tires and rusting vehicles that seemed to have rained from the sky onto other spreads I'd passed. The woodpile beside the front porch could have won blue ribbon in a wood-stacking contest. There was a rocking chair on the porch with a table beside it, on the table a small pile of magazines. I looked across the valley. The clarity of the mountain air compressed distance and I saw as through a lens. Low in the valley was a town, little more than a cluster of houses peering from green. Church spires and a few taller, mercantile-looking structures poked from the tree-tops. On the outskirts of the town was a two-story official-looking building with a circular drive and a large, full parking lot; it looked like a medical facility.

A cyclone-fenced perimeter surrounded Caulfield's house, the fence hung with signs: KEEP OUT, BEWARE OF DOG, NO TRESPASSING. There were no dog leavings in the yard. I stepped from the truck slowly and stayed behind the protection of the door, which also concealed the nine-millimeter in my hand. I had a .32 strapped to my ankle and a shotgun across the driver's seat.

Something rustled behind me and I turned, ducking. A ground squirrel flashed across the front yard and into the woodpile. My heart raced and I felt foolish as I faced the door. Holding my badge in my left hand I called across the fence. "Dr. Caulfield. I'm Carson Ryder from the Mobile Police. I'd like to talk with you for a few minutes."

I watched the door, the windows. Stayed alert for someone running out with a blazing shotgun. Nothing.

"Dr. Caulfield, could you please come to the door, sir."

I saw it. The merest slitting of curtain. I waved at a solitary eye. "I mean you no harm. I want to talk about . . . about the day it all went wrong."

A minute ticked slowly past. I noticed how loud the woods were with birdsong and insects. The door creaked open a few inches.

"Go away," the deep voice behind the door said.

"There's something we need to talk about."

"Find someone else to talk to."

"This is important, Doctor. It may have to do with what happened to your hand."

Birdsong and insects again. Then a hand stuck out the door. Or what was left of one. The voice yelled, "You want to talk about my hand? There it is. Does it inspire conversation?"

"I've got four dead men, Doctor. Three have no heads and I have no answers. Isn't that what you were trained to do? Help speak for the dead?"

Silence. I watched a jay flit between trees. "There's big trouble in Mobile, Doctor. I'm begging for your help."

The cabin door opened slowly and a slight man stepped out onto the wooden stoop. He wore an outsized black sweatshirt over khaki pants, dark hair combed neatly, a handsome face alternating between defiance and puzzlement. The right sleeve of the sweatshirt was rolled to his bicep, the left sleeve hanging loose to covered his damaged hand. Wary of a trick, I studied the sleeve, but the hand I saw couldn't have gripped a weapon.

I said, "I'd be appreciative of any time you could give me, Doctor."

He stared at the crown of a tall sycamore for a few seconds, then sighed and turned back to me. "Time is something I have too much of. Put away the weapon you think you're hiding and step inside."

I let myself through the gate and onto the porch, where his empty sleeve flapped me through the door. Passing across the porch I noted the magazines on the table were topped by a copy of the CDC's *Morbidity and Mortality Report,* required reading for a clinical pathologist.

"You're right," he said quietly from his side of the dining-room table. "I wasn't scheduled to be the prosector. My first procedure was set for the following morning. But when Dr. Peltier asked if I wanted to take the autopsy, what could I say? Of course I said yes."

Dr. Alexander Michael Caulfield wasn't anything I wanted him to be. Not wild eyed and babbling, not ice cold and geometrically precise. He neither lurked nor overwhelmed. His tables were laden with medical texts instead of knives. His wall wasn't plastered with photos of Clair or spattered with blood, but hung with black-and-white photos of mountain scenes. A low-fat cookbook on an end table somehow reassured me: Do vengeance-driven killers care about cholesterol? In short, Dr. Caulfield struck me to be, like the vast majority of us, a human being of middle distances.

"Did you suspect Clair was going to give you the helm?"

"No. My eye started twitching I was so scared. This is Dr. Clair Peltier watching, you know? I'd read every one of her articles, attended three symposia where she presented. I found out later that handing over the autopsy is her way of indicating confidence in the new hire's abilities."

"How did you find out about the job?"

"A board at med school listed openings by specialty. I saw the one for Mobile and applied. I met with Dr. Peltier twice before I was hired. I take it I was in a close race with another applicant."

"You came to Mobile?"

"I spent two days the first visit, two weeks later I spent three. The last day was when I was offered the position."

"Where did you spend your time during the mating dance?"

"Virtually all at the morgue. I took the grand tour, met the staff, watched several procedures. About the only time I wasn't at the morgue proper was meals with Dr. Peltier, and when I went back to my motel at night." He ran his fingers through his hair. "I need a sip of something. Get you a lemonade?"

"A quick one. I've got to head back, start digging again."

I blew out a long, disappointed breath when Caulfield left the room. Jeremy had definitely drawn the wrong card on Caulfield. It was a long shot, but since Jeremy had failed, long shots were the only shots remaining. Problem was, I had run out of targets.

Caulfield returned with two glasses of lemonade carried one-handedly on a tray, unsteadied by his wounded hand, as if he were unaware of its potential for support. I drank mine in a couple of long cool drafts and secured his permission to call if I had any other questions. As we walked out on his porch I noticed several bushes in the front yard cut back to allow full view of the distant, official-looking building.

"What's that big brick place over there, Doctor?" I asked, pointing.

"County hospital," he replied without looking.

"You ever go over there, look around, introduce yourself?"

He managed a thin smile and flapped his empty cuff at me.

I said, "Might be a place where a smart man might do a lot of good."

His eyes flashed, then averted. "Look, Detective Ryder, I've thought about going over there—" He stopped himself, as if he'd been working on the sentence but didn't know how to end it, words in progress, subject to revisions.

I stepped from the porch. "Hell, Doc, half the time I'm unsure of my own name, but I do know that one good brain and one good hand are a lot more than many people have."

Caulfield glanced at the building and took a deep breath. "Yeah. Maybe one of these days I'll show up on their doorstep. See what's what."

I walked to my truck and dug through my traveling bag until I found a cotton shirt. It was white, it was clean, and it was short sleeved. I tossed it up to Caulfield and he trapped it against his chest.

"Maybe it's time to shed the mourning shirts," I said. I climbed into the truck and started the engine. I put the truck in reverse and flipped a wave. He hadn't thrown the shirt on the ground, that was something.

"Detective Ryder," he called as I started to back away.

I stopped and leaned out the window. He said, "I was just

wondering, does that one guy still work at the morgue? The angry man?"

I nodded. "Walter Huddleston. Yes. He'll probably be there until he dies. I imagine he'll be a hundred and twenty."

Confusion furrowed Caulfield's brow. "Walt Huddleston the diener? Angry? Not that I ever saw; a charming man, we got on famously. He took me to lunch one day and we discussed opera; I'm a buff, but he shamed me with his knowledge. No, I'm talking about the viscerally angry guy, short fellow, kind of stubby body, thinning hair . . ."

My turn for confusion. "Will Lindy?"

Caulfield's eyes darkened at the name. "Lindy, that's it. He was friendly and businesslike when Dr. Peltier introduced us, but when we were alone he wouldn't talk to me, wouldn't look at me, just skulked and muttered. Gave me hard looks from a distance. I'm positive I saw him spying on me a couple times."

"Are you sure you mean Willet Lindy, the administrator?" It didn't make sense.

For the first time during my visit Caulfield looked truly unsettled. "The only thing about working there that gave me pause was him. Scary guy."

I nodded vaguely, but inside my head was a windstorm of shifting conceptions. Will Lindy, scary guy. The words didn't go together, were nonsense. Scary Lindy guy Will. Guy Lindy Will scary.

But Caulfield had come up with: Will Lindy = Scary guy.

A equation I had never thought possible for anyone to make.

Willet Lindy?

CHAPTER 31

Suddenly, I had no idea who Will Lindy was.

Was he the quiet, reserved Will Lindy I'd known for a year? Or Caulfield's Will Lindy: sullen and angry? My Will Lindy was unwaveringly polite, Caulfield's was a spy in the shadows. Mine was consummately pleasant; Caulfield's stared daggers from a distance. Which was the real Will Lindy?

Willet Lindy. Will Lindy . . . The name echoed in my head. Willet. Will. Willy. On Burlew's broad back: *Willy-Nilly*, and *Will it be big Boston or Little Indy?*

I heard the sound assert itself in my head.

Will it . . . Willet. Oh, Jesus.

Maybe it's not the meaning of the word, but the sounds.

Will it be big Boston or Little Indy? Will it. Willet. Then cut the *itt* from little and you had . . . l'indy. Willet Lindy, hidden in the mad scrawlings on Burlew's back. My heart raced in my throat as I weighed the possibility of coincidence, of my need to make sense of something, anything.

But what if . . .

What if Will Lindy doesn't want Caulfield at the morgue, for some reason hates him so much he can't conceal it. Hates him so much he wants to harm him. But he can't get to Caulfield: the man's with Clair most of the day and in an expensive and secure motel at night.

So he waits. After the hiring Lindy attacks Caulfield's hands. He knows Mueller, or simply selects him at random. Through his work at the morgue Lindy knows several chemicals can mimic a coronary. Plus he's demonstrated skills with everything from plumbing to electronics. A basic explosive device with a spring-loaded trigger and powder from a shotgun shell would be simple, the materials at any hardware store, directions rampant on the Internet. Clair is scheduled for the morning autopsy, but Lindy knows she traditionally offers the new hire the procedure. Lindy waylays Mueller, inserts the bomb, administers the chemical, and calls 911. Mueller ends up at the morgue, where Caulfield opens the body and triggers the device.

My God, this makes sense

Why does Lindy want Caulfield out of the way? Why doesn't he want him to have the job? Because he either hates

Caulfield for some unknown reason, or he wants someone else to have the position.

There's only one other contender.

Ava.

I jabbed at the phone, missing the numbers, nearly swerving off the road into blue sky over treetops. I pulled to the side of the road, took a deep breath, and tried the phone again.

Nothing. An electronic dead zone, cellular limbo. I jammed the truck into gear and fishtailed down the mountain, scaring hell out of a two guys in a truck coming the other way. They honked and cursed and stabbed their middle fingers. The road began to flatten. I tried the phone again.

"Nautilus," Harry barked. It sounded like he was on the far side of the universe.

"Harry, check out Will Lindy's whereabouts on the nights of the murders. I think Ava is the target of the messages, but keep Clair guarded too. I won't get back for at least four hours. Call me with up-dates and keep trying, I'm going to be jumping between cells."

Harry didn't linger. "On it."

I downshifted, drifted sideways in the gravel, straightened back out. "Harry, wait."

"Still here."

"Be real careful around Lindy, bro. I think he's an exotic."

"I'll treat him like sweaty dynamite. Get your ass back here, brother."

340

I tossed the phone onto the passenger seat and watched it bounce, onto the floor. In the split second of inattention my right-side tires slid into the rutted shoulder, yanked the steering wheel from my grip. Trees raced at me and I stood hard on the brakes, sliding sideways.

The truck dropped into the ditch, the left-side tires spinning off the ground. I rocked the gearshift from reverse to first. Not enough traction. Screaming and cursing and pounding the steering wheel, I dragged myself out just as the two guys I'd nearly sideswiped drove up.

"Sorry about the driving," I said. "Help me get back on the road, I got an emergency."

They jumped out, red faced and swearing. "Sumbitch try'n drive us off the side, we'll give you a fuckin' emergency. . . ."

The first guy's fist caught me behind the ear and sent me spinning into the second. He swung a looping right that I managed to block, cutting to the outside. I spun an elbow into his mouth and he fell to one knee. The first guy scrabbled in the truck bed and found a ball bat. He moved toward me as the bat drew slow circles in the air.

"Bust your fuckin' head open. . . ."

I pulled the .32 from my ankle holster. Their windshield was already cracked and the hollow point collapsed it across the truck's dash like crinkly fabric.

"Get my goddamn truck back on the road NOW!" I screamed, turning a headlight into dust for added emphasis.

Yes-sirring like Brit butlers, they had me roadworthy in thirty seconds. I shot out two of their tires and left them leaping over the guardrail as I climbed back into my truck. My phone beeped. I grabbed it, dropped it in my lap, picked it up.

Tell me she's safe.

Harry conveyed the facts without emotion. "Doc Peltier's here at the morgue. There's no trace of Lindy. He's a no-show at work. First time in three years."

"What about Ava?" I said.

"Her car's there, but . . ."

"She should be at home. Keep looking."

Over four hours to Mobile. I hung up and tried to remember everything I'd been taught in the police course on emergency driving. The phone rang. "Talk!" I bellowed.

Voices in the background. Harry speaking to someone. The phone changed hands and I heard an unknown voice. "Carson, I want you to head north. There's an old weigh station on the highway at the 217-mile marker. A chopper's set to meet you there."

"Who the hell is this?"

"Your favorite boss, Carson."

Tom Mason. I didn't recognize his voice; he was talking so fast he sounded normal. I kicked over toward the highway, figuring times. A half hour to the chopper, then maybe an hour and change to get back to Mobile. And then . . . what?

I was passing vehicles like they were bolted to the road

when lights sparkled in the rearview. State police. I figured I'd been busted by the rednecks in the truck and eased up on the gas, thinking of a fast way to sell my story. The lights lit up my truck cab and I pulled toward the shoulder, cursing.

The statie passed by with horn blasting and his hand waving forward out the window, *Keep going, keep going.* I jumped in behind and we ran a solid one-ten all the way to the weigh station, where I saw a big helo with the state seal on it. I flicked a salute to my escort and jumped into the state bird of Alabama, a Sikorsky. The pilot studied me through his dark helmet visor.

"I don't know who you are, buddy," he yelled over the banshee engine, "but you sure's hell got friends in high places." He tossed me a helmet and the chopper thundered aloft. I suddenly remembered the dedication ceremony at the morgue. Who was chatting up the attorney general like an old fishing buddy?

Clair.

The land flowed by like a green flood and I used the time to breathe down my fear and focus on Willet Lindy. Who had access to the schedules? Lindy. He could "aim" the bodies, kill on the nights when he knew Ava would be first up for the post, a fresh body ready for her inspection.

But what was Lindy's motive? What did he gain from his aimed autopsies? A perverse voyeurism? He'd never been in the autopsy suite while I'd covered a post. My mind raced

343

through the process of an autopsy, what it generated: Paperwork. Results. Conclusions. Speculations. Reports. The prosector did the postmortem, keeping track of the process . . . giving a play-by-play to the microphone.

To the tape recorder. Then to the transcriber. Then into the records. I saw the pilot twiddle a knob on the console and talk into his helmet mike. He reached over and pushed my helmet mike into position.

"You got communication."

I heard Harry's voice crackle in my ears and yelled, "What's going on, Harry, what's happening?"

"It's like Lindy and Ava fell off the face of the world."

A cold hand gripped my heart and began to squeeze. "Is Clair there?"

"Across the room."

"Ask her who handles the tapes made of the posts."

A few seconds of muffled voices and Harry returned. "Lindy's responsibility. He makes sure they get to the transcriber, then catalogs the actual voice recordings. Dr. Peltier says all the electronics stuff is wired to his office, voice and everything else."

"What's *everything else* mean?"

More indistinct voices. I heard Clair in the background. "What's the commotion, Harry?"

"Sit tight, Cars. New info arriving, strange stuff."

"About Ava? Is it about Ava, Harry?"

"Hang on."

Montgomery was five miles ahead of us. It was five

miles behind before Harry's voice crackled into my ears again.

"Lindy not only has voice recordings wired to his office, he has video input. Part of the security system installed after the bomb. Video cams in the halls, entrances, and so forth. They feed to screens and recorders in a big cabinet in Lindy's office."

The pilot had the engine maxed. "Louder, Harry, I can't hear!"

"Get this, Carson: Lindy's repositioned some of the cameras—you can't see them, they're like pencil erasers. He's got four cameras in the ceiling above and around table one, four different views. He's spying on the autopsies, Carson."

Another rustle and mumbling into my headset. Yelling, anger. Harry reappeared. "I found some people who might know more about Lindy. They're heading into town now. But there's a problem here."

I heard a familiar voice barking orders in the background. "Squill," I spat.

"He's pricked out to the max. Maybe I'll go take the bastard's head off."

"Stay cool, Harry. I can deal with Squill."

"He's taking over. I think I was just suspended."

"Any sign of Ava . . . Harry?"

I heard a popping sound and angry voices. Then Squill's voice filled my head. "How are you at bagging groceries, Ryder?" he said. The headset crackled. And went off.

In the distance I saw the gray-blue of Mobile Bay, dark clouds rolling from the west like a shroud.

"Big storm coming," the pilot said.

CHAPTER 32

"You're suspended, Ryder. That's just the first move. Then it's off the force."

Squill jumped me the second I stepped from the chopper into the parking lot of the motel on the northwest side of downtown. Beside him was his fresh monkey, Bobby Neeland. The new chimp had new shades. Harry's unmarked screeched into the lot behind them. I pushed past Squill and sprinted to Harry.

"Ava?" I yelled.

He shook his head. "Nothing yet. There's some odd stuff in Lindy's basement. We were looking it over when—"

Squill was red faced, voice barely controlled. Neeland looked like he was having a jolly time under the captain's umbrella. Squill jabbed a finger at Harry. "One more word to Ryder and you're gone, too, Nautilus."

Harry ignored Squill. "I got a woman in the motel for you to talk to, Cars. Here's her story—"

Neeland was in the full testosterone bloom of being Squill's selectman. He stuck his face in Harry's. "Listen to the captain, Nautilus. He wants your black face to shut up right—"

Barely turning from me, Harry buried his fist in Neeland's gut. Neeland made a few little wet sounds until his knees crumpled and he fell to the asphalt like a gunnysack of mashed potatoes.

Squill said, "You're both under arrest for assaulting an officer in the performance of his duties. It's the end of life as you know it."

Two cruisers bore down the street, lights flashing. Squill waved them over. Neeland tottered woozily to one knee, a green strand of snot hanging from his nose. Squill started counting coup on his pink fingers. "Assault, insubordination, lying . . ."

"Your inexperience is showing, Captain," I said, as calmly as I could muster. "Maybe you should have spent more time at autopsies."

He wheeled on me. "What are you babbling about, Ryder?"

I smiled. It wasn't what he expected to see. "Our little talk by the autopsy table, Captain. About DC Plackett and various other events? When you were candid. Remember?"

Squill stage-laughed. "You might want to speak with a

professional, Ryder, get some help with those delusions. You'll have the time."

The cruisers angled in, braking hard. Flashing light spangled our faces. I said, "Remember how the prosector talks all the time?"

"What?"

"At the morgue. The person doing the autopsy is always talking."

I pulled from my pocket the white envelope Ava had given me, tore off the end, puffed it open with a breath. I shook a black cassette tape into my palm.

"Did you think they were talking to you?"

I tossed him the tape and he made a fumbling catch. "The tape kept running after Burlew's autopsy," I said. "All through our little chat. Good sound quality. Even on the copies." Doors opened on the cruisers. "So, Captain, you can either tell everybody how you carved Deputy Chief Plackett from a dungheap, or . . ."

"Or what?" Squill whispered, his face drained of color.

"Or you can tell Harry and me what a great job the PSIT is doing. And to keep doing it."

Neeland made a croaking sound and threw up. Fried chicken and gravy spattered across Squill's shiny black shoes.

"Rumbling and tumbling," Harry noted.

"I want you to see something," Harry said. "Then we'll talk to a woman who knew Lindy when he was growing up." Harry passed me an eight-by-ten brown envelope as we ran toward the motel. "Check this out," he said quietly. "Got it from the sheriff's department in Choctaw County. Lindy grew up on a farm up outside Butler."

I opened the envelope and pulled out a faxed photo.

Ava. In a booking photo from the Choctaw County Sheriff's Department. Front and profile. Arrest number.

Almost Ava. The nose was a shade too long, the forehead a touch too high, and the eyes seemed like eyes from a taxidermist's inventory, something piscine, or perhaps reptilian.

Harry waited for my shock to subside. "Lindy's mother. Arrested for child endangerment and related offenses. Kept him chained in a pantry, for one." Harry sighed. "Plus other bad things. He was sixteen at the time. She died two years later in prison, cirrhosis."

I said, "When Ava walked into the morgue for her job interview—"

"Snapped our boy like a nickel pencil."

Harry knocked on the door of room 116. A dusty Choctaw County Sheriff's Department cruiser sat in front. I nodded my thanks to the deputy behind the wheel.

Harry said, "The woman is Velene Clay. She's fifty-three. Youth-services director around Butler. She's with her aunt who lived on the farm next to the Lindys. Not a big town."

"The aunt know anything?" I asked, wanting to shoulder through the door, yell, scream, get things moving, but if there had ever been a time to soak up impressions and details, it was now.

Harry shook his head. "She's almost eighty and has

Alzheimer's. That's why the motel: Ms. Clay couldn't leave her at home."

"Find anyone else who knew Lindy way back when?"

"He wasn't out a lot."

The room was warm, the AC barely breathing. Out of concern for the wire-thin woman in the wheelchair between the twin beds, I supposed. She had a crocheted shawl hanging from hard-boned shoulders and her white hair was combed but not subdued, strands poking out like frosty antennas. Emotionless blue eyes fixed on the blank television. Her hands moved in short jerks from her lap to her lips, smoking an invisible cigarette.

She turned to me. A flame of recognition of something. "Ha-aah," she said. "Ee-you. P'leasmn."

Policeman, I thought she said. The left side of her mouth drooped slightly, a stroke probably. I nodded and said hello. She returned to smoking and staring at the television. I had a vision of ancient programs trapped in the starchy sprigs of her hair.

"That's my aunt, Mrs. Benoit. I'm Velene Clay, sir."

I turned to a portly woman sitting at the table in the corner. She wore a simple yellow dress and had a tattered folder in front of her. The fingertips of both hands rested on the folder as though it were the planchette from a Oiuja board. Ms. Clay had been youth-services director in Choctaw County for five years and a caseworker before that. I asked for everything she knew about Will Lindy, looking at my watch to emphasize the need for speed.

She spoke hesitantly. "I first saw him when he was thir- teen. He'd run away from home. Not so unusual. He was brought to me for counseling. A bright, soft-spoken young man. But the first day I knew something was . . . very amiss."

Harry had heard some of her story over the phone. "Listen to this, Cars," he said.

Ms. Clay continued. "There was a waiting room outside my office. Chairs, magazines, toys for the younger children. I came through the door just as Willy dropped a magazine and bent to pick it up. My phone rang. I said, 'Don't move, I'll be right back.'"

Her fingertips twitched over the folder. It shivered toward me, it quivered back. "The call took twenty minutes. When I came back he was still bending over to pick up the magazine."

I said, "You told him, 'Don't move.'"

"He looked like a statue. I said, 'It's all right, Willy,' and he picked up the magazine and placed it in the rack as if nothing had happened."

Mrs. Benoit stomped her foot and moaned. She began jabbing the air with her phantom cigarette.

"Sorry," Ms. Clay said. "She's disturbed about something. We rarely travel. It's so hard on—"

"What else, ma'am?"

"The next time I saw him was in high school. He seemed to not have changed at all, a bit stouter. But still a tiny boy with the same eyes and the same expression. Blank one moment, engaged the next. Like a switch going on and off."

352

"Abuse?"

"He had marks on his wrists and ankles like he'd been bound. He claimed he'd gotten wrapped in the ropes of a tire swing, playing jungle boy or something. It was a very elaborate excuse, coached, I felt. I tried to broach the subject of sexual abuse, but at any mention of the body or genitalia he'd grab his abdomen and start moaning, saying he had to go to the bathroom. Then he'd just turn mute."

Almost imperceptibly, Ms. Clay's hands began moving the file toward me. "I had authority to inspect living conditions and went to his home and told his mama I needed to look around inside. I'd seen the woman in town, of course, spoken to her a bit during the first sessions. Always quiet and polite. It was a mask. She went crazy when I asked to come inside. The foulest language I've ever heard, every form of violent threat. She was like a rabid animal that spoke English."

"What was Lindy doing all this time?"

"Ya-hhhh," Mrs. Benoit said. She looked around the room as if noticing it for the first time. "Y-ahh," she moaned again, balling her fists and striking the air.

Ms. Clay said, "I saw him through the door. Just sitting in front of the TV, nose right up to it. No sound, but it was like he was hearing the TV just fine, but not hearing the to-do at the door. I noted his fascination with TV during office visits, preferring to stare at the screen in the waiting room instead of interacting with other children."

"You went inside the house?"

"It took a sheriff and three big policemen to carry her away."

I said, "It was strange, wasn't it? The house."

The folder crept the remaining distance across the table. "The police took pictures. I asked for copies, so I'd always know, you know. What might make a kid act like Willy Lindy."

"The bows," Mrs. Benoit whispered. "Bows."

I slid the folder from beneath Ms. Clay's fingers and opened it. Twenty photographs, numbered sequentially. The first was of a simple white frame two-story. Nothing behind but flat fields going out of focus, cotton. A heavy tree line in the distance, bordering the Tombigbee River, judging by what I took to be a couple of broken-down boats hauled up between the trees.

The photographer took us inside, documenting his passage. Furniture was sparse. Two hard folding chairs in the living room. One faced a television in the corner. The TV was on, a cartoon judging by the bright color. We moved into the dining room. A square wooden table, one chair pulled to it. The same in the kitchen. A dog's bowl sat on the floor of the kitchen, newspaper beneath it.

"What kind of dog?" I asked.

"They didn't have one," Ms. Clay said, avoiding my eyes. Another photograph, a pantry off the kitchen. Stripped bare of shelves. Nailed into the wall were various lengths of rope, tag ends friction-taped against fraying. The walls were gray. I saw the shadow of a small boy pass the wall. When I blinked the shadow disappeared.

"There wasn't anything upstairs," Ms. Clay said. "Empty."

I tucked the photo of the pantry at the back of the stack. The next photograph was a small wooden outbuilding.

"Out back," Ms. Clay said. "About twenty feet from the house."

A white door with two heavy locks.

The next photo took me into a small room with deep shadows and a stained concrete floor. Black tape covered the windows. In the middle of the floor was a banquet table drilled every few inches near its edges, rope threaded through the holes. Above the table a single hooded light, like a mechanical flower. Two pink snakes dangled from somewhere above with their heads compressing to stubby points.

"What the hell are those tubes?" Harry whispered.

The next photo followed the snakes to the rafters where they joined heavy bladders, one still distended with water.

Ms. Clay's soft sounds were damped by a tissue. "Poor Willy Lindy, poor, poor little boy."

"Bows!" Mrs. Benoit wailed.

"Excuse me," Ms. Clay said, dabbing her eyes and going to her aunt.

"Bows, bows, bows," Mrs. Benoit repeated, striking out with her fist as if she were trying to nail a shifting image into her mind. We excused ourselves and progressed to the next station in our pilgrimage of horror.

Lindy's house was a small, neat Craftsman cottage in midtown, tucked into a miniature forest of palmettos and ferns and wild grasses. Rain had started falling. We waved to the slickered cops on guard, passed the tape cordon, and entered. There was a wooden chair in the high-ceilinged living room, a TV in front of it. That was all. A small table and another wooden chair sat in the dining room. The decor had been foretold by the folder beneath Ms. Clay's fingertips.

Lindy's sleeping bedroom had a mattress on the floor. His clothes were in precise stacks in the closet, the hanging garments spaced to not touch.

There was a second bedroom and a large Master Lock hung open on the door. "Not locked when we came in." Harry said. "Like he was scooting fast."

I walked in. A wall-long table supported several electronic devices, including a computer and video monitor. Two of the devices had tape slots and I took them to be VCRs. A videocamera on a tripod sat in the corner. There were two lights on stands, reflectors clamped beside them. Cables snaked everywhere.

"Videotaping and editing equipment," Harry said. "Amateur but decent. Computer-controlled editing, special effects. Least that's what Carl Tyler said, he's the department's resident tech-brain."

Four tapes were stacked on the table. "You or Carl look at these?"

"No. I just wanted Carl to make sure this stuff wasn't booby trapped or any other weirdness."

"You're aces, bro. Let's rack 'em up."

Harry put a tape in the player. The monitor screen turned to blue-gray snow. A voice issued from speakers below the table. Harry fumbled with buttons on the monitor and the volume elevated.

"... *the stomach is tubular and empty, indicating several hours since the last meal....*"

"Ava's voice," I said, staring into the snow. "See if you can find tracking."

Harry jiggered a knob and the picture resolved into a close-up of bloody, gloved hands lifting a stomach from an open abdomen. The camera zoomed out, framing Ava as she worked, her hands inside the body. I recognized it as Deschamps's corpse.

"... *contents sparse, gruellike, indicative of ...*"

"What the hell is going on, Cars? What would anyone want with tapes of people getting cut into?"

I fast-forwarded. Deschamps's body, different angle; nothing more than the same autopsy shot from a different camera. I popped a second cassette into the player. Same thing, Nelson's body, not yet into the cutting.

"This guy gets off on autopsy movies?" Harry said. "Is that what this is about? Killing people to watch them get cut up?"

"There's more, Harry. The words mean something in all this."

I fast-forwarded. Several angles again. Lindy'd been playing with the controls as the tape recorded; some shots were skintight close, others distant, Ava and the corpse from knees to neck. Farther into the tape was more of the same. Lindy had pulled input from three cameras and dumped it all on this tape. Editing.

The third cassette was the same, only the body was Burlew.

"Three bodies, three tapes of scenes edited from the cameras above the table," I said, picking up the final cassette. "Let's try tape number four."

The cassette had a small star scratched on the case. I jacked it into the player. The machine clicked and whirred. The screen started black. A black-and-white mouth gradually took shape in the dark. The contrast had been punched up to full, the lips almost a moving abstraction. Opening and closing. Wet. Talking. A whisper.

Will Lindy's voice.

"Don't do that. It's dirty and you're not allowed. I'm telling my mama," he said, his voice a mixture of pleading and admonition. Distorted music flowed beneath his words.

"Oh, please . . . stop touching me. Help me, Mama. She's here."

The scene cut to a woman's fingers sliding down a man's chest, kneading and stroking, teasing over a bicep, caressing a rounded shoulder. The camera zoomed in to an extreme close-up and Ava's fingers played across a nipple. Lindy moaned and his voice increased in volume.

"She's here, Mama. The bad girl. Touching me everywhere."

The scene switched to another angle, one of the ceiling-mounted cameras above and slightly left of Ava, a quarter view from the back of her head. The field of view condensed as Ava's hands trickled down the abdomen and across the flat belly, stopping at the pubic hair. She stroked it. Pressed on it. Put her hands beside the base of the penis.

The camera angle shifted and became more oblique.

Stunned and breathless, we watched Ava lean forward and began fellating the corpse of Jerrold Nelson.

CHAPTER 33

The fat tires of the big ATV sank in a mudhole, spun, then bit. The machine skidded sideways before roaring toward the river. Less than a mile to go. His truck now rested at the bottom of a creek north of Chickasaw. A beautiful day, purple-gray clouds and sheets of lovely concealing rain. He cut around a fallen limb and jumped a soft hummock, rising from the seat to let his knees absorb the shock.

Behind him, strapped above the rear fenders, he heard Mama moan lightly. The sleep drug was beginning to wear off. He'd put it in her coffee and when she'd gotten disoriented steered her out the loading dock and into his car. The drug would be vaporizing in her body now—he knew this from personal trials—and she'd breathe it quickly away as she awakened. He had to hurry, an angry Mama was a very dangerous Mama.

In the distance he saw the cluster of trees keeping his boat from casual view. No one would find them. He would talk with Mama about the bad things that had happened in the past, then show her what he had become.

He would save her.

He had to cut the bad girl out. He was strong enough to do it now.

The clouds swirled like dark ghosts and the rain fell harder. Will Lindy aimed for the trees and pressed forward through the flailing rain. It was a beautiful day.

"My God," Harry exclaimed, as we watched Ava's jaws move back and forth, up and down. "Is she doing what I think?"

"Yes. She's reading, 'Warped a quart of whores, warped, whores,' over and over."

Ava appeared to change her facial shape and rhythm. Harry said, "It's different. Now she's reading—"

"'Rats. Rats. Rats. Rats.'" I said. "Or 'Ho ho ho ho.'"

"Without hearing her voice it looks like . . ."

"I know. And remember, I'm standing almost next to her, barely out of camera range."

Harry whispered to himself while holding his chin. "He selected words that swing the jaw."

The writing made sense now. Lindy wanted to Ava to

mimick the facial motions of oral sex as she leaned close to read the tiny, faint writing, her head concealing where an erect penis would be. From the high angle the motions were slight, but suggestive. He had edited between multiangled shots of Nelson's and Deschamps's almost identical lower abdomens to extend the scene, then looped it over and over. Ava's head bobbed, her jaw moved faster, then slower, as Lindy's wet moans poured into the room. His arousal didn't sound faked.

The scenes had been filtered to reduce clinical reality, the whites blazing, the shadows dark and muddy. Beneath it all were the music and eerily distorted sound effects, a throbbing and scratching to haunt a saint's nightmares.

Lindy's moans increased in speed and volume as Ava's head began bobbing furiously. I realized she had been leaning away from reading the inscription and he had reversed and fast-forwarded her motion repeatedly.

Lindy produced a blanketing orgasmic moan and the screen went black. A high-pitched squeal blasted from the speakers and Harry jumped. The video started again with close-ups of the dissection: scalpel slashing, gloved hands retrieving organs through the red slit.

Harry said, "Uh-oh."

Ava's voice: "Willy? Willet Li-indy."

I was right. Lindy had cobbled his name together from individual words and syllables. Were the other words just distraction, chaff? I held my breath and listened in horrified fascination.

"Will Lindy?" Ava said.

Lindy spoke with a child's voice. "Yes, Mama?"

"You were with that girl again, weren't you?" Ava's voice was slow and monotonous, computer-voiced in its inflections, a verbal patch-work from Burlew's back.

"I didn't want to, Mama."

"She makes bad things inside of you, doesn't she?" The flatness of Ava's voice charged the words with despair.

"I won't see her ever again. Promise."

"Willet, Willet, Willet . . . you know how the bad girl makes you lie."

"No, this time I mean it. I said I promise."

"We have to make sure, Will."

"No." Quivering.

"Time to get the bad things out, Will." A hand sliding into the wet cavity. It squeezed and kneaded.

"Don't hurt me again, Mama."

I wondered if this was how it might actually have been: Lindy's voice frantic and frightened, Mama's voice dull and mechanical, a terrified child versus an insane robot. One moment she's the Bad Girl, the next, she's Mama.

"She's deep in you, Will. Mama has to get her out."

"No, please. Please don't, Mama."

The gloved hands sliced and pulled. Scene dissolved into scene. A liver. Kidneys. Bladder. They glistened under the light, like mutant fruit. Most of the scenes were so close the stump of neck wasn't in the frame. When it was, I figured the identity-deleting beheadings must have allowed Lindy's fevered mind to simply fit his own head in place.

Harry spoke as softly as if in church. "Think she really cut into him?"

I said, "Maybe that's what he imagined when she was pumping his insides full of whatever."

"Did the woman crawl up from hell?" Harry asked, watching a lung emerge into the light.

"Horror crawled down through generations."

Lindy's voice moved up a register. "It hurts so bad, Mama."

"Pain makes us pure, Will."

The screen went black and quiet and the silence seemed total. Then Lindy's voice returned; older, cynical.

"I know something, Mama."

"What do you know?"

"I know a secret, Mama." The voices had been stereophonically channeled, Ava's voice coming from the right, Lindy's from the left.

"What do you know, Will?"

"Secrets, secrets." Taunting.

"What do you know, Will?"

Whispered: "You're the bad girl."

"What did you say, Willy?"

"I know you're the bad girl, Mama." He laughed, a voice thickened with lust. "Secrets, secrets. So many secrets."

Harry said, "Whatever's shaking out, it ain't gonna be good."

"You . . . just . . . shut up . . . now . . . Will Lindy."

"You're the bad girl, Mama, you're the bad girl, Mama, I know a secret. . . ."

Lindy's singsong rant pitched headlong into a scream that cut the air like a scythe, then shivered into black. There was only the whirr of the VCR as over a minute's time a body slowly appeared on the screen, surfacing from a coal-black sea. Nelson's body. The color was completely washed away, leaving only black and white and shape-shifting gray. The camera panned to a bicep, zoomed in close.

"Watch what I can do, Mama, watch me do *this*." Lindy's voice was a taunting whisper.

Nelson's bicep was replaced by Deschamps's arm in the same position, larger, thicker.

"I'm growing, Mama. Look."

Nelson's flat stomach turned into the more muscled abdomen of Deschamps. Nelson's thigh became the thicker thigh of Deschamps.

"Uh-oh, Mama," Lindy's voice challenged, "you better watch out now."

Nelson's shoulders ballooned as if by magic, gaining weight and definition.

"My God," Harry said. "It's a revenge fantasy."

Ava/Mama's cobbled-together words: "Don't, Will. You're scaring me. Don't scare me."

"You think you're scared now, Mama, watch this." Triumph rang in Lindy's voice.

The screen went dark and the eerie sounds grew deeper and more rhythmic. The screen lightened to a shot of

Burlew's powerlifter's body, thick and defined, the boulder chest, the ham biceps. Then a montage of the body from several angles. Dozens of shots squeezed into a few seconds, the camera zooming in as though drawn against the body.

"No. Will. Don't. I'm scared."

"It's your turn now, Mama."

A close-up of lips recalled the beginning of the video: Lindy's wet mouth spitting out words: "Did you ever think I'd come for you, Mama?"

Ava's voice contorted through a mishmash of jammed-together vowels, an ugly choking sound, the *ee*'s from "Pee." The hollow *o*'s of "Boston." The long *o*'s of "Kokomo." The city names had provided both needed syllables and a diversion.

". . . ahhhh-oooaa-uu . . . Don't . . . please . . ."

A cut to Lindy's face, half in dark, a wild grin beneath blazing eyes, his hands gesturing the viewer into the picture.

". . . oo . . . ahh . . . oooaauuhh . . ."

"Pain makes us *pure*, Mama."

". . . eeee-aa-ooo-ahhh . . . Will . . ."

"I will save you, Mama."

". . . oooooaaaaeee—"

The screen abruptly snapped into black and the sound cut off. A white hiss of blank tape filled the room.

Harry said, "What happened? The tape bust?"

"No," I said slowly, my mind watching another set of invisible lines push from the dark. "It's lacking the final scene. The climax."

"Mama's death."

"Damn you, Jeremy. Damn you to hell and back," I whispered at the empty screen, suddenly knowing why I'd escaped his room unscathed.

Harry said, "What, Carson?"

"Jeremy couldn't see who the killer was, but he saw who it wasn't," I said, recalling Jeremy's study of the police reports and interviews, his pinpoint-focus mind deciphering the minutia. I heard him rant at Ava when she'd suggested his input had saved lives.

"You see it as saving lives, witch. I see it as BETRAYING JOEL ADRIAN!"

I recalled the ease with which he manipulated me toward the innocent Caulfield, and the willingness with which I went.

I said, "Jeremy read the material and discovered or suspected the killer was on a mother-dominated mission of revenge or whatever. My brother saw the killer as a kindred spirit. He also saw that Caulfield didn't fit the mindset."

Comprehension dawned in Harry's eyes. "So Jeremy aimed you at Caulfield to give the real killer time to fulfill his mission, to put Mama in the movie. Jeremy didn't burn you because . . ."

I nodded. "Because he didn't fulfill his end of the bargain. He misdirected me instead."

"And now Lindy's somewhere with . . . Mama," Harry whispered. "Completing the fantasy."

I slammed my fist against the table, a gesture as futile as wafting off a storm with a paper fan.

"What will Lindy do?" Harry said. We sat in the car with no idea of direction. I braced my feet on the floor and tumbled twenty years back. Threat. Storm. What to do? Daytime: Run to the oak in the woods, climb to my fort. Wait. Night: Slide out the window, creep to the car.

I knew what he'd do: It was in me too.

"He'll go where he feels safe, Harry—his version of a tree-house. I've got to find out what that is."

"Will he race to—to finish the movie?"

"He's never rushed anything. We've got that."

Was I lying to myself? But Lindy had spent hundred of hours stalking his victims, combing through videotape, selecting scenes, stitching them into a five-minute crazy-quilt of retribution. No. He'd want his moment of confrontation to linger. As long as he felt safe. That meant no standoffs, no rushing attacks, no SWAT teams roaring up in a scream of lights and sirens and bullhorns. That would only accelerate his mad agenda. Yet when it was finished I suspected he could run laughing into a hail of fire and metal, pain and death nothing more than pixels on a TV screen.

But first we had to find him. What had Ms. Clay said? No. What had Mrs. Benoit said?

Bows.

Bows. I recalled Mrs. Benoit's growing turmoil as we

talked with her niece. *Bows*. She'd gotten excited whenever someone had said Lindy's name. Said, bows. Or something.

"Back to the motel, Harry," I said. "Crank it," I added, needlessly.

CHAPTER 34

I sat on the bed beside Ms. Benoit and laid my hand over her knee, a walnut under a blanket. She was still smoking and watching TV, oblivious to anyone else in the universe. I shifted closer until I was staring into her diluted eyes.

"Will Lindy," I said. "Willy."

Her mouth formed a pucker and released the word "Bows."

"Where's Willy, Mrs. Benoit?"

She leaned to one side and craned her face toward the TV. I moved between them. "Willy," I repeated. "Will Lindy. Where's Willy?"

"Bows," she said, more forcefully.

"Will Lindy!" I yelled into her face, hoping volume would

align her shifting plates of memory. Ms. Clay wrung her hands but didn't intervene.

"Bows," Mrs. Benoit said to me. Her hand shot to my face like a brittle claw and held tight. I tried to picture what she was seeing. She had lived beside the Lindys. On the Tombigbee River. Farmhouse. Outbuilding. Field. Trees. What else had I seen in Ms. Clay's photos? Water. The boat hulls in the tree line.

"Boats?" I asked Ms. Clay, her aunt's nails digging into my face.

Ms. Clay whispered across the room. "On back of the Lindy property by the river. Two old rotting boats, fishing boats I think, the ones with the big arms coming away from them? Nets? One was on its side, a rust shell. The other was upright, stuck in the mud. They're long gone, but maybe that's where he hid when he got the chance."

I nodded. "Boats?" I asked Mrs. Benoit. My eyes stared from between her fingers. She leaned forward until electric springs of white hair grazed my forehead. Her teeth clicked as she spat slurred words into my face.

"Tha crazy-eyed . . . li'l monkey . . . was always hiding . . . in them fucking . . . bows."

Two major rivers empty into Mobile Bay, the Mobile and the Tensaw. Between and surrounding them is the second-largest river delta in the country—tens of thousands of acres of marsh and swamp and bottomland, gators and snakes, relentless clouds of hungry insects. We slogged upriver at maybe twenty knots, all I could wrench from the big Merc with this much water surging back at us. I cocked my head down to keep the bill of my cap between the rain and my eyes. I was damn glad the boat had been blessed. Jabbing hard ahead with my finger, I yelled, "Watch the water, Harry!"

"For what?"

"Logs, stumps. Anything. Yell it out."

The same storm that Ava and I had made love in had moved northwest and bumped a front stretching down from Canada. The storm had stalled, spending three days flooding the upper portion of the Mobile River system's 44,000-square-mile watershed. A second storm moved in behind it, the one pounding us now. Harry yelled, pointed. A tumbling snarl of uprooted tupelo raced at our bow. I jerked the wheel. Tendrils screeched down the hull. Harry closed his eyes and whispered to himself.

Working with the county cops, MPD quickly discovered Lindy had sunk a goodly portion of his $73,000 annual salary into land. Seven parcels in Baldwin County, five in Mobile County. It took a gut-snarling two hours to identify the parcels and outline them on a map. Most seemed speculator parcels, raw acres in the middle of nowhere waiting for sprawl to bring developers to the door, paying dollars over dimes. More of Lindy's long-range planning. Teams of cops were spreading onto the parcels now, moving low, bristling with armaments.

Way up the Mobile River was Lindy's only parcel on water, two acres in the middle of nowhere with fifty yards of river frontage. There'd be a fish-camp shack, maybe. Or a boat. I was rolling the dice he'd be on water; it was his retreat, his sanctuary. We could have come in from the land side, but the map showed it tough slogging even for an ATV, slough and marsh. The weather was too wild for a chopper.

We'd asked only for the boat and the command staff gave it readily, happy to concentrate on their heavy-assault strategies, figuring Lindy would never head to his most inaccessible piece of land. Most suspected he was already in Mississippi or Florida and making survival choices based on logic and planning. To me he was years of sizzling wires checked only by paper-thin insulation. Seeing Ava had peeled the insulation away like dead skin, leaving loose wires sparking and crackling and making random and mystifying connections.

"We'll never get there if you slam into something," Harry yelled. "Can you cut it back a little?"

I looked at him. Caution wasn't a Harryism.

"I can't swim," he said, looking away.

The boat slapped a standing wave and for a moment we were airborne. Harry clawed at the windscreen as we slammed down and continued grinding upriver. I kept one eye on the water while scrabbling through the underseat storage. I found a bouyancy vest and threw it to him.

"Got a plan?" he yelled, squeezing into a ridiculous yellow vest at least two sizes too small.

"It'll be full dark in a half hour. I'm hoping he's running

power from a generator. Making noise. We'll slip up and take him down."

"If he's there."

"It's his tree fort, Harry. He's there."

"It's raining, Mama. Remember how you love the rain?"

The interior of the shrimp boat was dry, the rotting overhead replaced, joints caulked. It was a small craft, a thirty-six-foot wooden box perched on wormy four-by-four's, three hundred feet from the river, a hundred from the silted side channel. The boat was surrounded by trees, almost hidden.

The low-roofed central cabin was large enough to accommodate the bright metal table. Belowdecks was the heavy bank of car batteries for power. He had a gasoline generator for charging the batteries; he'd run it yesterday, all was set. The TV, a thirty-two-inch flat screen sitting on a shelf at the back of the cabin, wasn't as large as he wanted, but a person couldn't have it all. A drive-in-sized screen would have been perfect, bolt Mama to the hood of her old Buick and park her front-row center.

Lights, camera and . . . Look how I'm changing since you left, Mama! I can save you!

Mama was strapped to the table at her neck, wrists, and ankles. He'd had to leave her belly open, of course, though it gave him pause; Mama was strong as a bear when she got her blood up. He'd doubled the other straps just to be safe.

Lindy's hands began tearing open the dress, shredding it away. Mama was beginning to stir and moan. Now was when he'd have to be most careful. The police were out there somewhere, but compared to Mama's powers they were ants on the far side of the world.

Mama's breasts quivered in her bra as he pulled remnants of dress from beneath her. He let his eyes roam her skin and heard the bad girl inside her begin singing. He hummed loudly to blot it from his head. MMMMmmmmmm. This was when Mama was most dangerous. MMMMMmmmmmmmmm.

Willet Lindy hummed louder as he aimed the TV at the autopsy table and began wiring his magic show together.

The rain fell heavier as the light faded. Visibility was failing and disappeared entirely when blasts of wind threw rain into my eyes. I glanced at the river chart; we were close. I didn't want to overshoot Lindy's place and alert him to someone on the river. We were the only boat I'd seen since leaving the bay.

"Carson!"

Harry jabbed his finger ahead. I looked up to see a silver ramp charging our hull. I reflexively cut the wheel, but there was no way to miss it. An explosive *whump* and we skidded sidelong up the ramp, seeing water and then only tumbling sky. The engine roared as the boat pitched on its side and the disintegrating prop cleared the water. Sheared metal whipped the air like bullets. Brown water slashed over the gunwales. The boat roared onto the bank with a squeal of agonized metal and stopped dead, canted high on its side, lodged in mud. I pulled myself upright with the wheel. The only sound I heard was the rain. There was no Harry.

"Harry? Harry!"

I heard sloshing. "Damn. I can't walk."

I stumbled aft and saw Harry wading in from the river, struggling through the hard laminar flow at his legs. My feet slid over the side and I sank to my ankles in black muck. I struggled to Harry and pulled him to the bank.

"What the hell happened?" He said, wiping his eyes with a sodden sleeve. "I got flipped straight up and the next thing I know I'm in the river."

"We hit a capsized johnboat. You OK?"

He nodded and palmed water from his eyes. "Where we at? In relation to Lindy?"

The chart had been flung out with Harry. The rain pounded straight down now, hissing on water and swamp grass and drumming the body of our forlorn craft. I closed my eyes and tried to recall the markers. "Maybe a quarter mile. Only problem is"—I looked across thirty yards of surging water—"we're on the wrong side of the river."

I studied the water in the fading light, the same width from bend to bend. Swim up and into the flow, I thought, fighting the current like a riptide, never stopping; swim straight across and I'd end up hundreds of yards down-stream. If I wasn't pulled under.

"Show me how to swim," Harry said.

"It's not like that, bro," I said, watching a fifty-five-gallon drum tumble down the channel like a pop can.

"There was this community pool when I was growing up," he said. "They showed me how to dog-paddle. And I've got this"—Harry pointed to the yellow vest, the brightest thing in miles, incandescent. It was probably rated for someone a hundred pounds lighter. The white straps were too short to girdle his belly; they hung at his sides in a grotesque parody of a straitjacket.

"That ain't dog-paddle water, Harry," I said. "For you it's drowning water."

"What the hell is it for you?"

"Just wet, Harry. Don't worry."

I tore my shirt off, the buttons landing in the water, tumbling faces drowned in an instant. The rain pelted harder. It stung my bare shoulders like rock salt dropped from a roof. I stripped to briefs, a shoulder holster with the Beretta, a belt with an extra clip and a five-inch Buck hunting knife in a leather scabbard. There was a .30 Marlin in the boat, along with a 12-gauge, but every added ounce put me closer to the bottom. I had two good legs and about one and a third arms. It had to be enough.

The philosopher Heraclitus said you can never step into the same river twice, meaning by the time you step in a second time the water has changed. He was trumped by Parmenides who said you can never step into the same river once, it's changing as you step. I went through a thousand rivers before I got waist deep in the warm opaque water, vortices swirling on the down-water sides of my legs. Leaves and debris clotted against me and foretold the river's stranglehold before I'd even begun my journey.

I looked at the far side, dark trees cutting into purple sky and all shrouded gray by the rain. I thought of Ava, in a box in the middle of nowhere with a maniac, the rain pounding his delusions deeper into his skull. I took a deep breath and dived into the current.

It was worse than I'd imagined.

CHAPTER 35

He stood on the foredeck and looked across the marsh into gray light fading toward a black as lush as velvet. No stars or moon, no lights. Sometimes he could he see lantern light from a fish camp a quarter mile downstream, but the old man who used the camp walked with a cane and listened with a hand behind his ear. A lucky old man: Had he been a threat, Mr. Cutter would have syringed a heart attack into the old man's veins like he'd done to the grinning pervert he'd sent Caulfield. The depraved monster had approached Mr. Cutter at a bar when he was shadowing Nelson. It had been wonderful to lure him, inject him, push the simple explosive device into him with a broom handle. It was delightful what one could create with the powder from three shotgun shells, a sawed-down flashlight tube, a spark-trigger, a foot of monofilament, and a treble fishhook.

"My fingers? Where are my fingers?"

Willy Lindy smiled at his recollection of Caulfield's first and last autopsy. The devious young pathologist had tried to steal Mama's ordained job from her—the one that brought her back to Willy.

Now he was safe in his own world. Made even safer by the rain. The universe had given him his boat back, returned Mama, and now protected him from the outside world, allowing time. Time for Willy, time for Mama. Two weary travelers united in atonement, when sins of the past would be clarified through the revelation of image, redemption washing their souls in scarlet waves, leaving them safe and alone and together forever.

He heard Mama making noises in the engine room below. She'd want to know what was going on. He'd best go and tell her.

Show her.

"Cars! Watch out!"

I was halfway across, muscles screaming and burning, eyes blinded by grit and garbage, when the uprooted stump tumbled over me. It was the size of a car, its root system clutching as it rolled me under, roots like pliable iron, inescapable, like being welded to the face of a locomotive highballing beneath an ocean. I ripped and clawed at the tendrils surrounding me, pulled, tore. Screamed in my head.

A roar of bubbles, distorted sounds. The burn of fingernails peeling away.

The stump shuddered and spun and jammed me like a dredging shovel into the thick muck of the bottom, sponge-soft at the top, thick and sandy beneath. Mud filled my mouth and nose and ears as I waited for the crush, an orchestral roar blaring in my head. I skidded along the bottom with my final taste of life pouring from my lungs, thinking, *My last moment: bubbles across my face.*

The stump shuddered again, and rotated upward, taking forever before it broke the surface. Rain and beautiful air, me sucking it past the mud and sand, choking, vomiting, but air. I screamed at the clutching roots, wrenched. The stump rolled me slowly toward the sky as my hands scrabbled to discover where I was bound.

The shoulder rig, my mind screamed . . . *tangled.*

I fought the binding with torn fingers. Then heard the sound of splashing carrying through the rain. I saw Harry in the river, a dozen feet from shore, sixty from me and moving away, white plumes rising as he slapped the water. Seeing me overtaken by the stump, he'd dived in, found attempting to swim is more destructive than not swimming at all.

"Go back!" I screamed. "Harry, stop!"

I watched in horror as the current sucked him out into the main channel, spinning, splashing, choking. The stump rolled me down toward the water again.

"Hold your breath and float," I shrieked. "Your body wants to float."

His head disappeared, but broke the surface seconds later, ten yards farther downstream. He was slowly rotating, as if in a whirlpool, moving away. He went under again.

After that only flat and relentless water.

I cursed and wailed and tore at the harness straps, the water rising up my legs. It was just straps now, the Beretta scraped away by the bottom. My torn hands couldn't work the release, fingers like smoke at the ends of my arms. Water raged across my chest.

The knife was still at my waist. I fumbled it loose, pressed it between my palms, and sliced furiously at the straps.

At my neck, water . . .

A snap of nylon and

water filling my mouth again . . .

Free. Floating in the river, gasping, the stump tumbling to the depths, roots slashing the surface. I felt the thunder of its crushing skid against the bottom.

When I spun toward the far bank the knife fell from my bleeding fingers. I struck out wildly for it, catching the grip across my palm. I couldn't grasp it, could never hold it as I swam. I was gasping and shaking too hard to clamp it in my teeth. Kicking hard, treading water, swirling downriver, I angled the point between the flesh and the meat high on my thigh, jammed my palm against the pommel, and thrust. The knife slid into me and stuck hard.

I howled like a man possessed by whirlwinds and swam past anything I ever knew as pain, reaching the far side of the river bleeding, rigid with cramp, blind with mud and rage. I cried until my eyes cleared and crawled in the mud and watched the river roll by, now just a rumbling sheet of dark water. The pictures in my head were cold enough to ice the river, crust the black marshes with frost. The world was black and white and the only light came from drifting filaments at the farthest reach of the sky, faint capillaries of waning lightning.

I slipped in the mud that squirted between my toes, fell to my knees. I threw back my head and screamed. Then, rising against the rain, clad in only a muddy twist of cloth, my knife in the scabbard of my flesh, I stood and started upriver. I was no longer a Ryder or a Ridgecliff or any name patched over a human being, I was a blazing creation of hate and vengeance and white-hot fury, and in my mind one burning picture: wiring Willet Lindy to a tree and making the evil bastard SQUEAL and SQUEAL until tube worms and black honey poured from his belly like a river.

"Did you think you could sneak up on me, Mama?"

"Will? Will, what's going on? Let me go, Will."

"Could you see me from where you were, Mama? Did they have windows there?"

"Will, I'm not your mama. Look at me, Will. It's Dr. Davanelle."

His mouth at her ear, he could have bitten it off. "Did they tape the windows there, Mama? Did they have the black tape where you were?" He couldn't help himself, he licked her ear and almost swooned with delight.

"I can't feel my hands or feet, Will. Please let me up."

"I've still been good, Mama. I've been clean. Sometimes I make the pee-pee, but I've tried. I made something else, Mama, I made a magic secret. Remember our magic secrets, Mama? The ones I couldn't say?"

"Will . . ."

"I made magic pictures to show you how I am inside now, Mama. Watch, Mama. You me and the pictures. We'll watch the pictures and then I'll get the bad girl out of you, Mama. I promise I will."

One more little flick of his tongue at her ear.

"I love you, Mama. Yes, I will."

There was nothing to explain where I was. No map or GPS, no moon or stars. All I had was the sound of the river at my right arm and the suck of the mud at my feet. Insects covered me like a cloud and I stopped to coat myself with muck, but the rain washed it away. Pain sang from my hip and I eased the knife from my flesh in teeth-clenching increments, a warm flow of blood behind it. I flexed my fingers and realized my grip was returning. I looked down at my bare, muddy feet and was grateful that years of barefoot beach running had callused the bottoms—at least I could walk. A building poked from a small copse and I crept to it, my steps muffled by the rain and the water racing through the brush. A fish camp, deserted, little more than the tree house of my youth, a tarpaper roof amplifying the fall of the drops into a drumlike sound. It occurred to me that I'd heard the camp well before I'd seen its hazy outline, my ears picking up the sound of the rain on the roof from thirty yards' distance. I moved past the camp, then paused and listened. Rain on water and leaf and grasses, a solid hiss of monotone rain. I no longer heard the rain against the tarpaper. But I had heard the difference.

I walked on. One hundred trudging paces. Stopped.

Nothing. The same flat hiss. Another hundred paces. Listened. And again moved on.

Stopped.

I heard it. A brown cricket chirping in a field of black ones, or a cornet hidden behind a blare of trumpets. Something in the sound had changed. In front of me, behind, I couldn't discern. I stood like a blind man smelling smoke in a tinderbox forest, moving up a few feet, back, sensing the change, the direction, sifting for discrepancies. It seemed to be off my right arm, slightly ahead. I turned that way and walked.

Mama had known what the magic pictures meant. It was deep in her disguised eyes, the ones she'd painted green instead of the gray ones she used to wear every day.

Let me listen to her now. Lying.

"I'm not your mama, Will. I'm Dr. Davanelle. Ava Davanelle. We work together at the medical examiner's office. Remember? Stop and try to remember, Will. It's all there if you try and remember."

He's never heard Mama use a scared voice before. She

was trying to keep it flat, ironed down, but that scared sound was making tiny wrinkles.

"I remember, Mama. It's in the pictures. They're history pictures, the secrets. Did you see me grow up to be a big boy? Did you see my muscles grow?" He pointed to the gray screen of the paused television.

"Yes, Will, but that's not you—"

"I saw you come back and I knew you were mad at me still but I'm going to clean the bad girl out of you forever, Mama and—"

"Will, you'll get in trouble, in terrible trouble. You can stop this now."

"—then we can do it all over again, Mama, right this time, like the just-people that everyone gets to be, I want to be just-people, Mama, and you want to be just-Mama."

"Oh, Will, please . . ."

"I'm strong now and I can get the bad girl out of you."

He walked to the canvas bag he'd brought with them. He removed a few bright tools from the morgue, things they'd never miss, so it wasn't stealing. He arranged them on a clean white towel in a shining silver tray and proudly showed them to her.

He reached down and eased a strand of hair from her eyes.

"Don't cry, Mama, pain makes us pure."

Another sound entered the one I was focusing on. I ran ahead a few paces and saw shoreline, lapping water. That was the new sound: I was following a channel angling from the river, an anchorage perhaps.

I stepped back and focused on the sounds in the rain again, heard a rhythmic tapping, and followed it to wooden pilings at the channel's edge, tubular ghosts slapped with waves, invisible until I was a dozen feet away. Rain drummed a few remaining planks of decking on the old dock. My feet crunched rock and shell and I knew I was walking an abandoned launch ramp.

I moved from the distraction of the rain on the decking, held my breath, closed my eyes, and again became a listening machine. Another sound somewhere to the right, thin and hollow. I wished for a bolt of lighting, a moment of moonglow, anything to pierce the black. The sound disappeared once, but I backed up until I heard it again. I angled to the left and kept walking.

Until I saw the light.

I wiped the rain from my eyes and it remained: a strip of horizontal moonbeam hovering in the air. In the trees? *No*, my mind cried: in the faint outline of an old shrimp boat against the gray-black sky, its outriggers like raised spears and the hiss of rain on its wooden body a soft wail from deep within a mine.

CHAPTER 36

"Willy? Willy?"

"Don't talk to me. I have things to do. You can't talk to me."

"Don't you want to talk to the bad girl again, Willy?"

"MMMMmmmmmmm. MMMmmmmmm."

Lindy put his fingers in his ears and hummed louder. He'd tried this a long time ago but Mama ran his fingers through the stove flame and told him that's what happened to fingers that got caught in ears.

"You were so good to her, Willy. What if Mama lied and the bad girl was really the good girl?"

"That's a lie! MMMMmmmmmmm."

"Did the bad girl ever make you do things you didn't want to do, Willy? Or did the bad girl make you feel good?"

He shouldn't have reminded her about the bad girl in her. She was trying to use it against him.

"It wasn't good, Mama. It was sickness coming from me. MMmmmmmm."

"You were going to cut the bad girl from Mama, Willy? Are you sure?"

"Mmmmmmmm. Mmmmmmm."

"Maybe you wanted to cut Mama out of the bad girl."

"You're crazy! That's why you're bad, you lie."

"Take these stupid ropes off me, Willy. Come curl up with the bad girl. *Your* bad girl, Willy."

"Stop talking those words."

"You don't have to cut Mama out of me, Willy. I can just send her away. I can send her off the edge of the world."

"She won't go. She's STUCK here!"

"Not anymore. You scared her with your secret magic movie, your wizard movie. She's not even in this room, Will. Won't you come and let me up? Let's escape from here before Mama comes back."

Willard Lindy, Mr. Cutter, picked up a scalpel and whisked his thumb over the blade.

"It won't work, Mama. You used to say that too."

"No, Will, don't, Will . . ."

Her belly was so soft and warm.

The ladder to the deck of the boat was anchored in the mud beside a large four-wheel ATV. The boat's keel was a yard above the mud, the craft raised on thick planks for repairs that never arrived. It looked unstable and I was afraid of the boat shifting when I stepped on the ladder.

I heard a soft sound through the hull: Ava's voice.

The boat held firm as I climbed to the deck. The light came from a slender strip of window where one course of tape had not quite overlapped another. I heard a second voice now. Crouching, I slipped my eye to the window.

Willet Lindy standing over Ava. She was in a bra and panties, strapped to an autopsy table. Lindy wearing nothing but muddy suit pants and boots. I watched him define a trail down her abdomen with his finger, a scalpel poised to follow.

I dived against the door and the corroded hinges dissolved away. It was like diving into paper and I stumbled, arms flailing, across the slender cabin. I slipped in blood and mud dripping from my legs and fell hard, bouncing, pain screaming from my hip, my knife skittering away. The boat shivered on its pylons, yawing as if on water. A crunching sound from below and the craft listed. Food cans, water bottles, plates, tools, crashed from shelves onto the floor. The television slid forward and stopped, held by a cable. The remote pitched onto the floor as I sprawled, nearly naked, on the floor.

The tape started to rewind itself.

"*Eee-yawp, tis-tris sipppen . . .*" On the screen, the mouth of Willet Lindy appeared from black and began vacuuming its words. The real Lindy was above me, the dark eyes of a double-barreled shotgun staring at my face.

390

"Stay down!" he screamed. "Just stay right there, Detective Ryder."

He kicked me hard in the side with a steel-toe boot and I doubled over. "I cleaned and cleaned and now you're getting filth everywhere." He pushed the shotgun against my head.

"*Owp, eenyah, yeppuh* . . . ," the television Lindy said as he swallowed more words.

"Get across the room. Not standing. Crawl!"

I crawled.

"I've been watching you, Detective Ryder," Lindy said. "You've been sniffing around after Mama." On the TV Burlew's massive arms relaxed into Deschamps's biceps, deflated further into Nelson's arms.

"*Creen-yee-up, tenrip, ridish* . . ."

"Sit. There. Don't. Move."

I obeyed. If he pulled the triggers my head would turn to gruel.

"Why are you here?" he demanded.

"To take Dr. Davanelle home."

"*Mama* is staying here."

The TV showed Ava replacing organs in Deschamps's body like packing a parcel for shipping. One swift motion of the scalpel and the slit in the body was healed.

"*Tten-yupo, pinreep, toodo* . . ."

"I can't tie you up. Hold up your hands."

He was going to blow my hands off.

"Your hands or your head, Detective Ryder."

I had never heard of anyone who escaped death saying

391

the world became like this, hyperreal, almost luminous, like another sense coming on, feeling everything. Even the tiniest shift in the boat, as if someone else had crept into my final moment. Could it be?

Again, the shift, the smallest creak. A whisper of wood.

Someone outside?

Lindy's eye squinted down the black barrel. He hadn't heard. "Hold up your hands now!" he howled. I moved my hands slowly upward and to the side so the pellets might miss my face. Lindy's finger whitened on the trigger. I closed my eyes.

A yellow bird flew through the door. It bellowed. Lindy spun and blew it to pieces. The bird disintegrated into a soft snow of white foam and scraps of plastic, a former life vest.

I rolled across the floor and kicked Lindy's legs from beneath him.

Thunder at the door. Harry charging. Me rising, grabbing at the table beside Ava. The boat shivered under the motion and one of the shoring planks cracked. The boat shifted again and the tray of surgical instruments spilled across the floor. Lindy squirmed past Harry and cracked him on the jaw with the stock of the shotgun.

Harry dropped.

I grabbed a scalpel from the floor. Lindy spun toward Harry, the gun swinging up.

I roared and threw myself at Lindy, grabbing his neck with one hand, the other angling the gun up and away. It discharged through the roof and the kick spun it from his grip. I bent him backward across the tilting table. He tore at my eyes and hands, ripping his fingers on the scalpel, blood pouring between us. His belly was to me and I pushed the edge of the scalpel just below his navel as he screamed and snapped his teeth at me. I felt the resistance of his skin against the point of the scalpel. An inch of bright blade slipped inside his belly.

I had the power to slice him all the way down to his first breath.

"Mama, Mama, Mama, Mama . . ." he recited like a litany. I looked at Ava. She shook her head, *No, no, no.*

Lindy howled, "Mamamamamama . . ."

I felt my arms slacken.

"*Dee-yup, penit, tesheeup* . . ." On the TV screen Ava returned Nelson's insides.

The floor listed and I grabbed the table to steady myself. Lindy spun away and dived into the bilge hatch. I looked into it and saw only wired-together ranks of batteries. A sharp crack came from the keel and the boat shifted again, harder. The gasoline can by the generator tumbled and upended, dumping fuel across the floor and through the hatch to the engine room and bilge. The batteries shifted and clacked together. We were adrift in a boat soaked with gas and a hold full of jerry-wired batteries in the rain, our captain a madman.

One short, one spark . . .

The boat listed several more degrees. Joists screamed,

bulwarks strained. Harry and I dug at Ava's ropes, fighting to stand on the slanting floor. Failing metal squealed beneath us and the deck shivered and dropped another six inches. I fell. Harry grabbed the edge of the bolted-down table and continued tearing at Ava's bindings. Gasoline fumes burned tears from our eyes. Harry struggled at the ropes as I pulled myself up.

"Te-repped uten benetha . . ."

Harry roared with effort, his arms shaking with strain. I smelled the acrid stink of wires cooking off insulation.

Only her neck bound now.

A crack of wood and the boat teetered severely. The last holdings of the shelves emptied across the floor. On the tape Ava traced her hand over the bare body, nodded, and backed quickly from the picture. *"Amam, amam,"* Lindy said as the tape rolled to its beginning. His lips faded to black. The tape snapped off.

"Got it," Harry yelled, Ava in his arms, rising.

I heard the thunder of heavy wood breaking. The boat shivered for an instant, then knelt forward and buried its prow in the soft earth. We tumbled across the floor as cans and tools and debris clattered over us. Smoke suffused the gasoline-laden air.

But we were by the door.

We scrambled out into sweet, beautiful mud, and pulled ourselves through the grasses. The snap of a spark behind us became a tremendous sucking *whump* and the night blazed orange and gold. We stumbled to a hummock and knelt behind it, the heat pressing our wet faces. The interior of the old shrimper's cabin burned like a torch, but the rain-soaked wood outside was slower to ignite. Light blazed through the doors, the ports, the pilot house. For a few minutes the old boat resembled a magic lantern dropped from the stars to the earth, and we crouched golden beneath its light.

Then it simply fell to pieces and consumed itself.

EPILOGUE

". . . last thing I heard was Carson yelling about floating. So I took a deep breath and relaxed. Ever try and relax when you think you're gonna drown?"

"I'll pass," Ava said. A gull keened overhead and she studied its wheeling flight. Harry plucked another boiled peanut from the bowl on my deck table. He was eating them Harry style: bite off the tip of the shell, dribble a few drops of hot sauce into the opening, pop the whole affair in his mouth. He chewed and reflected.

"But I found I could just kinda bob along. When I went under I'd flap my arms like wings, float up to the surface, grab a breath, and then the water'd cover me again."

Harry flapped his arms to demonstrate. For a moment I

heard the sound of rain and saw him spinning away in the brown river. I caught my tumble into the past and fought back to the present. There needed to be time to reflect on the past, I figured, but not today. Today would be dedicated to This Moment Only, unencumbered by chains or ghosts or lines converging in the muddy dark.

"How far'd you go?" Ava asked.

Harry narrowed an eye, calculated. "Guess about a quarter mile. Then my feet hit bottom and damned if I wasn't crawling up a sandbar on the other side."

We were sitting on my deck. This was our first chance to talk in any detail among just the three of us. We'd spent the day following the event in the hospital, surrounded by doctors and inquisitive cops. Yesterday was more cops and the media. We answered the reporters' haphazard questions vaguely, downplaying our roles.

Ava leaned toward Harry. "You thought Carson was"— she paused; the word was hard for her to say, and wasn't that easy for me to hear—"gone?"

Harry looked at me and winked. "Boy can't do a whole helluva lot, but he can swim. I knew if anyone was gonna pop up on the far shore, it'd been Carson. I just kept moving upriver, knowing that's what he'd do. Then I heard a crashing sound up ahead."

I said, "Me going through that rotten door."

For a split second I was tumbling through the boat, sliding in mud and blood and coming to rest with a 12-gauge at my eyes. I shook the scene from my head.

Harry said, "Thought I'd go see who was disturbing my pleasant little nature hike. Then I see that damn boat up in the air. . . ."

Two full days behind us and the event was settling into a blur. My hands weren't too bad, or wouldn't be when the fingernails returned. The knife slit in the meat of my hip felt like someone had sewn bees in there. They gave me a crutch at the hospital but I'd left it in the car, more trouble than it was worth. I pushed myself up from the table.

Ava's hand reached for mine. "You OK?"

"I'm gonna go lean on the rail. My ass is stiffening up."

Her hand squeezed mine and I looked into her eyes. They looked good, clear and sharp and green as the sunshiny sea. She winked one at me and my heart skipped a beat. I patted her hand and gimped toward the deck rail. My idiot cell phone chirped from the table. I should have never let it out of the cooler bag.

"Grab that, would you, Harry?"

He said, "Probably another damn reporter. Or Squill trying to make nice again."

Though I didn't circulate the cassette, Squill picked up heavy tarnish. He'd been booted from investigations and assigned the title "media liason'; the press probably deserved him. He was again reinventing history and had called earlier confessing he had been completely duped by Burlew, so sorry. It was pathetic, but that was Squill.

"Ryder's place," Harry said. "Hello?" He stared at the cell, then looked at me and shrugged.

"Nothing. Wrong number, I guess."

Harry flipped the phone on the table and lumbered into the house to refill the peanut bowl. I leaned my back against the rail. Ava joined me, putting her elbows on the wood, staring quietly out into the Gulf. The sky was cloudless blue and a tight chain of pelicans moved low across the waves.

I said, "The first time you stood there, the wind blew your clothes tight against you and I had lascivious thoughts."

She slid a breeze-blown strand of hair from her eyes. "It seems so long ago."

"That I had lascivious thoughts? Odd, I thought I recalled several from this very morning."

"I had every intention of showing up sober. But fear got the best of me. Fear of myself."

"You were full of ghosts, some you invented, most were real."

She nodded, took a sip of ginger ale. "I've talked with Dr. Peltier. It's going to be different. Very different."

Clair was making peace with her own demons, no longer brandishing them at others. I'd spoken with her last evening, and knew today she was meeting with an attorney specializing in divorce. I was anxious to see how she looked when she looked free of Zane. Might her eyes turn even bluer?

I said, "You're going to the meeting tonight?"

"And tomorrow, and the day after that. Whatever Bear says to do, I'm doing. I like going; when I leave I feel lighter, like dancing on air." She she set down her glass and stood on tiptoe to put her lips lightly over mine. I heard Harry slide the door open, return to the deck.

"What's this stuff I'm seeing?" he said.

I paused, ran several combinations of words through my head.

"Kissing and blissing?" I ventured.

"Damn," he said, eyes wide in feigned shock. "The boy finally got one right."

I started to launch some grief his way but the phone twittered again. Harry set the peanuts on the table and lifted the phone. "Ryder's. Uh-huh. He's right here. Yes, ma'am, hang on just a second." Harry looked at me.

"It's a Dr. Prowse, Evangeline Prowse."

I nodded. Harry brought me the cell. I turned to face the waves and brought the phone to my ear.

"Carson? Carson, this is Evangeline Prowse." Her voice dropped low. "I'm sorry, Carson. I'm afraid I have some bad news? Terrible news."

"My God, what?"

The voice trembled. "It's Jeremy, Carson. He's dead . . . a suicide. He hanged himself."

I heard the words but couldn't make sense of them. "Jeremy? No, there's no way he'd—"

"Last night. Or early this morning. He left a note? It's addressed to you."

"I can't believe this, it can't be true. My brother would never—"

400

"Do you want me to read the note, Carson? I don't have to, it's personal. I can send it."

I took a deep breath, let it drift from my chest.

"Yes, go ahead. Please read."

The sound of paper unfolding. Then Evangeline's hushed voice.

"'Dear Carson, I apologize. I did not know it was your womb-man he was after. My translation of the materials was wrong in that area. I was sure he wanted the other one, the one in charge, Peltier. I don't know if that would have mattered in my sending you astray, but I think it would have. I hope so. Love for now and always, Jeremy.' That's the whole text," Evangeline said quietly. "I'm so sorry."

I stood in my box in the air above an island, looked down the strand, and considered Evangeline's call. With the sudden clarity of revelation the sun seemed to light the world from every direction at once, nothing had shadows. The water stretched forward like a vast carpet of green, the white of the sand, blinding. I looked at Ava and Harry, saw the concern in their eyes, shot them a thumbs up, *It's all right, everything's all right.* Much as I tried to contain it, a smile spread across my face. I lifted the phone back to my ear.

"You almost got it perfect, Jeremy; the intonation, the rhythm. But Dr. Prowse never goes by the name Evangeline."

Silence from my caller.

I said, "She calls herself Vangie. It's always Vangie."

I listened for any evidence of a kindred being at the far end of the connection. With waves in the distance and breeze through my hair, I pressed my palm against one ear, the phone against the other, and listened hard into the silence. Then, for a slender moment, the breeze fell and the waves poised soundlessly between rush and retreat. I closed my eyes and discerned the lightest hint of breathing, as near as the blood in my veins, as far as the burned-away years: I heard the swift and shallow breaths of a frightened child all alone in the dark. My voice said, "I love you, brother."

Then I hung up on the past. At least until tomorrow.